Twain: Tattered, Trounced, Tortured and Traumatized

Twain: Tattered, Trounced, Tortured and Traumatized

By

Jay Dubya

www.BookstandPublishing.com

Published by
Bookstand Publishing
Pasadena, CA 91101
3081_3

ISBN 978-1-58909-687-5

Other Books by Jay Dubya

Adult Fiction

Black Leather and Blue Denim, A '50s Novel
The Great Teen Fruit War, A 1960' Novel
Frat' Brats, A '60s Novel
Ron Coyote, Man of La Mangia
Pieces of Eight
Pieces of Eight, Part II
Pieces of Eight, Part III
Pieces of Eight, Part IV
The Wholly Book of Genesis
The Wholly Book of Exodus
The Wholly Book of Doo-Doo-Rot-on-Me
Thirteen Sick Tasteless Classics
Thirteen Sick Tasteless Classics, Part II
Thirteen Sick Tasteless Classics, Part III
Thirteen Sick Tasteless Classics, Part IV
Thirteen Sick Tasteless Classics, Part V
So Ya' Wanna' Be A Teacher
RAM: Random Articles and Manuscripts
Mauled Maimed Mangled Mutilated Mythology
Fractured Frazzled Folk Fables and Fairy Farces
FFFF&FF, Part II
Nine New Novellas
Nine New Novellas, Part II
Nine New Novellas, Part III
Nine New Novellas, Part IV
One Baker's Dozen
Two Baker's Dozen
Shakespeare: Slammed, Smeared, Savaged & Slaughtered
Shakespeare: S, S, S and S, Part II
Suite 16
Time Travel Tales
Snake Eyes and Boxcars
Snake Eyes and Boxcars, Part II
UFO: Utterly Fantastic Occurrences
The Psychic Dimension
The Psychic Dimension, Part II
Modern Mythology

First Person Stories
O. Henry: Obscenely and Outrageously Obliterated
Poe: Pelted Pounded Pummeled and Pulverized
London: Lashed Lacerated Lampooned and Lambasted
Hawthorne: Hazed Hooked Hammered and Hijacked
Hawthorne Hacked, Shakespeare Sacked & Thurber Thwacked
THEMES
PLOTS
PLOTS, Part II
The FBI Inspector
Prime-Time Crime Time
The Arcane Arcade
Thirteen Tantalizing Tales
The Timeless Time Machine
Homer's Odd Sea Odyssey
HOMER'S ILL ILIAD
War of the Worlds
The Invisible Man

Young Adult Fantasy Novels

Pot of Gold
Enchanta
Space Bugs, Earth Invasion
The Eighteen Story Gingerbread House

Contents

Description

Twain: Tattered, Trounced, Tortured and Traumatized is a unique collection of twenty classic Mark Twain short stories and anecdotal sketches that have been creatively rewritten and satirized into adult parody form, featuring adult content and language. When author Jay Dubya was a New Jersey public school English teacher, he often enjoyed teaching and reading Mark Twain's "influential literature" to his sometimes-enlightened middle and high school academic students.

Remarkably, Samuel Langhorne Clemens (1835-1910) was both born and died the same years that Haley's (Halley's) Comet had made its seventy-five-year revolution around the solar system. Clemens acquired his pen name "Mark Twain" from Mississippi River steamboat terminology of "twain" being a water-depth of two fathoms (twelve feet), the allowable safe level for a riverboat to navigate over a reef or shoal, and the depth was measured by a leadsman who threw a heavy lead weight overboard, and then after lifting it out of the river, would *mark* the *twain.*

Sam Clemens became a successful riverboat pilot under the direction of a captain named Horace Bixby, but after the Civil War broke-out, the Mississippi River was closed to commercial traffic. Being unemployed, Clemens journeyed out west to try his hand at gold prospecting in Nevada, and then at newspaper journalism in California. The writer gained international recognition with the publication of his classic. humorous short story "The Celebrated Jumping Frog of Calaveras County," first published in 1865.

Mark Twain is generally regarded as a humorist, but the author is also understood by literary critics as being a serious philosopher and an astute analyzer of the antebellum and post-Civil War American societies of his time. Twain's most famous novels are *The Adventures of Tom Sawyer, The Adventures of Huckleberry Finn, The Prince and the Pauper,* and *A Connecticut Yankee in King Arthur's Court*. Other important Mark Twain works are the books: *Roughing It, Life on the Mississippi,* and *Innocents Abroad*, and some short literary sketches from the last-mentioned three books have been used in organizing *this* satire/parody collection.

In 1870, Mark Twain married Olivia Langdon of Elmira, New York, and the couple had two daughters, Susy and Jean. After becoming rich and famous, Clemens built a fabulous mansion in Hartford, Connecticut that had a porch and staircase that made the spectacular dwelling resemble a Mississippi riverboat. .

“Mark Twain”

Everywhere I travel, curious folks keep asking me how an idiot like Samuel Langhorne Clemens had ever obtained my clever-sounding pen name Mark Twain. And over the years, I’ve gotten so fatigued and so pissed-off telling and re-telling the goddamned story redundantly, again and again, that I finally figured I oughta’ put it all down in writing so that nosy assholes and annoying jerk-offs all over the damned world will know for sure how I happened to adopt that particular intelligent-sounding appellation. Now here’s exactly how all that incredible *nom de plume* bullshit came about.

Before I ever tried my hand (or hands) at gold prospecting in and around Virginia City, Nevada (without finding any bonanza), and years before I ever attempted legitimate newspaper reporting way-out West in San Francisco, I had grown-up in good old Hannibal, Missouri, which was right near the banks of the grand-old muddy Mississippi River. Well, maybe I should start at the damned beginning, because I’ve always maintained that food should enter the mouth and exit the asshole, and not the other way around.

I was born a boy in Florida, Missouri (two states in one) on November 30, 1835, the same year that Halley’s Comet zoomed by the Earth. My family then moved to Hannibal in 1839, and I called the town Hannibal, St. Petersburg, in my classic novels *Tom Sawyer* and *Huckleberry Finn,* mostly because I didn’t like the idea of living inside any goddamned dead Carthaginian general.

My pa’ couldn’t take my absurd antics and semantics, and so dad died when I was twelve. I dropped-out of school (luckily it was only a one-story building), and soon worked for my older brother Orion, before he became a famous constellation. His newspaper was called the *Journal,* and naturally, that’s where I sorta’ learned to be a journalist wanting to journey.

In 1853, out of sheer boredom and rebellion, I unceremoniously left Missouri to live in St. Louis, Philadelphia, and New York City, but not in all of those fucked-up places at the same time. But growing tired of being an itinerant failure, I ate some humble pie, and reluctantly rejoined tyrannical Orion in Muscatine, Iowa in the year 1854. And then later that year, in Keokuk, where my industrious and ambitious sibling had started-up new newspaper enterprises.

Being adventurous and naïve, in the autumn of 1856, I hopped aboard a riverboat in Cincinnati, and headed-down the Mississippi to New Orleans, with intentions of me then voyaging down to South

America and striking it rich in the cocoa business, somewhere down along the Amazon River in Brazil.

While going south down the river, I met the steamboat's pilot, a gregarious fella' named Horace Bixby, who convinced (or should I say "persuaded") me to become his *cub* (even though Bixby wasn't a bear) on his riverboat, the *Queen of Dixie*. And in April of 1859, I was prouder than a peacock when I received my riverboat pilot's license to navigate the Mississippi.

But in 1861, the damned *Civil War* broke-out, and the river was closed to commerce and trade. So, that's when I decided to try my already proven bad luck at gold prospecting and/or writing. I had learned plenty of relevant and irrelevant horse-crap about human nature on the various riverboats upon which I had served, and figured I could apply that questionable knowledge to some fictional stories and novels. But I'm afraid I'm getting a little ahead of myself, so I think I oughta' reconnoiter and go back to my childhood, even though at present (in my old age), my recollection is suspect and pretty damned erratic, principally because I suffer from extreme amnesia and from mild senility.

My big mamma Mrs. Clemens had always constantly yelled and bitched, because I was habitually tracking in mud and dirt into her kitchen from the Mississippi's banks, where incidentally my friends and I would keep and hide our money and worthless treasure junk. Mom just couldn't fathom my great fascination with the notorious river, and always worried that I would drown before I ever learned how to swim, fly, or float. That's when Mom pressured me into working for Orion at his ramshackle printing shop, which I did for nearly ten long and very tedious years, until I finally rebelled against his petty despotism. Yes; Orion and I did have a few minor arguments and squabbles in the decade-long interval, so I believe I'll commence my significant narrative about me becoming the author Mark Twain right here and now.

"Damn it, Sam!" Orion exclaimed while standing inside the *Journal's* tiny side office. "I have a bone to pick with you, Bonehead! You'll never master the newspaper printing trade as long as you think you're Prints Charming!"

"What did I do wrong now, Orion?" I vehemently retorted. "Did I belch too loud instead of mildly and politely burping? Didn't my last fart meet with your demanding specifications? If ya' don't like the way I set-up the type," I arrogantly protested, "then I strongly suggest that you do it yourself, and let *me* be the boss findin' fault with your general incompetence!"

"Listen to this load of happy horse-shit you've just put into type!" Orion boisterously complained as my older brother held-up the first printed copy of that morning's back page. "Parson Seth Petters has religiously paid his annual subscription with two bushels of large yellow *bears!* You Dumb Fuck!" my sibling loudly hollered. "The goddamned word should be *pears*, not bears! Why the hell can't you keep your simple mind on your simple work? I think you're becoming daft!"

"Listen to that magical steamboat whistle coming around the river bend," I calmly answered, almost in a trance. "That baby's not just whistlin' *Dixie,* ya' know Orion! It's a callin' me like a siren's voice, and I hear it beckonin'."

"That riverboat ain't puttin' food on the table or payin' my office rent," Orion chided and scolded me. "That river's gonna' be the ruination of you, yet! Sam; come back here! If you leave this building, I'm gonna' switch you good when you return! Don't go in the muddy water over your head, because you're already wet behind the ears!"

Well, I scampered-out of the office like a dashing young man, and neglecting to slam the door shut, my haste nearly knocked-over Mr. Bartholomew Thaddeus Higgins, editor of the *Journal's* rival newspaper in Hannibal, the *Bugle.* Mr. Higgins seemed mighty pissed-off before I ever had the opportunity to further malign his sore shoulder during my frisky exit down to the waterfront dock to greet the arrival of the magnificent *Queen of Dixie.*

"Howdy Mr. Higgins," Orion courteously stated, covering-up his exasperation at my premature departure from the premises. "What can I do for you besides buy your failing newspaper, and rescue you from an embarrassing bankruptcy?"

"Don't fuck with me, Orion Clemens!" the livid encroacher yelled. "Just read what the hell your mediocre paper, last week's edition I believe, said about me!"

Mr. Higgins handed Orion a copy of last week's *Journal,* and specifically pointed to a column on the "Local News" page. "Here Asshole; read this fallacious and slanderous article! I oughta' sue your ass for libel over this fraudulent bullshit!"

"Mr. Bartholomew Thaddeus Higgins, the craven, blowhard editor of the *Bugle,* single-handedly rescued himself from drowning himself in the mighty Mississippi while foolishly having his more dexterous right arm tied behind his back."

"Go on Clemens, read the fuckin' rest!" Higgins screamed like a deranged and demented maniac. "By the time you're done reading, you're gonna' think I'm a goddamned *Sioux* Indian after you receive notification of the upcoming litigation from my lawyer!"

Orion read the essence of the printed article aloud to the already-chagrined, unexpected visitor. "The editor's sweetheart Molly Screw left him high and dry, so good old Bartholomew Thaddeus Higgins again waded-out into the Mississippi to end his emotional distress. But when Mr. Higgins discovered that he, the incompetent fool, was totally inept at drowning himself without getting his cheap toupee wet, the jilted lover-boy turned his corpulent ass around, and waded back to shore."

"But that's all a lot of fiction that never happened in reality!" Orion admitted, realizing that a potential lawsuit might actually be in progress. "I suppose this is the type of humor that my younger brother Sam values and employs. He has trouble discriminatin' between fact and fiction, yes, the rascal does. I wholeheartedly apologize for the slanderous commentary, Mr. Higgins. And I'll definitely write a retraction paragraph to that effect in next week's edition of the *Journal*. I'll even put the statement on the front page."

"Well, your moronic brother Sam's got Mississippi mud in his veins instead of genuine red cells," Mr. Higgins replied, indirectly accepting Orion's promise to retract and correct the false, published chronicle. "Tell your fucked-up brother Sam that I think he's more-full of shit than the goddamned St. Louis sewer system!"

* * * * * * * * * * * * *

Well, that same night, my mom found a note I had scribbled on paper tucked inside her sewing bag, which I had never seen sew anything, not even a damned sock or seam. I tried explaining in the brief missive that I just had to try exploring the river, and that I would always strive to constantly remain her "faithful-but-disobedient son". I sorrowfully signed the note "Sam Clemens", because I wasn't clairvoyant, and had no idea who the hell the phantom identity "Mark Twain" would ever be in my future life. And so, while touring the pilothouse of the glorious *Queen of Dixie,* I struck-up a casual conversation with garrulous old Horace Bixby, the ship's eminent pilot, who at first seemed to actually relish my gullible presence.

"Excuse me, Sir," I awkwardly began my introduction. "But I used to be a pilot myself in my older brother's newspaper back in Hannibal. For you see Sir; I used to take stuff from my brother's desk and *pile it* in the corner of the office!"

"Well Son, it takes much more than a clumsy sense of humor to expertly guide the *Queen of Dixie* up and down this dangerous river," Mr. Horace Bixby answered. "I always like to sing, 'Big wheel keep on turnin', *Queen of Dixie* keep on burnin'. Keep on rollin', rollin', rollin' down the river! Ha, ha, ha!"

"Pretty catchy lyrics!" I acknowledged with a smile. "Sir," I addressed the jolly man in a more serious tone of voice. "My name is Samuel Langhorne Clemens, and I have aspirations of becoming a riverboat pilot myself. Would ya' happen to need an apprentice to learn the art of piloting?"

The pilot's attitude suddenly changed from a jovial disposition to one of absolute petulance. "I most certainly would not!" Mr. Bixby yelled as if his testicles had swollen and really hurt badly. "And I don't like strangers, especially punk young kids like you, trespassing into my pilothouse and making either orthodox Christian or unorthodox Greek requests!"

"Maybe you don't understand my motives," I sincerely confessed. "I wouldn't be workin' for wages."

"Boy, are you sufferin' from some kind of mysterious mental disease!" Mr. Bixby bellowed, exposing his tonsils. "You gotta' *pay me* to learn this freakin' trade, five hundred dollars, cash in advance, you pathetic little Scamp! Now go back to Hannibal and get your Pa' to give ya' the necessary money."

"My Pa's been dead since I was twelve!" I truthfully exclaimed. "And I gotta' earn money to help support my Ma'. But I do have some money; seven dollars and sixty-five cents that I've been savin' up since I was seven. I was goin' to use it to buy a new uniform after I became a riverboat pilot."

"Close that door, Son," Mr. Bixby commanded, feeling sorry for my desperate plight. "If I know women, your mother's probably glad to get rid of you. Now then, you Junior Jerk-off. The next major port we land at, wire the money back to your mom. And don't fuckin' speak out of turn and interrupt me, you diminutive Asshole! Cubs don't speak when they're spoken to by a superior."

"Did you say cubs?" I inquisitively asked. "My Mom often said that I was so confused from poor school grades that I didn't know whether I was from the North Pole, or from Antarctica, and that's why I was bi-polar!"

"Ha, ha, ha, Sam," Mr. Bixby guffawed. "Your Mom knows geography just as well as she knows human nature. Now are ya' ready to be my bona fide apprentice?"

"Yes Sir, I sure am ready to be a cub," I gratefully returned, right before Mr. Bixby requested that I join him in a chorus of "Rollin', rollin', rollin' down the river"! "When do we dock in Chicago?"

Well, twenty miles north of St. Louis, the *Queen of Dixie* approached a rather difficult part of the river. I was at the helm steering the resplendent steamboat when Mr. Horace Bixby returned from taking a dump in the officer's crapola, and soon felt obligated to challenge my navigational judgment. "Where in tar-nation are ya' takin' her now, Sam? Don't ya' know that you're responsible for dozens of lives of passengers and crew members aboard?"

"Well Sir, I'm tryin' to keep the boat in the mainstream because I'm basically a product of mainstream society," I coyly retorted like a true wise-ass. "I suppose that…"

"Look, you aspiring Juvenile Delinquent!" Mr. Horace Bixby curtailed my facetious response. "You don't *suppose* anything when you're in proud command of a sacred riverboat. You have *to know* what the hell you're doing up-here in the sanctuary! You have to know every bend, island, shoal, landing, and reef by heart. How else are ya' goin' to fuckin' steer on a dark, cloudy, rainy night when there's only an ominous New Moon up in the sky, and no damned stars visible! Now be careful Sam! That's Angel's Point up ahead. Listen to the leadsman's call to help you guide this sucker!"

The leadsman was a worker that dropped a lead weight attached to a rope overboard to measure the true depth of the water. "Quarter less, quarter less twain!" the fellow chanted.

"That call means we're in shallow water Sam," Mr. Bixby instructed. "There's obviously plenty of shoal water out-there that's not more than six-feet-deep. Glance sharply over your starboard side shoulder and turn the wheel to the right!"

"Half-one! Half-one!" the apprehensive leadsman repeated. "Oh lawdy, lawdy, half-one!"

"Watch out Sam! Are ya' attemptin' to clamber up that bank there, Boy!" Mr. Bixby anxiously reprimanded me. "Set her back! Set her the hell back, or else we're gonna' skim the muddy bottom! It's no damned time for a bum steer Sam!"

"Quarter less, quarter less twain!" the neurotic leadsman's voice boomed.

"Hold her steady like it's your girlfriend's tits!" Bixby yelled. "I think you're gonna' get-out of these dire straits and successfully make it through Scylla and Charybdis!"

"Mark twain, mark twain!" the very relieved leadsman called-out. "Mark twain!" he reiterated, wiping sweat from his brow.

"Mark twain, safe water," Mr. Bixby announced, wiping his own sweat from his own brow. "That's pretty damned merry language on any damned riverboat, Sam. That's a measurement of two fathoms deep, or twelve feet. It's okay to pass through Angel's Point, now that you've made nearly everybody on board get the diarrhea!"

"Mark Twain! I happen to be enamored with those wonderful words!" I expressed to my conscientious mentor, Horace Bixby.

"Well Sam, it's a lot easier making an asshole into a riverboat pilot than it is making a riverboat pilot into an asshole; you know, the shitting part of a person's rectum!" Mr. Bixby literally clarified. "But Sam, there's nothing wrong with bein' an asshole! Let me tell you, young Clemens. Don't you ever be insulted when I call you an Asshole! I mean, what would the most beautiful woman in the world look like after twenty or so years if she didn't have an asshole to shit out of!"

* * * * * * * * * * * * * *

One blustery afternoon, I met a wealthy, itinerant vagabond from Elmira, New York on the deck of the *Queen of Dixie,* and when the young traveler whipped-out a gold fob chain timepiece that had a locket picture of a beautiful woman inside, I just had to ask that sartorially-dressed Eastern fella', named Charles Langdon, exactly who the vivacious female happened to be.

"Why that's my sister, Olivia, Mr. Clemens," Langdon declared. "And despite your apparent interest, she's the most sought-after debutante in all of Elmira."

"Well, Mr. Langdon. Someday you're gonna' become my brother-in-law, because I'm gonna' marry this here Olivia, and we're gonna' live in a comfortable house that I'll personally design to look like a Mississippi riverboat."

"Aren't you being a little presumptuous, Mr. Clemens?" Mr. Charles Langdon asked me before sipping some coffee from his *Queen of Dixie* cup. "After all, you don't even know Olivia."

"Just mark my words," I cockily replied. "After I make my fortune writing stories and books, I'll be able to woo any female existing parallel to me in my newly-gained social strata. Now then. Charles, I'll personally invite you up to the pilothouse and show ya' how to keep this here vessel in the center of the channel."

"Getting rather dark, isn't it Sam?" Langdon casually observed and mentioned as we climbed-up the ship's wooden steps. "But it isn't every day that I get to visit a pilothouse."

When we got to our destination, Horace Bixby was up-there being my helm substitute during my brief absence. "Well Sam, are ya' ready to tie her up once ya dock?"

"No Mr. Bixby," I confidently-but-negatively answered. "I'm gonna' take this tub past Hat Island despite the heavy fog. In fact, I won't be completely happy until we get the *fog* outa' here, ha, ha, ha! Get it Mr. Langdon! We'll get the fog outa' here!"

"You'll have to excuse Sam's perverted sense of humor," Mr. Bixby explained to Mr. Langdon in a slightly-embarrassed tone of voice. "But to young Clemens' credit, his jokes are often funny and self-deprecating."

Then, my knowledgeable mentor remembered something salient that his aged-ears had just heard. "Did I just hear you say you're gonna' pass by Hat Island in the goddamned fog? Sam, no pilot in his right mind has ever tried *that* risky maneuver! You'll be putting the entire ship and its passengers in jeopardy!"

"No pilot until now!" I haughtily boasted. "I've finally developed my skill to its maximum potential, Mr. Bixby."

"Mr. Clemens, Sir," a suddenly disturbed Mr. Charles Langdon politely interrupted. Why are you always turning and looking to the boat's stern? I must confess, you look so stern when you do that!"

"Alligators, Mr. Langdon. Yeah; I just witnessed an alligator latch onto the rear next to the giant paddlewheel."

"That sounds like a croc (crock) to me!" Bixby exclaimed. "Sam's noted for his exaggerations and his hyperbole, Mr. Langdon; not to mention his excessive bullshit."

"Of course, Charles," I added and complemented tongue-in-cheek. "Just several damned alligators hitchin' onto the stern for a ride ain't so upsetting, but then another sucker grabs onto the first one, and in no time flat, we're pullin' and draggin' along a whole procession of the damned carnivorous lizards."

"Sam, watch your steering and forget about this stupid-ass alligator bullshit!" Bixby imperatively admonished. "If this ship smashes into something big, then we might all be alligator food before we know what the hell has ever happened. Sam, you've just passed Hat Island! You've drifted past your landing, and the fog's as thick as tomato and rice soup! I've run this river two whole decades, and I've never attempted anything as brazen or as bizarre as this maneuver you're enacting!"

"Half-ahead and stand by!" I yelled-down to the crew and the lead-headed leadsman.

"Deep four! Deep four!" the petrified leadsman shouted-up.

"Samuel Langhorne Clemens, you're crazier than the biggest cashew in the local nuthouse!" Mr. Bixby alleged.

"Less twain! Less twain!" the leadsman hysterically screamed. "Oh, lawdy, lawdy, less twain!"

"Sam, you managed to make it past the first reef, but there's another one just ahead!" Bixby shouted, showing rare emotion. "Pretty soon the *Queen of Dixie* could be reduced to splinters and assorted toothpicks!"

"Half-one! Half-one! Only three-feet deep! I'm beginnin' to shit my pants for a third time!" the panicky leadsman shrieked.

"Let her have full power!" I yelled-down to the crew at the top of my lungs. "I'll skim this well-constructed sucker right past the treacherous obstacles!"

"Mark twain! Mark twain! Oh lawdy, lawdy, mark twain!" the paranoid leadsman screamed, narrowly escaping being victimized by his imminent cardiac arrest.

"Mark twain! Safe water!" Langdon echoed before taking a deep breath. "Why, Mr. Clemens. That demonstration was absolutely astonishing! I'd be glad to have an intrepid individual such as yourself' being my prospective brother-in-law."

"Sam, I've never seen a finer exhibition of piloting on the Mississippi in my entire life," congratulated Mr. Horace Bixby. "You rolled the dice, and your incomparable ability and guile salvaged us from impending destruction! Now I wonder if the unwary passengers know what the hell kind of super calamity had almost-annihilated them?"

"And you did it all in a supreme manner with that whole chain of alligators hanging on behind," praised Mr. Langdon. "I'm an avowed environmentalist, and I hope that none of them were injured colliding with that awful reef."

"I'm afraid that this exciting episode was just the beginning of what constitutes a tall tale Mr. Langdon," Mr. Bixby stated, shaking his head. "Someday, Sam's *tall tales* will become published *short stories*, I predict."

"Well Sam, if ya' ask my opinion, that's exactly what you oughta' be doin'. Writing a whole book of tall tales about your adventures and exploits on this fabulous river," Mr. Langdon suggested.

"Yeah, Charles. And I reckon I'll be writing under the extremely intriguing pen name Mark Twain," I answered with a degree of certainty. "I hereby *author*ize myself to do just that; once I get tired of bein' an accomplished Mississippi riverboat pilot!"

"Boyhood Reminiscences"

When I finally became old and famous after a lifetime of hard work, and coincidentally developing arthritis in my hands from writing manuscripts on paper too damned much, my very demanding publisher insisted that I author an autobiography of my screwball life, because common folks throughout the country wanted to know more shit about me than I fuckin' knew about myself. In organizing *that* monumental assignment, I was smart enough to use some of those early life experiences in my book *The Adventures of Tom Sawyer,* which took place (just like my childhood did) in the mid-nineteenth century along the Mississippi River. And so. me and some of my dumb-dick boyhood friends (and *our* outlandish real-life adventures) actually became Tom Sawyer's and also Huckleberry Finn's unique exploits later on in literary fiction.

My school reminiscences began when I was about six years old, and my mere existence soon manifested itself as a real pain in the ass as far as the adults in the somnolent community of Hannibal, Missouri were concerned. In those primitive early days, long before Abraham Lincoln had ever ascended to the Presidency, Missouri had no public schools, but private schools were quite common and popular. Hannibal boasted of two private institutions of lower learning, and the standard tuition for attendance (even for an irascible asshole imp such as myself) was a meager twenty-five cents a week, although my two-bit teachers often told me that my "babysitting expense" should've been quadrupled, with *that* meager bargain-basement amount of money also being paid by the parents of the average "good behaved Hannibal student".

Mr. Sam Cross (who was reputed to be both mean and cross all the goddamned time) taught the older kids their irrelevant academics in a frame schoolhouse situated up on a hill just outside town. Mrs. Horr conducted her martinet-oriented grammar school/log cabin at the southern end of one-block-long Main Street. Although the nasty schoolmarm was married, the old hag (with thick-rimmed glasses hanging upon her lengthy snout) never screwed around with any men (besides her husband) like her weird-sounding last name might suggest when spoken orally.

And so, I figured and accurately assessed at a very early age that Mrs. Horr was not a regular harlot, or an everyday prostitute, as was the infamous rumor all around the morning playground. And after sixty-five years of what could only be characterized as growth and immaturity, I still can recollect some significant incidents involving curious, little, nefarious me that had occurred under Mrs. Horr's austere classroom jurisdiction.

A particular episode happened on my first day of formal education. Being my normal non-compliant self, I easily violated several basic and easy to understand school rules, and Mrs. Horr warned me that continued mischief and recalcitrance on my part would automatically warrant the well-deserved penalty of receiving a "royal whipping" to be administered swiftly and directly to my tender ass by the snotty, pompous-acting churchgoing Bible-toting, old lady pedagogue.

After my second minor misdemeanor (which involved scratching my itchy testicles in front of the girls in the legendary cloak room), Mrs. Horr told *(instructed)* me to go outside and fetch a functional birch switch, so that the ancient bitch could proceed to beat the living and dead shit out of my asshole. Well, I was appointed to complete that important responsibility, And I truly believed that I was the most qualified student, and that I could practice more judiciousness in doing so than the average stupid-shit classmate, who out of pure jealousy and spite, might've been harboring grave animosity towards me because of my extreme popularity with the more-kinky girls, all of whom wanted to closely examine and inspect my itchy balls, and also examine my corresponding, miniature pecker apparatus.

I diligently searched the swampy mud located behind the fire-hazard log cabin schoolhouse, and soon discovered a cooper's shaving; the remnant of an old decayed barrel that had been originally crafted out of solid oak wood. The piece of "punishment tool" was a quarter of an inch thick, and two-foot-long; and it rose to a shallow curve at one end. I really liked the new-found rod because it was rotten, and I reckoned that the improvised object would break into shreds after making hard contact with my skinny bony ass. Upon my hasty return inside the dimly-lit log cabin, Mrs. Horr didn't at all like my personal selection, so right then and there, I knew that the old witch bitch wanted to administer a rather cruel beating, and that she was basically a vindictive, bloodthirsty sadist left over from prehistoric Puritan times, where stocks and bonds in the town square (and not the Wall Street type) were the goddamned rage to punish suspected classroom violators.

Despite my contrived attitude of overtly exhibiting meekness and self-depredation, Mrs. Horr didn't buy into or fully appreciate my choice of an appropriate torture weapon-device, so the hostile-to-me villainess called me by my full name of Samuel Langhorne Clemens, which fuckin' meant that my ass was grass even before she would ever begin to wallop the hell out of it.

"I'm ashamed of you Young Man; so therefore, Samuel Langhorne Clemens, you should be adequately prepared to experience some pain in your bottom because you're definitely a royal pain in everybody else's ass in this humble classroom."

Well now, Mrs. Horr appointed this kid possessing a gigantic gut and accompanying massive abdomen named Jim Dunlap to go outside and find a more suitable "birch switch" for her to beat the digested and undigested feces out of my vulnerable asshole. I was excessively worried from that moment on, because that belligerent kid Jim Dunlap hated my entire being ever since *that* morning out on the playground when I had told him that I thought he had a bad terminal health condition called "Dunlap's disease", where his inflated stomach "done laps over". Anyway, five minutes later, that junior jerk-off Dunlap returned inside the building with a pretty usable, sturdy switch rod; so I immediately comprehended that the obese punk was an expert on the matter, a moron-dumb-fuck who wanted to see me suffer severely, and become penitent and submissive to the wicked teacher's basic hostility.

Now, it was known all throughout Hannibal that Mrs. Horr had originated from up north in Rhode Island, and everyone in Hannibal was aware that she was a treacherous New England bitch that loved to switch the rear ends of devious little boys for personal gratification. The old abuser opened her little Inquisition hearing with a prayer read directly from the Good Book; yes, that weird fuckin' psalm that begins with some oddball passage like "Walking through the valley of death and fearing no Devil-generated evil." The conclusion to her brief requiem happened to be the screwed-up, pathetic prophetic words, "Ask and you shall receive!" Then, the raunchy, bizarre, barbaric woman, without me ever asking for a damned thing, tanned my hide so hard that I thought I was being turned into the leather remains of a slaughtered cow, and that I would wind-up becoming a part of another freaky kid's jacket, belt or shoe soles.

After I had gotten the shit knocked out of me by my new-found adult enemy, I soberly concluded that perhaps I should give the oddball "Ask and you shall receive!" philosophy an honest try. I solemnly prayed for some scrumptious gingerbread to eat as a reward for surviving my brutal Puritanical-style persecution, and coincidentally Margaret Kooneman, who just happened to be the town baker's daughter, had brought a slab of the delicious baked item to school on that propitious first day of kindergarten.

At age six, I was not only a penitent sinner, but also a junior culinary authority, in addition to being remarkably sexually precocious and inquisitive for my tender age. When I finally finished my silent "gingerbread prayer" to Heaven, I glanced behind to Margaret's desk directly in back of me, and her gingerbread treat was sitting there on the top slate while she was leaning over and retrieving a scrap of paper that had floated onto the wooden floor. I immediately became a convert to being a devout, grateful Christian, because I had been fortuitously rewarded for my religious reverence and steadfast devotion twofold.

First of all, I had the delightful opportunity to snatch the freshly baked gingerbread slice, and then quickly devour the delectable snack in three wonderful bites and swallows. Secondly, I got a fantastic glimpse of Margaret Kooneman's snatcheroo because her legs were wide open when she was leaning over and grabbing her coveted scrap paper; but unfortunately, even though Margaret wasn't wearing any type of underwear beneath her dress, I perceptively noticed that she only had a weird-looking Z-shaped slit between her legs, and no damned pussy hair was yet growing down there in her future pleasure garden. 'No wonder why all the girls in the class want to see my balls and pecker!' I then realized and understood.

* * * * * * * * * * * * *

I prayed incessantly the entire next week, but never received any more scrumptious gingerbread samples, or any more sensational young girl hairless crotch glances, so I became disenchanted, evolved into an instant atheist, and soon gave up prayer; my skeptical mind regarding the mystery mental communication as a thing that only magically worked once for a young mischievous fella' like myself. And amazingly, the miracle happening only once on my first day of school.

My more-than-tolerant mother experienced a great deal of trouble raising my ass through puberty, but I think she rather enjoyed the impossible challenge. My brother Henry, who was two years younger than me, was the ideal "lily-white conscience" kid who never caused problems and who wasn't one himself. So, mom looked at *my* mischief as a counterbalance to Henry's obedient and angelic nature. My negative deportment tended to furnish her with adequate relief and variety from Henry's trite contriteness and his general hatred of mayhem. My junior brother was not a normal, vicious youngster, but Henry definitely was too damned righteous, wanting to grow up to be a schoolmaster, a minister, a pope, or some stupid-shit adult like that.

Henry often reported my radical and rebellious misdemeanors to mom because of my negligence to ever indict myself, and in the novel *The Adventures of Tom Sawyer*, the fictional character Sid (who always squealed on Tom) was actually benevolent Henry in disguise. When I was approaching thirteen, I had often planned to push Henry out of my second-floor bedroom window and impale his never-spanked ass upon the white picket fence below, but then I logically figured that the extensive cleanup (with all of the blood, piss and shit all over the damned backyard) would have been too laborious for a lazy jerk-off like myself to have to perform.

One sunny, summer afternoon, just before suppertime, Henry brought it to mom's wicked attention that the thread that she had meticulously sewn my collar together with (to prevent me from playing hooky from school and going swimming down at the secret pond) had strangely changed color from black to white. Well, mom became quite piqued at my outrageous audacity, and based on insignificant circumstantial evidence, and Henry's speculative testimony, the woman viciously cracked me a dozen times on the head with her metal thimble, nearly riveting me right through the goddamned wooden floor planks.

When I finally got Henry alone outside, I believed that I had to mercilessly whip his ass for ratting on me, which my strong-willed conscience considered *his* fundamental disloyalty, his squealing being a grievous mortal sin of the greatest magnitude. And I had to exhibit to Henry my physical dominance over him during *my* pre-pubescent adolescence. But right when I began administering my justified retribution, mom detected the clamorous backyard commotion, rushed outside, immediately sided with that no-good-prick Henry without even initiating a brief investigation, and then savagely used two metal thimbles (on both her left and right index fingers) to make my totally abused scalp feel like a large bag of marbles as more and more nasty big skull bumps materialized.

Henry was such a despicable saint that the juvenile nutcase never once pilfered any sweet objects inside the kitchen cookie jar without first obtaining permission from mother. But one morning, an itinerant demon must've possessed my younger brother, because I caught him with his paws inside the bear-shaped jar, and upon his realization that I had nabbed him performing the pilfering act, the little, conniving bastard dropped the revered container from his grasp, and then, the ceramic old English mamma bear (along with its precious sugary cargo) splattered all over the new linoleum.

"Now I'm gonna' tell on ya' just like you always do on me," I threatened the guilty culprit. "Not only did I catch you with your hands in the cookie jar, I've also witnessed you breaking the damned thing, you idiotic, clumsy oaf!" I warned. "I hear mom enterin' the house right now. You're in big-ass trouble Henry, and now I'm goin' to enjoy you receivin' your first terrible whippin'! Maybe ya' better scamper upstairs and put on three more sets of underpants for sufficient padding to endure all the brutal agony! But never mind your fat ass! Breaking the damned cookie jar probably means you're gonna' get the thimble-head-denting treatment!"

Mother entered the kitchen, keenly observed the recently caused debris, and then stood there with her arms folded under her huge, flopping breasts that extended down to her ankles when mom was not wearing a bra. I figured I would savor the wonderful, joyous moment of Henry's beating, so I procrastinated before acting like the county prosecutor engaged in convicting a heinous felon. But mom never interrogated her two offspring by asking, "Who did this shit?"

Well now, I had made a grave error in situational miscalculation by not speaking-up and making the allegation as direct evidence against Henry, because mom instinctively presumed that I had been the wicked villain, so the livid parent aggressively gave me an assortment of cracks upon my already throbbing skull with her metal thimble, which I felt when excruciating pain descended-down my spine clear to my quivering heels. My bad experience was all pretty damned close to being executed.

"But Mom, you've punished the wrong person!" I exclaimed and explained. "Henry broke the cookie jar, I swear it! I saw him do it despite the fact that it was an accident!"

"Don't be absurd, Sam!" mom yelled in staunch defense of her erroneous disciplinary actions. "Henry is incapable of doin' such a terrible thing as pilferin' from the cookie jar without first askin' my approval. But Sam, I'm glad I thwacked ya' a few times on the head to make-up for some sneaky violations that you've recently committed that had somehow escaped my scrutiny!"

Another misadventure implicating Henry occurred when I was twelve and he was ten. A stairway outside the Hannibal house led to the upstairs' hallway, similar to what is called a fire escape nowadays. One day, Henry was climbing up those rickety steps, so I wasted no time and sprinted upstairs and locked the door from the inside, isolating the subservient asshole on the top steps outside the modest home. Then seeking revenge for his myriad trespasses against me (especially his tattling), I felt obligated to make Henry atone for his past transgression, so I started hurling wet black mud clods at him as he began ducking-down left and right like a target in a modern-day shooting gallery.

"You can use that tin bucket in your hand as a deflector all ya' want," I boldly hollered-up. "But that ain't gonna' protect your ass for too long, because I got at least a hundred more mud clod balls to throw up at your puny, scumbag body!"

The wet, smelly clods were loudly smacking against the house's weatherboarding, and soon mom appeared on the back porch steps conducting her usual visual and olfactory investigation. She and Henry immediately formed an alliance, and the pair began sprinting after my frightened ass, so I frantically bounded over the side white picket fence, and almost castrated my tiny testicles on the same four-foot-high boundary that I had unscrupulously plotted to impale Henry's body upon.

Several hours later, I surreptitiously ventured back to the family property, and was happy to observe that no one (conspiring to annihilate my entire being) was in sight. But then Henry suddenly appeared from behind a magnolia tree, and tossed a stone in my direction. The hard object ricocheted off my noggin and left a sizeable welt above the center of my forehead, the damage to my forehead having the spectacular shape and appearance of that Matterhorn Mountain over there in Europe.

Mom came running out of the house to evaluate the source of the commotion. "That's what you get Sam for always pickin' on poor little Henry!" the woman accused and concluded. "That's what the hell you deserve after you were throwin' those dirty wet mud clods at your younger brother. Now Henry," mom commanded, "go inside and eat a piece of that warm apple pie I just baked, and as for you Sam, get a bucket of water, some soap suds, and a couple of washcloths, and start cleaning-up that horrendous mud mess you've made up there on the weatherboarding!"

* * * * * * * * * * * * *

Besides being engaged in mild sibling rivalry with the family's apostle-in-chief, Henry, in late autumn of 1849 (during the height of the exciting California Gold Rush), my older sister (who wishes to remain anonymous in my monastic-type monk writings) gave a huge party, and invited most of the horny teenage males and females of the village, virtually all of whom were obnoxious, future village idiots, of course. Although I was biologically driven by my newfound sex hormones, my basic bashfulness felt overwhelmed in the company of mature girls that had tits with half-dollar-sized nipples puffed out on their magnificent chests.

My irascible sister had arranged for me to be part of the "jolly entertainment segment", and dress-up in a bear costume during a "fairy-play" that was to be performed. "You'll just stand there for eight minutes and then foolishly cavort around in circles like a gay homosexual carnivore for the remaining two minutes," I was directed. "Don't worry Samuel! I'm sure you'll be the hit of the party! The girls and I will be doing a forest dance scene from William Shakespeare's *A Midsummer Night's Dream!"*

At half past ten, I was told to go to my room and put on the furry bear outfit, and patiently wait to be called to perform my indispensable role. Then, if I wanted to further rehearse my amateur baptism into show business, I should advance up to the attic in full disguise, and practice marching around in circles like a completely fucked-up asshole impersonating an inebriated bear.

After arriving up inside the dark attic, I heard some giggling originating from behind a translucent dressing screen, and instantly recognized the high-pitched voices of young members of the opposite gender mumbling and conversing next to a candle-lit table. 'Perhaps this theatrical thespian bullshit is not so damned gay after all!' I plausibly reasoned. 'Maybe unlike my little gingerbread caper with Margaret Kooneman back in Mrs. Horr's first grade, this time if I'm lucky, I'll get to sneak a big-time peek at some mature hairy teenage pussy cracks!"

I had not yet donned my bear disguise, and so I stripped-down bare-ass naked to be able to facilitate my tedious clambering inside the cumbersome ensemble. Boy, was I in for the shame and embarrassment of my formative years of development, when my limited cerebrum failed to keenly anticipate the 'unexpected'.

No sooner had I gotten all my clothes off my anatomy that the translucent dressing screen tilted over and tumultuously collapsed to the floor, revealing in the dull candlelight six masked naked girls with real nice tits and furry brown bushes being exposed in their various personal body areas. The naked snickering young ladies simultaneously rushed my nude form, tackled and knocked me down, and one by one rubbed their hairy brown snatches against my nose, tongue and face. It was a boy's absolute delight, a sort of perverted college sorority-type, sex initiation being enacted on a gullible-yet-defenseless, petrified fourteen-year-old, willfully-victimized boy. Five long minutes later, the thoroughly amused girls all darted with their (lesbian/dyke) fairy costumes under their arms down the attic steps to my anonymous sister's room, where they would ultimately get changed for their anti-climactic nightingale performance.

'Holy shit!' I remember thinking. 'One of those brazen, conspiring smelly cunts might've been my older masked sister! I mean,' I considered with a frown of disgust, 'licking your older sister's hairy brown anonymous crotch is far worse than just having to kiss the bitch on her other lips!'

* * * * * * * * * * * * *

When I had left Hannibal several years later to seek my fame and fortune on the Mississippi River, I had all but forgotten about the peculiar attic female sex assault. At the time of my older sister's party, one of Hannibal, Missouri's dearest and prettiest teenage girls was the stunning and dazzling Mary Wilson, and every boy in the village (that could muster an impressive erection) wanted to get his noodle wet inside Mary's highly desired love tunnel. But I always stood in awe of the voluptuous, mature broad, and could only get an erection thinking about her luscious love tunnel when the adorable doll *wasn't* standing or sitting in my presence.

The scene now shifts to Calcutta, India forty-seven years after the long-forgotten attic incident. I had arrived in that distant country in 1896 as part of a formal lecturing tour I was conducting to promote my books and my authoring career.

As I entered my hotel lobby to check-in at the main registration desk, a heavenly angelic vision passed by me, and the young attractive girl my eyes had spotted looked identical to the radiant Mary Wilson I had known and admired back in Hannibal. 'That's impossible,' I decided. 'Mary's my age; even several years older, and she sure as hell would be subject to nature's cruel aging process, just the same as any other human being would be!'

Come to find out, the beautiful young damsel I had noticed in the lobby was the granddaughter of the Mary Wilson I had once known back in *our* hometown. Mary had learned that I would be staying at her Calcutta hotel, so she sent a messenger to deliver a handwritten invitation for me to join her at six for supper in the main dining room. I immediately sent a memo' back to Room 224 agreeing to meet my former dreamboat (whom I had greatly admired long before I had ever stepped foot on a steamboat). I had also known through reliable sources back in Hannibal, Missouri that Mary was now a widow and was possibly looking to renew some romantic ties with old acquaintances.

The now-wrinkled, wealthy, gray-haired woman met me at her table and we warmly shook hands. "Won't you sit down Samuel, er, I mean Mark?" she commendably requested. "It's been a mighty long time since we both left Hannibal!"

"Yes, it has been Mary," I merrily concurred. "Ya' know, when I was a youngster, I, like every other boy in the village, had a mad crush on you. I guess you've known that fact all along."

"Yes Mr. Twain, but before we reminisce old times and the glory of our memorable youth, there's something rather cute and relevant that I wish to tell you."

"Are you gonna' talk about that un-hilarious line that I had to deliver in the infamous Shakespeare' forest scene: 'What's so special about dried herring'?" I asked my former girl idol.

"Well, Mark, if you insist on knowing, I was one of the six masked girls that sexually molested you up in your house's attic," Mary confessed with a wide grin being evident on her countenance.

"Oh my God Mary! That splendid assault was the first time I ever tasted delicious pussy juice in my life, and I haven't stopped seeking more of it ever since!"

"Now Mark," Mary naughtily giggled. "I'm awfully afraid that my personal area is now a dried-up herring, just as your one and only play line suggests!"

"Who the hell gives a shit!" I exclaimed with a hardy laugh. "At my advanced age, you valiantly fight for every damned sniff of Heaven you can get!"

"Club Pilot on the Mississippi"

Samuel Langhorne Clemens (1835-1910) was undoubtedly one of the most influential early American authors, and was also a prolific contributor to United States literature. The literary genius was born the year Halley's Comet made an appearance, and died seventy-five years later, when the celestial object made another solar system pass past the earth and then around the sun.

Sam Clemens acquired the writing pseudonym "Mark Twain" from Mississippi River steamboat jargon. A worker on the riverboat would toss a lead weight attached to a rope overboard, and "mark the twain". If the water was two fathoms deep (twelve feet), then a riverboat could safely navigate past a shoal, or over a hidden underwater reef.

Growing-up in the quiet town of Hannibal Missouri, young Sam Clemens knew more about the Mississippi River's 'muddy waters' than the blues/jazz musician Muddy Waters ever conceived of. As an imaginative boy, Twain's prime ambition was to become a Mississippi riverboat pilot. His dream eventually did come true, and Clemens' classic, humorous, autobiographical story "Cub Pilot on the Mississippi" retells one of his first rich experiences on the *Pennsylvania,* a typical steamboat of the antebellum (pre-*Civil War*) era. Herein lies an unworthy, decadent corruption of one of Mark Twain's more popular tales with the ordinary word "Cub" being mischievously changed to "Club".

When I was a boy, and I do believe that happened some years before I became a man, my happy-go-lucky friends and I had one principal aspiration. We lived in somnolent Hannibal, Missouri on the west bank of the mighty Mississippi River, and each of the guys wanted to become a steamboat man, which in reality is sorta' fuckin' easier than actually becoming a steamboat.

I must confess, I had other fanciful notions circulating in my hyperactive cerebrum, but those hankerings were but transient, fleeting impressions, and mostly totally juvenile perceptions. When an occasional circus came to town, I wanted to be a clown. But then I realized that my grammar school teachers had always persisted in calling me "a clown", so why should I grow up to become what I happened to be already? So, when the damned circus pulled-up its tent and packed away its midway concession stands, I lost interest in becoming an acrobat, a lion tamer, a ringmaster, a midget, a bearded woman, and also a dumb-ass clown.

I recall a minstrel show coming to Hannibal, and my buddies and I were all enthused and psyched-up about the prospect of becoming traveling troubadours. But then that was during our 'minstrel period', and we all soon realized that only girls had that kind of stupid-assed bloody bullshit to deal with each and every month. And to tell you the truth, who the hell needs that kind of monthly bull crap? That's the only period during the entire month when pussy juice absolutely tastes worse than tomato juice!

My pals and I also wished that God would allow us to become formidable pirates, even though Missouri was plenty far away from Pittsburgh. Then, we figured we could ambush travelers taking the stagecoach into Hannibal and profit from selling them corn on the cob for a *buck-an-ear*. And if our captives refused our generous ransom terms, or didn't particularly savor the taste of corn kernels, then my creative young colleagues and I schemed-up an honorable penalty. The guys all reckoned we would rob the rambling bastards, and simultaneously rape the more-voluptuous stagecoach bitches passing through "our territory", all done in the noble tradition practiced by our notorious, villainous, high seas' heroes, Blackbeard and Captain Kidd.

Once, in my later youth, I wanted to be a riverboat cabin boy, so I could exit the steamship's kitchen area wearing a white apron and proudly shake all the crystal saltshakers and pepper-shakers, and then nonchalantly loosen the embedded breadcrumbs off the dining area's tablecloths. Finally, I fuckin' realized I could be a cabin boy just by staying at my pop's cabin in the woods, and in that stellar capacity, I really didn't have to wear any fancy white apron, or deal with the crummy passengers' crumbs.

Later, in my fairly-pleasurable youth, I thought I would prefer being a deckhand standing conspicuously at the end of the vessel with the lead weight in my hands to officially "mark the twain". That might've been tolerable for a year or two, but confidentially, who the hell wants to measure the depth of river water for the rest of his or her damned life? I needed to do something more adventurous and more dynamic in my future, like robbing trains, and amusing myself terrorizing the appalled passengers; or perhaps wrestling aggressive gorillas or ferocious grizzly bears at exciting summer carnivals.

Most of my childhood amigos eventually managed to find work on the local riverboats. The minister's son, who despised the four gospels with a passion, abhorred the total *Bible*, and hated *his* inflexible, straightlaced, holier-than-thou old man, smartly became a riverboat engineer. The doctor's and the postmaster's sons became "mud clerks", and that seemed quite appropriate for them in that both a physician and a postal worker deal with prescriptions and writings of some sort all the damned time. At least working on a steamboat seemed much better than going the traditional doctor route or as they say, "going postal".

The local liquor merchant's son became a bartender on a riverboat called *The Delta Queen*. On that same boat, the county judge's son became a *pilot',* whose first job each morning was to carefully move a barrel, a piece of equipment, or a cargo bundle from one side of the boat and then "pile it" on the other side of the spectacular vessel.

A real authentic riverboat pilot was the most wonderful elite position of all. The assignment commanded a sensational salary of perhaps two-hundred-dollars a month, even in those lean years of trivial wages prior to the catastrophic event known as the *Civil War.* Twenty-four-hundred fabulous dollars a year! That's six times as much as a preacher's annual salary was in those hard times, because as we all know, cheap words command cheap compensation for cheap services rendered.

But many of *our* overprotective parents and guardians were against us boys getting employment on riverboats. The dumb-shit Missouri adults pompously claimed that interesting stuff like gambling; itinerant people; drinking whiskey; fighting; enjoying immoral fellatio and cunnilingus; patronizing forbidden bordellos; participating in totally erotic, pleasurable prostitution, and fingering loose, flirtatious women's hairy love tunnels were bad influences on our characters. But that's exactly why the hell we all wanted to get hired and work on the riverboats! I mean, fuck morality! Who the hell wants to grow-up (I think it's impossible to grow-down) in any way, shape, or form to be a facsimile of their prudish mother or their sexually frustrated father? Even Hannibal's un-liberated parents envied *our* penchant for exploring freedom's limits, and also *our* noble desire to escape the listless mediocrity of the restricted lifestyle generally associated with middle-class WASP culture. I say, "Hooray for horny promiscuous women wanting to share their eager beavers"!

So, I ran away from home, escaping from responsibility; from rules of society, and from the dictatorial standards of Christian values, and sought sanctuary riding on Mississippi riverboats', which to me symbolized liberty and escape from parental influence and from social tyranny. I vowed to my conscience that I would not return home again to Hannibal until I achieved my childhood wish of becoming an eminent and esteemed pilot on the mighty Mississippi. The colorful, glamorous excitement that goes on inside a riverboat was also an incentive to want to leave the dull tranquility of rather rustic Hannibal, Missouri.

I proudly served under many honorable pilots during my three-year apprenticeship aboard the stately *Pennsylvania.* My education involved not only mastering the art of being a riverboat helmsman, but my fascinating function also entailed meeting people and learning about their occupations, interests, vices, and in the final analysis, all about the good and the bad of human nature. That was the kind of stuff good authors' greedily study, and by virtue of my stellar steamboat preparation, I had sufficient material to begin organizing a variety of short stories, and then later, tackling novels. And I readily admit, I owe it all to mingling with all kinds of whacko charlatans, slippery con-artists, cagey gamblers, attractive hookers, and sinister villains. Who the hell wants to read a novel with nothing but goody-goody-two-shoes praising each other all day and all night long as the key element in the fucked-up plot? That kind of lackluster, dull, lousy, high-falutin' fiction might as well be cemetery fodder with a big family burial *plot!*

Now then, a pretentious jerk-off named Mr. Brown was my immediate superior on the good ship *Pennsylvania.* Brown was a middle-aged, tall, bony, and thin, smooth-shaven, donkey-faced, miserly, stupid, mealy-mouthed, faultfinding, snarling, despicable martinet that made that bastard Napoleon Bonaparte seem like an innocent altar or choir boy. I always dreaded going on watch with the loathsome imbecile. I knew *he* was a malicious asshole looking for someone like me to daily shit-on, just to make himself look like an important disciplinarian to the judicious captain. I could be flying high after winning a bet, or thrilled after seeing a gorgeous female take-off her costume in the ship's entertainment dressing room. But as soon as I approached the inevitable pilothouse, my heart sank into my bowels, knowing that I had to contend with Brown's bossy, cynical, sarcastic, idiotic, and authoritative happy horseshit.

The first time I had a negative encounter with the captain's chief "*Brown*-noser" was in St. Louis, when the steamboat had just backed out from the wharf. I sprinted as usual up the rickety wooden steps to the pilothouse. Brown was standing at the helm, wondering whether he should piss, shit his pants, or loudly fart; and so, being cautious, I deliberately paused in the center of the room. My intent was to make a very prolonged and exaggerated theater stage bow, out of respect for the ship's chain-of-command, which was traditionally extended to anyone in authority.

I suspected that rude and crude Mr. Brown, as usual, decided to feel self-satisfied; his hands gingerly maneuvering the *Pennsylvania* from its dock. I also cleverly reckoned that the haughty asshole was deliberately ignoring my miniscule presence. My astute brain sensed that the neurotic shit-head was furtively aware of my appearance inside the pilothouse, but I dared not interrupt his pretended concentration. If a collision with another boat occurred, *he* naturally would surely blame the event on my distracting him from the performance of his vital duties. I tip-toed very softly and cautiously to the stepped "cub pilot observation bench", where "students of the profession" ardently learned basic, essential knowledge of the unpredictable river, and mastered the very intricate and difficult mechanics of riverboat helmsmanship.

A pregnant ten-minute silence elapsed without a word being exchanged between that sarcastic pecker-head Brown and me. I don't think that I was sitting 'on the bench' like a bump on a log, or like a court judge acting ostentatious, or anything out of the ordinary like that. Then the friggin' dumb ass turned-around and examined my body from head to foot, for what seemed like a good half-hour. I suspected that the reputed faggot wanted me to perform some gay activity on him, so I was mentally *cog*nizant and emotionally prepared to grab his scrawny head and insert it between two of the pilot wheel's *spin*dles. Finally, the friggin' gay jerk-off broke the ice and initiated a rather peculiar, unsavory dialogue.

"Are you Horace Bixby's new cub pilot?" the illiterate asshole asked as if he was addressing a baby bruin through iron zoo bars.

"Yes sir, yes sir," I defensively and politely answered. "My name is Sam Clemens."

"I didn't ask for your goddamned name," Brown snarled back, demonstrating great rancor and a deficiency in civility. "Speak when you're fuckin' spoken to, you, you obnoxious little punk! All I asked you was if you were Horace Bixby's new cub pilot!"

'Fuck you shit-head!' I thought but refrained from uttering. "Yes sir!" I volleyed-back with intense fire raging in my heart. "Yes sir!" I firmly reiterated.

After that initial verbal sparring, there was another pregnant pause, and that fucked-up ignoramus Mr. Brown again feigned sincerity and gruffly asked me, "Now sonny boy. What's your goddamned name again? Ya' got me so pissed-off that I forgot it!"

I felt like administering the stupid fuck a swift knee-lift to the testicles, but then I seriously doubted if the creep had any bona fide nuggets dangling-down between his skinny bowlegs. "My full name is Samuel Langhorne Clemens," I replied as mannerly as I humanly could under the bizarre circumstances.

"Samuel Langhorne Clemens!" the miserable fuck-head repeated like he had amnesia, dementia, or schizophrenia, or some other common asshole mental disease. "Where was ya' born Langhorne?" the repugnant creep asked without the courtesy of saying either my first or last name.

I felt like offering him something smart-ass like "I was born in a bed"; or "in a hospital"; or "in a hospital bed"; or "on Planet Earth," but amazingly, I exhibited remarkable self-control. "In Florida, Missouri, but I grew-up in Hannibal on the banks of the Mississippi," I answered as nicely as I could.

"Well, which damned state was it!" the preoccupied asshole boisterously insisted. "Was you born in the state of Florida, or was you born in the state of Missouri, or was you born in Mississippi, or was you born at all?"

"Er, Missouri," I affirmatively *stated.*

"Ya' shoulda' stayed there, ya' little snot-nosed twerp," Mr. Brown admonished without mentioning any of my name. In fact, in retrospect, the stupid shit never ever called me by name; always addressing me with "Hey you sonny boy!" or "Cabin boy, I wanna' tell ya' something!"

Brown then extracted my family history from me by asking a series of irrelevant questions that had no pertinence to the art and science of riverboat piloting. Mr. Brown's interrogation was interrupted when the fanatic had to steer around several sharp bends, and that enormous responsibility (and test of ability) made the very high-strung knucklehead even more self-conscious and petulant. The insufferable imbecile's face suddenly became beet-red, and every muscle from his forehead to chin began twitching as if the moron was having a terrible bout with St. Vitus palsy. Then, Brown, in lunatic fashion, nastily shrieked without provocation, "See here, you wise-assed simpleton! You gonna' just sit there collectin' splinters in your little fat ass all day?"

"Sir, I have no particular orders to enact!" I diplomatically volleyed-back. "I'm simply here to learn, and you're simply here to teach me something!"

"Ya' say ya' have no orders!" my principal adversary stormed-back like a livid maniac. "My; what a prissy little pussy piss-head you are! How come ya' ain't wearin' a goddamned dress, bra or petticoat?" the belligerent fuck belittled. Then, Brown went on an illogical tirade that when the fool finally finished his diatribe, the nincompoop sounded more like an incoherent asylum patient. "You've had no *orders*, ya' say!" Mr. Brown vehemently ranted. "You think you're some kind of dizzy blonde waitress or somethin', workin' in a goddamned gourmet restaurant? Ya' have *no orders!* This ain't the military son, and I ain't your daddy either, even though I might actually be, since I called ya' son. *Orders* is what ya' want, huh? I'll learn ya' to swell yourself up like a blowfish, or a pregnant bullfrog, and march around this here ship thinkin' you're a freakin' spoiled prince, or a friggin' rich duke. Get away from the damned wheel!" the tyrant imperatively thundered. "Ya' ain't that kind of big wheel yet to take over the *Pennsylvania's* helm! In fact, you'll never amount to anything besides the young discourteous punk ya' already are! Sonny boy, ya' ain't worth your weight in horse manure or termite shit!" the pathetic despot maliciously ridiculed. "That's for damned sure!"

I was stupefied and flabbergasted by the unsolicited and unwarranted verbal assault I had been innocently receiving. I moved back a step, feeling like throwing the egotistical bastard headfirst overboard into the murky, muddy water.

"Ya' ain't fit to be a cabin boy, let alone an ambitious cub pilot on the Mississippi," Brown nastily criticized. "Now, take this ice pitcher down to the Texas Tender. Ya' can be the officer's waiter down in their quarters for the rest of the friggin' mornin'. Better yet," the accomplished ballbreaker continued his impertinent lecture while again changing his detestable, ever-vacillating mind, "deliver the pitcher and then come back here to do some minor chores for me!"

I knew that the Texas Tender was the largest room on the boat where the officers stayed, sort of like a combination office and pleasure lounge. But I was new to the *Pennsylvania,* and didn't know exactly where the damned tender quarters were located. Since the tender was the biggest room on the boat, it was naturally referred to as "Texas". 'Texas on the *Pennsylvania!'* I whimsically thought. 'That's as fuckin' bad as Florida located in Missouri!'

When I finally completed Brown's ball-bustin' errand, I sprinted back up the rickety steps to the pilothouse to avoid further verbal abuse from the "crazed psychopath". Instead, the fanatical fiend yelled, "Hey you, dumbwaiter! Where were ya' sonny boy all that time you've been gone!" the shit-mouth boomed, intentionally breaking my chops and bustin' my sensitive balls simultaneously.

"Sir, I couldn't find the Texas tender, so I had to go down to the pantry and get accurate directions," I indirectly apologized by providing a wonderfully feasible excuse. "I beg that you can fully appreciate my predicament."

"Darned likely phony story ya' just fabricated!" Mr. Brown instinctively chided. "Now fill-up the damned stove with fresh firewood, and do somethin' useful for a goddamned change!"

Brown watched me load the stove like a red-tailed-hawk sizes-up its intended prey. Then, the junior dictator went into another nonsensical, inane outburst. "Put that damned shovel down!" the zany freak characteristically exploded. "You're the damnest numbskull I've ever seen in my life. Ya' ain't even got the wherewithal to load-up a goddamned, cotton-pickin' stove! Were ya' raised in a redneck barn by savage cannibals, or were ya' raised in a goddamned Neanderthal cave?" my volatile, incensed, immediate superior contemptuously rebuked.

That kind of haranguing from the egocentric Mr. Brown went on all throughout that morning watch. And for three whole months, I had to endure a multitude of *his* perpetual sarcasms. I dreaded coming on duty and daily being verbally maligned and butchered with his vitriolic remarks. Brown was like an insidious serpent, always in quest of a pretext to spit-out some hideous venom in my direction. The charlatan would start by commanding, "Here, take the wheel Rookie. I gotta' take a serious healthy crap!" Then, my testy mentor would change his unscrupulous mind and yell, "Where in tar-nation are ya' takin' us, sonny boy? Give me back the goddamned wheel! Give me back the goddamned wheel, I say!" the temperamental pervert fiercely clamored. That particular interaction would be repeated at least twice every day. I was never immune to either Brown's grouchy disposition, or to his continuous wrath.

George Ritchie was the other cub-pilot "learnin' the trade" on the majestic riverboat. The kid was from Pittsburgh, and seemed more at home on the *Pennsylvania* than I did, being from Missouri. Ritchie got along splendidly with his good-natured mentor, George Ealer; and truthfully, I envied the other cub because I had to contend with Mr. Brown's vile, cruddy shenanigans every single day. Ritchie had steered for Brown the previous year, and my friend and peer knew exactly what I had to tolerate and endure from that sorry excuse for a riverboat tutor, namely Mr. Brown.

Whenever I was lucky enough to take the wheel on Ealer's watch, George Ritchie would bust my sensitive testicles by successfully imitating Mr. Brown. "Snatch her! Snatch her!" my buddy would yell without either laughing or smiling. "Pull her down! Pull her down! Damnest greenhorn mud-cat I've ever seen on this here fucked-up planet! Sonny boy, ya' gonna' stay a rank amateur for the rest of your goddamned life!" George affectionately berated. "Don't cramp over that shoal! Watch-out for that damned reef! Give me the damned wheel you stupid whippersnappin', delinquent weasel!"

So, I always had to overcome abundant derogation and denigration, no matter whose watch I was assigned to, George's or Mr. Brown's. And sometimes, George Ritchie's good-natured badgering seemed almost as abusive and almost as abrasive as Mr. Brown's poisonous commentaries. I eventually realized that a cub had to take all the distasteful relegation that a pilot felt obligated shooting in *his* face.

I was expected to appreciate the time-honored riverboat tradition that "critiquing" (harassing) was a vital part of a cub's basic training, so that an apprentice such as myself would be able to keep his cool in any emergency.

George Ealer once confidentially told me that it was a federal crime to ever strike a riverboat pilot, regardless of *his* pessimistic disposition, and if I ever committed that type of heinous felony, I would be dispatched at once to a United States' penitentiary. And so, although I secretly wanted to make Brown into a genuine homicide victim, I reconsidered *that* specific option, and decided to stay the course and absorb all of the savage acrimony *he* could barrage me with. I was determined to survive anything that the arrogant asshole could throw in my direction.

Two trips later down to New Orleans, I got into some serious trouble involving the despicable Mr. Brown. The fucked-up dolt was steering the *Pennsylvania* south down the scenic river. Henry, my impish younger brother, appeared before my alert eyes, walking on the hurricane deck. Young Henry knew of the dramatic conflict going on between Brown and me, so my perceptive sibling yelled-up to the very volatile pilot, "Stop at the next landing and leave me off!"

Brown pretended he didn't hear Henry's innocent request, and the bellicose ignoring asshole went about his routine business as usual. The condescending ingrate never compromised his arrogance to simply recognize the vocalizations of an under-clerk like Henry, or of a cub pilot like me. I knew that Mr. Brown was virtually deaf, even though I perceived that he was dumb. Anyway, Brown always vainly attempted to disguise *that* very obvious dumb and deaf fact. I remained discreet, waiting to see if Brown would honor or ignore my younger brother's request to dock. I didn't want to defiantly challenge my "straightlaced professor" by repeating my sibling's intent to disembark at the next landing, a mile or so down the river.

Well, sure enough, the *Pennsylvania* cruised right past Henry's appointed destination. When we sailed by the designated plantation platform, Captain Klinefelter suddenly appeared on the pilot deck and intensively interrogated the already-frazzled Mr. Brown about the apparent oversight.

"Didn't Henry request to get-off at that landing back there?" the captain authoritatively inquired.

"No sir!" Brown neurotically stammered. "I heard no such request from that irresponsible pipsqueak!"

"Mr. Brown," Captain Klinefelter imperatively said. "Do you realize I'm the one that sent Henry up to the hurricane deck to do it?"

"He did come up to the deck," Brown deviously maintained, "but the little squirt never said a damned word about anything, but just stood there lookin' at me stupid-like the way that *his* immature, older brother does, all the damned friggin' time!"

The *Pennsylvania* was far away from any ocean, or from the *Gulf of Mexico,* so I couldn't understand why Captain Klinefelter would want to *harbor* someone of Brown's low-character ilk on *his* prestigious riverboat. I was shocked when the captain asked me a poignant question.

"Well Clemens; didn't *you* hear Henry's request to get-off at the plantation?" the chief officer asked. "Certainly, if anyone would heed Henry speaking, it would be you."

I knew that if I spoke the truth, then I was indirectly declaring war on Mr. Brown, and that the mercurial son-of-a-bitch would then wrongly deduce that I was betraying him. "Yes sir; I heard Henry tell Mr. Brown to stop!" I courageously responded, spontaneously aggravating my normally volatile instructor, and daringly baiting *him to* now go ballistic in the captain's midst.

"Shut your goddamned mouth!" Brown furiously hollered in my direction while in the benign captain's presence. "You never heard anything of the kind, and if ya' ask me," the infuriated nutcase continued his wild dissertation, "ya' are an insolent young punk wise-ass seekin' to take over my job by deliberately lyin' to Honorable Captain Klinefelter!"

An hour later, Henry casually sauntered into the pilothouse, unaware of the confrontation that had recently transpired. I knew that Brown would show no mercy toward my younger brother and would generalize that Henry was fair game, because *he* and I were genetically similar in the Clemens' family tree.

"Here, here, you fucked-up little squirt chimpanzee!" Brown began his standard didactic vituperation. "Why didn't ya' tell me we'd got to land at the plantation instead of just standin' there like a dimwitted asshole scratchin' your ass like it was infected or somethin'!" the dip-shit irately condemned my sibling. 'Ya' could always swim back to the plantation, if 'ya so desire!"

"But Mr. Brown, I did tell you to stop the boat!" my usually calm and inoffensive brother sincerely answered. "But ya' either didn't listen, or ya' didn't hear!"

"That's a fuckin' boldfaced lie!" Brown cursed and accused. "You lie better than a whore on a wool rug! Both of you Clemens' boys are young, inexperienced hemorrhoids. And you, Henry. You're nothin' more than a dreamin' schemin', no good, smart-assed, sonny boy, punk, just like your nasty older square-assed brother is!"

"That's a bold-face lie!" I exclaimed in honorable defense of Henry and me. "You aren't even fit to be a respectable pilot teachin' anybody anything about this boat, or about this river!"

Brown glared at me and was momentarily speechless at my unanticipated audacity, and at my enviable rhetorical ability. Then, the livid dick-head anxiously shouted like a maniac, "Shut the fuck up! I'll attend to your situation in a minute!" the ninny yelled at me. And next, the insane nutcase vilely criticized Henry by saying, "And you get your silly ass out of this here pilothouse right this minute! You're trespassin' where ya' don't belong and instigatin' trouble, just like your older brother does all the goddamned time!"

The inflexible "pilot law" had to be obeyed, because according to George Ealer and George Ritchie, if it wasn't respected, then Henry would have to spend a month in the county jail for leveling Mr. Brown and sending him to either the hospital or the morgue. When Henry obediently trudged to the door with his head crestfallen, my principal adversary performed a rather deplorable act. The emotionally unstable pilot picked-up a lump of coal weighing a full pound, and with unbridled fury, ran toward my brother and was about to smash the black object into the back of Henry's head. There was absolutely no time for Henry and me to form a *coal*ition against lunatic Mr. Brown.

I first picked-up a small low chair, and hit the *stool* pigeon on top of his noggin', making his dandruff-infected scalp bleed. Then, I picked up a nearby 'club' and violently clobbered Brown on top of his already aching head, exactly like a good "club pilot" should. The uncouth, hostile villain fell to the floor, and was found to be temporarily unconscious from the dramatic impact he himself had perpetrated. I just had had enough of *his* relentless invectives, but when Brown was about to injure my precious brother, I just could not harness my temper and felt compelled to retaliate.

Well, I fully understood I had committed the riverboat crime of crimes, and would more-than-likely bypass the county jail, and that a federal judge's verdict would no doubt sentence me to incarceration in a government penitentiary. 'At least I got *some* personal satisfaction out of this terrific altercation!' I remember thinking. So, I figured I would really get my money's worth of serving two years in prison. I angrily got-down on my knees and began brutally pounding and pummeling the living shit out of the uncivilized, dictatorial asshole, who was still lying prone and dazed upon the pilothouse floor. Fortunately, Henry heard and observed my rage, and my loving sibling interceded by wrapping his arms around my flailing fists. Then, my brother lifted me to my feet and proceeded to wildly tug me to the other side of the pilothouse.

A few seconds later, Brown regained consciousness, and instead of launching an attack on my physical presence, the jerk-off jumped to his feet, and the paranoid moron dashed over to the ship's wheel. In the heat of our out-of-control fight, I had forgotten that the riverboat was heading south with nobody at the helm for five full minutes; the ship was going about fifteen miles an hour downstream. Thank goodness that Eagle Bend was two miles wide, and the water twenty-five feet deep. Thank God no collision with shifting shoals or with existing dangerous reefs was imminent. The magnificent riverboat was in no immediate jeopardy from *steering itself* down that particular stretch of the mighty Mississippi.

Recovering from the shock of receiving the well-deserved thrashing of *his* life, Mr. Brown required a full minute to comprehend that the *Pennsylvania* had miraculously escaped the attendant perils associated with self-steering river navigation. Brown picked-up the giant spyglass that had been set atop his cluttered desk, and raising the instrument as if it was a weapon, the lunatic boisterously ordered me out of the pilothouse. I figured I had sealed my doom and would be ostracized from all riverboats as a result of my blatant insubordination to an immediate, intolerable, egotistical, narcissistic superior. "Get the fuck out of here right now you piss-faced hooligan!" Mr. Brown blustered with his bulging eyes appearing in their sockets as red as rubies.

But I was not afraid of Brown now, because I had just beaten the shit out of him, and was resigned to the idea of being conducted to a federal penitentiary as subsequent punishment. I tarried in the pilothouse, and easily found fault with *his* propensity to use colloquial English when becoming enraged. I said, "Mr. Brown, you should've suavely indicated 'Leave my premises right this instant you, recalcitrant individual'!" I rather perceptively and intelligently corrected *his* poor grammar.

Apparently, Mr. Brown was not acclimated to this sort of controversy involving an underling, so not knowing exactly what the hell to do in that situation, *he* put-down his venerable spyglass on top of his cluttered desk and resumed command of the wheel, generally ignoring my physical presence. Sensing that I had achieved the upper hand in our rocky relationship, I leaped-up on the cub's observation bench and intensely studied *his* body language, which immediately suggested to me that Mr. Brown's despotic spirit had been effectively vanquished by my undaunted tenacity. All *he* did for the next full minute was deliberately stare at the river in sort of a hypnotic trance, while shaking his head back and forth to gesticulate his disgruntled attitude, along with his basic disapproval of recent events.

Our intense scuffle had caused a racket that was heard on the deck below, and soon a dozen very alarmed shipmates and the concerned captain were standing inside the pilothouse. I trembled when I saw Klinefelter's face incredulously staring at both Brown and me.

'Now, my goose is really cooked!' I fearfully thought. 'I've taken away the captain's options, and he has no alternative other than to dismiss me from the ship and report my ass to the local constable!' I anticipated the maximum penalty, since I had endangered the lives of the passengers (without them even knowing it), and I could've inadvertently sunk the *Pennsylvania* and destroyed all of its costly cargo it was carrying downriver to New Orleans.

"Sam Clemens; I'll talk to you in the privacy of my office!" Captain Klinefelter austerely commanded. "I insist that you follow me right this minute!"

I was led to the spacious Texas tender's parlor. The captain closed the after-door, and next closed the forward one; his stern actions giving us the privacy he had promised up on the pilothouse deck where I had recently and satisfactorily kicked the brown crap out of ignoble Mr. Brown. I stood erect like a loyal soldier at attention as Captain Klinefelter adroitly interviewed me.

"So, Mr. Clemens," the good man deliberately began his narrative. "I see you've stooped to fighting with Mr. Brown!"

"Yes, Sir," I politely and meekly replied. "I guess I got tired of his constant abuse. He was going to hit…"

"Do you realize that what you've committed is regarded as a very serious offense?" the riverboat's captain impatiently interrupted.

"Your impulsive action could result in your dismissal from the ship, and a minimum year's vacation in jail!" the chief officer informed.

"Yes, Sir; I'm fully aware of that!" I blandly responded. "I really should've shown more self-discipline! Sorry, Sir. I suppose I was acting too impetuous."

"Are you aware of the fact that the *Pennsylvania* was plowin' down the river at fifteen miles an hour with no one steering it?" my Captain professionally reminded me. "Automatically piloted boats haven't been invented yet!"

"Yes, Sir," I guiltily admitted. "I should've known better I suppose. I guess I'm the ideal asshole!"

"Did ya' strike Mr. Brown first?" my very intelligent boss appropriately and professionally interrogated.

"Yes, Sir, I must confess that I did," I replied without a trace of remorse for my most egregious deed.

"With what did you hit Brown with? Your fists? A hammer?" Captain Klinefelter asked with a grim expression on his face.

"With a stool, Sir," I answered, thinking that Brown himself was a piece of *stool* inside an outhouse's shit hole pit.

"Did ya' clobber him really hard with the stool?" the captain curiously inquired, exhibiting the vocal skill of a highly qualified court prosecutor.

"Fairly hard!" I somberly attested. "At least hard enough to knock him down!"

"Did ya' follow that up?" Captain Klinefelter systematically asked. "By that, I mean, did you continue to hit him without using the stool?"

"Yes sir," I honestly testified. "I pounded him pretty well with both my fists, and bruised-up his face a trifle, and bloodied his nose, too!"

"Well, did you pound Brown more than much? By that I mean, did you fuckin' pound him relentlessly?" the captain further inquired.

"One might describe it like that," I verified.

"Well then," the captain paused. "Don't repeat this to anyone, but I'm really happy to learn that you, pardon my French," my superior hesitated to grasp the proper nomenclature, "that you kicked the fuckin' shit out of the no-good bastard. You did to Brown what I've always wanted to do to that dirty cock-sucker, but I was prevented from accomplishin' my goal by my high position on the ship, and by my good reputation on the river."

"Why thank you, Sir!" I exclaimed with great surprise as I glanced into a nearby wall mirror and detected a sparkle in each of my suddenly rejuvenated eyes.

"But Mr. Clemens, please don't let this incident go to your head!" the captain solemnly warned. "Remember that you've committed a great crime worthy of expulsion from this boat, and banishment from every other ship on the Mississippi," the commanding officer meritoriously proceeded to lecture. "And never be guilty of it again, do you hear? I rarely give any cub pilot a reprieve of any kind, let alone a major one of this nature."

"Yes, Sir. I'll always bear your words in mind," I promised my venerable mentor.

"Now, before the ship docks at the next port, I want you to do *me* a big favor," the captain suavely requested.

"Anything you say," I agreed to cooperate.

"I want you to go up to the pilothouse, and this time *really* beat the living brown feces out of Brown," the captain ordered with a very evident smile upon his countenance. "Do you hear me Clemens? Pulverize the lousy, obnoxious scumbag! A whelp like you is allowed one, and only one official crime on my ship, so go up-deck and finish the damned job you had started!"

I scampered upstairs and accosted Mr. Brown in the pilothouse. "Well, I hope the captain has laid down the riot act to you!" the asshole uttered while staring at the river below and not giving me the courtesy of looking me in the eyes. "Well, you impudent wimp; what do ya' want now, sonny boy!" the cunt-lapper chuckled without mentioning my name.

"I want to beat the livin' shit out of you again!" I boldly yelled as I clenched my fists and quickly administered to the dirty slime-ball a rather violent right cross that was soon followed by a vicious uppercut to the chin. "I'm gonna' hit you over and over for each of the hundred people that always wanted to smack ya' in the face, but didn't have a chance to finish the task!"

An hour later, Brown was all black and blue, and the paper-tiger bully hobbled over to the boiler deck where Captain Klinefelter was conversing with several sophisticated, well-dressed male and female passengers. Brown demanded that I should be put ashore at the next stop, and that the county sheriff should be summoned and notified of my "brutal assault and battery" that had been performed on him.

"That punk Clemens has a criminal mind," Brown asserted, "and I'm never gonna' turn a wheel steering this boat until that insolent ruffian is put in the slammer where he belongs."

"But that cub needn't come around the pilothouse when you're on watch, Mr. Brown," the captain casually replied. "I'll just re-assign young Clemens to George Ealer's watch instead of yours, that's all!"

Brown had too much pride to admit to Captain Klinefelter that I had twice beaten him up, fair and square. "Sir; I refuse to even stay on the same boat with that pugnacious, hooligan, delinquent thug!" Brown argued and complained. "One of *us* has gotta' go ashore and stay there permanently!"

"Very well then; have it your way," Captain Klinefelter cordially acceded. "Let Mr. Brown go and stay ashore, and let Samuel Clemens be a permanent part of my crew!" the ruling officer of the *Pennsylvania* justly decided.

During the remainder of the trip down to New Orleans, I knew exactly how an emancipated slave must feel after escaping the treacheries of the Deep South. For in a certain inexplicable way, I too had finally been emancipated by Captain Klinefelter's benign proclamation liberating me from arrogant Mr. Brown's perpetual tyranny.

"The Cat and the Pain Killer"

Tom Sawyer was extremely depressed. His favorite girl Becky Thatcher was not attending school, and the melancholy lad was mighty concerned that something drastic had happened to her. Perhaps she was going through puberty, and having her first period, or maybe she was pregnant by the sperm juices of another twelve-year-old boy popping his first load. Or maybe that distrustful son-of-a-bitch Huckleberry Finn was hitting on Becky, without ever sagely consulting Tom's unparalleled wisdom.

Young Tom Sawyer began finding himself (without the use of a mirror) surreptitiously hanging around in the vicinity of Judge Thatcher's mansion (well, a mansion by Missouri and Mississippi River standards), and the perplexed youth was feeling more than a tad sick and miserable because of Becky's prolonged absence from school, and possibly, her apparent absence from existence.

'Is she ill? What if she should die?' Tom thought and negatively considered. 'She's pretty rich, and she's rich and pretty; and Becky's quite popular, too. I hope the young doll didn't run away to join the circus as an acrobat, or as a fortuneteller, or dread that she has been captured by dangerous pirates or bandits. Maybe she's finally getting some hair around her luscious cookie, and running a mild temperature. Gee, if Becky is becoming an eleven-year-old prostitute without my permission or approval, I'll be really pissed-off,' Tom Sawyer assessed. I'll become so pissed-off that I might commit suicide, or maybe even homicide, and go to jail for life without ever getting fuckin' laid!' Tom dejectedly contemplated. 'What a horrible thought, that's sure to weigh-down my heart like a heavy anchor! I'd rather go to war and have my balls and dick blasted-off than to have to put-up with all of this silly love bullshit!'

So, the charm associated with the pleasures of Tom Sawyer living; and breathing; and eating; and sleeping; and dreaming; and pissing; and shitting was absolutely gone; totally vanished into oblivion. 'No more playing with my petrified dead bat, or throwing my ugly cat out of my second-floor bedroom window, because those sources of entertainment no longer amuse me,' Tom reckoned.

And Aunt Polly was alarmed that Tom was getting physically sick, and the on-a-mission lady tried a variety of new home remedies on him to determine what prospective cure was the most optimal and viable solution to correct his chronic misery. The domineering woman mercilessly unloaded a heap of her conventional verbal propaganda on poor Tom to accompany the creative snakebite medicines she was prone to buy, not at the town drug store, mind you, but from any on-the-run peddler jumping off the late afternoon steamboat and aggressively promoting the elixir's sale and distribution door-to-door on his way to the next town (and its gullible citizens), either up or down the enchanting river.

"Tom Sawyer, you have to first read a chapter from the Good Book, and then obediently swallow-down two tablespoons of the patent medicine I've just bought for you that's sitting on the kitchen table," Aunt Polly authoritatively insisted. "Now, I've read all sorts of literature about the need for resolving your major health problem in the monthly periodical I've subscribed to, and all the published experts say that you have to defeat a cold in its initial stages before you're bedridden and about to go unconscious after receiving an enema," the sagacious woman maintained. "And during your health crisis, don't forget to keep your room well-ventilated with your window half-open, even though it's almost the height of winter. And do some exercising, but not with your greedy little hands down inside your pajamas," Aunt Polly continued orating her relentless diatribe. "You might be going through a terrible growth process called 'puberty', and you're coming into what Reverend Thompson refers to as 'the Temptation Zone', with the diabolical Devil becoming more active and tantalizing in your mischievous life. Church services twice on Sunday will also aid and cure you in overcoming your current malady!"

"Aunt Polly, your family doctor must look like a duck with all of these quack medicines and cures that you believe in and try to practice," Tom nastily and defensively answered. "And as for the Devil and his subordinate demons, Huck Finn and me, and the rest of our gang will beat the crap out of those red-tailed varmints, either on Earth, or in Hell, or in Purgatory, after we all finally get there and organize our rebel army!"

"Tom, I do believe that you've already become susceptible to Satan's evil influence. I swear that I'm going to get the preacher to march over to this house and exercise an exorcism on you," Aunt Polly adamantly replied. "If he can't do it, I'm sure that the bishop can! You're probably the most defiant mouth in the South when it boils-down to being insolent. Now just pretend, Mr. Sawyer, that I'm the Angel of Healing, and agree to sample this new medicine that I've recently obtained. It's called Pain Killer; and it's guaranteed to remove all of those evil germs and wicked spirits out of your vulnerable, diseased system."

‘If the Pain Killer would make me have my first ejaculation and wet orgasm,’ Tom mentally reckoned, ‘then I might consider drinking down the whole fuckin’ bottle.’

But then young Sawyer became more rational and boldly challenged his guardian on *his* moral and logical battlefield. “Aunt Polly, you ain’t gonna’ get me behind the woodshed and pour buckets of cold water on my naked body, because you ain’t gonna’ be able to see my naked body anymore,” Tom Sawyer courageously argued, attempting to establish his independence and his about-to-happen teenage puberty rebellion. “I’m startin’ to get some important peach fuzz around my dingle, and pretty soon, I’ll be squirtin’ sticky sperm juice all over the damned place, especially on my bedroom walls, and maybe even up on the ceiling, should I produce a real gusher. And besides those potential acts,” the thoroughly upset lad editorialized, “I’ll no longer consent to bein’ wrapped-up in a wet blanket; so Aunt Polly, it’s lookin’ like you’re goin’ to be the only damned wet blanket and crepe hanger in this here house!”

“Tom Sawyer! You vulgar, obscene little Imp!” Aunt Polly yelled and scolded. “I’ll make sure that the harmful yellow infection stains ooze right out of your pores, and that you profusely sweat your entire body clean under ten pounds of heavy towels. But I’ll allow you to take your hot sitz baths in private, if you insist on not being scrutinized. And then, Young Man, there’s going to be numerous mustard plaster applications I’ll administer, and also a strict oatmeal diet, too!” the livid lady ranted. “But listen-up, Tom! You’re going to have to drink-down these two tablespoons of Pain Killer, or else I’m going to make an appointment for Minister Thompson to come to the house, and through an hour of intense Bible prayers and chants, the beloved Reverend will skillfully remove all of those pesky evil demons that are greedily possessing your body and your juvenile mind. Now, here you are Tom Sawyer. Take and gulp-down this wonderful medicine so that I can begin retrieving your soul from Lucifer’s covetous clutches!”

“Okay, Aunt Polly. But I think I’d rather pal around with Satan than buddy-up with either you or Preacher Thompson!” Tom vehemently protested. “Yuck! This junk tastes like liquid shit! It’s gonna’ rot my stomach and asshole away!”

“Tom, you watch your foul language and show more respect for your elderly Aunt Polly!” the aggravated woman commanded. “I’m thinking about making you join the church choir, or maybe go over to that Catholic Church across town and become an altar boy! That’s it!

We'll have the town doctor cut-off your testicles, and you'll instantly become a Castrati choir boy!"

"Great ideas Aunt Polly!" Tom vehemently balked. "That's just what I need! I don't want to be molested by either that faggot Reverend Thompson or by that gay pedophile Catholic priest, either. All I want to do is screw Becky Thatcher, get her pregnant, and then go into politics just like all of the successful, immoral assholes in this messed-up town do!"

"Sakes alive Tom! Your rudeness is incredibly intolerable! You need to rinse your mouth out with detergent after you take another dose of this delicious Pain Killer!"

"Aunt Polly wants a cracker, so why don't you find a good white man to sleep with and get yourself pregnant!" Tom impertinently answered. "At least that's what all of the black folks around town have been sayin' about you!"

* * * * * * * * * * * * *

Being excessively naughty and unscrupulous, Tom began asking his beleaguered relative for Pain Killer at every opportunity, and the fiasco eventually reached the point where the boy's constant utterances became a plain nuisance, and Aunt Polly was getting awfully suspicious of young Mr. Sawyer's all-too-furtive motives, and the old lady was often yelling into his face, "Quit bothering me with your asinine requests!" But the aged woman persistently distrusted her nefarious nephew, and closely watched the Pain Killer bottle clandestinely, endeavoring to catch Tom pouring its contents out the nearest window an ounce at a time; but Tom's guardian's vigilance and perseverance were to no avail. All that Aunt Polly could daily observe was the liquid level inside the brown medicine bottle upon the kitchen shelf gradually diminishing in volume, day after precious day.

But all the while, instead of mending his poor health with the magic Pain Killer formula, wily Tom was each and every afternoon assiduously mending a narrow crack in the wood-planked sitting room floor. One Wednesday afternoon, mischievous Sawyer was secretively filling the aforementioned crevice with some new Pain Killer, when Aunt Polly's near-death yellow cat Peter came purring into the vicinity, and then keenly eyeballed the cherry red liquid rather avariciously.

"Well, Peter; let's see if this powerful shit will make your peter erect!" Tom whispered out of fear of getting caught administering the all-potent drug to the rapidly deteriorating tomcat. “Let’s see ya’ lick this foul-tasting crap down your throat, and we’ll see if it rejuvenates you back into your youth when ya’ used to be the best damned fighting, sex-starved cat in the whole damned town. But don’t blame me if this shit makes you jump-up to the ceiling, hit your head hard, and then die as a result of you bein’ cured of distemper, or whatever the hell’s wrong with you. I warn ya’ Peter. This nasty mixture tastes a lot worse than cod liver oil, or even that horrible castor oil shit.”

So, then, Tom gingerly pried-open Peter’s mouth and poured-down an ounce or two of the omnipotent, putrid-tasting Pain Killer remedy. Well, that ornery tomcat sprang several yards up into the air, with its normally kinked, curly fur standing straight-up on its back and tail. And upon honoring the rules of gravity and hitting the floor on all fours, the suddenly-obsessed animal screamed incessantly, and wildly whirled around in circles at least two dozen times, violently knocking over flower pots, ramming against furniture legs, and pissing a long yellow streak while crazily and repeatedly scampering around the confined area in full velocity.

Next, Peter, being exhausted, ceased his frenetic frenzy, and then pranced around the room like one of those trained white Austrian stallions, flamboyantly showing-off his fantastic, new-found, energized disposition. But then the possessed cat accelerated again to full speed, tearing around the house like a creature possessed with demented demons, and in his self-created chaos, the furry marauder was plowing into any object or obstacle in his erratic path.

Aunt Polly immediately stepped into the normally tranquil sewing room, put her wet hands on her hips, and promptly (in an exasperated tone of voice) interrogated innocent-looking Tom about what all the commotion and racket was about.

“I don’t know what the heck’s gotten into Peter,” Tom politely and uncharacteristically testified, showing little remorse or humiliation for his naughty actions. “I think Peter’s entered his second childhood and wants to be the kitty in a poker game over in the smokey back room down at the pool hall!”

“I don’t know what ails that strange-behaving tomcat, but I’m glad to see that he’s getting over his general lethargy, even at the expense of breaking a couple of flowerpots,” Aunt Polly stated in a confused state of mind. But then, the old lady bent-down and discovered the telltale handle to the tablespoon sticking-out, and quite visible, under the sewing room’s table. The irate woman immediately fathomed exactly what had occurred to Peter, so she swiftly raised Tom up by his right ear, and repeatedly clobbered his cranium with the heavy tablespoon until his scalp and skull fully ached. Then, the extremely livid woman placed her metal sewing thimble upon her index finger, and made several impressive rivets and dents directly upon Tom's already-throbbing forehead.

"Tom Sawyer, why did you have to treat poor Peter with such unbridled malice?" Aunt Polly very loudly chastised her principal nemesis. "You know that the creature is nearly blind; can't hear a lick, and can't even smell his own feces! Stop deliberately torturing and abusing that poor animal."

"I only gave him the same damned medicine you was givin' me," Tom effectively debated the issue. "I was only treatin' old Peter like he was a human being. I done it out of sheer pity, because Peter ain't got a wonderful caring aunt like I do; a lady who gives me delicious medicine to cure my illnesses!"

Aunt Polly suddenly felt a wave of charitable compassion envelop her, and she soon experienced a pang of remorse (penetrate her forgiving heart) for the excessive punishment of her saintly and considerate nephew. The old bag's eyes watered, and she put her hand on young Sawyer's shoulder saying, "I'm sorry for hurting you, Tom. I was meaning the best for you and Peter, so that's why I unfortunately pounded and pummeled you!"

"Well, Aunt Polly; the Pain Killer really did Peter some good because his peter became erect, and now the cat can journey about and screw all of the pussy in the neighborhood; even pumpin' the hairy ass of the gay faggot male cat moochin' a living next door. And that psyched-up Tom-cat of yours is feelin' young and virile once again, thanks to the wonderful wizardry of your most fabulous Pain Killer formula."

"Oh Tom; get to bed early so that you can arrive at school tomorrow morning well-rested," his protective guardian advised. "I just know that you're going to grow-up to be a famous scientist, inventor, mathematician, or comedian some day!"

* * * * * * * * * * * * *

Anticipating a punctual rendezvous with Becky Thatcher, Tom reached school early the following morning. The impulsive lad anxiously loitered around the playground gate, hoping to catch a glimpse of Becky's frock approaching from the distance, but the boy's intense surveillance was noticeably unproductive. Young Sawyer had felt both swindled and hoodwinked by the whims of fate, if not being egregiously exploited by human nature. The kid twice entered (and exited) the play area and half-heartedly chased some friends around the perimeter, pretending to be a twelve-year-old successful hooligan, but out of the corner of his eye, Tom was stealthily doing espionage and reconnaissance work looking-out for any sign of his imagined sweetheart. Jeff Thatcher then paraded through the open gate and into the dirt and gravel area, and Tom accosted the free spirit, and felt compelled to ask him a question or two about *his* absent sister.

"Hell Tom; I ain't got the time of day for Becky, no way," Jeff responded to Sawyer's dire inquiry. "My parents treat her like she's some sort of special royalty, so the conceited little bitch thinks she's a princess and a goddamned queen-in-waiting! See ya' around Tom! I got my eyes on that cute little Mary Lee Chapman doll standin' all by her lonesome over there!"

Tom heard the teacher's hand bell ring, and reluctantly entered the schoolhouse with his head crestfallen. All during morning roll call, the boy's head rubbernecked toward the side window, looking for any sign of his missing girl-Venus. 'Maybe she's eloped with some older punk, and they've run off to Ohio or the Amazon!' Tom imagined. 'No; Becky wouldn't do anything drastic like that! She's too spoiled-rotten at home by her overprotective parents to ever consider doin' anything like that kind of dumb stupid shit!'

Soon, one last frock came ambling into the schoolyard, and Tom's heart nearly leaped out of his chest. Against the alarmed teacher's wishes, the overzealous lad jumped-out of his desk and zoomed out of the schoolhouse, dashing full-throttle towards the petite girl of his dreams. Young Sawyer intentionally grabbed a tardy boy's hat off his head, as the youth was entering the ramshackle building, and then nonchalantly tossed the object onto the schoolhouse's roof.

"My goodness Tom!" Becky Thatcher exclaimed in indignant disappointment. "Some rebellious asshole I know thinks he's mighty important around these parts and always showing-off."

"Look Becky," acne-faced Tom replied. "I see a big zit on your forehead, so that pimple either means that you're getting over the chicken pox, or having your first monthly period and goin' through what the local pious adults call 'puberty'. If that's the case," Tom said with a sparkle in his eye, "let's go inside Aunt Polly's tool shed after school so that we can play a friendly game of doctor, and curiously examine each other's newly-formed pubic fuzz!"

"The Fence and the Sunday School"

Aunt Polly entered the remote upstairs bedroom of her St. Petersburg home and yelled for her often-derelict nephew, "Tom Sawyer! Show your dirty face right this very second, or else you'll have your choice of either sleeping in the cellar, or in the attic tonight! Come-out from where you're hiding! You're always running away from work and responsibility! Grow-up, now! Act your age instead of your shoe-size!"

After a minute of graveyard-like silence, Aunt Polly continued articulating her threatening diatribes. "You just wait until I get my firm arthritic hands around your neck, you little impulsive Imp!" Aunt Polly screamed as the volatile woman poked under the boy's bed with her long dirty broom. "You're goin' to wish that you never had testicles and a rectum when I get done with you!"

Aunt Polly then observed the open bedroom window, and stuck her head outside to scan the garden, the backyard, and the distant woods for any sign of the mischievous, delinquent boy. But all that her roving eyes could detect was the stack of wood that her nephew hadn't yet cut, plenty of towering weeds that also hadn't been pulled, along with a whole tall-grass lawn that the irresponsible boy hadn't mowed. But Aunt Polly's keen ears soon detected a squeak behind her, and nearly decapitating her head upon the raised window, the incensed woman wheeled-around and skillfully collared the rascally lad. The livid aunt was holding her shaking hands around Tom's vulnerable throat in the classic professional wrestler's strangle grip.

"Ah Tom, I knew I should've checked to see if your ass was secretly stashed away in the closet!" Aunt Polly began her intensive oral indictment. "Did you think that this house is a ship, and that your closet was the hold where you could furtively stow away from the captain? What's that sticky red crap oozing out of your mouth? Are you pretending to be a vampire? It certainly isn't blood! And I'm not squeezing your skinny neck hard enough for that liquid crap to be internal bleeding!"

"It ain't nothing important, Aunt Polly!" Tom gasped and panted as his nose and throat struggled to inhale fresh oxygen. "It ain't nothin', ma'am! You're cuttin' off my air supply!" Tom choked and groaned. "You're cuttin' off my air, and I'm gonna' die, and you're gonna' go to Hell and have to work for the Devil!"

"Why that's the fresh jelly I just made for Mrs. Harper dripping-down from your lying lips!" Aunt Polly hollered as the incensed lady applied more pressure to Tom's aching larynx and upper trachea. "It seems that you're always in a *jam!* And what's that white powder trickling out of your pants' pocket? Is it some new kind of drug, or tobacco? Holy Moses Tom!" Aunt Polly exclaimed as she maintained her prodigious strangle grip. "There must've been a pound of sugar stuffed inside! The next thing I know, you'll be sleeping in your bed with some honky-tonk brown sugar! That's the last straw that broke the dromedary's back, Mr. Sawyer! Now I'll ease-up on your neck and attempt yanking your ear lobe off!"

The following day was a sultry Saturday July morning, and with the whole vicinity of the small-town bursting with energy and life, Tom Sawyer had been officially relegated to the assignment of whitewashing the giant fence that encompassed Aunt Polly's property. The lackluster, cedar structure was six-feet-high, and had a perimeter of at least four-hundred-feet, and young Sawyer had to paint the entire damned length, width, and height of the obstacle before he could go swimming, fishing, or running-away from home for the twentieth time that summer month.

'The damned punishment doesn't match the simple crime,' Tom complained to himself as the lad splashed his wide brush into the bucket, and then initiated his tedious daubing. 'Forget escaping to Ohio! The next time I run away from home, I'm leaving Missouri for good, and will wind-up in either Canada or the Bahamas, or in one of those other distant states.'

After lazily completing the first vertical board, Tom sat his rear end down under a tree to rest, and contemplate his un-dramatic fate. 'Shit! I could be fishing, or fighting, or smoking, or cursing, or gambling, or robbing stage coaches, and here I am; doing this stupid-ass adult work bull-crap!' Tom sadly regretted and lamented. 'This cornball job won't be finished until I have my first orgasm, which might not be until next 4th of July. If other kids see me doing this shit,' Tom conjectured, 'I'll be the laughing stock of the town, and the guys will all get together, drag my ass over to the gang's cave, and make me remove the dingleberries from their rear ends; and then lick their smelly assholes as a final insult! And I'm sure as hell not going to be engaging in that degrading horse-crap activity! I'd rather be doing it to total strangers, or to monsters up there in Canada, than to my ornery Missouri pals here along the Mississippi River!'

Tom stood-up and resigned himself to his already-prescribed morning (mourning) destiny. After five minutes of lethargic first-coat board applications, the delegated chore and task worker heard a familiar whistling and singing coming around the corner, and the approaching youth was non-other than Ben Rogers, a chubby self-centered kid notorious for breaking Tom Sawyer's balls at every given opportunity.

Young Sawyer stood erect as if the youth was an ambitious Michelangelo or Rembrandt putting the finishing touches on a spectacular new masterpiece, and Sawyer's intense concentration immediately caught the attention of Ben Rogers, who ceased biting into his delicious green apple, and curiously wondered what sort of mischief his occasional friend was engaged in doing. But all the while, wily Tom pretended that Ben Rogers had been walking, eating, and behaving in another non-perceptible dimension.

"Got to work your ass off, don't ya'!" Rogers began his predictable harassment. "I thought that you liked *fencing* with swords and sabers, and not with usin' a cheap brush and whitewash. It looks like dingleberry plucking and ass-licking time for you, Tom, once I tell Joe Harper and the other guys about this stupid-ass bullshit your aunt is makin' ya' do! You're gonna' be hi-jacked by a tribe of renegade Indians, and dragged on out to the secret cave where we'll make ya' earn your new brown tongue! Ha, ha, ha!" Ben guffawed, holding his flabby stomach intact. "It'll be just grand! Ha, ha, ha! You'll be givin' us a lickin', while we'll be givin' *you* the real lickin', ha, ha, ha!"

Tom ignored Ben's extremely sarcastic remarks, rubbed his chin in a philosophical manner, crossed his arms in deep meditation, and carefully scrutinized the un-majestic fence as if he were evaluating the genius of the *Mona Lisa's* brush strokes upon the canvas hanging on the wall of a famous museum over in Paris.

"There ain't no special mystery to this particular job," Ben pragmatically criticized as the boy's teeth crunched-down and took another bite out of his large green apple. "Your nasty Aunt Polly put you to work, and there ain't no more rebellion left in ya' to resist her dumb-ass authority. This definitely looks like a double round of dingleberry removal and ass lickin' for you, Tom!" Rogers chuckled and then smirked. "Joe and me will even get kids that aren't in our gang to participate in having their smelly assholes licked! Maybe even a few of the older girls, too, might want their stinky assholes and fur-burgers lapped! But their aromatic pussy holes will be off limits for you to munch on! Ha, ha, ha! This punishment of yours is absolutely wonderful bullshit, Tom, ha, ha, ha!"

Tom turned his head towards Ben and acted shocked to see the instigator/aggravator standing there on the pavement beneath the hot overhead sun. "Gosh, Ben. What the hell are ya' doin' here? I thought you might be involved in something borin' this mornin' like swimmin', or fishin', or jerking-off!"

"Well, for your confidential information Tom, I'm goin' to the swimmin' hole with Joe in about an hour. Harper tells me that there's been a couple of older girls with lots of hair on their cookies that go skinny-dippin' over at the cove on the lake, and my buddy and I will be hidin' in the bushes watchin' the girls' bushes, while they're gigglin' and splashin' around in the water. It sure beats the hell out of work, I'd say! The bushes aren't always used for ambushin', ya' know what the frig' I mean, Tom?"

"What the hell kind of work are ya' yappin' about me doin', Ben?" Tom audaciously challenged his fat, egotistical friend. "Sometimes your asshole comments are more puzzlin' than the damned mysteries of the Universe are, all put together! You don't know your ass from a hole in the ground, because you don't even know what the fuck a hole in the ground looks like; let alone your ugly asshole! Now leave me the hell alone while I continue enjoyin' this marvelous pleasure that I'm engaged in."

"You're tryin' to tell me that you actually *like* painting this enormous fence," Ben laughed, and then held his crotch to prevent himself from pissing his pants. "I suppose that ya' also like obeyin' your Aunt Polly's bullshit commands, too!"

"It's not every day that a Missouri boy gets to whitewash a huge fence, Ben!" Tom argued and maintained. "Think real-hard, but don't let your mini-brain explode out of your stubborn hard head, and thus ruin my magnificent paint job!" Sawyer chastised his highly critical pal. "When's the last fuckin' time you've done something as strange and unique as I'm doin' right now? I believe you've been subject to brainwashing about the joys of whitewashing; that's what the fuck I think!"

Ben watched Tom adroitly maneuver the wide brush over the wooden fence, and began to actually envy his friend's nonchalance as Sawyer stopped every three strokes or so to admire his own expanding accomplishment. "Say, Tom; forget those older girls with hairy pussies jumpin' around in the shallow water down at the lake. Let me try my hand at improvin' your fancy artwork! Leonardo da Vinci was one of my distant ancestors over there in France, or was it fuckin' Russia?"

"Bullshit, Ben! I can't trust this vital job to a rank amateur such as yourself!" Tom insisted, feigning prolific anger and resentment. "And Aunt Polly won't ever appreciate your involvement or contribution to this terrific project. She told me that only one acne-faced kid out of ten thousand is capable of satisfactorily whitewashing this colossal fence!" young Sawyer exaggerated. "She told me that not even fuckin' Hercules, or that giant son-of-a-bitch Paul Bunyan was capable of reliably finishin' this difficult job, and then achievin' perfect results!"

"Tom, please give me a shot!" Ben pleaded and insisted. "I'll give you the rest of my tasty apple! I promise not to tell the gang of how you're obeyin' your Aunt Polly's wicked tyranny! I'll even gently pull the dingleberries out of *your* asshole, and lick it three times for good luck, if you agree that there won't be any witnesses! Please, Tom. Let me whitewash the fence!" Ben Rogers again begged. "It's just like jerkin' off to get my first volcanic explosion; that's how I see it! I just gotta' try it, Tom!"

"Okay, Ben. Here's the goddamned brush," Tom indignantly answered. "And don't get any freakin' whitewash on the pavement, or else Aunt Polly will be blamin' me for your awkwardness. And if you do a decent job," Tom speculated and remarked, "I'll bet your final brush swipe will be at the *stroke* of midnight. And then Ben, your heart and mind will be in full ecstasy thinkin' all about the greatest attainment of your fucked-up dull and dismal life!"

Tom then sat under the tall shade tree, and savored swallowing down the remaining bites to the green apple, all the time deriving tremendous satisfaction from observing Ben Rogers' dedicated toil in the sweltering summer heat. But young Sawyer quickly realized and concluded that his genius had accidentally discovered a fantastic axiom relevant to early nineteenth-century juvenile life. 'If I can make an asshole knucklehead like Ben Rogers want to do something against his will, all I have to do is make that certain something hard to get, and the rest of the monotonous bullshit suddenly becomes quite easy to finish! It's as easy as swallowing-down raspberry jam!'

* * * * * * * * * * * * *

Tom was in a festive mood the next morning at breakfast, until Aunt Polly reminded the Devil-may-care youth that it was "the Lord's Day", and that the ornery boy would have to dress-up in his formal finery, and attend the grueling, monotonous routine commonly known as Sunday School. Even Aunt Polly's scrumptious pancakes seemed to lose their taste appeal, along with the accompanying sweet-maple-syrup, when the pious woman deliberately whipped-out her gold leaf Bible. and began reviewing the Ten Commandments as she had done each and every Sunday morning. Tom despised the Sunday morning sessions more than the young rebel hated severe stomach aches, measles, mumps, chicken-pox, indigestion, and constipation.

"The Good Books says…"

"I didn't know that any book includin' the Bible could talk," Tom objected and challenged. "The Good Book never says anything at all Aunt Polly, because it has no darned vocal cords and mouth, and can't speak a word, blessed or otherwise!"

"Well Tom, if you refuse to listen to the great wisdom that I want to read you, then you'll have to hear the holy knowledge from Mr. Walters at your Sunday School class. But first," the devout guardian ordered, "you must study with your conscientious cousin Mary, who'll be here to tutor you any minute now."

"I studied and memorized my verses yesterday," Tom's saintly brother Sid piped-up, just to deliberately pester and bother his pesky sibling. "See you later, Tom! You'll have to postpone until tomorrow killing those savage Indians, and those desperado outlaws you were plannin' on ruthlessly murderin'!" Then, the taunting "goody-goody-two-shoes" sped-out the kitchen door to play with himself' (by himself?) before his vengeful brother could utter a syllable.

Reluctantly, Tom shuffled off to his bedroom, located his small Bible upon his closet's top shelf, and blew-off the accumulated dust, thus griming-up his entire face. 'I got five Bible verses I have to memorize,' Sawyer remembered as the reluctant reader hurriedly leafed through the New Testament. 'Here it is. I'll select five short lines from the Sermon on the Mount. This studyin' job oughta' be easier than stealin' and eatin' raspberry jam, and certainly plenty easier than whitewashin' that atrocious fence! Maybe I can convince Ben Rogers to learn this shit for me!'

Ten minutes later, always punctual Mary entered Tom's bedroom, and the devious boy thought, 'It's a damned good thing we aren't kissin' cousins. Who the hell would ever want to screw this ugly bucktoothed little bitch?'

"Okay, Tom. I've been appointed by Aunt Polly to hear you recite some specific verses," the well-behaved girl haughtily teased. "Let's see if you know more than the average atheist does, or more than a deaf and dumb Arab knows about the Holy Bible."

"Blessed are the assholes, because they…"

"Blessed are the poor," Mary groaned and then corrected.

"Oh yeah; blessed are the poor assholes because…"

"Because the poor assholes are poor in spirit," Mary erroneously finished, finally realizing her verbal mistake by shamefully putting her hand over her mouth in disgrace.

"Mary, aren't you the mother of Jesus?" Tom sarcastically asked. "Is your husband's name Joseph?"

"Tom, you're the biggest sinner I know, and you're gonna' bask in Hell for all eternity. I'm sure of it!"

"If Hell was like Antarctica, or even like the North Pole, I'd be afraid to go there, but since I like the summertime heat, I'll be glad to stay there forever like you say," the cousin obnoxiously stated. "At least I'll be in fairly good company with Huck Finn, Ben Rogers, and Joe Harper fightin' and assassinatin' demons, gargoyles, monsters, assholes, and devils!"

After an hour of very difficult tutoring, Mary helped Tom button the starched-collar white shirt that complemented his wrinkled-up Sunday suit, and then brushed the thick white dandruff off of the cuffs, elbows, and shoulder fabric. "Here Tom. Here's your favorite formal speckled straw hat you can proudly wear. Just pretend you're an important king or someone of high royalty."

'I'd rather have Mr. Walters suck my tiny dick than listen to that fucked-up gay asshole's corny bullshit,' Tom secretly thought. "Oh well Mary," young Sawyer declared with an all-too-honest frown. "Which way to the local gallows?"

Contrary to her cousin Tom's dissatisfaction with Sunday School attendance, Mary absolutely both loved and relished the mediocre hour-long ordeal. The school's fundamental rules of motivation were quite elementary and understandable: If a boy or girl could recite two Bible verses, he or she received a blue ticket from Mr. Walters, or from his assistant. And ten blue tickets equaled one red ticket; and ten red tickets was equivalent to one yellow *redemption* stub, and upon amassing ten yellow stubs, the lucky ticket collector and verse-quoter would be eligible to receive a bona fide, plainly-bound, Christian King James Version Bible.

'KJV! Keep jerking vertical!' Tom thought and laughed. "Two thousand verses happen to be way-too-much information for my petite brain to learn," Tom told Mary on their ramble into the center of the village. "I have to go through ten whole redemptions to get to Heaven. I should only have to redeem myself but once!"

"I've won two Bibles, Tom," Mary reminded her derelict cousin. "And don't forget that Gunther, that German boy who just had the measles; he's won four or five, and doesn't even speak English too well! He just memorizes those sacred words and phrases and sentences for the glory of mastering religion, and eventually winding-up at the Pearly Gates!"

"Gunther would've been better off stayin' in Berlin and collectin' all the germs in Germany," Tom vulgarly quipped. "The dumb-ass jerk-off deserves to have the German measles! What the hell's the sense of ownin' five damned Bibles, anyway? You'd only have to give at least four of the suckers away to other dumb-ass, obedient assholes just like yourself'!"

Sid was running and eventually caught-up with Tom and Mary, and the three finished their jaunt to the all-too-familiar Sunday School building. Outside the meeting hall, Tom noticed a friend Billy Barker, whose father worked in a carnival sideshow as the designated loud-mouthed announcer who would bally prospective customers inside a tent to witness and appreciate all kinds of human freaks and spectacles.

"Say Billy, I know ya' got a yeller ticket? What'll you take for her in a decent trade?"

"What'll ya' give me?" Billy Barker asked. "I'll never accumulate ten of these suckers, and even if I was that crazy, who the hell wants a goddamned Bible?"

"I'll give ya' a piece of black licorice, a fishhook, and a pornographic picture of a nude lady with big tits and a hairy bushola!" Tom bargained.

"It's a damned deal!" Billy exclaimed and cursed. "I need something tangible to which I can jerk-off to! This neat clear picture of yours is the perfect thing to stare at while workin' my stick!"

Tom made a circuit of the assembled boys standing outside the hall, and soon amassed ten yellow ticket redemption stubs, thus qualifying him to earn an official Bible. And according to Tom's always-scheming, contrary-to-authority mind, the itchy boy could impress 'All of the horny holy roller girls sitting there in their hard wooden chairs and stealthily playing with their swollen buttons.'

The Sunday School class was a restless aggregate of troublesome and noisy rebellious boys, mixed-in with thoroughly domesticated and subservient horny girls. But in Mr. Walters' sage estimation, Tom Sawyer was without a doubt, the worst behaved nightmare of the entire group of twenty-nine "sagacious Good Book students".

After the neurotic kids were moved around and seated in alphabetical name arrangement, which happened each and every Sunday, Mr. Walters impatiently picked-up a piece of chalk, and then foolishly turned his back to write a salient parable upon the blackboard. All of a sudden, a boy to the right rear of the room yelled

“Ouch!”, and the pedagogue quickly determined that Tom Sawyer had been the instigator of some nefarious malice.

After ineffectively verbally reprimanding Tom’s “insolent deportment,” Mr. Walters somberly addressed the irascible male students along with the compliant females. “Now class, please sit-up straight; fold your hands, and listen carefully. I want your undivided attention. We have a new family residing in town, and they’re going to visit us shortly.”

“Why don’t they visit us in their right height?” Tom defiantly challenged his religious mentor out loud. “Why do these new people have to enter the room shortly?”

Before Mr. Walters could attempt disciplining the derelict young sinner, the eyes of all present inside the spacious room turned to the rear, where a well-dressed, affluent-looking family, consisting of a portly, short, dark-haired man wearing glasses; a dignified and refined woman, and their pretty blonde-haired daughter instantly occupied everyone’s attention.

‘That two-pigtailed blonde bitch is really something beautiful!’ Tom evaluated as the boy’s greedy pupils widened to their maximum diameter. ‘I’ll have to make a good impression on her without jumping or stomping on her shiny black right shoe. Now how can I get that knockout doll to notice little old me? I think I’ll soon have the damned solution well at hand.’

The stocky, short man was formally introduced to the class as Judge Thatcher, “the finest and most-powerful justice in the entire county.” And although Tom didn’t catch the man’s wife’s name, his ears perked-up when the horny kid heard that the pretty blonde girl’s identity was “Becky”.

Realizing that the Judge was curiously watching and evaluating the rather raucous class, Mr. Walters futilely shouted-out general directions as all the other undisciplined boys began imitating Tom Sawyer’s careless-care-less disposition. Several paper missiles erratically (and missile-aneously) zoomed across the expansive room, so out of fear of losing control of his charges before adult classroom spectators, Mr. Walters motioned for Judge Thatcher to step forward to possibly assist in conferring a formal Bible prize to a fortunate recipient. Naturally, the class’s clamor soon subsided with the appearance of the distinguished American citizen standing in front of the hot sweltering room.

“Judge Thatcher might like to have the privilege of awarding a Bible to any exceptional student that has diligently worked to accumulate ten yellow redemption tickets,” Mr. Walters nervously announced. “Does anyone in the class have ten yellow coupons in his or her possession?”

Tom raised his hand, stood-up, and unilaterally marched to the front of the room without ever being instructed to do so. “Here you are Mr. Walters, sir. Ten yeller ones, just what you had asked for! Yes sir; here those suckers are!”

The teacher’s face turned ashen as if a thirsty vampire had just sucked all of the blood out of his neck and head. The pedagogue hesitated, and then seeing the broad smile of approbation on Judge Thatcher’s countenance, Mr. Walters slowly counted Tom’s ten yellow tickets. The class burst-out into a boisterous round of spontaneous applause, and Tom couldn’t resist glowing in that radiant moment of personal triumph. The junior instigator turned to his right side, and noticed Becky Thatcher joining the overall recognition and passively clapping her hands, much to the incredulity and chagrin of already-humiliated Mr. Walters. Yes, in Tom’s presumptuous mind, total victory was about to be clutched, possessed, and cherished.

The ruffled instructor then introduced Tom to Judge Thatcher and the usually-delinquent boy, for the first time in his rational life, was spellbound and appeared virtually speechless.

“What’s your name, son?” the Judge cordially asked. “Don’t be shy about your major accomplishment. I’m quite honored to make your acquaintance.”

“T-Tom; Thomas sir,” the suddenly-paranoid lad stuttered and answered. “Thomas Sawyer.”

“What an inspirational and marvelous young man!” the Judge commended, not knowing Tom from Adam, Abraham, Isaac, Jacob Moses, or Doubting Thomas. “And Thomas; you had competently mastered memorizing two thousand verses. Knowledge is indeed what makes great and excellent men, yes it does! One day Thomas; you’ll attribute all of your fabulous success to your noteworthy and admirable Sunday School achievement.”

“Thank you, sir,” Tom replied, showing an element of modesty and genteel civilization.

“Now son,” the Judge stated in a more authoritative tone. “Could you kindly share several of your wonderful Biblical verses with this fine audience of your envious peers? No doubt, you know the names of all twelve apostles, including that diabolical rogue scoundrel Judas Iscariot. If it’s not too much of an imposition,” Judge Thatcher strongly urged, “would you mind revealing the names of at least two other prominent disciples, or excuse me for not utilizing the proper nomenclature, two other *apostles* that were assembled at the Last Supper in Jerusalem?"

Not one name could transfer from Tom's flustered mind to his muted tongue. Mr. Walters was becoming excessively frustrated and anxious from Tom's lack of a desirable response. The instructor grabbed Tom by his starched white collars and imperatively whispered into the lad's ear, "Look here you little wise-ass Bastard! Say something fuckin' right for goddamned once in your fuckin' worthless life!"

"Now come along Tom," Judge Thatcher coaxed and prompted in a more austere tone of voice than had been evident before. "The names of the first two disciples, or excuse me, in this case apostles, who technically were also disciples were...."

"David and Goliath, or maybe Adam and Eve!" Tom yelled-out during the culmination of his panic attack. And after the embarrassed young Sawyer sprinted out of the hall farting quite loudly four separate and distinct times, the rest of his class howled and shrieked with abundant laughter.

"Tom and Becky"

Tom Sawyer was miserable each and every Monday morning, because it meant another boring and tedious day of school drudgery. 'Shit!' the boy negatively thought as the upset lad felt his head. 'I ain't got no damned fever or wicked headache! If only I could vomit naturally; then Aunt Polly might consider keeping me home. Damn it to Hell! From September to June, being healthy is a mother-jumpin' curse I'd like to forget about!'

On his half-mile morning ramble to the all-too-familiar schoolhouse, Tom soon encountered mischievous Huck Finn, the local juvenile derelict who hated all women in lazy St. Petersburg, including the Widow Douglas, Miss Watson, and Tom's own Aunt Polly. But even though "ornery Tom" was forbidden to associate with "evil Huckleberry", young Sawyer greatly admired young Finn because the local legend (among his peers) was independent of adult authority, and didn't have to go to either school or church, all of his decisions made at *his* own stubborn and obstinate volition.

"Hello there, Huckleberry!" Tom merrily greeted. "Been jerkin' off lately? I'll bet you've already worked your stick at least twice this mornin'."

"Hello yourself, you dumb-fuck Asshole!" Huck rudely answered, slightly jealous and perturbed that Tom had a fixed destination and purpose. "Why don't ya' sew your two dicks together? Then you oughta' have enough length to go fuck yourself! Now, out of sheer compassion, I'll be a little more pleasant with your ass Tom and ask ya' if you'd go fishin' and huntin' with me all day long, instead of fartin' around with those other faggot-midget-shit-heads inside the piss-ant schoolhouse."

"I'd like to go along with ya' on your expedition, Huck, but that new blonde-headed girl in my class wants me to feel her tits and check out and rub her hairy pussy," Tom flagrantly lied. "Say now, whatcha' got inside that pouch you're carryin'? Gross rat turds, or male moth balls?"

"For your information, Asshole, these here are cat whiskers and some other important shit too confidential to mention," Huck rudely answered his one and only true friend. "It's a magic potion I learned from my Pap that cures warts."

"But you ain't got no damned warts, Huck?"

"I'm just practicin' some workable solutions in case I get some later on," Huck disclosed. "But ya' oughta' be concerned about learnin' the secret if that new blonde hair girl at school has any of them vaginal warts in her crotchola like I hear the older kids downtown talkin' up a storm about."

"Well Huck, how the hell does it work? I think I'm getting a wart at the top of my dick!"

"Well, here's what I have to do, and you can come along with me tonight if you'd like to be my personal assistant," the notorious troublemaker told his trouble-finder friend. "First, you and me will take the magic formula to the cemetery at midnight. The Devil's mean-ass red apprentices will show-up to steal the soul of somebody wicked that's just died, and I believe that that wicked dead asshole will be Hoss Williams who was just buried."

"Well Huck, do ya' have to say anything like hocus-pocus, or ab-ra-ca-dab-ra?" Tom curiously asked. "I saw a pretty neat magician use those corny words at a carnival last summer, and let me tell ya' Huck, they really worked."

"Yeah, when the evil demons are cartin' Hoss Williams's ghost down to Hell, all I gotta' say is, 'Devils follow corpse; potion follow Devils; warts follow potion; and then, no more fuckin' warts," Huck shared with his favorite pal. "It's almost guaranteed to work wonders every single time!"

"Okay; I don't want any wart growin' in my personal area to eventually become bigger than my dick!" Tom feared and expressed. "Can I go along to the graveyard with ya' tonight? I promise I'll be brave and won't be afraid of the fucked-up demons and goblins."

"Okay, Tom. Be ready at midnight to climb-down from your bedroom over at your Aunt Polly's place, and hop onto the back tin roof," Huck instructed. "But wait for my secret signal first before ya' start evacuatin' that haunted house you live in."

The stern teacher, Mr. Dobbins, was dozing-off in his rickety-wooden chair behind his front desk when Tom stealthily entered the classroom, tardy as usual. But a nervous fat kid named Jim Dunlap in the second row loudly farted, and then Mr. Dobbins awoke from his stupor, and instantly spotted the often-recalcitrant late arrival.

When a St. Petersburg teacher used a student's full name, that utterance was indicative of the fact that the designated kid was about to be disciplined, either physically, verbally, or both ways. "Thomas Sawyer; you punk insolent Imp!" Mr. Dobbins boomed and then snarled like a wolf. "Come on up here and receive the just punishment that you've earned!"

On the way to the front of the classroom, Tom observed Becky Thatcher's long blonde braided tails draping down beneath her shoulders, and the rascal also noticed one empty seat on the "girls' side" of the room next to where Becky was conscientiously sitting and industriously studying.

Tom knew how to get Mr. Dobbins riled-up to the maximum, and according to the instructor's past practices, Sawyer was aware of how to obtain the precise punishment that the boy's ever-cunning mind desired. "I stopped on the street in front of the general store and had a long talk with Huckleberry Finn on my way to the schoolhouse, and that's why I'm late," Tom honestly confessed.

"What did you say, Boy?" Mr. Dobbins incredulously asked. "Perhaps I didn't hear you right the first time."

"I stopped walkin' to school and had a nice long talk with my amigo, Huck Finn," Tom honestly repeated, much to everyone's astonishment. "He's a most amazin' hooky player, and a very smart and kind person, too. I'll swear to Heaven and to the Almighty on a stack of Bibles a mile high about what I just said, and that's the honest-to-Jesus-truth, Mr. Dobbins."

The astounded letter-of-the-law pedagogue got-out his notorious birch switch and cruelly slashed Tom really hard; first on his buttocks, and then lashing the little rogue really viciously across his personal area, nearly slicing the newly-formed wart right off the lad's tender penis. Tom winced-but-prayed that his penalty wish would soon become a veritable reality.

"Now Mr. Thomas Sawyer, you must go and sit your sore fanny on the girls' side of the room," the angry, prudish teacher further chastised the frequent rules' offender. "That's a very serious demotion for any self-respecting boy, who wants to amount to anything more than a hill of baked beans!"

Tom walked with his head crestfallen (pretending to have been effectively chastised) across the room and sat-down next to the gorgeous Becky Thatcher, who actually felt a degree of sympathy for the convicted tardy offender. But young Sawyer ignored the face of studious, well-behaved Becky, and also the faces belonging to the other whispering students, and the devious young fellow then gently opened a grammar textbook and pretended to be reading about nouns and verbs. But deep inside the interior of Tom's noble heart, the highly-focused youth couldn't have been more ecstatic or thrilled about actively exploiting his wonderful predicament.

Tom Sawyer had a soft peach in his pocket, and figured that everything would be peachy if he quickly placed the fruit on Becky's desk without her noticing. 'This peach fuzz makes me imagine the blonde fuzz that must be around Becky's terrific furry crack,' Tom naughtily thought. 'Forget mountain caves and tunnels. That's the kind of cavern that I really want to explore!'

Becky glanced to the side, and saw the pink peach upon her formerly vacant desk slate, and *snatched* it up while Tom contemplated the wonderful idea of the girl's fuzzy pink snatch opening and closing. And now that Becky had something of his and owed him at least a perfunctory "thank you" in exchange, Tom got his head and right hand low to his desk and began drawing a nude boy with an abnormally large erection holding his hard-on straight to the furry love tunnel of a naked girl, and Sawyer then naughtily scribbled the words "I love you! Let's shack-up and get laid!" at the bottom of the pornographic sketch.

"I want to see what you've drawn and written," Becky whispered and implored. But Tom refused to show her his tremendous artwork and his imaginative literature, so the girl slid young Sawyer's right elbow over, perceived the suggestive nude drawing, along with the accompanying solicitous sentences, and then the blonde girl let-out a loud shriek, and next quickly slapped Tom across the face.

Mr. Dobbins, who was jotting some homework notes on the black slate chalkboard, came running over, grabbed Tom by the right ear, and then dragged him across the classroom to an empty desk in the boy's section. Although Tom's ear tingled and throbbed, the naughty recipient of punishment also felt a 'nifty-feeling tingle' inside his dingle, too.

* * * * * * * * * * * * *

Tom stared blankly out the classroom window, enviously watching two love bird blue jays stitching together a tree nest, and then promptly thought about Becky Thatcher's nice blonde nest, which must be even nicer than his old girlfriend Amy Lawrence's dark brown muffin. 'Becky's busy over on the other side of the room pretending to be reading her geography book,' Tom observed and hypothesized. 'When noon recess comes around, and all the kids go home for lunch, I'll try and persuade Becky to stay inside the schoolhouse for a little romantic discussion. Maybe she'll even let me see and rub her tiny tits?'

When the students were dismissed for their lunch break, Tom swiftly stood and caught Becky by the arm as the pretty girl was exiting the classroom. 'Go outside with the other kids, and when you get to the general store, turn down the lane, and come into the playground through the rear entrance. I'll be waitin' for you there, and then we could have a secret talk."

Mr. Dobbins had gone into another quiet side room to swallow-down his ham and cheese sandwich, and to reach into the office's desk and imbibe his standard six ounces of bourbon in order to make it through the afternoon session, so Tom and Becky had *their* classroom all to themselves.

"Do ya' like rats?" Tom weirdly asked Becky. "Next to pussies, I really like rats. But it sure as all heck beats me, Becky, because I'm a little confused about the situation. I'm still tryin' to figure out how all those colonies *rat*ified the Constitution."

"No Thomas, I totally hate rats. But I do like chewing gum," the well-behaved 'good girl' politely and formally answered the bold young rascal. "And if you're planning on asking me whether my father used to construct straw roofs over in England, the answer is absolutely 'No'! My father is an important Judge in the area, and the name Thatcher is prominent all over Missouri! And no Thomas Sawyer; my father doesn't own any Sunnybrook farm either!"

"Well, I got some week-old gum in my pocket that we can chew-on while we're also chewin' the fat," Tom said as the love-struck boy offered the Thatcher girl a stale slab. "Tell me Becky; have ya' ever been to the circus! I love to watch the ladies in the skimpy costumes on the flyin' trapezes! And I wanna' be a clown when I grow-up, and that's why I'm getting this really good practice for my future career right here in Mr. Dobbins's classroom!"

"Yes Thomas," Becky formally addressed her principal suitor. "My loving parents have brought me to see the circus over in St. Louis three times already. And the next time I see a silly clown fooling around and playing havoc on everyone else, well Thomas, I'll be certainly thinking about you."

Tom sighed and then asked his new-found love, "Becky, have ya' ever been engaged? That's the first big step into getting married and then getting laid!"

"Thomas Sawyer, of all the unmitigated audacity!" Becky exclaimed, repeating what her snobbish mother often said when reacting to something Mrs. Thatcher found to be unacceptably outrageous. "I seriously think that before you even ever consider getting engaged, and I'm speaking symbolically of course, a boy and a girl would have to first kiss each other."

"On the kisser?" Tom roguishly asked, and then mentally speculated. 'God; I'd love to kiss Becky on her more exciting set of lips located directly between her gorgeous legs,' the little scoundrel imagined and assessed.

"That's right Thomas! The boy and the girl would have to kiss each other on their kissers!" Becky verified.

"Okay then, Doll. I'm gonna' kiss you on your kisser, and that'll mean that we're almost engaged and ready to be married, and then ready to get laid." And before Becky could clench her fist to slug young amorous Sawyer, or physically resist his impulsiveness, the aggressive boy planted a heavy smooch directly upon her lips. "Now we're sort of goin' steady Becky, and we'll always be together cavortin' at parties and gang bangs!"

"What did you say, Thomas Sawyer? Of all the unmitigated audacity! Did I hear you correctly?"

"Er Becky, I meant to say that since I just kissed you, as you almost suggested, you'll always be my best friend, forever and ever."

"Am I the first and only girl you've ever kissed?" the Thatcher doll asked her new-found beau. "Tell me the truth, and if the answer is 'yes', I'll let you kiss me again!"

"Well, to be perfectly honest with you, last year I kissed Amy Lawrence, but that short romance is all over now," Tom admitted and then noticed something wrong. "Becky, please stop crying. I don't love Amy any longer. I love only you!"

"You're a monster! Get away from me right this instant! You're making me cry my blue eyes out!"

"Becky, here's the drawing of me and you having our first standing sex act," Tom offered the weeping girl his illustration and accompanying prose scribbled at the bottom. "Take and keep it as your personal treasure to always remind you of me!"

Becky abruptly grabbed the sheet of paper, ripped it to sheds, and then continued her prolonged sobbing. That particular rejection made Tom feel angry, alienated and insulted, so the confused love-fledgling fled out of the classroom, leaving Becky crying a cascade of crocodile tears down her tender cheeks.

Tom was so full of energy that needed to be released that the distraught youth speedily dashed past the Douglas Mansion, and then past the Cardiff Mansion, desperately searching for his one true salvation and redemption from social disgrace and romantic failure, the one and only inimitable Huckleberry Finn.

'I'll meet-up with my hero Huck tonight, and we'll jaunt-out to the cemetery at midnight to cure this itchy wart on the tip of my dick that's really bothering the hell out of me. I'll even allow Huck to look at it, even though the pervert once told and promised me that he wasn't any damned pecker-checker!'

Tom quickened his pace and headed into the nearby woods to smoke his pipe and engage in a bit of self-sympathy. 'And then Huck and I will go sailing and fishing together, and maybe even jerk-off together. We'll either become pirates, or kill a few buccaneers or privateers all by ourselves without the constable or the police interfering into *our* private business. I can't wait to start my new life on the high seas,' Tom theorized with a smile as the emotionally disheveled kid loaded some rancid-smelling tobacco, and then lit his secret corncob pipe. 'Huck Finn's right. It's great being mischievous and independent. Some-day, I'll come back to this hick village of St. Petersburg wearing my tall black boots, and my red sash with dangling pistols, daggers, and swords tucked inside my thick leather belt. Then, I'll enter the church, and with everybody quiet and wondering what I would say or do, including astonished Aunt Polly, I'll then loudly yell out to the entire congregation, "Fuck you and the goddamned world, and also fuck that conceited rich bitch, Becky Thatcher, too!"

"Muff Potter and Injun Joe"

Since there weren't many bloodthirsty marauders, swashbuckling pirates, or hostile buccaneers terrorizing people along the Mississippi River in the vicinity of somnolent St. Petersburg, Tom Sawyer and Huckleberry Finn had arranged to get together around midnight for a walking excursion to a rather frightful place. Tom had to share a bed with his brother Sid, and didn't want his tattling sibling to know that he was going to sneak-out of the upstairs bedroom, shinny-down the drainpipe, hop onto the back porch's tin roof, and ultimately rendezvous with his fellow adventurer, who would be impatiently waiting for him below.

Every sound in the dark was discernible, even the chirping of the crickets, and the creaking of the roof rafters connecting the upstairs rooms' walls and floors. Next, a distant canine's persistent barking was detectable, the village church bells tolled twelve times, and then the sound of glass shattering against Aunt Polly's backyard woodshed was soon followed by a familiar voice saying, "Scat you lousy devil!"

Tom leaped-down from the back porch's tin roof, met Huck on the dark rear lawn, and the two amigos exchanged pleasantries, and soon headed-out to the local weed-infested graveyard as had been secretly scheduled, arriving at the eerie destination at half past midnight.

The cemetery was in a shambles, with its rusty wrought-iron fence crumbled-down in some areas, and the black-metal spikes being grotesquely distorted and twisted in others. But the shabby-looking barrier still made a crude rough-looking circumference around the spooky tombstones arrayed upon the dark, lonely hill. A low wind swirled through the foliage-laden elm and oak tree branches, and Tom and Huck imagined that the voices of recently deceased spirits could be occasionally heard moaning, muttering, cursing, and mumbling amidst the weird-sounding tree rustling.

"There's Hoss Williams's newly dug grave sittin' up there on the top of the haunted ridge," Huck pointed-out to his loyal-but-neurotic companion. "Let's now park our ugly asses against a couple of these huge elm trees, and we'll wait for something supernatural to happen. It's awful quiet and spooky out here at night, Tom," Huckleberry noted and excitedly expressed. "It's not really an ideal place for you to take Becky Thatcher if ya' wanna' have some late-night sex. If you're anything like me," Huck Finn mentioned and stressed, "you' won't be able to get doin' it under such hostile conditions and abnormal surroundings. And I don't think Becky could get it up for you either in this horrible place. At least that's my personal opinion."

"Sex ain't nothin' compared to excitin' graveyard chills and thrills," evaluated and stated Tom. "Say Huck; this horrible place ain't no paradise for the livin,' especially after dusk sets-in. Do ya' think that Hoss Williams can hear us talkin'? I mean, not him hearin' us, but his ghost."

"Of course, he can," Huck answered in a low-but-certain tone of speech. "But old Hoss Williams was a two-bit gambler, a four-bit thief, and a lousy no-good lifetime sinner. So, I don't suspect that his condemned spirit is any damned holy ghost!"

"Quiet Huck; you Dumb Fuck!" Tom advised and cautioned. "Did ya' hear that oddball sound approachin'? I think the Devil and his don't give a shit, escorting demons are comin' here for sure. The evil spirits are here to remove Hoss's ghost and transport it straight to Hell. And if the fucked-up, crazy demons see us spying on them, too," young Sawyer speculated and said, "they might just also kidnap our delicate asses. And then we'll have to cut their dicks and balls off with our pen knives during a big, bloody battle. I mean to say Huck, who the hell needs that kind of shit? I just want normal adventures with normal living people."

Three ominous-looking figures slowly ambled-up the hill, with their silhouetted forms barely visible in the light of the full moon. The lead man was carrying an old-fashioned tin lantern; its scattered light serving to guide the trio to their main objective. Fortunately, the boys' remote presence had not been detected.

"Those fucked-up demons trudgin' this way look-like dumb-fuck human men to me," Tom observed and fearfully whispered. "I'd pray if I could only remember how the hell to do it! How come Huck, I can't remember any of those fucked-up verses I had studied in Sunday School?"

"Say, Tom. I recognize the goofy-lookin' guy with the lantern. It's Muff Potter; one of my Pap's friends, perhaps his only friend," Huck clarified. "They're the two biggest lushes in all of St. Petersburg, and Pap's the only jerk around that can drink Potter under the table with rye, bourbon, gin, scotch, vodka, brandy, or even regular beer," Huckleberry bragged. "And I can now faintly hear Potter's voice and can rightly tell that he's already half-intoxicated. And that second jerk-off pushin' the wheelbarrow is…."

"Injun Joe, who sometimes keeps reservations at the downtown hotel, and wears a large hat during the winter to keep his wig-wam," joked Tom. "But wait a minute; the third guy carrying the two spades is none other than…"

"Young Dr. Robinson, who recently graduated from medical school, and is startin' up a practice on Main Street," Huckleberry realized and mentioned. "Let's see what they're up to Tom. And don't speak too loudly, or the three trespassers might hear our stupid bullshit, and decide to bury us alive! I mean, I wanna' live long enough to become rich and famous, and be buried in a fuckin' white marble mausoleum!"

Injun Joe put-down the wheelbarrow the town thug had been pushing, and he and Muff Potter began digging with their spades into Hoss Williams's shallow grave. The doctor placed the lantern toward the wooden headstone, and the three intruders were so close to the boys that both Tom and Huck (hiding behind the elm trees) felt that *they* could be easily seen or discovered if a sound were accidentally made. Muff Potter and Injun Joe dug quickly and assiduously. The suspense was mounting as the shovels kept removing the soft dirt and gravel. The fascinated-but-terrified boys watched the surreal activity from their crouched-down positions.

"Hey, Tom. I think Muff and Injun Joe are grave robbin' for Dr. Robinson," Huck whispered into his buddy's ear. "Some doctors have trouble getting' ahold of body parts to dissect and do weird experiments on. I'll betcha' that's exactly what the hell we're witnessin' right now!"

Then, one of the spades made contact with the wooden coffin, and next Muff Potter and Injun Joe used a set of thick heavy-duty ropes to hoist the heavy rectangular box up to ground level. After prying-open the lid with a convenient crowbar, the men removed Hoss Williams's pallid-looking corpse, placed it into the wheelbarrow, and then covered the body with a blanket.

"Too bad Lady Cadaver wasn't buried here, because I'd like to see her naked body, day or night," Tom said, not fully fathoming his own subconscious thought that had unintentionally surfaced, and had been incidentally revealed to his spying friend. But Huckleberry was not-too-impressed with Tom Sawyer's unorthodox sense of humor during a time of dire crisis. Then suddenly, the small felony of grave robbing quickly evolved into what unexpectedly constituted a major heinous crime.

"Now that the excavation has been done," Injun Joe said to Doc Robinson, "I'll have to charge you five-dollars more before Muff and me cart old Hoss out of the graveyard and over to your office. I mean, Muff and I are workin' overtime, and that ancient wheelbarrow is hard to steer with its wobbly wheels, especially when the sucker is loaded!"

"You connivin' Swindler! You lowdown dishonorable Crook!" the enraged young doctor accused the avaricious thug. "We had agreed on the final price; cash in advance, and you've already been paid that handsome sum! A gentleman always honors his contracts, either verbal or written!"

"Listen carefully, Dr. Robinson. Five years ago, I was a trifle short on cash and food when I had gotten out of jail, and I came beggin' like a leper at your father's kitchen door," Joe orally rehashed, growing more incensed with each word uttered. "Your fucked-up old man had me thrown into the clink for vagrancy, claimin' to the constable that I was a 'no good bastard drifter'. Forget your high-falutin' education for a cotton-pickin' minute. Did ya' forget *that* fucked-up incident I had with your old man? Now tell me; did ya' honestly believe that *I* had forgotten about it?"

"Look here, now Joe," Dr. Robinson vehemently argued. "I'm not responsible for my father's actions. I see that you're quite unfamiliar with the *United States Constitution.* Each individual has to account before the Lord of his own record of deeds and misdeeds. That's always been my conviction."

"Forget all the political and religious bullshit!" Injun Joe belligerently shouted directly into the doctor's face. "Jesus Christ ain't climbin' down from His death cross to help ya' out, should I decide to hurt or kill your ass inside this here graveyard," the volatile redskin yelled, shaking his clenched fist close to the physician's chin. "And if ya' dare self-righteously talk about your holier-than-thou conviction, I'll talk to *you* about my second conviction; the one where your pop sent me behind prison bars! Your goddamned old man had me put into jail when I didn't deserve it, and ya' don't give a five-dollar shit about *that* event! Your pop fucked me up good, and now if ya' don't give me more dough, I'm gonna' get even and fuck *you* up!"

Suddenly, Dr. Robinson became infuriated and forcefully punched Injun Joe in the gut, knocking the vile villain flat on his back. Muff Potter immediately dropped his knife and swiftly ran over to defend his criminal friend against Dr. Robinson, who then instinctively lifted Hoss Williams' headboard straight out of the loose ground, and the town physician forcefully pounded the hard wooden object on top of Potter's skull.

In the meantime, Injun Joe had recovered from receiving his wicked shot to the abdomen, and hastily crawled over toward the ongoing altercation, coincidentally discovered Muff Potter's knife lying upon the ground in the pale moonlight, and then the heartless former jail-mate rose to his feet and violently plunged the sharp long blade into Dr. Robinson's chest, savagely killing the grave-robber almost instantly.

"Injun Joe always settles his scores," the repugnant Cherokee descendant yelled to the prone body lying on the soggy turf. The ruthless thief next stole the doctor's wallet and watch, and at that same time, Muff Potter finally was regaining consciousness. Injun Joe gathered his evil wits, wickedly placed the bloodstained murder weapon into Muff' Potter's right hand, and when the drunkard groggily sat-up while finally coming out of his stupor, Injun Joe fraudulently informed Muff that the owner of the knife had committed homicide by gruesomely killing Dr. Robinson.

"I can't remember a goddamned thing except that I was involved in a pretty nasty fight," Muff related his rueful narrative to the real dastardly murderer. "It's these terrible bad spells I've been havin', getting all dizzy-like, and faintin' all the damned time. I gotta' give up alcohol, Joe; that's what the hell I need to do! Say, Joe; you won't tell anybody about this fucked-up incident, will ya'?"

"You've always been square with me Muff, and I promise I won't squeal on ya'," Injun Joe answered as Potter began whimpering and sobbing. "Now stop cryin' like a goddamned emotional weak woman, and get the hell out of here as fast as your frail legs will carry your skinny ass. Get the hell outa' town, I say'; that's what the hell I suggest ya' do!"

Muff Potter wasted little time dashing-out of the dank, dreary cemetery. His escape path was soon followed by Injun Joe, who then was walking with a less strident gait. Tom and Huckleberry waited a full-minute before the pair mutually scampered out of the graveyard in the direction of the old tannery building, located on the west side of the sleepy village. Upon safely fleeing inside the old deserted factory, the boys held a brief consultation.

"Tom," Huckleberry began the dialogue, all out of breath. "If Dr. Robinson's dead, like I think he is, then either Injun Joe or Muff Potter is gonna' hang from a tall oak."

"But Huck, Muff thinks he's the one that had committed the horrendous murder, and if push comes to shove, Injun Joe is gonna' lie like a mortal sinner in the courtroom to save his own skin," Tom insisted with the full moral weight of his conscience bothering him. "We're the only ones that know what the hell actually happened, that is, besides that dangerous lyin' bastard Injun Joe. Will we tell the truth, Huck? Will we tell the constable or the town judge what we both saw?"

"Judge Thatcher is now on vacation with his family out of town, so we can't discuss the vital matter with him," a befuddled Huckleberry Finn answered. "And if Injun Joe escapes from jail after we testify against him, the rotten son-of-a-bitch sure as hell will come after our asses, and kill us both as if we were just two annoyin' mosquitoes! The constable and the judge can't protect us from his revenge; no way Tom!" Huck maintained. "Say; we gotta' sign a pact in blood sayin' we aren't gonna' tell anybody nothin' about what the hell we saw tonight! Do it, Tom, you frightened Turkey! Do it now before Injun Joe assassinates us both!"

Tom quickly removed a piece of red chalk from his pocket, picked up a clean shingle from the dirt floor, and then roughly scribbled: "Huck Finn and Tom Sawyer swear that they'll both keep mum about what they saw tonight, and the witnesses both wish to drop dead should either of us squeal."

Next, Tom retrieved a sewing needle from his right pants' pocket and pricked his thumb, squeezing a drop of blood, and Huckleberry Finn soon mimicked the "autograph-ready process". And after Tom signed his signature to the pledge in red blood-ink, the youthful partner showed Huckleberry how to print the initials H. F. on the bottom of the shingle, because Huckleberry never learned how to read or write.

Tom Sawyer eventually returned to civilization, after two in the morning, to Aunt Polly's residence, clambered-up the wooden post to the back porch's tin roof; shinnied-up the frail drainpipe, and reentered the home through the open upstairs bedroom window. The following morning when Tom finally woke-up from his stressful nightmare, Sid had already-evacuated the bedroom to perform his usual annoying reporting to the matriarch of the dwelling.

"Tom, I'm very disappointed in you brazenly leaving this house last night and gallivantin' your lazy butt all over St. Petersburg!" Aunt Polly yelled after the surprised and still-shell-shocked boy sat down for breakfast. "Why must you continue to break my elderly heart with all your relentless, juvenile shenanigans?" the old woman asked and wept, endeavoring to send Tom on a classic guilt trip. "When are you going to learn that there are more serious things that are of a life-or-death nature, other than the foolish mindless nonsense you and that worthless scamp Huckleberry Finn do together after midnight! I mean, all of St. Petersburg's finest citizens are always talking about your dual mischief!"

"I think Tom and Huck are a couple of perverted homos!" normally-reticent Sid opined and declared. "At least that's the latest gossip floatin' all around the school playground!"

* * * * * * * * * * * * *

Tom was bedridden for two whole weeks because the boy had come-down with a bad case of the measles, and wished all during his recovery that he had never come into contagious contact with the holier-than-thou German kid, Gunther Schultz, at Sunday School, which was bitterly regarded and evaluated by both Tom and Huckleberry as "a truly very bad-luck place." But the major topic of discussion all round St. Petersburg was Muff Potter's scheduled upcoming trial. The drunk had been captured, thrown into jail, and formally accused of killing Dr. Robinson with *his* knife inside the town graveyard.

When Tom was back to feeling and behaving normal again, the neurotic boy met Huckleberry Finn in the woods near the abandoned tannery, and the two aspiring bandits conducted a serious discussion about recent town legal developments. Naturally, Huck was glad to see Tom "up and about", and the pals had occasion to first commiserate, and then review basic strategy.

"Say, Tom. Did ya' know that the new constable arrested Muff Potter. He's bein' held in jail, and bein' officially charged with killin' Doc Robinson?" Huck informed his near-healthy friend. "The law has really muffed that one by arrestin' old Muff!"

"Pardon my ignorance, because of my absence from society Huck, but who's the new constable?"

"Why the new constable is Stan Bull from Constantinople, a tiny town outside of Troy, New York," Huck informed his colleague in nuisance. "At least that's what the local scuttlebutt is sayin' about Bull's butt! Ya' ain't gonna' tell the police what ya' had seen at the cemetery, are ya', Tom? Remember our contract signed in blood. We pledged to keep it a secret for all eternity, and if ya' tell, both you and me are obligated through our oath we gave to each other to die."

Tom had more of a developed conscience than Huckleberry did, and any mention of Dr. Robinson (or the bizarre circumstances surrounding his extraordinary demise) sent a shudder directly into and right through the boy's vulnerable heart.

"I reckon you're right about our solemn contract, Huck," Tom recalled and acknowledged. "But just hearin' the name Muff Potter sends me into a cold shiver, and I feel like the measles is gonna' overtake my weak condition again. I mean, Huck; it makes me feel like climbin' up inside somebody's asshole, because thinkin' about the atrocious murder makes me feel like shit!"

"Ya haven't discussed the matter with anybody else, like Sid, or your Aunt Polly, have ya'?" Huck shrewdly interrogated. "That would be treason, and good reason for me not associatin' with your squealing ass anymore! Then, I'd rather keep company with Injun Joe than with you, if *you* ever violated our sacred agreement."

"But don't ya' feel sorry for old Muff?" Tom rhetorically asked. "The poor old drunk just fishes, and idly screws around, and only gets enough money to loaf outside Mr. Kooneman's bakery and to drink whiskey in the town saloon, just so he can go out and fish in the river and repeat the dumb-ass cycle all over again. And I know Muff's stood by you Huck, and defended your ass, and your Pa's, too, a couple of times down inside the pool room!"

"And I remember that Muff helped fix your kite once against your Aunt Polly's wishes, after the raunchy bitch had told you to go fly one, because the old bag was mighty pissed-off at you," Huck recollected and added. "And then, Muff once tied some hooks on my fishin' line when you and me were out lookin' for a hooker to get laid for the first time," Tom's bizarre friend pontificated. "I really wish *we* could break Muff outa' jail, but then we might get caught and questioned by Stan Bull, and then tell on Injun Joe, and risk becomin' non-human-beings by bein' stabbed to death just like the young ambitious doctor was. At best, Tom; you and me would become fugitives from justice, and then mean-ass bounty hunters would be out on the prowl to either kill or capture us both."

"Even though I hardly know more about math' than I do about religion and the Good Book, you're a hundred percent right Huck," Tom logically concurred. "Even though Muff's innocent, we gotta' keep quiet about the situation to save our own precious hides. Injun Joe is more dangerous than the small pox, the large pox, and the chicken-pox all fuckin' put together! And that son-of-a-bitch lowlife Cherokee is goddamned lethal, more freakin' toxic than arsenic, and that's the goddamned long and the goddamned short of it!"

Despite the encouragement and the moral and immoral support he had received from Huck Finn, Tom was miserable and melancholy, and the mental sufferer frequently worried about Muff Potter's fate. And for the next several days, those depressing thoughts dominated the worried lad's guilt-feeling mind. And all throughout late July, Tom Sawyer vigilantly hung-out near the town courthouse, awaiting news of the decisive verdict of falsely accused Muff Potter.

The next hot sultry morning, the entire population of St. Petersburg flocked to the courthouse chamber, and upon gaining admission, crowded the inside public-hearing-room to seating capacity. Even Tom gathered sufficient courage to enter the building, and become a member of the concerned and curious audience. The jury members eventually filed-inside; sat in their respective chairs, and then Muff Potter was escorted to his seat, with his hands bound in chains while the true culprit, Injun Joe, sat quietly on the right-hand-side of the gallery, casually chewing a wad of tobacco.

Once the judge entered the overcrowded, mediocre, nondescript courtroom, everybody stood out of respect and remained upright during the traditional "Pledge of Allegiance" recitation. As the lawyers on both sides shuffled their papers, tablets, and other paraphernalia on their separate tables, the austere-looking judge asked the first "witness for the prosecution" to come forward and testify against Muff Potter.

"Yes, I saw Muff Potter washing-up his bloody hands in the creek the same morning when Dr. Robinson's body had been discovered lying in the graveyard," the bearded, old, toothless geezer claimed. "He seemed mighty anxious to get the red stains off his palms, and then the varmint hightailed it out of there."

"Your Honor; the prosecution now is finished with this witness," the county attorney declared. "But we have several more individuals on our list to call to testify."

"Okay, would Mr. Potter's attorney care to cross-examine today's first witness?" the judge perfunctorily inquired, according to standard and acceptable Missouri legal procedure.

"No, Your Honor. The defense has no questions to ask the prosecution's eyewitness."

The next testifier claimed that he had found Muff 's knife lying next to Dr. Robinson's lifeless body, and then Potter's seemingly aloof defense attorney declared that he had "no questions to ask". The courtroom crowd sensed that a serious miscarriage of justice was in progress, and the people sitting in the gallery began respectfully mumbling and conversing amongst themselves.

And then a third and a fourth witness also testified against Muff Potter, and the lawyer defending the accused each time had "No questions" to ask as the judge presiding over the rare St. Petersburg murder trial, who was becoming increasingly nervous when the restless audience began to openly heckle and criticize Muff Potter's seemingly incompetent and unsympathetic defense attorney.

“Order in this court!” the judge yelled, loudly banging his gavel upon his high lectern. “Now that the prosecution has rested its case, before of course, making its final statement, does the defense have any witness to call before this court? Please avail yourself of this one-time opportunity!”

“Your Honor,” Muff's laconic defense attorney said. “At the outset of this exceptional case, I had stated that Muff Potter was subject to getting intense dizzy spells, and that the strange physical continuous condition had made the defendant prone to periods of blacking-out, and then waking-up not recalling what had just transpired. But the defense has now changed its initial position and wishes to prove the defendant as being innocent of the crime of murder as has been falsely and erroneously charged. To prove this to be true beyond the shadow of a doubt,” the now confident defense lawyer asserted, “I'd now like to call the honest and noble Mr. Thomas Sawyer to the witness stand.”

Every face in the courtroom (including those belonging to Muff Potter and Injun Joe) had an appearance of absolute astonishment and awe, as both women and men alike gasped in unison. Everybody present had the sense that something very suspenseful and dramatic was about to happen.

“Do you solemnly swear to tell the truth, the whole truth, and nothing but the truth?” the stern-looking bailiff asked Tom after the boy had placed his right hand upon the Bible.

“I do!” Tom exclaimed without getting married. “I do!” the young defense witness repeated in a nervous tone of voice before assuming his seat. Everything was as quiet as an empty library room.

“Thomas Sawyer,” the defense attorney began his litany. “Exactly, where were you on the evening of June 17th just before and after the stroke of midnight?”

“Well, sir, before midnight I was getting ready to be on my way to the cemetery, and right after midnight, I was inside the graveyard,” Tom anxiously answered as the witness took a glance at Injun Joe's nasty-looking frown, and then intensely felt fear re-entering his already-palpitating heart. But then, Tom noticed Muff Potter's face turning from extreme apprehension to a look genuinely reflecting inspirational hope.

“Were you anywhere near Hoss Williams' recently-dug grave that evening, and if so, what were you doing there at midnight?” the determined defense attorney questioned. “Please speak loudly Mr. Sawyer so that all in attendance can hear your honest responses.”

"Well, sir. I was nervously hiding behind some tall elm trees when I saw Injun Joe, Muff Potter, and Dr. Robinson approachin' Hoss Williams's grave," Tom testified as the boy's knees and legs started to shiver and knock. "I was there inside the cemetery at midnight, because I was searchin' for a magic potion to cure warts I had heard about from a friend."

The crowd inside the courtroom broke-out into a roar as the judge pounded his gavel and demanded, "Order in this courtroom, or else I'll have the bailiff remove all violators of my directed rule! Order in this court, I say!"

After the gallery had quieted down again, the defense attorney proceeded with his line of interrogating the youthful witness. "I understand that you were with a companion at the cemetery, who can verify your story, but for now, his identity shall remain anonymous, but he'll be called to testify at the proper time. Now then, Mr. Sawyer. What happened next? And don't be afraid to tell the truth, and please don't be intimidated or influenced in any way! The whole truth must be heard!"

"Well now, Muff Potter and Injun Joe dug-up Hoss Williams and then after liftin' the coffin out of the ground, the two men pried-open the lid; removed the body, and put the corpse in the wheelbarrow. Then Injun Joe asked Dr. Robinson for more money, and the two men got involved in a serious argument. Next, Dr. Robinson punched Injun Joe and knocked him down, but then Muff Potter came to his friend's defense. But Mr. Potter had dropped his knife, and was not carryin' it. Dr. Robinson clobbered Muff on the head with Hoss Williams' wooden grave marker, and the hard blow sent Muff into dreamland. And then," Tom said and paused, staring directly at the guilty culprit now restlessly sitting in the gallery to the right of the judge, "Injun Joe crawled-over, picked-up Muff's knife from between the weeds and stabbed Dr. Robinson in the chest. And then, Injun Joe placed the knife in unconscious Muff's hand and...."

As quick as greased lightning, Injun Joe sprang-out of his chair, darted to the courtroom's partially open window, leaped forward and crashed right through, breaking the plate glass during his very wild and frantic escape. The treacherous criminal was now a renegade from justice, on the loose, and more-than-likely bound to be seeking revenge on Huck and Tom, but especially upon young Mr. Sawyer, for proficiently indicting the unscrupulous villain inside the St. Petersburg courtroom.

"The Cave Experiences"

The older kids of St. Petersburg had gone on a Saturday riverboat field trip down the Mississippi, and got off at a popular scenic landing. Having certain hormone-driven romantic inclinations, Tom Sawyer convinced Becky Thatcher to accompany him on a major hike to explore a large cave, situated far away from the other children, who were quite content, secure, and relaxed eating ice cream and hanging around the crowded dock.

But when the steamboat whistle blew, signaling for the kids to board for their river ride back to town, Tom and Becky had not made it back to the excursion, and it wasn't until the following morning that *their* adult family members were finally able to piece the simple puzzle together, immediately after Sunday church services.

Judge Thatcher's overprotective wife was exiting the church's center aisle with Mrs. Harper, and the rich woman innocently asked, "Is my Becky going to sleep all day at your place? She's missed her Sunday church!"

"Your beautiful daughter, Becky?" Mrs. Harper questioned with a degree of alarm showing in her verbal response. "Why she didn't stay over my house, but *my* daughter had mentioned that your child had gone on yesterday's recreational riverboat ride five miles downstream, and that she hadn't seen Becky on the return trip back to St. Petersburg. But I'm sure there's some feasible explanation confirming Becky's whereabouts!"

Mrs. Thatcher turned ghost-white, and almost-collapsed into unconsciousness as the judge's wife sank her frame into the nearest pew. Aunt Polly noticed the affluent woman's discomfort, so Tom's concerned aunt wondered if the judge's normally-dignified wife was feeling okay. "Good morning, Mrs. Harper, and Mrs. Thatcher. I guess Mrs. Harper that my irascible nephew Tom must've been a minor handful staying over with Joe last night, and that his peculiar phobia about attending church is why he's not in attendance for the service; or for that matter, showing his remorseless face for Sunday School class."

"Tom didn't stay at my house," Mrs. Harper uneasily replied. "And neither did Becky Thatcher. This entire scenario sounds like a juvenile conspiracy to me!"

Mrs. Thatcher started weeping in the pew, upon thinking that Tom and Becky had stupidly eloped somewhere, and that the lowlife asshole was pumping her beautiful daughter's blonde-haired pussy dry. But then, an even worse thought crossed the woman's ultra-suspicious mind. 'My precious Becky might've been kidnapped, along with that repulsive Tom Sawyer, and I might not ever see her alive again with that crazy criminal and heinous murderer Indian Joe in hot pursuit of *that* impudent, mischievous boy!'

Then, the holy and religious German boy, Gunther, was located playing with himself up in the choir loft, and was thoroughly interrogated by the worried adults. The strange, effeminate lad stated that Becky and Tom had ventured into a large cave down river, and then Mrs. Thatcher became even more delirious, and her mercurial emotions instantly shifted full-speed into high altitude hysterics.

In less than one hour, a search party of over two-hundred-men had been organized, most of the ambitious hunters on the expedition motivated by wanting to locate Becky Thatcher, and thus earning a huge reward from the grateful wealthy judge and the Justice's presently distraught wife.

All night long, the gossipy, superstitious townspeople yearned for some good news about the two young and daring explorers, but then on Monday afternoon, disappointed groups of fatigued men returned to the village empty-handed. The general consensus was that Tom and Becky were indeed lost in the immense cave, and that "the children" were too remotely trapped inside the gigantic interior for even the most experienced searchers to ever locate.

* * * * * * * * * * * * *

But after playing a routine game of hide and seek in one of the cave's deeper-innermost recesses, under the dual flames of dull candlelight, the pair had inadvertently descended into a very deep abyss, where the maze-like passages were complex, ultimately forming a very complicated labyrinth. Hundreds of bats were suspended upside-down from the dark cavern's colossal-sized ceiling, and the candles' light prompted the nocturnal creatures to instantaneously evacuate the chamber in frenzied flocks. The disconcerting and frenetic flapping of the bats' multiple wings caused Becky to shriek-out in horror.

"Tom. I think I just peed my panties!" Becky complained and cried. "That's the first time I ever wet myself! How disgraceful! Gross and un-lady-like!"

'Oh shit!' Tom thought. 'There goes my chance to smell Becky's blonde crotchola! Who the hell wants to do that now that the frightened bitch has pissed herself!'

"Tom, say something!" Becky elicited. "I've never known you to be so quiet; and during a terrible time of crisis, too! There're more bats flapping-away up ahead, and if they all decide to poop on our heads at the same time, we could be smothered in bat dung, and both of us could die very horrible and disgusting deaths!"

"It's a good thing those dirty creatures can't fly inside our heads, or else we'd both have bats in our belfries," ineffectually jested Tom. "We'll climb through this narrow side opening, and enter into the next rock chamber," pretentious Tom instructed the panic-stricken girl. "I think we can escape the panicky bats in there. Hey look Becky; there's a huge underwater lake over to our left. At least we'll have some fresh water to drink until some on-a-mission searchers eventually find and rescue us."

"Look, Tom. My candle flame's been extinguished by the low flying bats," Becky sadly indicated. "That's my second old flame besides you, Tom!"

'Right now, bitch, I'm so fuckin' scared that I have a wick dick that I can't even piss out of!' Tom thought as the scared-stiff lad evaluated the current status of his shriveled-up pecker. 'What a fuckin' bummer! Now, I can't even take an ordinary piss; let alone pop my first goddamned, glorious sperm load into Becky's wet pink pussy slit!'

"Tom, this is no time to be so quiet!" Becky scolded her disreputable, mischievous companion. "Please say something nice, Tom, before I die of sheer boredom. I think we should ignore the fickle bats, and go back into the larger chamber. I believe, Tom, that our chances of being rescued would be better-off inside the bigger cavern, that's apparently closer to the main entrance."

"I was such a fool!" Tom admitted to his favorite girl. "I didn't make any damned marks on the rock walls, and now we're really fucked, er, I meant to say 'we're royally screwed', Becky. Let's cup our hands, drink some of this fresh water. and then return to the other part of the cave we had just exited. Look at it this way, Becky!" the zany boyfriend stated. "At least *you* can piss your pants! I can't even do that simple-ass thing right now!"

"Thomas Sawyer, you're a totally crude and rude boy, just like everyone says you are!" Becky exclaimed and pouted. "Despite the fact that we're no longer in civilization and must now temporarily live by nature's rules, you must still show me more courtesy and respect, because I'm still a cultured and educated young lady. Do you understand my position?"

'Maybe I don't want to marry this arrogant, selfish, spoiled-rotten bitch after all!' Tom seriously considered. 'I'd have to work too hard for too many years, and have to court this conceited, stuck-up princess, and then marry her just to get my first lousy piece of ass! Huck's right!' Tom conjectured. 'I should find the nearest slut, and pound her swollen pussy with my erect tool like there's no tomorrow, and do it until my sore dick aches and finally falls off.'

* * * * * * * * * * * * *

Becky started crying again, and Tom realized that the cave-explorer lacked the proper emotional skills to soothe and comfort her wild outburst. Hunger pangs were beginning to set-in, and Tom comprehended that he had to either obtain food in a hurry, or find a way out of the enormous series of endless dark, dank tunnels. But suddenly a faint distant sound was discernible.

"Becky, did ya' hear that?" the boyfriend whispered. "It's like a low grating noise. I gotta' go see what's causin' it!"

"Please don't leave me alone for too long. How are you going to find your way back, Tom?" Becky panicked and asked. "I shouldn't have listened to your crazy nonsense in the first place and should've stayed on the dock eating ice cream with the other kids!"

"I have this ball of kite string in my pocket," Tom explained. "I'll tie one end to a small boulder and use the rest to go as far ahead as I can. Then, I'll use the same string as a guide to find my way back to your vicinity."

"That's plagiarism!" Becky objected.

"What the hell kind of dumb shit are ya' talkin' about now, Becky? Speak ordinary English, will ya'!"

"Tom, if you knew any school academics at all, you'd be aware that in mythology, the Princess Ariadne had given the Greek hero Theseus a ball of string to use to travel into King Minos's labyrinth on the island of Crete, in order for the champion monster-slayer to find his way back after killing the dreaded beast called the Minotaur, that incidentally had the hideous grotesque head of a bull and the body of a muscular man!"

"Sounds like a lot of educational fantasy bullshit to me!" Tom remarked. "Maybe if I run into a damned Minotaur down here inside this enormous cave, I could finally relieve my kidneys and not have to worry about dyin' from internal piss poisoning!"

"Tom, don't forget to come back for me," Becky urged as she kissed the valiant lad on the forehead. "And please; try to not use any more profanities!"

"Unlike that Greek bull-monster you just described Becky, this next trip of mine will be more than a *minute tour*," Tom' replied to his special girl, trying to add a degree of levity to the increasingly crucial situation. "I just hope I don't get any messy stinkin' bullshit on my shoes while walkin' around down here in the dark!"

Twenty steps up a steep precarious incline, the underground corridor seemed to narrow and perhaps soon terminate. Tom stuck his head through a small opening, and twenty yards ahead, the cave trespasser observed a human hand holding a candle above a rock while inspecting a cross that had been crudely drawn on the overhead hard wall. 'Holy shit!' the astounded boy fathomed. 'That son-of-a-bitch down there is Injun Joe!'

Tom carefully followed the length of his fully unwound kite string, and luckily managed to return to Becky, who immediately wrapped her arms around her hero's neck and head while whimpering incessantly. Her intrepid boyfriend's nostrils took a long whiff of the stagnant air, and Tom's nose immediately understood that his cherished girl had somewhere taken a healthy crap during his brief absence.

'Oh great!' Tom negatively thought. 'This whole marriage idea isn't all that I had originally imagined it to be! Here I haven't even gotten my goddamned finger wet yet, and my highly coveted girl is pissin' and shittin' all over the damned place, when my own constipated asshole is clogged-up all the way to my throat. And when I can't even think about pissin' a drop out of fear of explodin' my kidneys into a thousand different pieces! And then, besides all of this crazy shit,' the roguish boy determined, 'inside this huge cave there's still that no-good treacherous prick, Injun Joe, that I gotta' fuckin' worry about and contend with!'

* * * * * * * * * * * * *

On Tuesday evening, the village of St. Petersburg's chatty inhabitants were in a state of despair, and already mourning the "terrible demise" of Becky Thatcher and Tom Sawyer (in that exact order). The tired and frustrated searchers had virtually given-up their heroic quests when miraculously, just after the stroke of midnight, the village's bell-towers and steeples rendered forth great exuberant peals, and the streets soon filled with felicitous, half-dressed citizens hugging, kissing and checking-out each other's momentarily exposed genitals. "Becky and Tom have been found!" the townspeople shouted and rejoiced. "The children are alive, safe, and sound! Miracles indeed are possible!"

Tom stretched-out his aching body on a park bench, and reported for all interested listeners to hear that he and Becky had fortunately discovered an opening in the cave wall, and the courageous survivors followed two separate passageways the entire length of Tom's kite string. And then the boy's eyes eventually caught a glimmer of a far-off speck appearing in the night sky, that he and Becky had recognized as a star twinkling. Finally, after cramming his anxious shoulders through the cave's small aperture, Sawyer was able to identify the wonderful Mississippi River below, gently rolling past the mountainside. And after assisting Becky with achieving her egress, the pair meticulously climbed-down the hill, and the two were once again a part of "mainstream America".

After six days of well-deserved rest, Tom being healthy again, trekked over to the Widow Douglas's house to visit his old friend Huck Finn, who had a rather startling revelation to disclose to his good buddy.

"Well Tom, two nights ago Judge Thatcher announced that nobody in St. Petersburg has to ever-again worry about anyone in their family getting lost in that God-forsaken cave any more. I gotta' admit, his speech was pretty damned dramatic."

"What the hell do ya' mean, Huck?" Tom queried. "How could that be fuckin' so?"

"Because Tom, the Judge was so damned upset about his little baby doll Becky nearly perishin' in those harsh underground conditions that the rich guy hired a team of builders and masons to go downstream and seal-up the cave's main entrance. The newly installed door is triple-locked from the outside, and it's made out of heavy sheet iron," Huck divulged. "And that'll surely last over a thousand years of heavy wear and tear."

"Great balls of shit fire!" Tom euphorically exclaimed. "Injun Joe is trapped inside the goddamned cave! And the judge has just signed the jerk-off's death warrant without friggin' knowin' it! There's no way in hell that anyone, including that shrewd and evil Injun Joe, could live more than a few days inside that hell hole without havin' adequate food and water."

"Well, you're right on that account, Tom," Huck confirmed. "When you was laid-up recuperatin' from your great cave ordeal, Judge Thatcher found-out from his daughter that the remote place was Injun Joe's hideout. Yesterday, Judge Thatcher had the door re-opened, and the workmen found the Cherokee's limp body lying motionless on the ground. Joe's dead, Huck! Thank God Joe's dead and gone! The Indian's face was close to the crack of the door, and right there the dirty bastard took his last breath! But the Judge isn't worried about any legal repercussions about *him* accidentally killin' the dangerous criminal, because of Injun Joe's long record of countless felonies, including the recent murder of Dr. Robinson!"

"Huck, we've always been partners and damned good friends, so now, I have a plan that'll make the two of us as rich as Becky Thatcher's well-educated old man. And we don't even have to go to school, and graduate from any fancy academy or college to do it!"

"What's this fantasy horse manure you're talkin' out of your mouth now, Tom?" Huck challenged. "Can't ya' ever settle-down and smell the roses, and just leave well-enough alone?"

"Listen-up, Huck!" Tom imperatively commanded. "The huge cave was Injun Joe's secret hideout, and I know where he's buried his stolen treasure. It's in a side chamber underneath a cross marking, and then buried below the #2 scribbled on the rock wall. I seen' it all with my own eyes when I was lookin' for a way out of the giant, dark maze. If the treasure's there Huck, we're gonna' be rich sons-a-bitches!"

"But Judge Thatcher had the main entrance re-sealed after Injun Joe's body had been removed for a proper burial," Huck recalled and stated. "I'm afraid your glorious dream is of no use, now! No way we're gonna' be able to get inside that cave."

"That's what the fuck you think, you knuckleheaded Dolt!" Tom retorted and then laughed. "You forget that I had found a second exit high-up on the mountain ridge. Don't ya' understand? A goddamned exit could also be a friggin' entrance. So, tomorrow morning Huck," Tom directed, "you and I are gonna' paddle *your* retarded rowboat downstream and claim Injun Joe's treasure as our own. Are ya' fuckin' game?"

"Shit, Tom!" I haven't been this enthused about anything since I've been breathin' oxygen and pissin' yellow fluid! I'm tired of livin' out of a goddamned hogshead, when I ain't bein' disciplined by that ferocious Widow Douglas when I gotta' stay at her house. And I'm also tired of my deadbeat old man comin' around and smackin' and beatin' the shit out of me for no reason at all, except maybe jealousy whenever he gets overly drunk. Let's get rich together, Tom, and then we can tell the world and everybody else in it to go and fuck themselves!"

The two gallant adventurers did row downstream, did locate the "secret magic cave portal", and did enter the formerly formidable cavern from the upper ridge. Upon utilizing Tom's excellent memory, the pair eventually found the designated chamber containing Injun Joe's cross marking, and under steady candlelight, the dual encroachers meticulously dug beneath where the auspicious cross and #2 were clearly indicated.

A fabulous treasure chest was amazingly unearthed, and soon, Tom and Huck returned with their fantastic booty to St. Petersburg, where the explorers were instantly received as prominent heroes. Judge Thatcher properly invested the gold coins found in the treasure chest, and Tom and Huck learned to live like fat cat princes off of the fine interest money the local bank paid them for their wonderfully sizeable cash deposits.

"Tom and Huck's Gang"

Samuel Langhorne Clemens (1835-1910) was undoubtedly one of the most influential American authors, and was also a prolific contributor to United States literature. Sam Clemens was born in the year 1835 when *Haley's Comet* (Halley's Comet) made an appearance, and the literary master died seventy-five years later, predictably when the celestial object made another solar system pass past the earth, and then began another journey around the sun.

Sam Clemens acquired the writing pseudonym "Mark Twain" from Mississippi River steamboat jargon. A worker on the riverboat would toss a lead weight attached to a rope overboard and "mark the twain". If the water was two-fathoms-deep (twelve feet), then a riverboat could safely navigate past a shoal, or over a hidden underwater reef.

Growing-up in the quiet town of Hannibal Missouri, young Sam Clemens knew more about the Mississippi River's 'muddy waters' than the celebrated blues/jazz musician Muddy Waters ever conceived or imagined. As an impressionable boy, Twain's prime ambition was to become a Mississippi riverboat pilot. When the *Civil War* broke-out, the mighty Mississippi was shut-down to commercial boat traffic, so the unemployed riverboat pilot went west to first try his hand at gold prospecting, and later Clemens chose to become a newspaper reporter.

Mark Twain was a trendsetter, because the writer was one of the first authors to present characters speaking dialogue using poor grammar (the way ordinary people would converse), rather than the stilted, formal, academic author's style practiced by his literary predecessors, and also by his envious New England contemporaries. "Tom and Huck's Gang" is a thoroughly corrupted version of the beginning of Mark Twain's classic novel, *Huckleberry Finn*.

You probably don't know about Huckleberry Finn unless you've read a slanderous bullshit book by the name of *The Adventures of Tom Sawyer*. But I honestly believe all that particular bull-crap doesn't really friggin' matter an inch up a pig's ass. In that singular *Tom Sawyer* classic novel, some truths were exaggerated, but nevertheless, the essential facts were all goddamned bona-fide fucked-up truths from stem to stern.

I mean, just about any shit-head on this totally weird planet fibs and lies at one time or another, unless of course, their names happen to be the Widow, or Mary (not the Blessed Virgin), or *Aunt Polly*, who never wanted any goddamned cracker to eat. Tom Sawyer's Aunt Polly and the Widow Douglas are both told about in that first spectacular book, which (as I've already mentioned) is mostly true and contains a few deliberate *stretchers,* but no damned ambulances anywhere in it.

Now, here's the way that exciting *Tom Sawyer* manuscript concluded: Tom and me skillfully found the money that the ferocious robbers had hidden in the cave, and instantly, we both became rich as all hell. We got six-thousand-dollars each, all in gold. It was a lot of friggin' money when all accumulated on one table to look at and appreciate. Tom wanted to buy a national whorehouse franchise with his end, and I planned to hire a famous engineer and then construct a new type of portable outhouse suitable for utilization during circus and carnival events. But the all-too-sagacious Judge Thatcher had other designs.

"Boys," the wise Judge announced. "I believe you two lads got more *bucks* that amount to more doe (dough) than any hunters' club could ever wish for. Now I strongly suggest you two wet-behind-the-ears lucky dumb-ass kids invest your money scrupulously, rather than speculate puttin' it into a bordello franchise; into an illegal gambling casino, or into a national chain of newfangled metal outhouses for people with asses of all sizes."

"Well, Your Honor, what does ya' have in mind?" Tom crankily asked. "Huck and I are as darin' and stubborn as all hell!"

"Well boys," the Judge pontificated. "You two ain't got no say in the matter because, you're both under-aged, obnoxious turd-heads. I'm gonna' rule that the money be put into the bank, and you two lucky stiffs are gonna' each earn a dollar a day interest on your *principal*, even though your little two room schoolhouse ain't got no damned principal."

Then, the Widow Douglas took me (Huckleberry Finn) into her personal custody and predicted that she would civilize my ass, so that I didn't grow up to be a Vandal, a Visigoth or a *Hun,* even though she believed I had no observable homosexual tendencies, perverted or otherwise. The damned spinster was too decent, and too honest, and too kind in all of her ways, so it was sure rough living under her oppressive Spartan dominion. So, when I couldn't stand her demanding rules and her stern regulations, I hastily ran-away to gain freedom and independence from what I intelligently considered "fucked-up adult morals".

I got into my old rags (that I preferred wearing rather than formal school and church togs), and I happily lived out of an old abandoned hogshead down by the town livery stable. I was satisfied jerkin' off in a big old barrel, rather than pulling my meat in some fancy bed with four curtained posts erected around its frame. But then, Tom Sawyer hunted me down and said that he was "hankerin' to start a *band* of robbers" that would attack innocent civilians without using any friggin' musical instruments.

"Want to join my robber gang?" Tom persuasively asked. "You'd make a damned fine outlaw!"

"Maybe," I answered while coyly playing hard-to-get. "But why don't ya' form a gang of rapers, or a gang of hostile gay and lesbian bashers? I mean Tom; I ain't never licked a girl's beaver before, straight or lesbian, and I really never beat the shit out of a faggot minister tryin' to abduct me in the church choir loft!"

"We might do those things in addition to robbin' rich people like Robin Hood did in *Sherman Forest*," Tom authoritatively replied. "But instead, I think we'll rob from the rich, and keep all the damned easy money for ourselves. To hell with the damned poor, and with their damned stupid problems, and with their dumb livin' habits."

"What do I havta' do to join your thoroughly-neat gang?" I inquired. "Screw a woodchuck?"

"Ya' gotta' get out of this stupid barrel you're livin' in, and go back to the Widow Douglas's place," Tom assertively and firmly reprimanded. "Once you're respectable again, you'll qualify to be in my gang of fearful robbers. We're only gonna' do white collar crime to gullible white collared people, ya' understand?"

The Widow Douglas cried and slobbered all over me, and called me a poor lost lamb when I returned to her undesirable custody. The old bag also called me a "son-of-a-bitch", and a "no-good dirty little pecker-head" under her breath on Sundays, before goin' to church and receivin' communion. The demandin' widow made me dress in new clothes all over again, and I hated sweatin' in general; and I resented sweatin' my balls and ass off in that silly tight formal uniform. Truthfully, I was all *cramped-up* without even havin' my first monthly period.

Anyway, the old, damned-ugly practices of honoring customs and rituals commenced again. The Widow rang the dinner bell, and I had to report for supper on time, or else have to wash and dry the goddamned dishes and clean-off the really big supper table. And I couldn't begin eatin' my food until the old witch would tuck my head-down where I would have to listen to her say some incomprehensible holy words over the victuals. I mean to say that in the barrel filled with my personal belongings, items got all mixed-up, but in the Widow Douglas's rigid universe of ten thousand dumb-ass habits, things like laws and traditions got all muddled-up, and I had to honor each one of the strict prudish woman's goddamned Puritan WASP values.

After supper, the overprotective, overbearing widow got-out her *Bible,* and busted my balls good, reading all about Moses and the ancient Pharaoh. And I had to sit there sweatin' in my formal clothes, even when I had to take a long piss or a healthy crap. But then, I found-out that Moses and the Pharaoh had both been dead for many centuries, so I didn't take no more stock in her bullshittin' articulations, because I don't like hearin' about dead people that posed no particular, immediate, imminent threat to either Tom Sawyer or me.

I asked the self-righteous widow if I could smoke, so she set my old hogshead clothes on fire with me in them and laughed, "Smoke all ya' want Huckleberry! Next time wear your cute little blazer!" And I had to listen to her loquacious lectures about how smokin' was a vulgar habit that wasn't clean, or sanitary or healthy. I did have a maximum tolerance for her nauseous dia*tribe*, often wonderin' what Indian council she belonged to."

"But ya' don't know anything about smokin', or about sex?" I futilely criticized. "How come ya' could tell me what the hell to do about things you ain't no damned expert at!"

"Huckleberry; now don't you get overly sassy with me!" the austere widow threatened. "Next time I set you on fire, I'll let the blaze burn right to the end until you've been reduced to charred bones and ashes, just like the unfortunate residents of Sodom and Gomorrah had perished!"

"But ya' always read and talk about Moses killin' Egyptians in that *Red Sea,* and ya' don't say anything nasty about the jerk, because he had all those pyramid people slaughtered with God's help!" I ranted without achievin' any favorable results. "But ya' always find fault with me smokin' when all I'm really actually hurtin' is me, and not me drownin' an entire army in chariots chasin' my ass all over the desert! And besides, I see ya' takin' snuff and getting high, which in my honest opinion, Widow, is twice as damned deadly as puffin' masculine tobacco!"

Well, in order to reform my vulnerable soul, the determined Widow Douglas began talkin' about the "Good Place" in the afterlife. The old maid explained that all a person would have to do all day long was go around heaven on a cloud playin' a silly harp, and singin' praise forever all the way into infinity.

"Do ya' think Tom Sawyer will also be in heaven?" I asked the inflexible old Bible-totin' lady.

"No, Huckleberry. I don't think that Tom will amass the grace credentials to ever be qualified to live in heaven," the widow lamented and maintained. "Thomas Sawyer is too rebellious, insolent, defiant and insubordinate."

'That's good!' I mentally concluded. 'I wanna' be with Tom in the afterlife in a thrillin' place where we both could screw around, get drunk, get laid, rape women, and rob angels and saints on surprise raids from hell.'

The widow's sister, Miss Watson, was a slim, frigid, old maid, but certainly more tolerable than the Widow Douglas ever was. Miss Watson came to town to live with her martinet sister; wore glasses that looked like swimming goggles, and besieged my ass every night with the contents of a stupid spellin' textbook. Every evening after prayer readin', Miss Watson would break my stones about how to spell stupid-ass words like "dynamic" and "revolutionary". I instinctively went from nervous, to fidgety, to rebellious in imitation of my personal hero, Tom Sawyer. Miss Watson's imperial, condescending rhetoric was deadly dull, and her ridiculous nomenclature reminded me of the preacher's damned deadly and dull fire and brimstone sermons articulated during wholly monotonous Sunday church services.

"Don't put your feet up on the furniture," Miss Watson commanded like A Prussian officer.

"Don't slouch-down like that, Huckleberry Finn," the Widow automatically would chime-in.

"Sit up straight!" Miss Watson would imperatively add.

"Don't stretch your arms over your head in public," the Widow impolitely insisted.

"Try to always behave," Miss Watson snootily lectured. "Conformity breeds good manners."

Then, the two old bitches described in detail the "Bad Place," and after I told them "I want to go there and meet the really interestin' people that have lived on the earth," I got dual simultaneous uppercuts to the jaw, that the combination sending my ass reeling over the impeccable parlor's very ancient couch.

The two old hags didn't realize that all I desired was a change of scenery from formal rules and from their perpetual dictatorial tyranny, but the weird disciplinarian old bags would defensively go into their hyper-aggressive behavioral mode, and then effectively and systematically beat the shit out of me.

"That's very wicked Huckleberry!" the Widow boisterously chastised. "What you're sayin' is very wicked and sinful!"

"Christ, m'am!" I yelled in defense of my often-abused ego. "Beatin' the shit out of me is what is sinful and wicked. Words ain't never killed no one all by themselves!"

"The Widow and I are both preparin' to go to the glorious Good Place!" Miss Watson shrieked like a virgin maniac. "That's why we're tryin' our best to reform you to conform to good Christian teachings!" the female nutcase bellowed, before tossin' me up against the wall like I was some sort of very dangerous criminal.

"I ain't never goin' to go to heaven and be with you two Amazons," I yelled-back. "I don't need the crap and piss beatin' out of me for all eternity, if you two ugly bitches are there!"

Miss Watson and the Widow Douglas both kept verbally badgerin' and browbeatin' my stellar personality and my pristine character, and when matters didn't go their way, the old hags resorted to clobberin' and maimin' my entire body. I got tired of their sanctimonious and irrelevant bullshit, which they alternately falsely called "Christian morality" and "Western Civilization". Sometimes, the two insane hoary women would fetch the niggers into the house, and the group would pray together to escape goin' to hell, and then everybody would go to their respective beds dreamin' of heaven, and forgettin' all about the evils of child abuse, exploitation, human misery, and slavery.

I climbed the steps up to my room and intensively stared at a clean sheet of paper on my desk. 'I gotta' think of somethin' cheerful to write, tellin' the two witches of my intentions. I'm scootin' away from home once and for all!' I pondered and decided. I sat restlessly in the chair over near the window, and seriously contemplated what the hell I wanted to tell the two psychotic churchgoin' bitches.

I wished I were dead and in hell with my pal Tom Sawyer. I glanced-out the window and noticed the stars shining up in the night sky, and listened to the leaves and branches rustling against the house and shutters. I heard an owl hootin', and accordin' to local superstition, somebody in town had just died; and then my ears perceived a whippoorwill and a dog makin' oddball sounds, tellin' me that somebody else was about to croak other than a sick frog. 'I wish they're makin' noise about Tom and me both kickin' the bucket,' I imagined. 'That would be the greatest joy, if *we* could get the hell outa' this life and swiftly go to the Bad Place together!'

Then, the cold shivers came over me, when I heard a ghost-like sound originatin' from the woods behind the widow's wood-frame house. 'That ghost is unhappy in its grave, and must go around grievin' while scarin' the shit outa' all Hannibal's citizens,' I reckoned. Next, a spider crawled up my shoulder, and I flicked the sucker into my candle's flame, incineratin' the bothersome bastard and pretendin' that its body was delightfully roastin' in hell along with Tom and me.

'That's a bad thing,' I realized. 'A mighty bad omen indeed.' I recalled the perfect remedy for the totally bad luck event of burnin' a damned spider, so I took-off all of my clothes, and ran stark naked backwards doing three complete rotations of the bedroom. Next, I crossed my chest three times for good measure, and I finally tied-up a lock of my long hair to keep witches from meddlin' into my personal affairs. 'Tomorrow, I gotta' find a lost, rusty horseshoe, and nail it up against my bedroom wall, just to neutralize the damned evil spirits that had been generated from me torchin' the damned spider in the candle flame,' I vowed.

I sat-down while havin' a bad case of the heebie-jeebies, and shook all over like I had one of those nasty adult sex diseases in the advanced stages. I removed my pipe, and lit it up to puff some satisfyin' tobacco, tar, and nicotine into the air to serve as incense to help cancel-out the evil spirits caused by the black spider's fiery death. The house was as still as silent hell, and so I wished that I was dead too, just like the friggin' lucky spider was. I then heard the bell in the town clock-tower thud twelve times. 'Midnight!' I uneasily thought. 'This is when death stalks everyone weak, or anyone nervous. I better stay strong and focused!'

Then, my ultra-sensitive ears detected a distinct snap, and something mysterious stirrin' outside the house down near the ground. I sat still as a statue waitin' to meet my imminent doom. My acute hearing then heard what sounded like a dying cat squealing "Meow, meow, meow!" directly below my window.

I immediately knew how to respond to the magnificent code bein' transmitted. I scrambled-out the opened window, and plopped my bare feet down on the shed's tin roof. Then, I shinnied-down the drainpipe, and hustled into a cover of trees and bushes. Sure enough, my good buddy Tom Sawyer was waitin' to greet me.

Without a moment's hesitation, Tom and I stealthily meandered around the dirt path to the Widow's back porch. We had to be careful how we were treading, because stray dogs and cats often took craps in that area alongside the house, and I was still barefooted. And I fully realized that getting shit on the soles of a person's feet is even worse than getting nasty-smellin' animal turds stuck to the bottom of a kid's shoes. I know because that disgustin' shit has happened to me more than once.

When we surreptitiously passed by the kitchen window, I stumbled over a root, and my tripping produced a noisy thump. Tom and I slinked-down and laid still as if we were mutilated corpses. Jim (Miss Watson's big human property) came-out from the kitchen in response to the sound his ears had heard. The big oaf craned his powerful, muscular neck out, and nervously called, "Hoo dare!"

'Doesn't that dumb black bastard know any damned verbs?' I thought. 'He's fuckin' speakin' American English in a different freakin' language!'

As I was sayin', Tom and I were camouflaged behind two bushes, and the big black jerk was standin' right in the middle of the backyard vegetation. The black giant was within touchin' distance, and I didn't dare breathe, fart, gulp, or sneeze. Jim stood there for a full five-minutes, until the frightened ogre got-up the gumption to again speak his type of jargon.

"Hoo dare?" Miss Watson's slave anxiously asked. "Hoo the hell dare? Is you a ghost?"

My ankle began itchin'; my ear began itchin'; my ass began itchin', and soon my balls began itchin' somethin' fierce, too. 'I'm gonna' die if I don't scratch my whole damned body pretty soon!' I uncomfortably reckoned. I recalled that I was not supposed to scratch anything, includin' my ass and my balls at a funeral, or at a church service, where quality people were congregated (besides the inferior hicks from the sticks). I only itched in the wrong damned places at the wrong damned time, and that's another freakin' reason I wanted no part of society's incomprehensible rules, customs, traditions, extraditions, and laws. My fertile imagination was rudely interrupted by Jim, who was neurotically speakin' his slave dialect of English-non-English.

"Say dar; hoo is you out dare? Whar is ya'?" the huge lummox called. "There're no dogs and cats takin' dumps out here right now! But I did hear somephin'. Well, I'm just gonna' set my ass-down here and listen 'til I hears it again."

Jim stretched-out upon the ground under the stars, in the area separatin' Tom's hiding bush from my hiding bush. All the while, I was thinkin' about lickin' Becky Thatcher's bush regardless of what her pappy the Judge would say about my perversion, which was actually a genuine need to-get-laid-or-blown that dwelled pretty deep in my heart. Soon, Jim stretched-out his massive body on the dirt, while the inside of my nostrils began itchin' like a son-of-a-bitch. I clenched my teeth and bit my tongue, makin' my mind focus on the damned pain rather than on rubbin' my damned snout right off my face. Luckily, Jim began breathin' heavily, and then the black monster dozed-off five minutes later. His loud irregular snorin' made the ground vibrate like there was a colossal earthquake in progress.

Tom Sawyer was a daring kid that loved danger, and made every adventure more-risky and complicated than it really had to be. My best friend gestured with his head, and winked with his eye, the dual motions signalin' for me to clandestinely follow him. We crawled back toward the quiet house on our hands and knees, and I felt a plethora of garden ants scurryin' all over my arms, legs and ass. Twenty-feet away from snoring Jim, my pal Tom had the enviable audacity to whisper something so preposterous that I thought it was humorous.

"Let's tie Jim to the tree he's lyin' near," my most-excellent chum inanely suggested. "I think that darin' task would make a great adventure, and would be another feather in our caps, right Robin?"

"I don't wear caps," I obstinately retorted. "And besides, Jim's liable to wake-up and cause a ruckus," I objected. "Then the Widow and Miss Watson would really bust my stones if the two wrinkled old ladies found-out I was leavin' the house against their will."

"Okay, I'll concede round one to ya'," Tom reluctantly stated. "But now, Huck, I gotta' tell ya' an even better idea. I'm gonna' sneak into your house up the drainpipe, and enter through your bedroom window. Then, I'm gonna' visit the Widow Douglas's bedroom and steal those three candles ya' was braggin' about yesterday. I need 'em to have my first official gang meetin'."

"But the widow is sleepin' in her bedroom?" I vehemently balked, not realizing that I almost woke-up snoozing Jim. "The Widow's awake, and she'll think you was me stealin' her sacred candles that she lights when reading her damned *Bible*."

Tom called me a "cowardly yellow-bellied snake", and then my determined pal silently set-out for the aforementioned drainpipe. My devious companion demonstrated a chimpanzee's agility, as the brave kid maneuvered up the fixture, eventually clambering onto the green tin roof, and next climbing through the window into my bedroom. I waited in the dark listenin' to the irregular rhythm of Jim's dissonant snorin', forty or so feet away. Five minutes later, my loyal comrade returned down the flimsy drainpipe, carryin' his purloined three candles.

"Huck; I left a shiny nickel on the bedroom table to cover the candle expenses," my courageous associate informed. "An honest kid always pays his debts! I think I'm gonna' write my own Commandments after we get the gang started!"

"But the Widow will think it was me that took the candles and left the stupid five cents," I distressfully answered. "And then I'll get bashed and battered around like I was fightin' one of those ferocious bears or kangaroos that come around once a year with the circus. Who needs that shit?"

"Guess what Huck?" Tom asked while snickerin' and gigglin' his rear-end off.

"I haven't a clue," I disgustedly replied. "What's so vital ya' got to say?"

"When I entered the Widow Douglas's bedroom in the dark, she was havin' some wild sixty-nine session with her seventy-three-year-old sister. The Widow was lappin' away on the bottom and Miss Watson was munchin' away on top."

"You're bullshitin' me!" I gasped. "Their pussies must be drier than the Sahara Desert to begin with!"

"I seen it all with my own eyes, and heard the lustful sounds with my sharp-hearin ears," Tom adamantly insisted. "Those two old bitches were so into it that I had no trouble exchangin' the nickel for the three candles, and then hightailin' it out of the damned bedroom. That had to be the most surprisin', and the most disgustin', raunchy thing I ever did see or hear."

Tom and I promptly left the property in the opposite direction, and soon marched-up a familiar steep hill. "Miss Watson's slave knows plenty about witchcraft and black magic spells," Tom confidently related. "Tomorrow, if you're still alive, you be sure to ask the Widow and Miss Watson if Jim detected anything strange happenin' around her house."

"That's right Tom," I concurred. "Jim always keeps a magic five cent piece tied to a necklace around his neck. Other blacks come from miles around just to marvel at the cheap piece of shit. Jim claims the necklace could fetch witches and demons," I added, "but he never told the other darkies the exact words that would successfully summon *them* to Hannibal."

"But the visitin' superstitious Negroes was afraid to even touch the nickel," Tom indulgently laughed. "They thought the devil was inside the silly five cent piece. That's what I need now, Huck," Tom facetiously remarked. "A girl that's a five-cent-piece! Even Becky Thatcher would do!" Tom added while deliberately breakin' my vulnerable balls.

"Jim sure knows how to scare the shit out of his fellow slaves," I admitted, while pretending to ignore my juvenile colleague's allusion to my beloved girlfriend. "His balls at times must be bigger than blown-up balloons! I gotta' admit, Tom, that Miss Watson really owns an interestin' slave there, that's for damned sure!"

Well, when Tom and me ascended the hilltop on the fringe of the Widow's property, we looked-down into the village and noticed three or four oil lights and lanterns twinklin' where the sick people were takin' medicine, or where the dead folks were bein' mourned. The constellations were shinin' and beautiful, and the moonlight allowed the old faithful, mile-wide Mississippi River to sparkle next to the somnolent hamlet. The overall illumination was so awe-inspiring that Tom and me even forgot about Jim inhalin' green-headed flies while snorin', and about Miss Watson and the Widow naughtily doin' perverted senior-citizen lesbian sixty-nine.

My intrepid buddy and I descended the steep hill and proceeded down a well-worn path, which was a pretty nifty shortcut into town that we always used. Joe Harper (who was very *bizarre*) and Ben Rogers were hiding in the old tan-yard waitin' for us. The four of us then trekked to the riverbank and unhitched a skiff belongin' to the already-sleeping town mayor. Then, we competently rowed-out into the channel, not realizin' that our combined weight might sink the damned small, weatherworn boat right into the muddy Mississippi. The prospective gang members took turns rowin' the skiff, and finally, about two and a half miles downstream, we went ashore exactly where a big exaggerated scar marked the site of our pre-planned hillside destination.

"This is the secret hideout," Tom proudly informed the two other assholes and me. "It's my favorite place to come and jerk- off!"

"Shouldn't ya' jerk-off and then *come*?" Ben Rogers cleverly challenged.

"Shut your damned trap, if ya' wanna' see tomorrow morning!" Tom angrily answered our idiot friend. "I'm supposed to be the only goddamned comedian in the gang!"

The four of us carefully climbed the precarious hill, and crawled between several treacherous sticker bushes; and then our gang's bossy leader made us all take an oath of allegiance to *our* organization's clandestine cause. "Ya' gotta' promise to keep this all meeting a big secret, and not even tell your girlfriends, your wives, or your consciences," Tom sternly commanded. "And if one of ya' assholes squeals, I'll personally beat the shit out of ya', even when I only was suspectin' that ya' would be squealin'."

My best pal then led us through a narrow hole that existed in the rocky terrain, which was situated right behind the thickest growth of bushes. Then, we lit our four candles and crawled on our hands and knees like escapin' prison convicts. Twice, out of reacting to the suspense, I stupidly almost-swallowed my candle flame and wick. That particular dumb military-like crawling maneuver continued for almost two-hundred-yards, until the four participants reached the mouth of a really swell cave (that didn't look that swollen).

The inductees followed Tom through several tight passages until we ducked under a wall, and wriggled into a well-concealed hollow. On the other side was a chamber where we could all finally stand-up without havin' to look at someone else's ass while crawlin' like a procession of hypnotized infants. It was really damp, cold and sweaty inside the "cavern' room" as Tom had so loquaciously labeled the rock chamber.

"Now we're gonna' start this band of robbers called Tom Sawyer's Gang," my idol began his splendid explanation. "And everybody that wants to join my gang must solemnly take an oath and write his name in blood."

"But what if I don't want to use blood?" Ben Rogers foolishly objected. "What if I wants to use somethin' else?"

Tom Sawyer was one smart cookie. My pal knew that him and me had already gone through puberty, and could squirt semen all over the damned place, but that Ben and Joe couldn't, because the two punks were younger, and didn't even have hair under their arms or on their tiny balls to be able to ejaculate. "Okay Ben," Tom austerely replied. "If ya' all are afraid of usin' blood to sign your name, we'll all then use our own semen. That way we can all jerk-off and use our body fluids to do the trick. Since semen is almost transparent, it'll be just like usin' invisible ink!"

"No thanks!" Ben Rogers mildly protested. "On second thought, blood's perfectly fine with me."

So then, Tom whipped-out a folded sheet of paper from his pants' pocket, and marvelously read a historic oath he had written during a recent moment of inspiration. "Every kid must stick to the band and not tell anybody any of our sacred secrets," my closest friend proclaimed like a colonial town crier, or a loudmouthed somebody like that in olden days.

"What does ya' mean by secrets?" Joe Harper questioned.

"I popped my thirty-first load yesterday," I bragged, "so I guess the fact that *you,* Joe, doesn't yet have hair around your pecker would be one of the club's secrets too, along with Ben bein' a disgustin' gay virgin."

"Good example, Huck," Tom agreed and complimented, showing a degree of admiration. "In fact, it was a perfect example. Now let me continue with what we're gonna' swear to do, and also not to do. Now, if anybody tells anyone in Hannibal any secret of our gang, then that kid will not eat, drink, sleep, piss, or shit until *he* kills everybody in his friggin' family as a penance. Is that simple fact fuckin' clear?"

"As clear as I can piss my bladder empty without any yellow appearin' in the fluid," I appropriately stated. "Yellow definitely shows cowardice!"

"And the sign of our gang is gonna' be a double cross, because-that's what we're goin' to be doin'; we're gonna' trick, rob and double-cross everyone else in Hannibal. Now then, you three genuine, non-religious assholes know exactly how we're goin' to keep the goddamned devil away from snoopin' on our fraudulent activities," Tom emphasized. "And if an unfaithful gang member squeals on anyone else, that dirty rat must carve the cross deeply into both breasts of all his family members, after he kills 'em off, one by one."

"Isn't that rule a little harsh and cruel?" Ben Rogers nervously questioned.

"Well Ben, if ya' don't kill your family in twenty-four hours, then Huckleberry and me is gonna' cut your dick and balls off, and use 'em as fish bait. Ya' got any more asinine, nonsensical objections to raise?"

"Er, none at all!" Ben amiably agreed with a worried expression showing upon his face. "After I pop my first big load, I wanna' still have a dick and balls left to do it at least twice a day!"

"And anyone else outside the band that uses our adopted symbol, which is the Sawyer Cross, must be sued," Tom proceeded with expressing his extraordinary bullshit. "And that includes the damned preacher, and the fucked-up town undertaker. too. Do ya' country-bumpkin shit-heads all understand that pertinent bullshit?"

We all mechanically nodded our heads showin' our fathomin' of Tom's infallible declaration, and totally affirming our dumb-ass, wholehearted endorsement of his fallible insanity.

"And furthermore," Tom dramatically read from his prepared written oath. "Any kid in the gang that tells any confidential secrets, in addition to havin' his dick and balls cut-off and used for fish bait, then that stupid-shit will have to also have his throat slashed at the jugular; his carcass burned in the blacksmith's furnace, and his cursed ashes scattered all over this here secret cave," Tom pompously lectured. "Then, the craven asshole's name will be blotted off the club's list, and the dishonored fuck-head will be forgotten by the remainder of the members in-good-standin', until the day *they* officially die."

"Is that all?" Joe Harper incredulously inquired before taking a deep gulp that made his Adam's apple do an involuntary yo-yo routine three times.

"There's one more important particular I gotta' mention," Tom haughtily continued. "If a member reveals any secret of the gang, an evil curse will haunt that evicted and disgraced member's family for the next thousand generations."

Everybody agreed that Tom had orchestrated one fantastic oath to swear by, because next to playin' with our miniature erect dingles, we all loved to indiscriminately curse and swear.

"Did ya' think of all that neat bullshit all on your own?" I asked infallible Tom Sawyer. "Or did you find-out all of those terrific ideas in a library book?"

"No, Huck, you dumb-ass fuck!" our gang leader defensively answered. "I read some of the things outa' stolen pirate books, and others from certain robber journals. But actually, every high-toned gang here in Missouri has a similar damned code of ethics!"

Ben Rogers then thought of an irregularity that could have been embarrassin' to me. "Huck Finn here ain't got no family to kill, if *he* tells any of our confidential secrets," the conniving, little bastard declared. "What's ya' gonna' do about *him?"*

Tom contemplated the potential conflict for a moment. "Well, ain't Huck got a father?" our fearless leader retardedly retorted.

"Sure, he's got a biological father, but the deadbeat's abandoned Huck," that detestable little prick, Ben Rogers, maintained. "Huck's pappy is always lyin' drunk and wallowin' with Farmer Gray's hogs every time I see him in town. But he's been missin' from civilization for over a year now, either dead, or gallivantin' all over creation."

"Isn't Ben tellin' one of *my* secrets?" I yelled and balked.

"Yeah, but he's tellin' it to gang members, so that don't violate any of our oath!" Tom objectively clarified.

The fellas' discussed my unique predicament concerning a lack of family to kill, and the guys were going to leave me out, sayin' that everybody in the club ought to have a family, or a legitimate father to kill, or else the entire scenario would not be fair and equitable to each of the other members. Everyone was *stumped* without even having a damned sawed-off tree-trunk anywhere nearby, so we all sat there like moronic jerk-offs. I felt like I was about to burst into tears, or go into a hysterical tirade, and violently beat the shit out of Joe and Ben, and then make them suck my dick, when all of a sudden, a flash streaked across my mind, and I was miraculously enlightened.

"Hey guys," I ecstatically yelled. "What about Miss Watson to offer for sacrifice? You guys would have fun executin' an old formal nasty *Bible*-totin' bitch like her!"

"Oh, she'll do!" Tom defended my suggestion in direct support of my desperate-but-creative proposal. "I ain't never killed no eighty-year-old practicin' lesbian before. But I guess I gotta' stab or shoot her from behind, before the queer old lady turns-around and gets her *licks* in with the Widow Douglas!"

Then, upon Tom's very excellent instruction, the four of us all stuck a pin in our dicks and squeezed the blood into a small cup that our leader had brought along just for consummating the formal initiation ceremony. And with the accumulated blood extracted from the four members' dangling peckers, we then had sufficient red ink to sign our names to the official document. My limp penis really badly hurt, because Tom said the blood had to be obtained from the heads of our sensitive dingles, and not from the damned shafts.

"Now," Ben Rogers articulated in an adult-like mellow voice. "What the hell's the line of business for this damned gang? Are we gonna' rape and screw grandmothers, or are we gonna' terrorize dispensable senior-citizen lesbians like Miss Watson and the Widow Douglas, and possibly even our leader's wonderful Aunt Polly."

"Well, to start off with, until we get some valid operatin' experience," Tom replied while chewing on a length of straw extending-out from his mouth, "we're gonna' rob rich people, and hold them hostage. And if the captured aristocrats give us any verbal shit, we're gonna' murder them, real savage like."

"But there ain't many really rich folks in Hannibal to keep the gang busy for more than a week!" Joe Harper ridiculously argued.

"And if we only steal cattle and rob houses," Ben Rogers interrupted, "we will be..."

"Look turd-head!" Tom yelled at the obnoxious kid, who was tryin' to impress us with his general ignorance and arrogance. "Stealin' cattle ain't robbery, and breakin' into houses ain't robbery, either. Those damned juvenile practices are only examples of burglary. Burglars ain't got no damned style or class. We're desperados, daring highwaymen," Tom eloquently editorialized. "We're gonna' stop stages, and buggy carriages on the road while wearin' masks, and then we'll first kill all the men and shave the women's pussies just for fun."

"Must we always shave women's pussies and then kill them?" Ben Rogers declared. "I don't think we oughta' kill women with fine hairy pussies; especially beautiful blondes; that's what the hell I'm thinking! We could glue the pussy hairs together, and sell them as men's toupees!"

"Well," Tom elaborated. "We could bring the women with the hairiest pussies here to this cave and hold 'em for ransom. That would be a lot of fun I suppose."

"Ransom?" Ben Rogers innocently asked. "What the hell's that?"

"I really don't know for sure," Tom insincerely replied. "But that's what the hell pirates and gangs do in those damned books I was tellin' ya' about, so naturally that's what the hell we've gotta' do to have any style and decent class."

"But how can we do it if we don't know what it is we gotta' do?" the apprehensive Ben Rogers queried with a very confused look on his damned grotesque-looking face. "This gang is gonna' be doin' some illogical things!"

"Look, Asshole. Have ya' ever gotten laid and popped a heavy load inside a pretty girl or lovely lady?" Tom challenged.

"Er, no!" Ben admitted in pure humiliation.

"Well then, virgin Asshole. I've done that damned easy thing many, many times," Tom boasted. "But the first time, though, I didn't know what the hell I was doin'. But it all came naturally to me after I got started. The same thing's gonna' happen with ransomin'. It's gonna' come natural to ya', once ya' start, I guarantee it!"

"If ya' say so," Ben conceded with his head crestfallen. "If ya' say so!" the asshole obediently reiterated.

"And furthermore," Tom elucidated. "Since ransomin' is all done and already explained in books, we can't do anythin' any damned different, or else things will get all muddled-up. We gotta' believe what the books say, whether we think the published words are fucked-up, or not! That is, we gotta' believe every damned book except the damned *Good Book* that the fucked-up Widow and Miss Watson always read like their worthless lives depend on it."

"Oh, Tom, that's all quite grand and wonderful," Joe Harper butted in. "But how in tar-nation are these hostages goin' to be ransomed if we don't know how to ransom them? That's the thing I want to get at. Now, what do *you* reckon this ransomin' bullshit really is?"

"Well Shit-head," Tom angrily answered. "If we keep the prisoners until they're officially ransomed, it probably means we keep them hostage until they're officially dead. Now stop annoyin' and aggravatin' me with your trivial horse-crap!"

"Now, look who's talkin' bullshit!" Ben intrepidly chimed-in. "Those hostages will drive us broke, always havin' to be fed and attended to. They'll be eatin' up all our food, and then always tryin' to escape our custody. I say we just kill 'em and save ourselves plenty of money and aggravation."

"Okay Ben," Tom said with a wide grin. "As commander of this here gang, I'll appoint *you'* official executioner, so that *you* can kill all the adults we capture and take hostage."

"Er Tom," the neurotic Ben Rogers stammered. "I was only suggestin' that one of us would have to stay-up all night and all day guardin' the captives. But if that's what's necessary until we figure-out exactly what *ransom* means, then I guess we'll have to do it before decidin' to kill or execute our friggin' captives."

"Tom's right!" I interrupted, sticking-up for my closest chum before we ever attempted our first stick-up. "If it says in books that we gotta' ransom people, then that's what the hell we're gonna' do before we kill anybody. I mean," I stipulated. "Don't you silly assholes think that the people that wrote and made the books know what the hell they're talkin' about or doin'?" I rhetorically argued. "And besides; the Widow has a dictionary in her living room, and I'll look the word 'ransom' up, and then report its definition at our next damned meetin'."

"Okay, with me," Ben Rogers enthusiastically subscribed to my fantastic proposition. "And if 'ransom' means shavin' ladies' hairy pussies, I'm gonna' ransom as many of 'em as I can get my hands on. I mean; women have much more hair on their cookies than girls our age do; I'm pretty certain that *that's* for damned sure!"

"That's a great idea!" Joe Harper acknowledged. "We'll have Ben kill all the damned men, and then we'll ransom all the women and have enough fine curly pubic hair to go into the wig business. Other than that, I ain't got nothin' exceptional to say or report."

"I don't want to kill nobody!" Ben squawked. "I just wanna' shave and lick the ladies' hairy pussies! But first though, I think I should practice shavin' and lickin' my mom's pet housecat!"

"But ya' joined my gang, and you'll have to abide by *my* rules!" Tom screamed at the puzzled and disenchanted squirming kid. "And I aim to kick *your* ass black and blue, and black again, if ya' dare defy my authority! Get the message, Asshole!"

Ben shut his mouth tight, and Joe and Tom really gave *him* the raspberry, even though a kid named Huckleberry was present. And poor Ben Rogers had to suffer Tom and Joe's perpetual tormentin', or else the annoying brat would have to be beaten-up (by them) in front of me for my distinct pleasure.

So, then Tom Sawyer was unanimously elected President of the gang, and Joe Harper was installed as Captain. I was appointed Vice-President, and Ben Rogers was elected "Three to one" as "Chief Wimp and Sissy". And we all were elated when Tom announced that each of us would get to be "Sergeant-at-Arms, Legs, and Pussies" on a wonderful weekly rotating basis.

"Pap and Huckleberry"

Pap was always a pathetic loser and a complete failure, but worse yet, my derelict father was extremely jealous of me and my success. My Old Man thought I had become fabulously rich from Tom Sawyer and me finding Injun Joe's treasure in the down-river cave, and Pap got mighty pissed-off when I told him that Judge Thatcher was governing and monitoring the bonanza, and that I hadn't yet gotten my first interest payment from the bank. I knew all along that Pap's sole motivation for showing any particular interest in me was to extort and connive from my possession my accumulating fortune. That general, perplexing explanation just about encapsulates the magnitude of my ongoing dilemma.

So, one day Pap showed-up unexpected at the Widow Douglas's place when the Old Bat and her sister Miss Watson were buying groceries in the village. My unscrupulous Old Man kidnapped my ass, and the rest of my body, and took me down-river to hunt and fish, which I actually preferred doing, since the Widow and her fucked-up ugly old maid sister were suspected of being Bible-toting lesbian partners that made me do crazy shit (that I absolutely and positively despised). I truly loathed getting dressed-up on Sunday mornings to go to church; hated sitting-up straight at the kitchen table while eating; disliked taking a bath every damned night; resented brushing my teeth and combing my hair, and I also detested having to wipe my smelly asshole twice as clean as it should be at least six fuckin' times a day.

Going away with Pap was actually a pleasant departure for me from the Widow's deplorable dominion and tyranny, except that my father would get exceptionally drunk and when he did, the addicted fanatic would savagely beat the crap and liver bile out of me. Just the night before, while we were inside his upriver shanty/cabin, Pap became smashed on rye whiskey and thought I was the Devil in disguise. My father chased me all around his dilapidated log cabin shack with his sharp knife for two whole hours, and tried killing me with vicious swipes and lunges. I didn't sleep a wink all night, even though Pap was snoring louder from his terrible sleep apnea than any damned series of thunderclaps I've ever heard. My paramount fear was that the irresponsible drunk would wake up inebriated, become excessively disoriented, and then recklessly stab me dead (as I slept) while his affected mind was still under the influence.

So, I had to figure-out a practical plan to escape his style of dominion over me, just like I had been temporarily emancipated from the Widow Douglas's petticoat despotism. Above all else, I keenly desired achieving freedom from Pap, freedom from the Widow Douglas, and freedom from so-called organized civilization in that particular order. And if I had my fuckin' druthers, I would live in the woods with Tom Sawyer, and each day screw pretty girls, lick their hairy pussies, rob rich assholes riding in stage coaches, and us being merry passengers on exciting river-boats, where we could gamble; smoke pipes; fight pirates; laze-around the backwoods, and then jerk-off when Tom and I had nothing better to do.

"Listen here Huck; wake-up and get your clean ass erect!" Pop yelled at me the next morning inside his grubby river dump. "We gotta' catch some catfish so that I can trade them for cash; go into the village and buy me a fresh bottle of rye," my old man commanded. "Get your lazy ass up off the cot right this instant, I say! Now that you're filthy rich, ya' think you're better than your old man! Ya' think ya' could afford the lazy rich man's lifestyle, do ya'? I'm gonna' teach ya' some respect and discipline before I'm fuckin' done with ya'!"

At that moment, I was happy that Pap was sober, and that the lush hadn't sliced me up like lunchmeat or chopped liver, thinking that I was one of Satan's minions, or maybe actually thinking me being the dreaded Lucifer himself. "Pap, your drinking of booze is gonna' be your ruination," I sincerely attested. "Why can't we just be good friends; go huntin' and fishin' together, and have a decent relationship. You're fun to be with when you're not hittin' the brown bottle, and that ain't no damned lie, either."

"Ain't no fun bein' on the wagon, Huckleberry," Pap argued in defense of his alcohol habit. "Might as well be dead and buried; I'd be so damned miserable all the day long. Temperance is for fuckin' churchgoers that don't realize we're all headed for the ground, and the hungry insects and worms, without ever gainin' any damned salvation. It's all a big fuckin' lie, Huck! If there is a fuckin' afterlife, I guarantee ya' son, that the fucked-up Devil runs all of its departments. Once you're on the wrong side of the grass, you're dead, and that's all she wrote."

I didn't wish to get into any religious or philosophical debate with Pap, knowing how irrational he often was, so I figured I would cleverly switch subjects in midstream. "Somebody was tryin' to break into the cabin last night, so I stayed-up ready to defend your castle against whoever the hell it was," I deliberately fibbed. "Luckily the asshole got tired of failure and ran away when I yelled some cuss words through the door. I was only imitatin' you Pap, and my strategy worked to perfection."

"Ya' shoulda' rousted me up from my siesta. I would've given the son-of-a-bitch the thrashin' of his life!" Pap answered with a degree of bravado evident in his tone of voice. "Ya' know Huck; violence is the best defense against crazy fucked-up people that know nothin' else except lowlife criminal activity. Thank goodness I have my own customized morality existin' outside those fucked-up church rules. Now Huck," the rambling un-eloquent orator continued his demented tirade, "nothin' ain't accomplished by us just bullshittin' all mornin' long. Go out to our lines layin' in the river, and see if we catched any fish. I'm hungry as all hell, and could eat a caravan of elephants," Pap exaggerated. "And besides that, any extra fish I can sell for money and profit, I'll use to improve the condition of my liver."

Pap unlocked the one and only door so that I could then exit his miniature prison. My eyes looked toward the Mississippi, and I observed some driftwood randomly floating downstream. So then, my alert brain realized that the river was in its predictable June rise, and that sometimes-abandoned boats or pieces of log rafts could be easily retrieved, with the wood often being sold to sawmills to make lumber. But my ulterior motive for scrutinizing my physical environment was to seek asylum from Pap's perpetual ruthlessness.

Much to my surprise and joy, a dark red canoe came drifting by. Now sometimes the canoe might have an occupant that owns the damned boat, and when you go chest high into the river to catch it, the tricky asshole will sit-up and laugh his dick and balls off at your stupid frustration, futility and disappointment. But this baby I saw floating by was almost brand new, and about fourteen-foot-long; even longer than one of those elephant dicks Pap always talked about and wanted to fry in a stove or oven to eat. 'This son-of-a-bitch escape vehicle must be worth at least ten-dollars!' I gleefully estimated and concluded.

Well, luckily, the damned canoe was indeed empty, so I carefully climbed-inside, wet clothes and all, and I used the paddle to maneuver the boat to shore, where I hid it in a secret cove, all densely covered by tangled vines and willow trees (that had to be weeping for me), which was a secluded area that even my shrewd father was unaware of.

'When Pap goes rowing-off in his skiff to St. Petersburg to sell his fish and to buy more rye whiskey,' I schemed, 'I'll use this here canoe to go to Jackson's Island and live and camp-out all by myself.

Yes sir,' I imagined.' That's the ideal type of life for me. I can eat, sleep, shit and piss whenever the hell I want, without any damned adult supervision or interference.'

Pap exited his shanty with a limp and approached my vicinity, carrying his rusty shotgun. Fortunately, my erratic parent never noticed my clothes being wet, but instead, criticized my lack of initiative about checking the fish lines in the river. As usual, I tolerated his verbal abuse because I knew Pap was sober, and that when he was that wonderful way, my dad would beat the shit out of other men his own age, and leave me the hell alone as far as his violent temper was concerned.

But Pap was happy to learn that *we* had caught five catfish, and so we detached the dead creatures from their various lines and entered the log cabin to consume a tasty breakfast. Then, my routine-oriented father drank from his small water bucket, and decided to start pontificating about his perception of reality. His redundant monologues were always duplications of themselves.

"The next time some greedy fuck-head tries breakin' into my cabin, you wake me up, Huckleberry, so that I could pulverize the goddamned bastard and bust his head open, ya' hear me, Huck!" Pap yelled. "I'd shoot the no-good cock-sucker with my shotgun before I'd ever waste my valuable time beatin' the crap out of him with my bare fists! A man's gotta' defend his pride and his property, ya' understand that important bullshit, Son?"

Around noon, Pap and I were standing along the riverbank when nine attached logs from a runaway raft came floating by. So, we climbed into his skiff and skillfully retrieved the suckers. Now Pap was satisfied with his found treasure, and soon desired to spend his prospective booty. It wasn't his fashion to wait around for additional worthy debris to come drifting by during the June rise. My captor was quite satisfied with whatever he could discover that would fetch him a new bottle of rye whiskey back in "civilization".

"Why don't ya' buy moonshine instead?" I courageously asked him. "My suggestion is on the practical side. It's plenty cheaper, and your money will go farther, father."

"Why the fuck don't ya' learn to keep your big fat trap shut!" Pap rankled in a sort of rage. "Quality is always better than cheap quantity. Any regular asshole knows that; so, it all probably means that you don't even qualify to be an asshole, Son. Ha, ha, ha Huck!" Pap mercilessly guffawed in reaction to his own Socratic-like wisdom. "Ain't that the goddamned truth, though? Now leave me the hell alone, you junior juvenile delinquent Asshole. I'm gonna' lock your butt inside my shack, and then row my reliable skiff three miles over to St. Petersburg, and make my important retail purchase. And when I return," my unmeritorious mentor predicted, "we can do the same monotonous shit all over again tomorrow mornin'."

I waited for a full half-hour, after Pap finally left the cabin, before I went to work enacting my unique escape idea. First, I used a saw that I had furtively hidden under my cot to make a precision-type hole (just big enough for me to squeeze through) in the base of the wall behind a table, which had rickety legs. Next, I gathered together some bacon, beans, a hunting knife, coffee, sugar, coffeepot, fishing lines, matches, two blankets, an axe, a tin cup, and a jug of drinking water. After making my exit hole, I meticulously transported those items from the shanty to the hidden canoe, all within two hours. After finishing those difficult tasks, I utilized Pap's axe, and from outside the cabin, I cleverly smashed-in the door to make it appear that robbers had entered and kidnapped me. Then, a revolutionary thought tantalized and dominated my brain, and I jubilantly acknowledged that my plan could be successfully implemented.

'I know what. Instead of robbers' kidnapping me, I'll make it look like I was killed and mutilated. If I'm lucky,' I seriously reflected, 'my damned plan will fool the hell out of Pap, the police, the sheriff, and everybody else, too.'

Pap's shotgun was loaded, and I surreptitiously slinked into the nearby woods to blast the daylights out of some unsuspecting prey. Sure enough, a wild pig was snorting around in the underbrush, so I aimed and killed the fat oinker with one premeditated pull of the trigger. I wasted no time butchering the animal as best I could, loading the more essential meat into the canoe for my upcoming supper on deserted Jackson's Island.

The tin cup was soon filled with putrid-smelling pig blood, and I ingeniously splattered the red liquid all over the shabby cabin, making the area look like I had been brutally killed putting up noble resistance to the evil robbers' intrusion. Then, I carefully slid the sawed-out log back into position, and quite truthfully, I was mighty proud of my artful achievement in that the improvised configuration looked exactly as if it hadn't been tampered with by a creative and crafty asshole, such as myself. But then, I intelligently acknowledged that there were still more vital aspects to my grand design that had to be efficiently executed.

Next, I mechanically dragged what was left of the decimated pig down to the riverbank, leaving a thick trail of blood to further confuse crime investigators. The rest of the red slimy anatomy I tossed into the canoe. After hopping inside myself, I gingerly paddled my new-found mode of transportation into the river, and very methodically headed along the coast in the direction of St. Petersburg, which was also the way to Jackson's Island, which was situated directly in the center of the majestic Mississippi. All throughout my thrilling expedition, I occasionally hid along the banks of familiar creeks until I finally noticed Pap rowing his small boat in the opposite direction (with his newly acquired quart of rye) on his way back to his primitive cabin.

'Freedom just ain't another damned word in the dictionary!' I comprehended and concluded. 'Liberty is the most vital thing a man or a boy could ever have! Without it, I'm just a goddamned obedient, unhappy slave, just like Miss Watson's black servant, Jim! And who the hell in their right mind wants to spend the rest of their meaningless life being goddamned property?'

I paddled gently upstream for around three more hours, and when dusk passed and darkness fell, I floated by the ferry landing and could hear people's voices conversing and bullshitting about certain human society nonsense like religion, politics, sports, and formal education; all of the gossiping adults having academic, vain, hollow, shallow and inconsequential discussions that always led to nowhere, with plenty of verbal bullshit polluting the atmosphere.

After I slowly and silently drifted past the aforementioned ferry landing, I conserved my flagging energy, and gradually paddled-out to the middle of the river. I then stood-up in my canoe, symbolically declaring to myself my own independence. To my right I could see the twinkle of lanterns that represented nighttime St. Petersburg, and beyond *that* familiar spectacle, straight ahead, I smiled when my blurry vision perceived a heavily-timbered land mass that I immediately and merrily identified as my personal salvation, refuge and paradise; my land of freedom, Jackson's Island. That marvelous sight made me paddle ahead with much more fervor and vigor.

'Freedom from civilization and all its illogical rules, laws, and society problems!' I plausibly reckoned, and then momentarily paused to imagine some more. 'I think I'd be happy being the last goddamned asshole alive on Earth, and me enjoying my existence, managing the business of survival all by my goddamned lonesome!'

Then, my determined mind switched to considering more mundane considerations. 'I'll land this canoe on the Illinois side of the island, where I'm less likely to be detected by passing barges, boats and steamships,' I defensively reasoned. 'Yes, that's what I'll do! I've been here twice before with my loyal, faithful pal Tom

Sawyer, and only he'd be smart enough to guess where the hell I am if Tom still believed that I was still alive. I'm three full-miles away from St. Petersburg, and I fuckin' like it that way, and wouldn't settle for any other alternative.'

Upstream, about a mile distant, my wary eyes saw the outline of a monstrous lumber raft approaching, with a huge lantern lit in its center. And as I stealthily hid my ass in the high bushes, I heard a jerk-off employee saying, "Stern oars there! Heave her head over to starboard! Fuckin' hurry-up I say!"

After the awesome lumber raft eased by my dark vicinity, I no longer felt threatened by trespassers, so I plopped myself into an open area and took a long-much-deserved snooze, dreaming about smoking my pipe; eating a delicious breakfast; escaping Pap and the Widow Douglas's dual dictatorships; feeling gorgeous mermaids' beautiful big breasts; and finally, jerking-off; because even the ordinarily wonderful thought of screwing a pretty girl (as part of organized society) seemed repugnant and alien to me during that special moment of personal emancipation.

"Huck Finds Jim"

I was pretty damned content being my own boss when I had gradually fallen asleep on Jackson's Island, but then being a light dozer, I was roused by the sound of distant men's voices coming from the southern tip of the isolated, uninhabited small land mass. I grabbed the nearby shotgun I had taken from Pap's cabin, rose to my feet, and slinked-down like an Indian, apprehensively moving towards the disturbance's origin. 'These can't be members of a search party already out looking for me!' my distrustful mind evaluated. 'Hell, I've only been missing from Pap's cabin for around six lousy hours.'

As the deep-toned voices became louder and more distinct, I got-down on my knees and began slowly crawling towards their source. During my military-type reconnaissance, I soon came across two tough-looking varmints standing around a campfire, so I decided to stay quiet and eavesdrop on their conversation.

"I don't think he'd be able to make it out here on his own without some sort of a boat," the first man declared and shared with his companion. "And besides, this forsaken place is too hard for anyone, even him, to be able to swim to. We'll stay here another hour to get warm, and eat some grub, and then get back to our boat. To tell you the truth, Hank, I'm hankering to go back to town and gettin' tired of searchin' without makin' any progress. There's only so much aggravation I can tolerate."

"You're right on that account, Dan," Hank dejectedly answered. "I'm pretty darned discouraged, too! We might as well head back to St. Petersburg empty-handed. This ain't the first time I've fuckin' gambled on me earnin' a decent reward, and then have lost."

I crept back to where my supplies were stationed, hid all my provisions behind bushes and trees, and then trekked to where the dark red canoe had been hidden. I surreptitiously camouflaged it with reeds, branches and twigs, and then left a small opening for me to slither my ass inside along with my loaded shotgun.

'I've got a handful of replacement shells in my pocket, should I need to use them in a jiffy,' my survival-oriented mind rehashed. 'I hope I don't have to kill any desperate bounty hunters that are out lookin' for my butt, so that the pursuers can get a reward for bringin' my sought-after punk ass back into civilization. Gee whiz! I gotta' stay quiet to avoid a confrontation. Even burpin' and fartin' are out of the question until those two mean-lookin' jaspers eventually hop into their boat and leave the island.'

At sunrise, I awoke from my irregular slumber, and cautiously ambled from the stationary canoe to patrol and scout the island. Off in the distance, I saw two men in a skiff moving slowly towards St. Petersburg, and I then sensed that I was safe and sound from being apprehended. But much to my utter astonishment, my ears heard a certain rustling in the bushes, and so I pointed my shotgun into the brambles and was surprised to see a familiar black face frantically begging for clemency.

"Jim! What the hell are you doin' here on Jackson's Island?" I greeted Miss Watson's tall, muscular slave, who was down on his knees and stupidly appealing for mercy like some cowardly ancient Greek suppliant that Becky Thatcher, Amy Lawrence, and Margaret Kooneman have read about in their academic school textbooks. "How come you're here and not sleepin' like ya' should be in your bunk, or dozing on Miss Watson's back lawn?"

"Don't hurt me, Huck! I'm scared of ghosts, and that fact ain't no damned superstition, either! I always liked dead people, Huck; honest I have!" the petrified slave incoherently chattered. "Now please Mr. Finn; you just go back into the river where ya' belong, and leave my black ass alone before I shits my lungs and heart out!"

"What the frig' are ya' jabberin' about Jim?" I challenged the strangely behaving Negro. "You're strong enough that you could snap my spine in half in one mighty crack with those powerful arms of yours! And kindly explain to me. What's this stupid bullshit that you all of a sudden think I'm a damned ghost?"

"Huck, I ran away from that crazy lady Miss Watson, because I got tired of her strict orders. And also, I got tired of listenin' to the Widow's heavy bull-crap!" Jim nervously explained as if making a church confession. "I decided I can't take that female horse-shit of theirs any longer! So, I got pissed-off, and when my little boat began sinkin', I jumped-off and swam all the way out here to the island to escape to freedom. You just gotta' understand, Huck. Freedom's a pretty damned important thing to me, and accordin' to what I've heard, I can get it if I can make it to Ohio! But what the hell do you care? You're now a ghost, and don't give a shit any more about dumb-ass livin' people's problems!"

"Jim. You're speaking almost good English. How come?"

"Well Huck. People think I'm a dumb-ass, uneducated slave, so I acted like one to avoid suspicion."

"But you still haven't explained to me why you think I'm a fuckin' ghost," I reminded Jim. "Jump-off of square two and hop back to square one."

"Well Huck, ya' know how gossip floats around the village like smoke from a damned ragin' forest fire," Jim replied in a rather sophisticated simile. "Well, it's been reported all over town that you was killed inside your Pap's cabin, and that your body was probably thrown into the river. That's why the hell I still think I'm listenin' to and talkin' with a ghost, or a goblin, or a ghoul, or some other spooky thing like that."

"Ha, ha, ha!" I hardily laughed. "My trick worked! For your information Jim, I'm not a fierce goblin, or a wicked spirit after all! And I promise you, Jim. I'm quite alive and breathin', and proudly standin' here with you, in the flesh. Look now! Your' eyes can't see through me, right! I'm what the scientists call bein' three-dimensional. You can't see my asshole, while peerin' through my thick intestines, can ya' Jim?"

"Well, I'll be damned as sure as sin!" Jim ecstatically exclaimed. "It is you, Huck! You ain't no fucked-up ghost after all! Now I gotta' tell ya'; I'm so hungry I can eat a horse, a mule, and two ponies to boot. I've been livin' off of wild strawberries and huckleberries ever since I set foot on this place, and I need to swallow-down some other kinds of more nourishin' victuals, so that I have the strength to move on up to Ohio and freedom."

"Well Jim, don't turn into a cannibal and eat me, because my name is Huckleberry, ha, ha, ha! You ain't the only person searchin' around for freedom and independence," I educated the runaway slave. "I'm also seekin' liberty from the Widow Douglas's formal rules; from Miss Watson's chronic religious and temperance bull-shit; from Pap kickin' the crap out of me at every opportunity when he's drunk; and from the evils of church; from the horrors of school, and from fucked-up American society in general."

"Well Huck, if it wasn't you killed in that shanty, then who the heck was it?" Jim wondered and asked, inadvertently scratching his head to subconsciously emphasize his confusion. "I always suspected you was as smart as that connivin' rascal Tom Sawyer. Now, I knows ya' are!"

"I'll tell ya' what, Jim," I assured the paranoid runaway. "I'll let ya' know all about my recent escapades over a hot breakfast of bacon, coffee and beans. As long as you're travelin' with me, I'll treat ya' like an equal until *we* get your ass safely to Ohio."

"Why that's mighty fine of ya', Huck!" Jim praised me, his new-found fellow traveler. "That Miss Watson was sayin' she was goin' to sell me to a merchant the old bitch knows down in New Orleans for eight-hundred-dollars, so that the Widow Douglas's old hag sister could buy a new King Jimmy Holy Bible, and then donate the rest of the money to her greedy, pedophile church minister. What the fuck's wrong with this mixed-up world, Huck?"

"Nothin's wrong with the world, Jim," I philosophically answered. "It's just the fucked-up people that live in it that's the goddamned problem! Say Jim; are ya' sure ya' swam the whole four miles from the village out here to Jackson's Island?"

"Well Huck, if ya' needs to learn the truth, I borrowed the Widow's old skiff, but two-miles out, the sucker began leakin' somethin' mighty terrible. And so, I had to jump-out of the piece of shit, and swim the rest of the way all by myself."

I was especially impressed with Jim's knowledge of signs and superstitions, but I questioned his beliefs in that most of his omens were negative and ominous, but a few were of an optimistic nature. "Well, how does a body know when good luck's right around the corner, and when you're not goin' to die in some epic calamity like an earthquake, a hurricane, a flood, a locust plague, or the sun explodin' and gobblin' up the Earth?"

"Well Huck, a young fella' like you can know that good times are comin' when ya' get hairy arms, a hairy chest, hairy armpits, and hairy balls!" Jim claimed and insisted. "That's the signs pointin' to a young, white asshole like yourself becomin' rich."

"Well Jim, I'm startin' to sprout hair in all those special places ya' just mentioned, and you're right," I answered in amazement. "Tom Sawyer and I found Injun Joe's loot stashed in a cave, and I *am* rich, just like you say. Are all Negroes as smart as you are without ever goin' to grammar school or college?"

"Reckon the whole damned cursed race is, Huck!" the slave sadly replied in disgust. "But in your case, I think that since your body hair's showin' up in good supply, I thinks you gonna' be rich a second time around. Just you wait and see!"

Jim then informed me that his wise advice usually worked on others, and not on himself, since he had invested his life's savings of ten-dollars in a cow and a mule, and both had died soon thereafter; even though his body hair was in great abundance, and even though the slave had obtained a loan for fifteen-dollars at the local bank. But then, that fine financial institution had gone bankrupt after lending Miss Watson's slave the money, so bad-luck Jim had lost on other bad-luck investments, in which the unfortunate slave still owed the defunct creditors. And when Miss Watson found-out about Jim's speculations and about his insurmountable debts, the old bag decided to farm him out to New Orleans at a bargain price.

* * * * * * * * * * * * *

Jackson's Island was only around three miles long and a quarter of a mile wide, so I wanted to explore the entire topography in the event that Jim and I had to construct a fort, or build a decent caged-prison to keep bounty hunters or pirates in that we might capture, and then have to torture in order to get vital information out of those dangerous hostages. We climbed-up a pretty-precarious forty-foot-high ridge, and in no time discovered a utilitarian cave that we determined to be fit for habitation during a severe storm or monsoon. And we also believed that the high-elevation hollow would be an excellent dry spot to keep our necessary provisions inside.

And then the powerful-looking-but-meek Negro fascinated my curiosity by "educatin' me' with some of his common-sense, non-book-learned knowledge.

"Ya' see those upset birds over yonder flappin' their wings and behavin' wild," Jim related and lectured. "That sign shows me that rain is gonna' happen' soon, so we better hurry quick to the canoe and carry your gear and stuff up to this cave, where we'll both be protected from the upcomin' storm. Those excited Canadian blue jays from Toronto and those St. Louis cardinals already-know what the hell's comin' our way, and they're warnin' each other in bird talk to fly around real fast-like, and find shelter. That's their way of talkin' to each other durin' an emergency."

"I'm sure glad I coincidentally ran into you," I complimented my new colleague in adventure. "You know shit that the average feller' never even thinks about."

And so, Jim and I hustled and worked like obsessed maniacs in completing the task at hand, and within an hour, we had conveyed everything except the well-secured canoe to the desolate cave that we had discovered. Soon, we built a roaring fire with matches I had taken from Pap's shanty, and we expertly cooked some delicious fish that Jim had previously caught for dinner. And then the two of us bravely rode-out the incredible thunderstorm that followed, with the downpour featuring flashes of lightning and booms of thunder, making my eyes and ears regret that the son-of-a-bitches that were attached to my head and face were ever functioning properly.

“The wind’s nearly suckin’ me out of here!” I screamed as I reactively retreated to the cave’s posterior. “If this is what a goddamned good blowjob is like, I’m gonna’ leave this sort of crazy shit up to mentally-challenged assholes like Tom Sawyer, Ben Rogers, and Joe Harper!”

“Watch-out that the lightnin’ doesn’t bolt-up your lily-white ass, Huck!” Jim warned and inadvertently punned with a poker face. “It might seal your asshole shut for good, and then you’ll never be able to crap again for the rest of your white-boy life, because you’ll die before ever hittin’ twenty years of age!”

“The thunder sounds like giant empty barrels rumblin’ down stairs,” I observed and commented. “Definitely more like barrels than like casks or hogsheads!”

“I hope none of those fucked-up barrels barrel into my black ass,” Jim remarked. “There’s got to be other ways of havin’ a goddamned barrel of fun than experiencin’ dangerous shit like that!”

The storm finally subsided, but the river kept rising and rising for the next two weeks, until the burgeoning tide began overflowing its banks, and then flooding half of Jackson’s Island. Flood waters were reaching depths of three-to-four feet deep in the low-lying sections, where swamps formerly were prevalent. This phenomenon was occurring more on the Illinois side, but on the Missouri side (where high bluffs and our cave were located), everything seemed normally safe and fairly copasetic. “Hurry Jim! That’s a typhoon a-comin’. Typhoons don’t give a shit whether their victim is a tycoon or a raccoon! It’s all the same bullshit to Mother Nature!” But luckily, the fierce windstorm soon veered-off to the south of Jackson’s Island.

Jim and I were fortunate to find *our* red canoe in fine condition, and my black colleague and I paddled all over the island, where we used to have to walk to get around. The whole lowland scenario was flooded, and there were confused rabbits and squirrels sitting on the branches of broken-down trees, wondering where their next meal was to come from; or perhaps contemplating if they were going to be a hungry hawk’s next dinner, being all exposed to carnivorous predators as they were.

An abandoned raft of eight white pine planks tied together came bobbing our way. And Jim and I easily salvaged the usable mode of river transportation from the merciless Mississippi’s current. He and I decided that, with a few minor alterations and modifications, we could use the fine raft as our primary means of maneuvering around the river heading north up to Ohio, where Jim could be emancipated into democracy by some devout abolitionists, or Quaker do-gooders. At least that was *our* mutual goal at that moment.

But just before dusk, on the west side of the island, a frame house that had been dislodged from its foundation came drifting along, so Jim and I paddled-out in our red canoe to investigate its contents. My new black friend clambered-inside through an exposed window just above the waterline, and I carefully followed his stellar example. We noticed a tilted bed, an upside-down chair, and lots of articles and assorted junk like playing cards, masks, and empty whiskey bottles, scattered all over the planked-floor, which was slanted at an angle like one might be inside a carnival haunted fun house. In the far corner of the shadowy room, there appeared to be an unconscious man, and Jim nervously held his hands to his own mouth, forming a makeshift megaphone, and said in a stammering voice, "Hello, there, Mr.!"

The figure on the floor didn't move an inch, and my first reaction was that I was looking at some human-sized circus or stage dummy. And then Jim inhaled a deep breath, and threw some blankets, sheets, and old rags over the man, before I could inspect any damned part of the deceased. That was the first time I had ever seen a dead body, and I detested the macabre feeling that the hideous experience gave my soul. Jim told me to get back into the canoe, and that my black friend would sort-out some items that we could use in the future, all gathered from our little floating house encounter.

Some of the things that we obtained from the wrecked home were a lantern, a brand-new Barlow knife, tallow candles, needles, pins, a spool of thread, beeswax, some nails, fish lines, hooks, a woman or girl's dress, a usable comb and hairbrush, and some fancy sewing buttons. Finally, we left the slowly-drifting home and paddled-out toward our raft, and ultimately to the safety of remote Jackson's Island.

"Huck, now that that house we stole from is a couple of miles away," Jim said in a melancholy tone of voice, "there's somethin' bad I gotta' tell ya'."

"What is it, Jim?" I asked in an ordinary tone of voice. "Are ya' gonna' tell me that you communicated with the old dead guy's ghost, and that it gave you a voodoo sign of some sorts?"

"No Huck. I gotta' tell ya' that the old dead guy layin' there on the floor was your Pap. I don't think he's gonna' hurt ya' any more Huck, although I don't know exactly how mean your Pap's ghost is gonna' be!"

"Huck as a Girl"

Being curious and feeling chipper and audacious, I wanted to learn about what the news and the gossip in St. Petersburg was concerning me being suspected of being killed, and of Jim running away from Miss Watson's cruel custody. I dressed myself up as a girl wearing the dress that me and Jim had found in the house floating down the river during the flood. And next, I rowed the red canoe to shore to see what information my espionage could gather.

'I can't hang around the pool room or around the saloon, or else somebody snoopin' by will recognize me, either as a boy or as me disguised as a girl,' I thought before knocking on the door of a shabby-looking, recently occupied farmhouse just north of St. Petersburg. 'This is just about the only feasible way I can think of to hear the latest scuttlebutt about me and Jim. I wonder if the folks living in other towns are as nosy and inquisitive about other people's business as the rumor mongerin' nutcases in this one-horse village are? Well now, someone's answerin' the door.'

"Why come in, Young Lady," a surprised-looking matronly-but-enormous woman said to me. "Sit yourself down in that corner chair over yonder, so that we can chat, real respectable like. What might your name be? Sally? Jane? Sally Jane? Sally Mae Jane?"

I stared rather incredulously at the huge lady, who looked like half of an Amazon wrestling team that would travel around the countryside looking to smash and cremate any hillbillies or lumberjacks sitting in their circus sideshow audience. "Er, it's Sarah Williamson," I fibbed as best as I could, in a high-pitched voice. "I'm not from this here neighborhood, or from this here town, either. I live over in Hookerville, seven miles downstream, and I've walked the whole distance, and am pretty darned tired and hungry. That's why I'm briefly payin' ya' this here visit."

"Well now, Sarah. How come ya' left home to trek way up here?" the woman of the house politely asked. "Is there some kind of family problem that forced ya' to seek help? Are ya' runnin' away from home, because some adult's been abusin' ya'? Are your parents confirmed transvestites?"

"Well, my poor pa died just a few days ago, and my invalid ma's down-sick with a high fever, and she's all out of money for groceries and provisions. And I've come visitin' around these parts to seek-out my Uncle Abner Moore, who lives way on the other side of the village," I rambled and exaggerated. "Would ya' happen to know my Uncle Abner? He's a right decent man!"

"No, but my husband and I and our lesbian daughter just moved here a couple of weeks ago, and we only know our horny neighbors in the immediate vicinity," the lady loquaciously replied. "Take-off your bonnet, Young Lady, unless of course you have a mean bee residin' inside it. I suggest that ya' should stay here for the night, and head-out tomorrow when the sun's shinin' again."

"I'll just rest here for a half hour or so, and I prefer keepin' my bonnet on my head to give me good luck on the rest of my trip," I insisted. "And I'm not scared of the dark one bit, although I'm pretty superstitious about some other stuff."

The obese woman then told me that her mean-ass husband would be returning home soon, and that she'd send him along with me to protect my ass from incest-practicing drunken hillbillies that roamed the area, and who often sodomized any naïve wayward kid, either male or female. And after a half hour of discussing her family's history of poverty, toil, sacrifice, and failure, the garrulous, corpulent woman finally got around to disclosing the news that I keenly desired to hear. That's when my ears finally perked-up.

The know-it-all fat woman pretended to be more informed about my biography than I had actually been aware of myself. "These two lucky scamps, Tom Sawyer and Huck Finn, found ten-thousand-dollars (really only six) of treasure in a cave, and that rotten boy Finn won't even give five measly dollars to help-out his destitute father, who's totally down on his luck," the talkative woman haphazardly explained her twisted interpretation of my recent life. "And now that Huck Finn is reported murdered and dead," the homemaker distorted and maintained, "under the inheritance laws, his Pap's gonna' be entitled to the treasure bonanza that the new Judge is closely watchin' for young Finn in a secret bank account."

"Ya' say this punk kid, Huck Finn, is dead?" I asked. "Who killed him? Robbers or pirates?"

"Some gossipers down in the village say it was his Pap that did him in while arguin' inside the family cabin on the river. But then, a slave ran away from his poor elderly owner right here in St. Petersburg, and now the popular talk is that this barbaric slave, Jim's his name I believe, had killed Huck Finn, who had bravely tried to capture the Negro and get the bounty money for his return to his rightful owner, some old maid livin' with her God-fearin' church-goin' sister, the Widow Douglas, I believe."

The chubby farm woman, a veritable gazette of misinformation, further revealed that Jim had run-away at the exact time Huck was reported killed, and that there's "a splendid reward of two-hundred dollars" out for Finn's father, who was suspected of murdering his son, and that an even-bigger reward will soon be posted for the Negro Jim, for also possibly brutally killing my renegade ass.

"Do ya' have any other news about this boy Huck's father?" I inquired. "It all seems interestin' to someone not familiar with the local gossip and customs."

"Well now," the babbling hefty woman continued after handing me several hard stale cookies. "The old man Finn went to the Judge just yesterday, and asked him for some money to go up and down the river, and even over to Illinois to search for his missin' son. The Judge felt sorry for the old fella', and gave him some cash, but the old man went out and got drunk. That's made the town's folk think that either desperate robbers, or the fugitive Negro had killed Huck Finn, and not the boy's drunken old man, who incidentally is still regarded as a remote suspect."

Then, the old portly woman told me that her money-hungry husband was going to get several ambitious friends, and join a posse to go-out and capture the dangerous slave named Jim, for a sizeable yet-to-be-published bounty. "It's widely believed that the Negro is shacked-up somewhere on that deserted Jackson's Island, and my hubby and his determined friends have got their guns loaded, and plan on rowin' out-there at daybreak to locate and arrest the black runaway; that is, after the sheriff sobers-up and gets around to deputizin' the men. Yes, everyone's bettin' that the bounty on the runaway will be three-hundred-dollars cash, which is a hundred bucks more than the price for catchin' that connivin' old man Finn."

I was extremely nervous during the entire conversation, so I took-up a needle and started sewing. But then I realized I had to first thread the needle and find some material to stitch together. The observant, stocky woman peered at my perceptible frustration, and immediately, her suspicion was aroused about my true identity.

"Three-hundred-dollars is a handsome sum to get for so little work," I remarked as the sharp-witted lady carefully scrutinized my difficulty in threading the needle. "Ya' say that your husband's goin' over to Jackson's Island tomorrow mornin'?"

"If he and his pals can get deputized tonight, the gang of men are gonna' leave by boats before midnight," the woman confidentially divulged. "They'll catch that runaway slave while he's sleepin' if they can, so that he doesn't get killed or shot during the vital apprehension. Now then; what did you say your name was?"

"Er, Mary, Mary Williamson," I hesitated and then stuttered. "Hoss Williamson's daughter!" I stammered and fabricated, inventively alluding to a dead corpse recently reburied in the St. Petersburg Cemetery.

"Honey," the frightful-looking woman with the excellent memory persisted. "It seems to me that when ya' first entered this room, ya' told me your name was Sarah."

"Oh, I guess I forgot to tell ya' that my full name is Sarah Mary Williamson, and sometimes I go by Sarah, and other times, I go by Mary," I cleverly lied. "I'm afraid that's where the mix-up is. And that's why you became a little confused! And now that I'm fully rested and refreshed, and don't have to pee or defecate, I think I oughta' be movin' on to Uncle Abner's place that's just a few miles west of here."

Well now, the domineering farmwife (whose spouse must've been into some serious animal husbandry by the looks of the woman) had this terrible rat problem in her house, and every time one of those repulsive vermin popped-up (or if she had a major hallucination and imagined one rearing its rodent head), the fucked-up lady held a heavy lead bar. And then the hideous-looking bitch would take aim and wildly chuck the metal bar at the rat, nearly decapitating the first rodent that stuck its ugly head out of the side corner.

But then the bizarre old lady announced that her right shoulder ached from a rheumatism flare-up, and soon handed me the lead bar to duplicate her weird target practice. "There's one over there!" she exclaimed, pointing to a crevice between the floor and the wall. "Kill the flea-ridden, plague-carryin' son-of-a-bitch before the rat runs to the nearest hole, which is probably my highly valued clit slit!"

I aimed and hurled the lead piece, and the object caromed-off of the targeted rat's head, slaughtering the disgusting vermin right on the spot. The crazy woman commended me on my extraordinary marksmanship ability, and then the insane two-ton female dampened my spirits by issuing some amazingly accurate comments.

"Pretty versatile delivery!" the fat housewife praised my tossing talent. "Ya' oughta' live down there in Boca Raton, Florida because you conked that ugly rodent right on the jaw, yes ya' did! But you're a little poor-ass liar on two counts," the mammoth farmwife directly accused me.

"Why's that?" I nervously asked.

"First of all, a girl or a woman doesn't sew and thread a needle like you had so poorly demonstrated. And now secondly," the intimidating old bitch elaborated. "Ya' don't throw anything like a young girl does, but instead, ya' skillfully tossed that lead bar with some real male hormone intensity. And when I saw ya' wearin' that fucked-up dress and bonnet," the demented, vulgar woman added, "I knew right along that ya' must be one of them new fangled cross-dressers I read about in the papers. So, that's just fine with me, because I like to cross-dress too, and so does my lesbian daughter in the back-room, and so does my bisexual husband," the deranged female continued her peculiar dissertation.

"Well, what the hell do you have in mind?" I nervously inquired.

"Perhaps we could get a foursome goin', but first ya' gotta' strip-down so that I can inspect your private parts to determine whether you're a male or female. And then, we can decide whether you're a straight male; or a homo' faggot, or a male that thinks he's a female; or a female who thinks she's a male, or any combination of those fucked-up factors I just mentioned," the off-the-wall female cretin equivocated. "But it's all the same to me and my horny family. Straight sex, or perverted sex, or perhaps both quality experiences; it just doesn't matter to us about the goddamned silly details. Who really gives a half-a-shit on Jupiter or Venus, as long as the pleasure objective has been accomplished in a rapturous sort of dramatic climax? Wouldn't you agree?"

"What kind of demented bullshit are ya' tryin' to say, Lady?" I yelled in my regular male staccato voice. "I feel pretty threatened right now, and I absolutely detest the idea of perverted sex!"

"Come on, now; what's your goddamned name? Is it Bill, or Bob or Barnabas? Tell me, or else I'll rape your skinny ass right here and now, and see what the fuck gender ya' really are, usin' my own two eyes!" the lady sadist predicted. "Regardless of the gender of your genitals, I'm gonna' get my rocks off either way!"

"Look, Lady. I'm gonna' become a preacher, and maybe even become Pope someday, so I hate strange sex, and all sorts of pedophiles, and the like, and I think it's plenty sinful just contemplatin' it," I ineffectively argued and lied. "Ya' just gotta' trust me on that count, because I ain't shittin' ya' one iota!"

"Okay then; level with me! What's your fuckin' real story, and don't try and bullshit me, or else I'll cauterize your asshole shut with my husband's cattle and horse brandin' iron, and you'll never be able to shit again for the rest of your life!" the daft woman shouted. "Tell me the truth, or else you'll be molested so bad that ya' might not live through the whole ordeal to ever have a fine sample of tomorrow mornin's wild family sexathon."

I told the old sexually perverted, gargantuan hag that my mother and father were both dead, and that a country justice-of-the-peace had leased my ass out to a mean old farmer who had physically and sexually abused me. So, I ran-away from his misguided jurisdiction, and traveled thirty miles to the present farmhouse's front door. "But the part about my Uncle Abner is true, and my real name is Ben Rogers, and I only have a half inch dick when it's fully erect, so I'm by far no damned pleasure machine; regardless of what sex or combination of genders ya' believe yourself to be!"

"And did anyone give you directions to this country house of bisexual prostitution?" the massive, crazy woman asked. "This place has gotta' remain top secret, until we get some high payin' customers as clients like judges, and bankers, and politicians, and successful preachers and parsons!"

"No Madame," I cutely answered the dyke brothel owner. "I just stopped and interrupted an old man changin' a wagon wheel several miles back, and the geezer told me that if I took the right fork in the road, that I would wind-up in Goshen. But honestly, Madame. I never saw a fork in the road, nor a damned silver spoon, or a freakin' golden knife for that matter, anywhere."

"Goshen! Did you say Goshen?" the aspiring bordello proprietor bellowed. "The Goshen's hundreds of miles away from here! Ha, ha, ha! We' ain't even nowhere close to the goddamned Gulf of Mexico that's way below New Orleans; let alone close to the mother-fuckin' Goshen! Ha, ha, ha."

But then the raunchy wildebeest bitch blocked my access to the front door, and her grotesque-looking, three-hundred-pound lesbian daughter appeared out of the back bedroom and easily blockaded the hallway. So, I figured I should either stall for time by cooperating with my captors, or get sexually molested, and perhaps have my dingle and testicles ripped-off during some violent, sadistic, sexual ritual like the priests, nuns, and mother superiors often do in monasteries, rectories, and convents.

"Now if you're really a genuine country boy, I'm gonna' ask ya' a few important questions, and if you're fortunate enough to get the answers right," the fucked-up, huge lady articulated, and then paused before popping a tobacco chaw into her mouth. "My daughter and me will let ya' go free for bein' too damned straight for our needs. Now then Asshole, when a cow's lyin' down, which end of her gets up first after she's rested?"

"Obviously the hind or ass end Madame."

"Well, you smart-ass Junior Jerk-off. What about when a horse is lyin' down in the pasture? What end rises first when it gets its hoofs back up on the ground?"

"The forward part, if it's not horsin' around out there," I smartly responded like the true wise-ass I am and always was.

"And which end of the tree does the moss and algae grow on? Tell me or else I'll make ya' lick Dorothea Sue's and my cunts, and then my daughter Dorothea Sue's smelly cunt again, usin' your entire parched tongue!"

"The moss always grows upon the north side of the tree, when it's not growin' East Side, West Side, all around the damned town!" I stupidly quipped.

"Now there's only one more pertinent question for you to successfully pass the oral quiz," the formidable Madame continued her farm background litany. "If fifteen lesbian cows are browsin' on a hillside, how many of them eats with their heads pointed' in the same direction?"

"The whole fifteen, regardless whether they're lesbian or straight heterosexual livestock!" I accurately answered, passing the really easy oral farm test with flying colors.

"Well now, I reckon you're indeed a boner-fide country boy that isn't tryin' to hocus me," the mentally-disheveled Madame said in a disappointed tone of voice that was reinforced by Dorothea Sue's glum and frustrated facial expression. "Now, what the fuck's your real name, and I'll let ya' scamper the hell outa' here?"

"George Peters, when it ain't Ben Rogers or Joe Harper!" I stated. "And sometimes its Gunther Schultz, too!"

"Well now, little George Peters. If I were you, I'd go enroll in cross-dressin' charm school, and learn how to present myself correctly as a legitimate-looking, young female," the contemporary lady-behemoth declared.

"And furthermore, my name's Madame Grace Lofton, and my sex-starved nymphomaniac, lovechild, lesbian daughter, Dorothea Sue and me, would like to wish ya' good luck on your journey. And we hereby bid you adieu and safe passage on to Goshen, or to wherever the fuck you're headin'."

"Thank ya' Madame Grace!" I facetiously replied. "If I ever get around to it, I'll send my rich friends Tom Sawyer and Huck Finn over to your fine whorehouse here, for some extraordinary afternoon or evening delight!"

“Ya’ just do that George, and if ya’ do, Dorothea Sue here will give ya’ as a bonus, our handyman’s special the next time ya’ stop by: and that’s defined as a decent hand job; a genuine blowjob, and a normal straight-sex screw job! Isn’t that just Jim Dandy?”

I gratefully existed the oddball premises, and was thrilled to have my pecker and testicles intact. And I quickly doubled my trail tracks, and slipped-back to where my red canoe had been shrewdly concealed and hidden in the reedy swampland. I swiftly removed my blue and white bonnet from atop my head, and next stripped-off my dress, thinking that I was glad I didn’t have any girl’s tits and pussy, and then have to wear such a goddamned cumbersome costume each and every day to hide and protect them from public scrutiny and from boys’ throbbing erections.

I prudently rowed-out into the Mississippi, and when I arrived near the river’s middle, I heard the village clock dully bonging eleven consecutive times. My narrow red boat glided into the desolate cove, where my original Jackson’s Island camp had been situated. After securing the trusty canoe to the dependable “Old Faithful Willow”, I anxiously scuttled toward the familiar ridge, and climbed the promontory in a rush. Jim was sound asleep, and I roused him up, scaring the bats and the demons right out of his already-delirious subconscious.

“Get your black ass up, Jim! The bounty hunters are on our trail! They’re after us, and won’t surrender their pride until we’re both either in jail, or dead! And I can think of plenty of better ways of hangin’ around other than swingin’ by a goddamned thick rope from a tall oak tree!”

Jim never asked any relevant questions or uttered one tiny word, cuss or otherwise. I could tell that the runaway slave was really scared, the serious way the fugitive-from-distorted-justice packed our gear, and mentally concentrated while carefully doing it. We lugged all of our equipment and utensils down to the raft; tied the canoe to the side parallel timbers, and then cautiously and slowly shoved-off into the river’s darkness; our minds and souls fearful of (and refraining from) lighting either our lantern, or even one of our tallow candles.

“The Duke and the Dauphin”

Jim and I used some available sticks, nails, and cloth to make a small tent on the raft, where I could easily hide the runaway slave whenever serious-minded bounty hunters would come near. But we had one very close call on the west side of the river, when two grubby-looking men toting raised shotguns approached us in a skiff. The curious varmints wanted to search the tent for a stowaway slave, but I told them my Pap was inside suffering from advanced smallpox, and then the pair of demanding dense-dunces rowed their small boat away as if the assholes had just seen the Grim Reaper’s bony skeletal face staring at them.

One day on the river, I ventured-away from the raft and paddled the red canoe into a wide creek to find some wild sweet huckleberries to pick for breakfast. ‘Huckleberries are better tasting than dingleberries any damned day of the week,’ I remember thinking. I was nonchalantly paddling up the creek, surveying with my eyes the jagged cypress woods on either side, when I heard separate voices yelling, and then saw two idiotic boneheads running on a cow path towards my ‘borrowed canoe’.

The pair of suspicious-looking nutcases was shouting and begging for me to take them aboard, because their very lives were in some sort of fucked-up jeopardy. The marathon dashers both panted-out their separate pleas as the duo scampered along the creek’s bank, hollering that they were being unjustly chased for committing no egregious violations, and that a desperate crowd of dedicated vigilantes was in hot pursuit of their vulnerable asses.

“I don’t hear any vicious bloodhounds howlin’ or horses gallopin’ coming after your ugly flabby rear ends!” I yelled-back at the two scruffy-looking out-of-breath shit-heads. “If you’re both dead serious about bein’ rescued by me, each of you nincompoops dash through that cluster of bramble bushes over there ya’ see, in front of ya’, and then wade into that shallow part of the creek up ahead. I’ll evaluate the situation and maybe let ya’ both into my canoe.”

Sure enough, the two fucked-up itinerants splashed their butts inside the rocking canoe, and then we heard dogs, horses and a bloodthirsty mob shouting and heading our way. Soon, we were a full-mile distant from the boisterous clamor and chaos, and were moving in the direction of the floating raft, without any wild, sweet huckleberries (or late wild sweet strawberries) in *my* possession.

One of the newcomers was around seventy-years-old and had a baldhead, at least four missing teeth, and the fool sported thick gray whiskers. The hideous-looking jasper wore an old battered-up slouch hat; an obsolete-looking, greasy, blue flannel shirt, along with ragged blue jeans that had evidently experienced better days. The grimy old-timer was also wearing ancient boots, and a long-tailed blue denim coat with slick-looking brass buttons dating back to bygone colonial times. His younger, fatter companion, around thirty-years-of-age, was dressed just as raggedly, and both traveling, in-a-hurry assholes were carrying cheap inferior carpetbags that were not too rugged.

I introduced the two nameless strangers to Jim, fibbing and telling the vagabonds that the affable Negro was my Pap's loyal slave, and that I was returning him to a second small plantation the family owned on the Missouri side of the river. As the four of us sat around in a circle upon the crowded raft and struck-up an informal conversation over some coffee and beans, which we consumed for breakfast, I soon discovered that the two imbeciles *we* had just taken aboard didn't know one another, and figured that both fleeing shit-heads were being chased out of two separate twin towns when the stooges accidentally had converged onto the same dirt intersection.

"What got you into conflict with some volatile local yokels?" the seventy-year-old itinerant mentioned to the thirty-year-old transient. "Were ya' perpetuatin' some kind of hoax or fraud on the idiotic village hypocrites?"

"Not exactly," the second pretentious mendicant answered before swallowing-down a mouthful of baked beans. "I was casually and successfully sellin' a special formula to take the tartar off of teeth, and the secret ingredients worked real-satisfactory, too. But one batch I was retailin' also accidentally took the enamel off the customers' fangs! I stayed hucksterin' my excellent product an hour longer than I ought to have been doin', and just as I was evacuatin' the village," the questionable testifier continued his tale of woe, "I encountered you Old Man on the dirt path crossroads, and you pathetically begged me to sprint along with ya' until we mutually found safety and shelter together. That's my whole mediocre yarn wrapped-up in a nutshell."

"It's a good thing the formula you were sellin' didn't make the tartar any tarter, or else everybody in that dumb-ass village you ran out of would've been in need of new sets of teeth," I laughed and clapped my hands. "What's your melodramatic story Old Fella'?" I asked the other more-elderly guest sitting like a miserable Indian chief to my right.

"Well, Young Fella', I'd been runnin' a legitimate temperance revival for about a week, and was makin' plenty of converts to my just cause, and my glorious presence was me being the pet of the petty-petite-pretty-petticoat woman folk who tended to dote on me; and the hussies were offerin' me all kinds of sex, especially when their husbands and boyfriends were out huntin' for rabbits and alligators," the old fart exaggerated. "And what I'm tellin' ya' is no contrived lie, either. I was takin' in, on the average, ten-dollars a night at ten-cents a head, but then word got around among the population that each night before sayin' my bedtime prayers, I was drinkin' a pint of Kentucky bourbon from a bottle tucked under my pillow."

"You sound like an absolute drunk to me!" I insisted. "What the hell happened next after the community gossip?"

"Well, just this mornin'," the "Old Gent" proceeded with his inane narrative, "I was roused by a nice accommodatin' slave, who told me that a committee of churchgoers was formin' a fanatical lynch gang. The angry mob first wanted to tar and feather me, and then attach my delicate ass to a rail with designs of tossin' my chaste body into the river, until I would nearly-drown, and then after puttin' me through *that* horrible ordeal, hang me, rail, tar, feathers, and all from the giant magnolia tree in the town square. So, naturally, I hightailed it out of there and met my young-anonymous friend here, who was also in an obvious rush to escape from his own private dilemma."

"Old Man," said his younger, and just-as-unscrupulous companion. "What do ya' say about us two geniuses joinin' forces, and combinin' our unique talents and becomin' fifty-fifty partners in some joint business ventures? We'd make a terrific double-team capable of flim-flamin' most of the average, uneducated, gullible morons along this river."

"I ain't opposed one iota to that sage suggestion you've just proposed," the old whiskerando answered without negotiating any particulars of their mutual arrangement. "What's your strong suits when it comes to connin' and scammin' the naive public?"

"I started-out as a printer by trade, and am a renowned expert at it when I focus all my attention and energy on what has to be accomplished," the younger petty crook claimed and bragged. "I also do a little general patent medicine business on the side. But actually, I specialize in elaborate Shakespearean theatrical productions, mostly on the tragedy play side," the slippery as a wet snake swindler informed us. "I've also, with noteworthy facility I might add, taught singin' and international geography in St. Louis academies and universities, and I know plenty about the advanced science of phrenology. I'll examine the bumps on your head for a mere modest one-dollar fee, but since you're now my lucky partner," the young turkey spoke to the old buzzard, "I'll duly sacrifice and perform *that* vital duty for you for a measly fifty-cent courtesy service fee. Can ya' match those essential business world skills I've just enumerated, Old Man?"

"Why yes!" the envious, greedy, old fart sneered and uttered. "I've had considerable education and practice in the doctorin' field, and have extensively lectured on the subject as far away as London, England and Edinburgh, Scotland. And besides that, I've cured many severe cases of cancer, heart disease, paralysis, neuritis, neuralgia, polio, vaginal warts, dysentery, small pox, large pox, yellow fever, scarlet fever, rheumatism and syphilis. I'm also an international authority on fortunetellin' and conductin' worthwhile séances, and if I may humbly add, in truth, I'm a mighty good tent revival preacher and faith healer, too."

I could tell from the outset that both of my new mentally-deranged raft passengers were irresponsible bull-shitters and untrustworthy con-artists, even though each claimed to be otherwise. But I was particularly fearful of the younger bum, who had been insisting that he was good at printing, because the last thing in the world I ever wanted to happen was to have reward bounty posters of either Jim or me (or both of us) plastered in every damned hick community along the river. Nobody sitting like Indians on the floating raft said anything for a while, with Jim and me trying to comprehend the magnitude of the extreme verbal horse manure that our alert ears had just heard.

* * * * * * * * * * * * *

I sensed that a monumental power-struggle of major proportions was about to erupt between the two presently nameless-but-egotistical new arrivals seated upon the small timber raft. The younger wandering vagrant started the odd dialogue exchanges by saying, "Alas, my mentally deficient colleagues in travel!" the wily jerk-off sobbed as the thin, garrulous jerk wiped the corner of his left eye with a dirty rag, seeking Jim's and my sympathy, and the old man's admiration. "To think that I must be so deplorably degraded and humiliated to have to travel amidst such lackluster company."

“Ain’t our company good enough for ya’?” the older gent challenged his arrogant new-found business partner.

“I didn’t know we had a company,” Jim injected into the already queer conversation. “What we maufacturin’ anyway? How about little black slave baby dolls, or maybe we’ll start growin’ watermelons and green okra?”

The younger, degenerate, self-aggrandizing cretin ignored Jim’s ludicrous inquiry and resumed his chronic bitching and complaining. “I don’t blame any of you three amateurs for wanting my unenviable predicament,” the asshole half-apologized. “But at one time, I was high and mighty royalty possessin’ wealth, property, title, and the loyalty of many devoted subjects and predicates.”

“What’s with the cornball broken heart shit?” the young bum’s older derelict partner yelled. “None of us seated around the breakfast table here is an artery, vein, aorta. or capillary in need of a goddamned heart surgeon!”

“I’ve never before shared with anyone the true secret of my majestic and noble birth, along with its accompanyin’ admirable and royal birthright,” the young prevaricator attested. “But by the rights and privileges of regal hierarchy, I *am* a duke; more specifically, my great-grandfather was the eldest son of the famous Duke of Bridgewater, but unfortunately had to flee Britain, at the end of the late 1700s, and soon ventured to this remote, primitive country commonly referred to as America, in order for him to escape political insurrections against his Divine Rights’ authority.”

‘Is that why you’re livin’ here in this country when you should be residin’ in England,” I innocently-but-skeptically asked.

“Yes. My royal ancestor, had to leave his only remaining heir, my dyin’ father, at the same time of his hasty departure from Europe.” Then, disingenuous Bridgewater studied our astonished faces for a pregnant moment, and decided to deluge us with more of his irrelevant bullshit. “And furthermore, kind sirs, I *am* the linear biological descendant of my father’s necessitated abdication, and therefore, I *am* the rightful new-but-impoverished Duke of Bridgewater. Alas my eminent, Gentlemen,” the down-on-his-luck idiot Duke summarized, “I’ve been reduced to the company of scurrilous felons adrift on a doomed-to-sink raft!”

Jim, who was adequately trained by Miss Watson to respect, obey, and cater to superior white folk, was perfectly willing to be the Duke of Bridgewater’s subordinate servant, whenever the slave would be a voluntary chattel in *his* illustrious, phony, counterfeit presence. Bridgewater told Jim and me that we should boost *his* faltering ego by calling him "Your Grace," "My Lord", and "Your Lordship" whenever *we* could accommodate his endless need for attention and general approval.

"And with *my* flexible discretion, any of you three clowns could occasionally call me just Bridgewater, because that's sort of a title of respectability anyway. And it's not, in itself, necessarily a common name," the lying Duke condescendingly stated and advocated to his relatively-astonished audience of three.

But all the while, the Old Vagrant onboard the raft remained plenty silent, because of the Young Duke's extravagant claim of being descended from aristocratic nobility. And my keen perception sure as hell detected jealousy on *his* facial features, but the scheming, grimy varmint at that moment said little about it.

But in terms of my own interpretation of matters upon the raft, I was disgusted that I had been relegated from being the captain of the floating vessel to now being a meager crew member servant, along with Jim, and quite confidentially, I deeply resented the arrogant Duke's insulting manifesto/edict that Jim and I had to be *his* personal valets. But then the Elderly Fart felt obligated to speak his peace.

"Look here, Bilgewater," the Old Shit defiantly uttered before involuntarily loudly farting a large quantity of stench-laden intestinal gas. "I'm very sorry to hear about your regrettable demotion into destitution, but you aren't the only victim that's had trouble just like you've been describin'. Now, listen-up Bilgewater, and you other two imbeciles, too. I'm the legitimate and entitled Dauphin of France."

"You is a dolphin!" Jim exclaimed. "You does look a little like a tropical fish! If you's really a dolphin, I might just want to chop you up and cook your better parts in a hot fryin' pan."

The self-indulgent Prince/King overlooked Jim's nonsensical interpretation, and proceeded with delivering his rather-fascinating monologue. "Yes, my Friends. It's as true as Gospel; yes, it is. I'm the poor Dauphin that disappeared from France many years ago, Louie the Seventeenth, and I'm the accursed son of Louie the Sixteenth, and the beautiful-but-beheaded Marie Antoinette."

"Then, how's come you're here on the Mississippi near St. Louis when ya' oughta' be livin' over there in Kentucky in Looyville?" Jim stupidly commented. "That's what the heck facts I wanna' know!"

"Look, my benevolent Servant," the Dauphin answered Jim. "I'm the last of the Charlemagne dynasty, and ironically, we all seem to die nasty in our dynasty. That's really the reason why I got the hell out of France, and quickly zipped over here to this prehistoric, primitive, barbarian country of uneducated dumb-fucks!" the

Dauphin criticized and belittled. "And all of *that* accumulated trouble, aggravation, and mortification has brought these gray hairs to my balding-head; and these gray whiskers to my handsome countenance. But once I'm again domestically and internationally recognized as the true King of France," the Dauphin bellowed in a stronger tone of voice, "I'll gladly entertain any and all of you three dimwits at the family's magnificent palace at Versailles. You Paris-sites will all just love seein' the incomparable Corridor of Mirrors. It's simply spectacular!"

Well, the ego-tripping Dauphin unexpectedly began falsely crying, and Jim agreed to call *that* fake son-of-a-bitch "Your Grace", "My Lord", "Your Lordship", and "Your Majesty", too. And my cunning perception could detect right-off that the phony Duke was envious of the next King of France, because high and mighty Bridgewater had been instantaneously outranked on the royalty ascendancy hierarchy scale by his deceptive partner/rival. My personal attitude was that both the King and the Duke should be crowned with powerful right crosses to their un-royal heads.

But then, the fickle-minded Dauphin observed that the equally-corrupt Duke was angry, and so the Royal French One addressed Bridgewater in a demeaning, sarcastic and ridiculing tone of voice. "Did you recently bathe your grotesque-lookin' face in vinegar? Stop with the sour puss, Bilgewater! It's not my fault I was born a prince, and that you were only hatched into this abominable world as a potential duke. Why worry about dumb-ass trivialities like that? Just make the best of the situation, that's my favorite motto!" the fake Dauphin loquaciously chided the indignant Duke. "It's not such a bad scene here goin' down the river with these two incompetent buffoons. Give me your hand in friendship Bilgewater, so that we can be friends in addition to bein' viable allies and business partners."

"Do Jim and me have to genuflect every time we come into the presence of you two sophisticated aristocrats?" I cynically asked the Duke and the Dauphin.

"Only if *I'm* sittin' on my royal throne inside the tent, all alone on the raft upon your entrance!" the egocentric, first-in-command King imperatively replied.

It didn't take me too long to determine that my two new raft passengers were liars, frauds, connivers and petty thieves, and were certainly not any important or eminent Duke or Dauphin. But I wanted to keep Jim's identity as a runaway slave a secret, and I didn't desire to have any annoying quarrels occurring on my little square, wooden Mississippi River vessel. If nothing else, I had learned one crucial human relationship lesson from Pap, and *that* essential principle happens to be: The best way to get along with people of the Duke and the Dauphin's disgusting ilk is to let them each have his own selfish way, and then just hope that the braggarts don't kill one another in *our* strange voyage along the adventurous Mississippi River.

* * * * * * * * * * * * * *

The Duke and the Dauphin were both addicted schemers, and soul brothers in illicit activity. In one small town, the devious swindlers staged a fake production of *Romeo and Juliet,* and I was forced to play the leading lady's role dressed in an evening gown. The net profit from the scam was over two-hundred-dollars, and then the three of us had to flee out of the hick town before serious injuries had been inflicted upon our highly sought-after bodies.

In another lazy village along the river, the Duke and the King overheard some prominent citizens speaking about the death of another distinguished local resident named Peter Wilkes, who had left considerable property and cash in his estate to his three grieving daughters, Mary Jane, Susan, and Joanna.

The ruthless Duke and King showed-up at the manor house with a phony-unauthorized will and claimed to be Peter Wilkes' two long-lost British brothers. And naturally, the three disconsolate girls had never before heard of any "two foreign uncles". The dastardly pair of distrustful connivers had convinced the three sisters that the two rip-off-artists should avoid an expensive litigation, and turn over several-thousand-dollars to the "mourning uncles", along with the estate's slaves, and also certain sundry valuables to be auctioned-off to the highest bidders. And "the profits" were to be eventually distributed amongst the five beneficiaries.

But me and Jim were disenchanted with all the fallacious and callous ongoing proceedings, and so, I turned the two royal impersonating assholes over to the local sheriff's office, but before the Duke and the Dauphin could be satisfactorily arrested and incarcerated because of dumb-ass bureaucratic paperwork, the slippery jaspers fled to the raft, and Jim and I had to actually contend with those two repugnant assholes some more.

To get even for me squealing on them about the shrewd extortion of the three victimized Wilkes' girls, the vindictive Duke turned me in at the next river town on charges that I had falsely killed myself to protect Jim, a wanted runaway slave. As a result of the fake Duke's accusations, Jim was being held as a "dangerous fugitive from justice" in a small concrete prison having a dirt floor on the nearby Phelps' farm. And when I eventually arrived there (after evading the local constable's clutches), to figure-out a way to free him and get my black friend safely to Ohio, Mrs. Sally Phelps exited the house in an emotional frenzy and began hugging, kissing and slobbering her mucus all over my face and neck. The maudlin farmwife had mistaken me for her seldom seen nephew, my buddy Tom Sawyer, who coincidentally had been scheduled to make a rare visit to the country farm that same day.

Well, I told "Aunt Sally" about what was happening back in St. Petersburg with Aunt Polly, and with the Widow Douglas, and with Sid, and with Cousin Mary, and I was having a right decent time impersonating my good friend "Thomas". But when the real in-the-flesh Tom Sawyer showed-up on the Phelps' property, I told "Aunt Sally" that I was Tom's dumb-ass tattling brother Sid, and remarkably, the gullible woman believed my somewhat-imaginative and contrived story, and warmly congratulated me for my originality in skillfully fooling her.

"Listen, Tom. We's gotta' set Jim free, because he's been captured and bein' held, so that *that* old maid bitch Miss Watson can reclaim him, and sell Jim's ass off to that greedy shippin' merchant down the river in New Orleans," I related to my good friend all in one remarkable breath.

"Well now, Huck, I'll organize a simple plan to spring Jim loose from that makeshift hoosegow," Tom mentioned. "Just follow my instructions and everything will come out in the wash."

If anyone knows anything at all about Tom Sawyer, the genius kid absolutely despises when something is too easy to perform. Everything's always got to be complicated and intricate (from his perspective). All Tom and I had to do was remove the keys from the Phelps' kitchen board ledge, unlock the padlocks, and let Jim hightail it at full speed to the river.

But instead, Tom and I spent three whole weeks laboriously digging a long deep tunnel under the "jail shack", and when Jim finally crawled his way out to freedom, some hostile neighboring farmers showed-up and began firing their shotguns at all three of us fleeing fuck-heads, who were collectively darting our scared asses through the nearby woods, seeking safety and protection. Tom was pretty damned proud of his successful complex plan, and of Jim's escape, but his biggest trophy was the minor leg wound that Thomas Sawyer had received while being shot at.

"Jim got three-miles down the river, but then Miss Watson's slave was re-captured," I grimly reported to Tom. "That poor guy has got more nasty bad luck than Julius Caesar, or Nathan Hale ever had."

"Well, Huck," Tom giggled while recuperating in one of Aunt Sally's comfortable beds. "There's something significant I got to tell ya'. Two days ago, Miss Watson had died while visiting my Aunt Polly's house in St. Petersburg, and the old bag had it written in her will that Jim would be freed upon her death."

"So, we really didn't have to go through all of the crazy bullshit about diggin' the tunnel for three whole weeks, and then you getting shot in the leg during Jim's excitin' escape!" I exclaimed. "All of this was done for the sake of adventure, right Tom?"

"Exactly Huck," my good friend replied with a broad grin. "Who the hell wants to live to be a hundred and one like grouchy Miss Watson, and then die after leadin' a totally long, borin' life? I'd rather take my chances any friggin' day of the week on getting shot at, and then survivin' the dangerous incident."

"Well, since Jim's a free man now," I seriously reflected for a brief moment and declared, "I'm gonna' tell Judge Thatcher to give him forty-dollars of *my* money from Injun Joe's treasure, so that the good-hearted fella' can start a new life as a free man."

"Good fuckin' idea!" Tom earnestly complimented me. "And Huck; ya' make sure ya' use some of your treasure loot to learn how to read and write. Someday ya' just might want to write all of this incredible bullshit down in some sort of dumb-shit fictional autobiographical novel!"

"Okay Tom, my good buddy," I sincerely promised and agreed. "But first, ya' gotta' get better in a jiffy, so that we two ornery jaspers can go out onto the Mississippi and have some more fucked-up, two-fisted, action-packed adventures together!"

"Among the Spirits"

One of those gimmicky, mentalist-type, séance readers came to town three nights ago, and I accompanied a reporter for the evening newspaper to attend the stellar event. My friend, Bob, told me that he had seen a gambler by the name of Gus Graham shot-down by a mob of vigilantes in a southern Illinois town around ten-years before, and that Gus Graham was probably the only person in San Francisco that knew about the circumstances, and that Bob wanted to confront and challenge the séance' medium with the specific murder situation, facts and details. Now I have to confess that this novice journalist is a staunch Democrat, and thinks and writes like a liberal member of that inelegant tribe of mixed-up, brain-dead politicians.

Bob carefully wrote his old acquaintance Gus Graham's name on a plain sheet of paper, folded it up neatly, and then placed it in a hat that was being passed around the dimly-lit, smoke-laden lecture hall. All told, the name "Gus Graham" was among five hundred or so appellations that had been submitted for a rare communication session between the gifted medium and the dead persons being contacted in the mysterious afterworld dimension. The pile was dumped into a heap upon a stage table, and then the veteran woman medium asked, "Is the spirit of Joe Diablo present? How about Fred Jensen? What about Gus Graham?"

My friend Bob yelled-out that he wanted the medium to specifically communicate with the deceased Gus Graham, so she attempted to accommodate his grand desire.

"Did you die in 1851, '52, '53 or '54?" the attractive, savvy gypsy lady sitting behind a crystal ball asked into the silent crowded room.

"Rap, rap, rap," came the answer from the other world.

"Did you die of Colitis? Diarrhea? Dysentery? Small pox?"

"Rap, rap, rap," was the supernatural generic response.

"Did you die in Mississippi? Kentucky? Sandwich Islands? Tierra del Fuego? Illinois? Texas?"

"Rap, rap, rap!"

"In Adams County, Madison County or Randolph County?"

"Rap, rap, rap."

"It seems that your deceased person Gus Graham isn't being cooperative," the medium yelled-out into the general audience, and particularly to my friend, Bob, the neophyte journalist. Her peculiar announcement was followed by some heckling and jeering, but then a couple of sincere German gents stood-up to give the medium particular information about a dead person; the two questioners being a foreign father and son team with the last name Ollendorff.

Old Ollendorff spoke in German that only his son (also in the audience) understood. “Ist ein geist hieraus?”

The obviously serious question was followed by three Other World raps, and a resultant burst of laughter generated from the audience, who wasn’t expecting a comedy routine type of show.

“Franz Shumann. Vollen sie schrieben?” Old Ollendorff politely asked.

Three off-stage raps were the standard orthodox reply, which of course affected another wave of chuckles and jeers.

“Finzig stolen,” the traveler from the suburbs of Berlin said and added. “Linsowfterowlickterhairowfterfrowleineruhackfolderol?” the elderly German clarified his original sincere request.

“Yes,” the solicited deceased soul cheerfully and incredibly answered through the very serious-faced, stoic-minded medium in direct telepathic contact with deceased Franz Shumann’s spirit.

The mostly male audience grew more boisterous and animated with every additional German question that the discourteous Americans didn’t understand, and obviously didn’t give a shit about understanding. In support of his aged and senile father, the younger Ollendorff tried to determine the date of the deceased person’s death. “Was it 1811 or 1812?” the son asked in English, as the assemblage of raucous Americans simmered-down a bit now, since they finally comprehended something discernible and relevant.

“Everyone here listening in this theater; I had written-down the name of somebody that’s still alive and very healthy,” Young Ollendorff testified for all to hear. “Franz Shumann is a dear friend of mine, presently living in Vienna, Austria and he…”

“Sit down! Sit the hell down!” the medium screamed at the on-a-mission young German and his Deutschland father.

“But Lady, I just want to clarify that….”

“I said sit the hell down and shut your insolent and disrespectful trap! You aren’t here to make fancy speeches!”

Of course, the audience became rambunctious, and most attendees roared their approval of the contentious verbal exchange. “But please, Lady Medium. The spirit cheats because Franz Shumann is alive and healthy!” Young Ollendorff maintained amidst a howling blast of verbal hysteria.

“Take your seat, Sir, and I shall explain the entire matter once everyone, including all of you disbelievers, calms down!” the gypsy woman ineffectively chastised. "Now, Sir; you and your father asked your ridiculous questions with the ideas of fraud and deception governing your hearts. You're both making sport of a very serious event that is now in progress. Both Hell and Purgatory are full of doubters such as yourself and your father, so naturally, that's where you're going to wind-up because you basically lack faith and hope in the hereafter. You're both too sarcastic and cynical to ever be admitted into Heaven's grace!"

At that moment, nobody booed or jeered, because everyone in the place, sinners and Democrats included, all had aspirations of residing in Paradise for all eternity, and we all found the concept of either Hell or Purgatory to be repugnant to our indigenous value systems. But then, some of the more audacious, non-God-fearing imbeciles in attendance yelled-out a spectrum of conflicting instructions to the flustered Young Ollendorff, "Va-moose, Asshole!" "Sit your ass down!" "Say your peace, Jerk-off!" "Stick to your stupid-assed guns!" "Stay right where you are until you're satisfied with the fucked-up answers!"

"If that man remains standing for the purpose of harassing me and my craft, then I'm leaving!" the lady medium insisted in the form of an ultimatum. "Not one of you sitting and standing out there has the right or privilege to come into this hall and insult me and my science. Contact with the dead is closely associated with my gypsy religious creed and beliefs," the swarthy-skinned woman maintained and chastised. "And I'll not tolerate any further abuse of my cherished religious principles! And furthermore, I'll not entertain any more questions in German or any other language that I'm not familiar with!" the irate fortuneteller articulated her stern admonishment loud and clear.

Just then, a well-dressed, debonair-looking gentleman signaled for me to approach the edge of the stage platform and asked, "Sir, are you a Spiritualist?"

"Absolutely not!" I honestly replied. "And if your next question is askin' me if I'm biased or prejudiced in any way, shape or form against any Spiritualist, or medium, or ghost, the explicit response is still 'absolutely no'!"

"Then, why are you sitting with all of those pessimistic and antagonistic men?" the show's obvious shill challenged me. "They're a terribly bad influence to a man's faith, integrity, and character!"

"I'd repent if I wasn't a tolerant preacher man seeking the Gospel truth!" I answered and fibbed, much to the elation of my clamorous companions seated in my immediate vicinity. But then I amassed the courage to request the grim-faced medium a question, and the gypsy woman reluctantly acknowledged my raised hand.

"Is the spirit of John Smith present?" I asked amidst abundant applause and levity. "I'm sorry, but one can never depend on the reliability of any dead Smith showing-up to communicate like that Adam Smith guy, who described the characteristics of modern economics. I mean to say, you might erroneously get into contact with the historic personage Captain John Smith, who was married to Pocahontas, or maybe another irrelevant John Smith, who might've been a colonial blacksmith; a goldsmith; a coppersmith, or a tinsmith, or any other damned smith that works with shapin' metal!"

"Please ask your deceased John Smith a specific intelligent question," the aggravated and chagrined gypsy medium seated in a chair upon the stage prompted. "It's getting later into my performance, and I'm not very effectively convincing any of you repugnant, loathsome, uncooperative, Doubting Thomas individuals sitting out there of my extraordinary Other World contacting ability."

"Well, John Smith, where the hell did you die?" I naturally asked. "And are you happy existing wherever the hell you are right now?"

"At least a hundred different voices shouted out the names of different diseases ranging from cancer and tuberculosis, to gonorrhea, and then another hundred "Smith voices" all yelled in unison "No!" to the question pertaining to their individual happiness in their new afterworld environment.

"Is it especially warm where you are?" I asked amidst some audience mumbling, muttering and grumbling. "Or perhaps, your new surroundings are not so hot!" I idiotically jested.

Some angry and invisible John Smith fella' seized the medium's right hand, and the gypsy lady wearing the speckled bandanna cooperatively scribbled down, "It's got no name, but the place is plenty torrid!" Everyone in the audience hushed-up when they learned and realized that *that imaginary* condemned-to-eternal-damnation John Smith was probably transmitting his telepathy from "the very bad hot place".

"How many other Smiths are down there with you?" I firmly asked out loud.

"Thousands, maybe millions of us," the medium wrote-down and then announced to the many cynics, skeptics, and Diogenes' wannabes' populating the jammed-packed, standing-room-only lecture hall. "In fact, there's eighteen million Smiths down here and counting, with the lengthy procession that could be extending all the way from San Francisco to Shanghai, China! In fact," the medium switched from the slower written-word to the more convenient and expeditious spoken word, "the Prince Lucifer Apollyon calls all newcomers to his steaming volcanic domain, either the surname Jones or the surname Smith, until Satan finally gets to know the new arrivals on a first name basis."

"What do the spirits call their dead abode?" I curiously inquired.

"The Smithsonian Institute!" the beleaguered medium interpreted and seriously filtered John Smith's authentic response. But after the entertained audience again toned-down, I learned from the female gypsy that my dearly departed friend Mr. John Smith had died a very violent, seizure-oriented, self-inflicted suicide death, resulting from his wife's incessant henpecking and relentless browbeating, which to my utter amazement, was all positively true.

Another more aggressive man stood-up and interrupted my séance inquiries by requesting information about a Joseph Smith friend of his, who had passed-away a decade before. But the besieged medium patiently explained to the inquisitive varmint that *his* Joseph Smith had also died a violent death by choking on a chicken bone after he got into a religious argument at supper with a Universalist, a Presbyterian, and a Unitarian-minister. And the deceased Joseph Smith, who was by trade a traveling Methodist parson, who employed all sorts of unorthodox Christian methods, said through the medium that he had no tangible body, and that a bullet could pass from his mouth and exit directly through his asshole without ever touching a muscle, a nerve, or a goddamned blood cell. The specter Joseph Smith also revealed through the gypsy that the ghost doesn't have to come into his heavenly mansion when it rains, because he can't feel any raindrops falling onto his intangible head, shoulders, arms, or body.

"What's the difference between Heaven and Hell?" the old jasper asked his departed pal Joseph Smith.

The medium answered that the two extremes were mental conditions; Heaven representing happiness, and Hell misery and emotional anguish. And however, a person was in this life, that same attitude and experience he or she would also exhibit when deceased. The gypsy medium also informed her fascinated and now quiet audience that there were varying degrees of happiness in Heaven, and varying degrees of suffering in Hell, depending on what kind of life the individual had generated while being alive. But one could attend school in the afterlife to matriculate into a more satisfactory level of either Happiness or Misery, but a person could never graduate from Hellish Misery into Heavenly Happiness, or vice-versa.

And so, according to the remarkable medium, once a person was doomed to contend with fire and brimstone for all eternity, the best-case-scenario he or she could achieve would be a lesser amount of either him or her being stung, burned, and charred in Hell by fewer cinders, ashes, and embers.

And finally, I learned through the informative suspect gypsy medium that there was still a strict distinction between the genders in both Heaven and Hell, but since everybody in the afterlife was in a spirit form without any physical body to take care of, biological pleasures such as food and sex were no longer practiced in either Heaven or in Hell, and *that* very unsettling concept made everyone present in the audience want to live as long as we could on this planet's surface, without dying and ultimately going anywhere, either good or bad.

"Does anyone ever achieve perfection in the afterworld?" the fellow standing in the rear of the auditorium asked Joseph Smith through the all-too-solemn medium.

"Are you kidding, Asshole?" Joseph Smith replied through has earthly spokeswoman. "There're an infinite number of degree levels in both Heaven and Hell, and if you want a perfect religious karma, stop being a Christian and convert to the Hindu faith, if you strongly desire to attain Nirvana!"

“Guying the Guide”

While merrily touring and enjoying the wonders of Italy with some other uncouth and uncultured fellow Americans, our guide (that *we* had affectionately nicknamed Roman Ferguson) expected us to revere Renaissance civilization along with the myriad accomplishments of Michelangelo, as much, if not more than he did. Quite frankly, my fellow tourists and I were getting extremely fatigued and restless after listening to the plethora of Roman Ferguson’s perpetual, sugarcoated bullshit.

I learned from Fergy’s daily walking lectures that Michelangelo was a great man in the fields of canvas (and tarpaulin) painting, marble sculpture, architecture, chapel ceiling painting, poetry, and the artist just about excelled in everything that the dedicated phenom’ ever did, including breathing, eating, farting and shitting. But we were all so deluged with Michelangelo, and the all-too-excessive praise, always flattering *his* esteemed reputation that it got to the point where the over-the-top glory was becoming quite nauseating to myself’, and also to my un-enamored and unimpressed American traveling companions. I mean to say, we were fed a constant diet of Michelangelo after every breakfast, every lunch, every dinner, every dessert, and after every tea, even though we were fuckin’ touring around inside Italy, and not inside England.

In Genoa, that artistic son-of-a-bitch Michelangelo designed everything we observed, and basically everything that our overzealous guide “Roman Ferguson” described and narrated. In Milan, either Michelangelo, or one of his protégé students, designed everything we saw, or that Ferguson laboriously depicted. His pupils (including the ones in his eyes) designed every fuckin’ thing including Lake Como and the Italian Alps.

In Padua, in Verona, in Venice, and in Florence (who was not a Tuscan woman, incidentally), Michelangelo was excessively mentioned and revered. I believe I even heard Ferguson declare that the Italian genius had designed bologna in Bologna, and had given Leonardo da Vinci the blueprints for the *Last Supper* and the *Mona Lisa,* because the brilliant Michelangelo was way-too-busy working on more important shit than to get tied-up laboring on *those two* mediocre, time-consuming, painting projects. I suppose in retrospect, that’s why just three days *before* I had gotten a severe case of indigestion looking at and trying to admire the *Last Supper* wall painting on that wall of the Monastery of Santa Maria delle Grazie, back in Milan.

In the city of Pisa, Michelangelo designed everything (including the public toilets) except the Leaning Tower, but the famous sixteenth century Italian would have been given credit for designing *that* spectacular edifice, too, if it were perfect and perpendicular to the ground. And had good old athletic Michelangelo thrown Galileo off the top of the Leaning Tower along with the astronomer's telescope and two bocce balls of different sizes and weights, then naturally, the distinguished and renowned Renaissance artist would've been even more famous than he is today.

. The incredible "Renaissance Man" also engineered the piers of Leghorn, and the customhouse regulations of Civita Vecchia. And in the Eternal City of Rome itself, the talented bastard also designed the Pantheon; the Coliseum; the Capitol; the Tarpeian Rock; the Barberini Palace and Beauty School; St. John Lateran; the Capagna; the Appian Way, and also the Roman Way; the Seven Hills; the Baths of Carcalla; the Claudian Aqueduct; the Cloaca Maxima; the Tiber River; the Swiss Guard uniforms; the Pope, and with no exaggeration, also St. Peter's peter.

Just the other day, one of my fellow Americans, whom I'll benevolently refer to as Dr. Dan, alarmingly said to Ferguson, "Look Fergy! Enough is enough! Simply say that the Creator up in Heaven made all of Italy from a design submitted by Michelangelo!"

And as recent as yesterday, I finally found mental peace and tranquility when our sanctimonious, assigned tourist guide "Roman Ferguson" finally answered one of Dr. Dan's questions correctly, by admitting and informing us that Michelangelo was dead and buried somewhere in Italy.

So, Dr. Dan and myself decided to take out some good old American-style vengeance on snobbish old "Roman Ferguson", who was *roamin'* and marching our group through miles of paintings and sculptures inside the vast corridors of the Vatican Museum.

We all marveled at the ceiling and wall frescoes of the Sistine Chapel, which incidentally is in the Vatican Museum area and not a part of St. Peter's Basilica, or not even a vital part of St. Peter's enormous peter.

"Is this the famous Cistern Chapel?" Dr. Dan deliberately asked and confused Ferguson. "No wonder the ceiling is chipping away from all of the water coming from the cistern!"

Now Italian tour guides are taught formal English, and have no appreciation of either colloquial slang or the American sense of humor. "The name of the Chapel is Sistine, Sir, and not whatever word you had just called it," Ferguson politely corrected Dr. Dan, the guide having no clue that *we* were together trying to bust his stones.

"What was Michael Angelo's last name?" I momentarily confused our native Italian, Fergy.

"What do you mean, Sir?" our all-too-courteous guide asked. "Michelangelo was his name, and that's all I can tell you."

"Well now," I clarified. "My full name is Samuel Langhorne Clemens, and the guy that painted the ceiling of this here chapel has the famous name Michael Angelo. What's his last name now that we know his' first and middle names, or is his first name Michael and his last name Angelo?"

My question was put on hold by our befuddled guide, with Fergy claiming that his acumen didn't understand the gist of my very intelligent academic inquiry.

"Are those ceiling frescoes up there from San Fran-fresco?" I jested, receiving a frown and a sort of painful grimace facial expression from Ferguson.

Then, the beleaguered Fergy showed us a statue and quickly and emotionally exclaimed, "Statoo brunzo!" (bronze, statue).

"Was *that* beautiful marble configuration also created and made by Michelangelo?" the slightly-cantankerous Dr. Dan wanted to know, intentionally prevaricating his inquiry. "That amazing fella' has his hands into everything around here!"

"No Dr.," Fergy answered, feigning suavity, but obviously still in a puzzled state of mind about the veracity and sagacity of the average American. "That's a very difficult question. I really don't know who made the bronze statue, but I'll find-out from someone else and tell you later."

Then, we were escorted across the Tiber River to the ruins of the Roman Forum, where I impertinently asked Fergy, "In regard to Julius Caesar, were the Roman citizens *for 'em* or against him? I suppose that some of the Roman Senators were not for 'em, because the rebellious politicians brutally assassinated Caesar, especially brutal Brutus, beneath the statue of Pompey, which I understand is actually a volcanic mountain (Pompeii) geographically situated just south of Naples!"

And before the very annoyed and perplexed "Roman Ferguson" could respond to my inanely stupid interrogatives and declaratives, Dr. Dan courteously asked him, "Was the Roman Forum also designed by the great and illustrious Michelangelo?"

"No, Dr Dan. It was built a thousand years or so before Michelangelo was ever born!" Ferguson replied, wondering if most alien-thinking Americans were born on Mars.

"And what about the Egyptian obelisk you referred to as Cleopatra's needle back at the Vatican? Did Michelangelo also design and construct that magnificent object?" Dr. Dan queried.

"No Dr.," Fergy said, his mind somewhat in disarray. "It was built in Egypt, and then brought here to Rome to honor Cleopatra; I'll say around two thousand years ago."

"Do you mean that the incomparable Michelangelo only is responsible for creating certain *parts* of Italy, and not the whole damned country?" I boldly challenged Fergy. "Didn't the man have time for anything else like food, women, cross-dressing, and sex?"

Our emotionally distraught and mentally encumbered guide was totally hogtied, and Dr. Dan and I were enjoying every damned minute of his terrible frustration. Fergy valiantly tried delivering the standard memorized preamble, introducing his strange audience to his next object of interest, for Ferguson knew *his story* by heart and had mastered nothing else outside of it.

Good old Fergy knew the history of each and every statue and painting our guide had diligently showed us, and the cultural encyclopedia redundantly parroted his recollection and knowledge. But any question from beyond the perimeter of his "awareness zone" would throw him off-track, and our flustered guide would derail like a runaway train, and then have to go back to his original station platform to begin his monotonous and boring spiel all over again, starting from his first memorized sentence.

In the final analysis, Ferguson was used to inspiring awe and admiration from his guests/clients, and when Dr. Dan and I resisted entering into the enchantment ecstasy that our illustrious tour guide was normally used to establishing without any satirical resistance, the poor overwhelmed fellow soon became lost in a sea of American-generated cynicism.

Dr. Dan and I had excavated a very evident weakness, a chink in Fergy's thick suit of armor, even though our guide was Italian and not Chinese, and to demonstrate our shared American audacity to one another, devious Dr. Dan and I decided to advantageously exploit *that* vulnerability (Ferguson's lack of English slang knowledge) at every given opportunity.

My ball-breaking buddy Dr. Dan is cool as a cucumber in his general demeanor, and keeps a stoic, expressionless poker face whenever he asks an obviously obnoxious question, and that special delivery technique of his tended to further disorient our pompous Italian tour guide. While wandering about in Genoa, Fergy took us inside a historical museum, and showed us a classic parchment signed by none other than Christopher Columbus.

"See here now, this document was signed by the great Christopher Colombo himself!" Fergy gushed with great pride and reverence. "What do you Gentlemen think about that?"

Dr. Dan and I both looked indifferent as if we had just seen ugly graffiti scribbled upon a New York City wall. Then, my medical friend and traveling colleague asked, "Fergy; what did you say the name of the fellow who signed this ordinary-looking paper was? I can't seem to accurately remember."

"Why it was Christopher Colombo, the very great Christopher Colombo himself!"

"Was Columbo a good friend of Michelangelo?" Dr. Dan asked, marvelously making his glorious anachronism pronouncement tongue-in-cheek.

Before Fergy could respond to Dr. Dan's comic utterance, I stupidly asked with a straight face, "Tell me Fergy; did this fellow Colombo write this letter all by himself, or did he have any help from Julius Caesar, of course before *he* was assassinated, er, I meant to say, before Caesar was assassinated and not this infamous fella' you call Colombo!"

And before Fergy could admonish me with some more of his monotone academic rhetoric, Dr. Dan followed my rather atrocious statement with, "Kindly tell us, Fergy; how come this Colombo fellow has such inferior handwriting? I've seen kindergarten boys back in the United States with better penmanship than that which appears on this old, faded and tarnished yellow paper."

"But this was written by the great Christo..."

"Look here, Fergy," Dr. Dan interrupted as our dual badgering continued to double-team our stunned guest lecturer. "I don't give a flyin' fuck who the hell wrote this piece of shit! Do you think we're a bunch of fucked-up, stupid, retarded American morons? Cut the goddamned phony bullshit, will ya'? If ya' have any specimens of excellent handwriting to show us, I'll gladly examine them, because as a hobby, I happen to be a much-heralded and published expert in the calligraphy field. Now tell me, before I lose my temper," Dr. Dan faked potential hostility. "And before I become angry and extremely violent, where the hell are the superb examples of superior Italian handwriting? I wanna' see those dumb-ass son-of-a-bitches right now so that I can readily determine whether they're authentic, or blatantly fraudulent?"

Ferguson sensed that Dr. Dan and I were pissed-off and exhausted from hearing all of his academic cultural drudgery, and the guide formally excused himself so that he could relieve his kidneys and bowels, and then successfully compose himself, and intrepidly return to our indispensable company, all refreshed and ready to receive more provocative and insane harassment to be systematically administered by fearless Dr. Dan and myself.

"Ah Gentlemen, allow me to show you a magnificent bust on this pedestal. It's of the great Colombo, who as you know, discovered America," Fergy confidently orated upon his return from using the local lavatory facility, which was a dark deep hole in the stone floor to piss and shit into.

"Wouldn't *that* mediocre work of art look better if the pedestal were on top of the bust?" the wily Dr. Dan demanded. "I mean Fergy, I'm a veteran medical doctor, and I've seen better busts on six- year-old girls, and on ten-year-old women!"

"Didn't Christopher Columbus discover America before America discovered him?" I obnoxiously asked our very vexed guide, as I methodically exhibited a tremendous degree of senility. "Or did a city in Ohio discover Columbus?"

"Now Fergy, we just came from America a week ago, and we heard nothing about your extravagant claim that this itinerant degenerate from Genoa ever once discovered America. It sounds like a lot of rubbish to me; absolute poppycock!" Dr. Dan eloquently contributed to *our* verbal bombardment. "Is this fellow Columbus still alive, so that I may personally interview him about this totally incredible discovering America bullshit?"

"Oh my God!" Fergy yelled in exclamation, attracting instant attention to our small group from among the other more respectful tourists and their guests inside the historical museum. "The great Colombo has been dead for over three-hundred-years, and most certainly, the great explorer is not alive for you to ever interview him! Don't you understand? Christopher Columbus is dead!"

"Did he die of the mumps, chicken-pox, rooster pox, or the measles?" I solemnly and somberly inquired. "Or how about acne, heartburn, or psoriasis? In fact, Fergy, when I first saw you after breakfast this morning, you were a sight for sore-eye-asis!"

And before the befuddled "Roman Ferguson" could recover from his stressful shock, and then cordially respond to my preposterous statement, Dr. Dan asked, "Please tell me, Fergy. Which end is the

Columbus bust, and which end is the pedestal? I think I'm a trifle mixed-up here!"

"Santa Maria!" Fergy vehemently yelled, shaking his hands in front of his enormous chest. "This is ze bust up here, and this is ze pedestal down there!"

"I suppose that this is the first time this gentleman Colombo has ever been in a big bust, police being involved or otherwise!" Dr. Dan seriously observed and opined. "Yes Fergy; he does look deceased, doesn't he? But for the life of me, I can't understand why you Italians have put this Colombo up on a pedestal for everyone else to admire, when in truth, he's such a big fuckin' deal here in Italy, and hardly even known at all back in the United States!"

"Look Fergy," I continued my personal tour-guide insurrection. 'We know that the word *Italics* is derived from the word Italy, because, entomologically speaking, Italy is where the use of Italics had originated. Now then, in a similar fashion, did the Roman Emperor Caligula invent Calligraphy?"

"I regret that I do not know that particular answer, Mr. Clemens," our by-the-book tour-guide very politely answered with his head semi-crestfallen.

Then, my new pal Dr. Dan chimed-in to further double-team and frustrate our assigned Italian guide. "Well now, Fergy. Thirty years ago, an American genius named Alexander Graham Bell invented the telephone. Is it true that the Pope's private phone number is: 'Et Cum Spiri-220'?"

Fergy could not master the subtleties of that silly American joke, and thus was totally ignorant of the American sense of humor that featured mostly sarcasm, irony, cynicism, slapstick comedy, and exaggerated criticism. But throughout the remainder of our stay in Genoa, Ferguson looked quite pallid, and his overall behavior needed overhaul; and his spirit was vacillating somewhere between the bewildered zone and the nonplussed zone.

But then, while our tour group was visiting another lackluster museum, this one of an archeological nature, Ferguson attempted to regain his pluck and confidence. The Italian cultural encyclopedia stridently approached Dr. Dan and me with renewed vitality, professionally showing us an Egyptian mummy on display.

"This mummy discovered near the Great Pyramids is the best preserved in all the world," Fergy noted and then smiled. "It's in the most splendid condition that one could ever expect or imagine!"

"Fergy, what did you say this deceased gentleman's name was?" I insisted on knowing with a stone-like expression on my visage.

"Name? He has no name! He's a mummy!" our Guido-type guide yelled, causing a bit of a disturbance scene inside the all-too-quiet archeological museum.

"Was the gent born here in Italy, or was he a German, or a Frenchman, who just happened to die here in Genoa?" Dr. Dan interrupted my ignoramus-type of perverted interrogation. "Perhaps this unfortunate man was a Roman general who knew Julius Caesar and Michelangelo, both on a first name basis?"

"He's a goddamned mummy and was born in fuckin' Egypt!" Ferguson cursed, showing some signs of being human, and finally understanding how to think, speak, and act like an American.

"Is he still alive?" Dr. Dan wondered and asked, being fully amused at our guide's history histrionics. "It looks like part of his chest is still breathing!"

"He's fuckin' deader than fuckin' Caesar, and fuckin' Colombo, and fuckin' Michelangelo, all fuckin' put together!" Ferguson screamed a string of profanities like a raving lunatic. "All of you fucked-up Americans are fuckin' fucked-up, uncultured, and uncivilized fucked-up maniacs!"

"Now you're talkin' our kind of English!" I wholeheartedly commended the still-infuriated Roman Ferguson. "Forget all about this daily all-too-refined cultural wine and cheese bullshit, Fergy! These boring tours are worse than an eight-and-a-half-hour painful appointment at the dentist's office!"

But reliable old Dr. Dan had the best suggestion of all. "Now let's all go find a good Italian tavern that serves black-angus American steaks, along with pizza and frosted pitchers of cold beer," the classy physician recommended. "And now that you finally understand what red-blooded American men are like Fergy, *we* could finally fuckin' enjoy each other's fucked-up company!"

"Curing a Cold"

The common cold is really quite common among commoners, aristocrats, paupers, and royalty alike. I don't know why the damned thing is actually called "a cold", because the sufferer usually has a high fever along with a temperature, so the friggin' appropriate terminology ought to be "a warm" instead of "a cold". Curing a cold is no elementary task. In fact, once during my teen years, I remember innocently opening a window and "in flew Enza".

I'm presently attempting to organize this invaluable manuscript to benefit the average citizen, and instruct him or her about what the hell I've learned about valiantly battling the common cold. If one traumatized sneezing victim could glean just one helpful method from this inspirational essay, then my sage writing has served its purpose, and *that* particular mental reward should be compensation enough for my intensive labor.

Oh, the simple joy of being a Good Samaritan Christian and feeling holy and sanctified about performing a remarkable, unselfish, humanitarian deed! And so, with *that* noble ideal in mind, I boldly advance my special principles of self-doctoring, which abundantly flourishes outside the proper jurisdiction of the meddling and non-compassionate medical establishment.

When I was already a disconsolate asshole living in Virginia City, Nevada, my house caught fire; burned to the ground, and almost simultaneously, my spirit sank into an abyss that eventually resulted in me succumbing to and getting a very severe cold. I was thinking and worrying about my material losses, and basically, lost track of the fact that my frazzled nerves were indeed disintegrating my body's resistance to the onslaught of harmful infection.

"Bathe your feet in hot water and then *go to bed*," a friend suggested as a remedy. "But remember; only fill the pan or tub water up to your ankles."

"I ain't got no goddamned bed, because it was destroyed when my house burned to the ground during the infernal inferno," I balked and squawked. "The whole damned mess is now a pile of cinders. How about if I spend the night at your place?"

"I reckon not," my non-empathetic amigo abruptly answered. "I don't wanna' catch your goddamned cold, so keep the raunchy son-of-a-bitch all to yourself. You can stay over once you fuckin' get better! Until then, keep your fuckin' cold inside *your* body!"

Another sympathetic acquaintance voluntarily advised me to first take a cold shower-bath, and then thereafter to "feed the cold and starve the fever". I followed both of those erudite recommendations, and wound-up becoming a temporary resident lying horizontal inside the "Quarantine Ward" of the Virginia City infirmary.

Upon being released from the infirmary a week later, I sat in a neighborhood restaurant coughing my lungs out, when the owner came over, collected his meal fee for my half-eaten supper, and fearing that he would catch my terrible contagion, the defensive-minded proprietor tore down his outside overhead shingle. Next, the owner swiftly locked his door with me remaining inside his eatery, finishing gobbling-down my rather mediocre dinner. Luckily, I eventually managed to escape my incarceration through an unlocked back window inside the establishment's rodent-infested kitchen.

On my way to register a week's stay at the local hotel, another bosom friend (whose face actually looked like a female breast) stopped me on the street, and informed that a quart of warm salt water swallowed-down rapidly would definitely alleviate my cold symptoms in a hurry. I did as the recommender had prescribed, and then nearly regurgitated-up my soul and my spleen as my recently eaten dinner soon became scattered all-over downtown Virginia City.

And so, for any unfortunate individual egregiously afflicted with the scourge of common cold symptoms, please ignore all of those home-cure methods that I've thus far, so meticulously, chronicled. As for the choice between quickly imbibing a warm quart of salt water or experiencing a major earthquake, I'd gladly take the more propitious earthquake cure to violently shake the nasty cold, before ever conscientiously employing the goddamned chugging-down hot salt water technique.

After borrowing a half dozen handkerchiefs from perfect and imperfect strangers, and next blowing all six of them into atom fragments with my incessantly-sneezing nostrils, in front of the city livery stable I encountered a believable old woman who must've been at least a hundred-and-fifty-years-old, if any credence is to be placed on general appearance; on facial wrinkles, and on sagging flabby tits. The elderly bitch named Doreen Smith claimed that she had lived for almost a century in a remote territory of the northern country, and that she knew all about old Indian cures, unique shaman incantations, and certain infallible totem pole charms.

"Here now, Sir," Doreen said to me in her luxurious hotel room. "I'm in the process of mixin' you a marvelous concoction of molasses, aquafortis, diluted turpentine, and various secret drugs and ingredients too numerous to mention. Take a wine glass full of this potent shit every fifteen-minutes until you get an erection. I've just given you the general recipe for the perfect male aphrodisiac!"

Well, I was so desperate to feel better that I gulped-down the first dose and instantly, my pecker began rising like the mythological Phoenix, and suddenly, I had the keenest desire to wildly screw the old hag through a damned mattress. But then, when I began coughin' up green phlegm, and sneezing snot all over her aroused body, the old bitch leaned-over from her brass bed, grabbed a black iron frying pan, and knocked me out silly with one savage swipe onto my vulnerable noggin. My dizzy mind was reveling in supernatural-like meanness, as I imagined myself robbing graveyards and maniacally sodomizing geriatric whores with dried-out cunts. But then two days later, I woke-up from my extended nightmare; the result being me all exhausted and all-out fatigued from my incomparable forty-eight-hour, unconscious, formula-drinking-rampage. But amazingly, I found myself cured of my cold!

Just like a small pony, I felt a little hoarse. My voice had somehow descended to below a zero volume, and I had to converse and ask questions as if I was the bass singer in a barbershop quartet. My intonation was so low that I had to verbally communicate with myself' (instead of my normal talking to myself) in sign language while peering into a mirror. And this accurate description of mine is by no means a gross exaggeration. I was an even bigger mess than the scattered debris resulting from a loud dynamite explosion.

Another close pal put me on a very strict "four-day cold diet". Here's what the hell the no-good prick articulated. The first day, I had to drink three ounces of gin every hour. The second day of remedy, I needed to drink three ounces of gin, and eat a quarter of an onion every hour. The third day, I had to imbibe three ounces of gin, eat a quarter of an onion, and faithfully take three tablespoons of molasses every hour.

"And on the fourth day, Sam, do the same as on day three every goddamned half-hour, and I guarantee you that your fuckin' cold will be totally cured."

Besides acquiring what other Virginia City inhabitants depicted as "Buzzard's Breath", I wound-up imprisoned in the town infirmary's "Quarantine Ward" for another full week of requisite rehabilitation. It had gotten to the point where I felt like heading back to the Virginia City Hotel and screwing the daylights out of the century-and-a-half year old wrinkly-faced, prostitute hag bitch, if I could ever escape the dreaded "Quarantine Ward".

Upon being released from the miserable hospital wing, I accompanied a dumb-ass ally of mine, Jim Wilson, out to Lake Bigler for a change of venue, and a doctor-recommended switch in climate. The two of us rode way out there (a distance of thirty or so miles) in his snazzy Pioneer Coach, and we hunted, fished, bullshitted around the campfire, and square-danced all day and half, the whole damned night. But to my lousy discomfort and regret, my chronic illness became even worse. I wished that I were a calf out on the range because truthfully, I was fit to be tied.

It was hard for me to refuse trying Jim's special home remedy. "Take a nice sheet bath, because you're *full of sheet* to begin with," Wilson melodramatically counseled and jested. "It's almost midnight; the crisp air is frosty, and that's the ideal atmospheric condition ya' ever wanna' have when you're fuckin' sick," Jim communicated. "I'll wrap this long white sheer sheet soaked in ice water around your bare-naked body, and I'm willin' to bet Sam Clemens, that you'll be feelin' like a strong young buck no later than noon tomorrow."

I consented to undergoing the radical non-medical experiment, since my troubled mind was in such disarray from all of the excruciating pain my chest, lungs, and head had been gruesomely experiencing. Truly, I felt like an Egyptian mummy, because I was freezing to death, and honestly and candidly, at that particular moment, I actually envied those ancient buried Pharaohs in pyramids, because the stiffs were wrapped similarly as I was in that pathetic white sheet. But conversely, the mummies were already dead, and felt no goddamned agony or pain like I had been feeling. And besides, to tell the truth, I've never been wrapped too tight in all my goddamned life.

Never before did I ever have such anguish as that night. I violently writhed about on a blanket like an intoxicated squid, when the chilly sheet-rag made contact with my warm flesh. My chest was gasping for air in a like manner to a chimney bellows, as when expiring men desperately inhale and exhale their last breaths on their deathbeds. The marrow in my bones became frozen, and my testicles had instantaneously shriveled-up to the tiny size of June sweet peas. My diminutive, flaccid, dick felt like a shrunken Arctic icicle, and I was afraid that I would inadvertently begin pissing out sleet along with solid, yellow ice chunks.

"Ya' remind me of a Negro I once saw bein' baptized," Jim Wilson commended me during the height of my extremely difficult predicament. "The black dude had accidentally slipped from the parson's grasp, and then floundered around in the deep, muddy lake;

thrashing his arms around in an erratic pattern," Jim casually pontificated while I felt like I was dying. "Now Sam. The dumb bastard couldn't swim a lick, and nearly strangled himself out of being excessively frantic. After gyrating about in a total frenzy, and then spouting water like a disgruntled whale, the incensed black asshole angrily exited the dirty lake, and proceeded to beat the livin' shit out of the very surprised parson. The partially-baptized black fellow's fists nearly decapitated the sanctimonious son-of-a-bitch preacher; all of that intriguing excitement happening moments before the black sacrament-receiver next viciously and wickedly hurled the alarmed minister into the aforementioned murky water, only to splash about incessantly all by himself."

"I see," I fully understood while unfortunately experiencing the onrush of paralyzing physical, emotional, and mental shock. "The pissed-off Negro asshole administered a well-deserved brutal beating to the piss-head minister."

When the unprecedented cold-cure white clear sheet bath ultimately failed to remedy my misery, a week later, a woman friend visiting Virginia City from Carson City told me that I should relish applying a large eighteen-inch-square mustard-plaster to my chest. But I was rooming in the hotel with young Jim Wilson, who coincidentally became mighty hungry in the middle of the night, and nearly consumed the hair and nipples off my breasts as the dumb-shit avariciously feasted away on his culinary mustard-plaster delight. "For Christ's sake you idiotic cannibal; you're fuckin' eatin' me alive!" I strenuously objected to my insane roommate's peculiar appetite. "Come to your senses before you fuckin' devour my tits!"

"Spaghetti and meatballs can't compete with this delicious flavor!" Jim seriously and crazily maintained. "Maybe tomorrow night ya' could rub this tasty mustard shit all over your fat ass!"

My debilitating disease became more aggravated with each successive cure endeavor. I decided to leave the insanity of Nevada and travel by stage over to San Francisco. A prostitute staying at the downtown hotel gave me probably the best cure remedy I had ever received, so pay close attention to its valid importance, because everything I've mentioned so far has been absolutely useless.

"Drink a quart of rye whiskey every twelve hours for medicinal purposes only," the fancy, expensive, knowledgeable, veteran hooker constructively proposed.

And then, a well-intentioned-fellow I met in the hotel lobby (who turned-out to be the horny harlot's pimp) intelligently persuaded me,

"Drink a quart of bourbon whiskey every twelve hours for medicinal purposes only."

Well now, that full gallon of delicious dual liquors I drank each day eventually cured my damned annoying horrible cold, once and for all. And so, in the final analysis, my sophisticated advice is to ignore all of the aforementioned cures provided in this explicit article, except the last proven excellent one that can be beautifully expressed in a pretty pertinent maxim: "Forget eating goddamned orchard apples! A gallon of whiskey a day keeps the fucked-up doctors away!"

"An Encounter with an Interviewer"

After I had somehow accidentally and miraculously become famous all over the goddamned world, I mercifully granted an interview to a young city slicker reporter, who apparently was feeling his oats, and I believed that the rookie writer knew a little bit about authoring and editing. But simple newspaper reporting (and its corresponding journalism aspect) is plenty more simplistic than serious fiction writing, along with serious creativity, happen to be, because editorial page journalism essentially involves opinion writing based on elementary, lower-level thinking skills such as interpretation and analysis. And newsworthy front-page newspaper articles simply concern utilizing the easy-to-answer pedestrian questions: who, what, when, where, why, and how?

But conversely, creative fiction writing (short stories and novels) exists on a much higher "thinking plateau" than does Neanderthal newspaper writing. And also, creative fiction organization has specific relevancy in dealing with what's known in the public domain as "invention, creation, and self-actualization".

Now, I happen to know all of this pertinent (and impertinent) bullshit because I started-out as a lowlife newspaper journalist, and then evolved, ascended, and finally transcended into a creative novelist and an inventive short story author. I mean to say, in a literary sense; a book *author* always trumps the notion of being an ordinary newspaper *writer* any damned day of the week.

In conclusion, there are some book *writers* out there that claim to be *authors* while writing mundane and un-inventive non-fiction biographies, autobiographies, and historical accounts, but the true authentic *authors* from Shakespeare and Cervantes to Poe and Melville write absolutely dynamic and imaginative creative *literature* that is called *fiction.*

One fine spring day, a dapper, overconfident, young newspaper fella' stepped into my San Francisco hotel room, and after politely introducing himself and handing me his fancy engraved business card, the presumptuous asshole cockily announced that he was associated with the *Daily Thunderstorm*, a low-budget publication of which I never had any previous knowledge or association.

"Mr. Twain. I hope it's no harm or inconvenience that I've come up here to the tenth floor to courteously interview you," the callow, pretentious jerk-off began his unsolicited solicitation. "It's indeed an honor for me to interact with such a distinguished and eminent world-renowned *author*."

I stepped over to a fairly-clean bookshelf in my hotel room, opened-up and studied a dictionary for seven or so minutes, and then said to the rather annoying neophyte, "Kindly tell me, Sir. How the hell do you spell it?"

"Spell what?" the perplexed, vernal ball-breaker inquisitively asked.

"How do you spell the word *interview?"*

"Mr. Twain, why would you want to know how to spell it?" the fucked-up jerk-off queried and challenged my veracity.

"Look Asshole, I don't want to know how to spell it. I just wish to know what the hell the fucked-up word *interview* means. Is that perfectly clear to your unimpressive pea brain?"

"This whole scenario is absolutely astonishing," the kid reporter observed and stated as the novice journalist feverishly scribbled-down some ridiculous hieroglyphic-type notes. "Mr. Twain, I can tell you what the word *interview* actually means if you…"

"Well then," I added and preempted the nasty tongued shit-head. "How does *interview* philosophically differ from, let's say, the word 'outer-view'?" I pondered and postulated. "What the hell's the rudimentary difference to the average lexicographer? Tell me Mr. Davis," I continued, reading from the writing rookie's fancy business card. "Does the nomenclature *interview* start with the letter *I?"*

"Why certainly!" the confused and momentarily disoriented young punk answered. "Why certainly!" vernal Mr. Davis repeated like a dumb-ass parrot phlegmatically memorizing his most important recital line.

"Well now, you'll have to excuse my ostensible hesitancy, but this here dictionary is rather antiquated, and it's what is ordinarily termed *Unabridged*, meaning that it doesn't have many *cross-over* references and definitions," I poignantly clarified. "Do ya' now comprehend my veteran gist? I mean Mr. Davis; we can't get the goddamned English language vernacular and the goddamned English language colloquial integrated, synchronized, or coordinated, because fundamentally," I nebulously elucidated, "the two disparate entities can never be exactly *congruent.* That is to say, Mr. Davis, to symbolically and accurately express myself and my principal intent in easily recognizable Euclidian arithmetical terminology. Wouldn't you concur?"

"My dear Sir, I beg your pardon," the young rookie jerk-off replied. "But your line of reasoning is rather obtuse and oblique. I have trouble deciphering your stilted language."

"On the contrary, Young Man," I querulously chastised. "People, both my close friends and my remote acquaintances, have often described me to myself as a profound individual who induces and inspires rapture; wouldn't you tend to agree?" I rhetorically asked. "Now then, Mr. Davis. Despite your feigned sagacity about esoteric matters, I find your tact and your diplomacy to be both quite artificial and indubitably lackluster. And in addition, you don't seem to be half as erudite as I had originally evaluated you as being. Do you perceptually and cognitively follow my infallible logic?"

"Why Mr. Twain, I do believe that you are endeavoring to insult my intelligence and…"

"And I speculate that I'm the first notorious personage that you've ever had either the privilege, or *diss*-privilege, of interviewing," I interrupted the fledgling writer, who obviously reminded me of myself being a completely arrogant know-it-all asshole journalist just a mere thirty years before *our* little hotel room exchange. "Now please ignore my random conjecture, and explain to my ignorant hard-of-hearing ears how this complicated interview process works? For example, do we have a qualified referee or umpire officiating?"

"Why Mr. Twain," the exasperated young fellow uttered with observable consternation. "Customarily, the whole event transpires with the well-prepared interviewer asking a battery of questions, and then the interviewed person cooperatively answers each item as honestly as he or she could. It's all the rage you know, in significant urban and urbane places like New York, Chicago, Los Angeles and Cleveland," the hotel room visitor insisted. "Now, Mr. Twain. If I finally have your attention and full compatibility, I'd like to ask you some calculated questions to evoke and elicit some salient points about your public accomplishments and about your private history."

"Oh, with pleasure," I amenably replied. "However, there exists one caveat, Mr. Davis. I do possess a rather mediocre, if not inferior memory; perhaps what might be identified by prominent psychologists and phrenologists alike as a singularly irregular recollection; or maybe even what other outstanding practicing shrinks describe as 'borderline senility'. Sometimes," I paused and emphasized. "My vague memory goes from a canter to a gallop, and then from a gallop reduced-down to a commonly low foxtrot by amazingly avoiding the canter phase altogether. So, it's no special wonder that my recall competency often gives me an amount of abundant grief. Do you follow my gist?"

"Please now, Mr. Twain. Do the best that you can in organizing your responses; that's all that I can fortuitously request," the young whippersnapper declared before wiping a pound of sweat from his brow. "Now Sir, how old are you'?"

"Well son, if you count the latest vernal and autumnal equinoxes, and the annual latest winter and summer solstice phenomena, I'm approximately nineteen, and will enthusiastically pass the landmark twenty-year-mark next June."

"Indeed, Mr. Twain. Without your birth certificate in my possession, upon close scrutiny, I would've taken you to be at least sixty-five years of age. Where were you born and when did you begin to *write?"*

"Well, Mr. Davis. It's a good thing my mother hadn't given birth in a hot air balloon, or else I would've been airborne somewhere over Florida, Missouri. And if my biographical data is accurate, I started to write in the latter part of the school year when I was in second grade. I think it was in the calendar year 1836."

"Logically speaking, Mr. Twain. How could you be only nineteen if you started writing in 1836, and the present year is now 1890? That's mathematically impossible!"

"I don't know exactly, and in retrospect, I agree that it's all astoundingly inexplicable. But in the final evaluation, it does seem mighty curious and controversial," I profoundly responded with a miniature grin appearing upon my devilish countenance. "As you might conjecture, Mr. Davis. I was never good at arithmetic, algebra, geometry, trigonometry, astrology, astronomy, home economics, and geography, in that particular order. That is to say, if ya' know what the fuck extraneous bullshit I'm futilely trying to communicate. For as you might already comprehend, the more fuckin' words an academic scholar learns, the less he's able to communicate with the remainder of his species."

"Well then, Mr. Twain. May I ask who you consider to be the most remarkable man you've ever met. That is, so to speak, some sort of outstanding person that you might label as your greatest American hero that you'd like to model your life after?"

"Without a doubt, and without any histrionics about our patriotic history," I cleverly elaborated, "that most excellent historical character would most definitely have to be the one and only Aaron Burr, who incidentally never invented the goddamned burrito, or even the goddamned cactus plant!"

I could readily perceive that my flustered guest was becoming damned-exceedingly frustrated at listening to my abominable condescending cynicism, pessimism, and belligerent skepticism. But then the bellicose little bastard tried to lambaste me with his suspect comprehensive knowledge of American history, especially the life of eminent Vice-President Aaron Burr, who had loyally served his country under the Thomas Jefferson regime.

"Honestly, Mr. Twain. Every grammar school child in America is aware that Aaron Burr had died way back in 1836, and that you could've never met the man if you are only nineteen in this gay year of 1890. I would say that there is a major discrepancy in your recollection of chronological events," the opinionated shit-head challenged. "Perhaps you need to undergo clinical hypnosis to fully refresh your vague and hazy meeting with Mr. Burr."

"Well Mr. Davis," I uttered before nonchalantly lighting-up the tobacco inside my pipe. "I recall meeting the venerable Aaron Burr sometime after he had shot and killed Alexander Hamilton in that infamous pistol duel on July 11th, 1804, back east in Weehawken, New Jersey. But I do believe our assignation was also sometime after good old Aaron was tried for treason in 1807 before Supreme Court Justice John Marshall. Say Young Man," I incisively expounded. "Did you know that in the Old Testament of the Bible, that Moses's younger brother was also named *Aaron?* Now I do believe that's a remarkable coincidence, yes, it is!"

"But Mr. Twain. Logically, if Aaron Burr had died in 1836, and you were born, according to my newspaper's records, in 1835, you couldn't have ever been mature enough to make Mr. Burr's acquaintance, especially since you've already claimed that you were nineteen at the time."

"Look Son, never let the facts interfere with the presentation of a good story; that's the cardinal rule of novel and short story *fiction authorship,* and it's the very last fucked-up rule of magazine and newspaper *non-fiction* journalism! Now then, impotent-brained Mr. Davis," I professed and insinuated. "If you know more about my life than I happen to know about myself, why the fuck are you wasting your goddamned time interviewing me? Are you disrespectfully questioning my integrity and my credibility? Aren't you enviably cognizant of my stupendous literary reputation? Are you an accomplished dunce or some kind of a developing dolt? Which is it, you unimaginative Imbecile!"

Davis humbly and graciously apologized for his blatant, antagonistic attitude towards me, and requested that I proceed with my splendid dissertation on the topic of the great American hero Aaron Burr. I sternly warned the acrimonious young asshole not to interrupt me again, or else the goddamned interview would be abruptly terminated.

"Well now, I happened to be attending Mr. Burr's funeral, and contrary to *your* undeniably deficient chronology, I wasn't there in attendance wearing diapers," I continued my part of the solemn dialogue. "When I somberly approached his coffin, Burr asked me not to make so much noise as to disturb his restful repose."

"Mr. Twain, that's utterly impossible!" Davis incredulously exclaimed. "If Aaron Burr was stone-cold-dead inside his coffin, surely he wouldn't be able to object to you making any sort of external clamor, whatsoever. Your current fascinating-but-incredible presentation is both preposterous and incongruous!"

"Burr wasn't *in Congress* as you've just alluded!" I sharply answered. "He wasn't even in the Vice-Presidency. He was fuckin' dead in his coffin, Mr. Davis!"

"But he had to be dead, and still, he was speaking to you! Was it his ghost addressing you?"

"Well, Mr. Davis. Some of the more sober witnesses that were inside the funeral parlor said that Mr. Burr was dead, and others, who were drunk, insisted that the deceased wasn't. We were all glad that it was good old Aaron lying there horizontal before us, and everyone in attendance celebrated the fact that we were all safe and sound, and still actively breathing, bullshitting, and mourning."

"Okay, have it your way," Mr. Davis conceded and replied, shrugging his shoulders in defeat and despair. "For the record, what is the precise date of your birth? I have the year at my disposal, but not the exact date!"

"It was on a Monday, October 31st, 1693," I rather realistically explained. "Now you might argue against that spectacular idea, saying that it's impossible for me to be one hundred and eighty years old, but if you were to confidentially confer with either Aaron Burr or Alexander Hamilton on the delicate subject, I'm sure that both of those honorable gentlemen would positively and wholeheartedly verify my statement."

"Well then, in the interest of sanity, how many brothers and sisters do you have?"

"There's Henry and William, and I can't seem to remember the rest; especially the females in the Clemens' clan. I seem to have a mental block about that nonsensical family bullshit, ya' know. But then, my younger sibling William died, being all upset about Aaron

Burr kickin' the bucket. But then again, one side of the family maintains that William's death was a tremendous unsolved mystery, and that the intricate puzzle could never be solved by anyone, fuckin' dead or alive, including my hero Aaron Burr," I solemnly communicated to Mr. Davis. "But I do remember that the family had promptly buried poor old William in the Hannibal, Missouri Cemetery, but I can't seem to recall whether he was dead or alive when that very sad interment had taken place."

"Well then, Mr. Twain," the completely-bothered, pissed-off, and ruffled *Daily Thunderstorm* reporter answered, and then cringed inside his hard wooden chair. "Indeed, I'm quite baffled, Sir. If your sibling William was dead, and your family mourned and buried him, then how could that mind-boggling sequence of activities ever be misconstrued as a mystery?"

"Ah, Sir, you're definitely smarter than I had initially given you credit for being," I falsely complimented the naïve, dedicated-to-his-proletarian work-ethic, asshole. "You've hit the bulls-eye with your wise-ass bullshit! You see, Mr. Davis. William and I were identical twins, and we got mixed-up in the bathtub when we were only two weeks old. Now, one of us was accidentally drowned, and some of the family members, particularly my mom, think it was me that had imbibed too much dirty, soapy water. So therefore, Kind Sir," I continued my noteworthy and dynamic oration, "you might actually be interviewing a fucked-up dead person as we speak! Now, needless to say, Mr. Davis, the difficult mystery of who had died that night in the bathtub has cast a grotesque gloom over my entire life, ever since *that* horrendous tragedy had transpired."

"Well, Mr. Twain. I believe I now have sufficient material to document and supplement my upcoming 'Human Interest Story' about your fantastic adventures," the fucked-up journalist tritely stated, quickly rising from his comfortable green cloth chair. "But if I may, I have one final interrogative that I wish you would satisfy. What was it about Aaron Burr's questionable character that has you thinking that he was such an extraordinary man? Was it because he was rumored to be conspiring with revolutionaries to begin establishing a new country somewhere in the South, totally separate from the United States of America?"

"Oh, not at all!" I declared with a smile. "You're bein' entirely too abstract and academically theoretical about this entire Burr bullshit scenario. After the reverend officiating at old Aaron's wake gave his awe-inspiring sermon, and with the funeral procession ready to depart for the dismal cemetery, and with Aaron Burr's body all properly arranged in his horse-drawn hearse, the former Vice-President loudly spoke from inside his coffin sayin' that he wanted to take one final gander at the earthly scenery. So then, the suspected traitor climbed-out of his coffin, and rode-up front all the way to the graveyard with the hearse driver."

Then, all of a sudden, Mr. Davis promptly excused himself from my illustrious company, and excitedly rushed to the door. The greenhorn reporter was such a pleasant aspiring journalist, I sagaciously assessed; and to tell the truth, I hated to see the rambunctious, uncouth, callow journalist-asshole hastily exit my luxurious hotel room.

“Lost in a Snowstorm”

Samuel Langhorne Clemens (1835-1910) was undoubtedly one of the most influential American authors ever, and was also a prolific contributor to United States literature. Sam Clemens was born the year Haley’s Comet (Halley’s Comet) made an appearance, and the literary master died seventy-five years later when the celestial object made another solar system revolution past the Earth, and then sped again around the sun.

Mark Twain was a trend-setter because Clemens was one of the first authors to present characters speaking dialogue using poor grammar, the way ordinary people would converse with regional accents rather than the stilted, formal, academic style practiced by his literary predecessors, and also by his pompous New England literary contemporaries.

I never liked blizzards or volcano eruptions, but instead, always preferred hurricanes and massive earthquakes. But here is one zany snowstorm tale I’ll never forget. One morning, it was snowing like a son-of-a-bitch when the three of us boarded the decrepit *Overland Stagecoach*, which could not float on the ocean, so naturally, the stagecoach usually always went over land. The snow was already several inches deep, and the dirt trail could not be seen by the horses, if ya’ get *the drift* of what the fuck I’m tryin’ to accurately describe here. Visibility was only about three-hundred-foot or so, and it really didn’t matter if the three stagecoach passengers were blind or not during that particular wicked shit-eatin’ trip that I’m lucky to have lived through and now write pertinent details about.

Ollendorff was an old, snotty, arrogant, senile Prussian asshole, and Ballou happened to be an elderly blacksmith that were travelin’ with me to Carson City. Ollendorff thought he knew everything about anything, and bragged that he could tell when the stagecoach driver would deviate one inch off the goddamned center of the dirt road. All during our lengthy ordeal, I suspected that both Ollendorff and Ballou, prior to being born, neither of the two morons could find his way out of his mother’s birth canal.

“How can ya’ be so sure of your claim?” I asked the garrulous, old European fart. “Do ya’ have some kind of compass implanted in your goddamned cerebrum, or maybe inside your epididymis?”

“Be careful!” the decrepit, inflexible Prussian cautioned. “I happen to be just as much an expert on fucked-up deviants as I am on fucked-up deviation!”

Then, the driver accidentally came-upon a fresh trail, and Ollendorff egotistically shouted, “Boys, I knew my senses are as good as that mental compass we were just talkin’ about! The driver spotted someone else’s recent tracks in the snow, and we ain’t lost one iota out here, meandering around in the wilderness.”

“I’d believe the driver sayin’ those words before I’d ever believe an old fossil-faced-fool like you!” Ballou asserted and challenged the militant Prussian. “Ya’ just ain’t got no credibility here in America, and I think ya’ ain’t got none back in wherever the hell ya’ came from, either.”

“Ballou’s right!” I insisted, just to further break Ollendorff’s supersensitive balls and to continue the bullshit conversation. “Now if we were travelin’ somewhere in Prussia instead of in the Nevada Territory on this lackluster North American continent, then I would be half-inclined to give ya’ credit for makin’ an intelligent observation. Speakin’ of a continent Ollendorff,” I continued with a wry smile featured on my countenance, “by your putrid body odor, Ballou and I both think you’re incontinent!”

The driver put the horses into a trot, and although I knew we was lookin’ at a mirage through the snowflakes, that flakey dude, fellow passenger Ollendorff, insisted that we were gainin’ on our predecessors (ridin’ in the imaginary speedy stagecoach ahead of us), because the discernible tracks embedded in the snow were apparently becoming more distinct.

“Why don’t ya’ just drink another pint of rye whiskey?” Ballou mentioned to the indignant Ollendorff. “You’re as drunk as the Lord at the Last Supper already, and I’ve seen walls not half as friggin’ plastered as *you* already are!”

“Ballou’s right!” I keenly added, to further bust the Prussian’s balls. “I believe we’re followin’ a phantom stagecoach, or possibly a mystery Conestoga wagon, or somethin’ ridiculous like that.”

“Look you two excessively dumb-shit Americans,” Ollendorff criticized in some kind of distinct perverted German accent. “The damned tracks in the snow are looking fresher and newer all the fuckin’ time. And now, instead of two sets of wheels, there appears to be four. We’re not alone on this treacherous journey to Carson City, that’s for goddamned sure!”

“I’ll bet it’s a company of stout-hearted soldiers from a nearby frontier fort,” Ballou theorized and suggested about the new-found wheel tracks. “Those Army guys know this territory better than we traveling assholes do.”

"Get a grip!" I ranted before taking another swig of blackberry brandy to finally end the main course of my impromptu and improvised dinner. "Soldiers ride on horseback, and those veteran eunuchs, who have lost their testicles from bouncing up-and down inside horses' saddles, well, those pony riders don't leave damned stagecoach or Conestoga wagon tracks in two-foot of snow durin' inclement weather. It's a good thing you're not an optometrist Ollendorff, because you'd make a spectacle out of yourself daily!"

In another hour, the visible wheel tracks advanced from four to six sets, and Ollendorff felt compelled to mercilessly chastise Ballou and me for being agnostics (or maybe even atheists) to his omniscient claims. "That platoon of soldiers is expanding as more troops are joinin' the regiment," the Prussian idiot confidently declared. "If worse comes to worse, the soldiers will feel obligated to rescue us from impending tragedy."

"Yeah; there's gotta' be at least a hundred soldiers out there ahead of us, deliberately getting lost in this goddamned snowstorm, too!" Ballou humorously maintained. "Got any more fucked-up claims to make Ollendorff?"

"You Americans are so damned cynical, it's absolutely sickening!" the irate Prussian admonished Ballou and me. "You two wouldn't believe Christ if he came-down from the cross and was sittin' here tellin' ya' exactly what I'm tellin' both you freakin' constipated, nutcase nitwits right now!"

"Right!" I sarcastically ridiculed the snotty, conceited European. "As if Jesus Christ has nothin' better to do than hop off His cross and miraculously appear inside this here stagecoach to tell us that you Ollendorff know what the fuck you're talkin' about. I think I need to take a healthy shit after poor Jesus hearin' all this fantastic poppycock, and then givin' us His supernatural advice!"

"The military has wagons attached to horses too, you know!" the regimented Prussian argued in his special brand of jabberwocky. "Why do you fucked-up Americans think you have a monopoly on logic, or on truth?"

"Right, and a thousand Indians in the vicinity feel like fightin' the soldiers from the fort right this minute in the center of this massive mother-fuckin' desert blizzard!" Ballou comically yelled and then laughed. "Grow a goddamned second brain, will ya', Ollendorff?"

The driver abruptly halted the *Overland Stagecoach,* and the cowboy sauntered to the cab and declared, "Boys; I can't see the damned trail any-more, and I suspect we might be goin' in circles followin' our last trail. What's your pleasure?"

"Alcohol!" Ollendorff defensively proclaimed.

"Gamblin'!" Ballou instinctively added.

"Loose women, good sex, big firm tits, hairy beaver, and perfect smoking tobacco!" I reflexively confessed.

"I knew I should've kept futilely ridin' into Death Valley instead of tryin' to be serious with you three degenerate jerk-offs!" the petulant driver chastised. "I was much happier bein' all content, sittin' up there exposed in the freezin' cold, tryin' to get you three mental-case fools to Carson City."

Two minutes later, the stagecoach jerked forward, and then Ballou again felt it appropriate to bust Ollendorff's sensitive testicles and scrotum sack. "I ain't never seen nor ever heard of such a fucked-up, self-centered imbecile as you are," the old blacksmith ranted to the emotionless, stoical Prussian. "Ya' probably try to take a piss every time your dick gets hard!"

Ollendorff was indeed pissed-off, but without having any noticeable erection. And the fuck-head dared not belligerently defy and challenge the muscular old blacksmith to a fistfight inside the stagecoach, because we were caught in a monster snowstorm, and still over a hundred miles away from the nearest hospital or the closest mortuary.

"Look!" I indicated to my riding companions while pointing to the right. "There's the bank of that frozen stream that we've already passed three times in this mean-assed snowstorm. If my thinkin' is correct," I hypothesized and mentioned, "the next inn oughta' be only five hundred *kilometers* or so away," I estimated, deliberately using a European distance measurement instead of the standard American word "miles" to further aggravate the traveling Prussian seated diagonally across from me.

The *Overland Stagecoach* smashed right over and through that frozen stream, and headed-out into the middle of nowhere. Everyone temporarily professed confidence in the clueless driver's good instincts, and in his sense of direction and overall experience, considering this was only his first trip to Carson City. To our utter astonishment, the three of us momentarily spotted a second swift-moving stagecoach directly in front of us, and the object was speeding along as if the vehicle was on a sleigh, rather than moving along on mundane wagon wheels.

"I still say that's a mystery illusion we're followin' up ahead," I mentioned to initiate another meaningless conversation with my extraordinary, opinionated companions. "I know a fuckin' phantom when I see one!"

"You have the faith of a condemned cynic and are a certain candidate for the infernos of Hell!" Ollendorff accused. "You were probably baptized in a contaminated swamp by some uncertified infidel, or by an unqualified, defrocked priest or pagan rabbi!"

"I think you two imbeciles would get along better if ya' just jerked each other off!" Ballou obnoxiously stated. "I've seen better rectum wipers in the *National Historic Asshole Museum,* that's conveniently situated in downtown Boston!"

Our driver's horses were no match for the other "phantom stage's team", and the fleet object soon disappeared into the vast relentless snowstorm. Ollendorff insisted that the current "matters really didn't matter", and that our driver could still follow the freshly-made tracks that were being laid down by "the disillusioned stagecoach pilot, and by the reckless delusional ghost driver".

"Despite the blizzard, those recently made ruts in the road are deep enough for our driver to easily recognize and follow," the Prussian idiot insisted. "It doesn't matter if the fuckin' artificial tracks are a goddamned mirage!" the drunken bastard conjectured and firmly stated.

"I think your freakin' mind is in a pathetic, damned rut," Ballou answered and admonished Ollendorff. "I'd believe you more if ya' was a tad more drunk than ya' are right now!" the argumentative old blacksmith further reprimanded the austere Prussian.

"Pretty soon it'll be night, and our driver ain't got no lantern to follow the imaginary trail left by the phantom horses and by the specter driver!" I concluded and emphatically stated. "We're fuckin' lost in a snowstorm!"

Night did descend on that remote part of the Nevada Territory, but the snowfall was still thick, as the severe winds cycloned around in the lingering twilight. Visibility had been reduced to fifteen human paces, and the glistening snowflakes had virtually covered the desert sagebrush, making each of the objects look like sugar or salt-covered edible mounds. The first stagecoach's grooves had been reduced to mere traces in the deep snow, and for the very first-time, concern filled the three passengers' hearts, instead of levity or rancor.

Now the snow-laden sage-brushes were mostly around three-to-four-foot-high, and some of them formed a lane of a sort of surreal avenue out there in the desolate desert; so, I told my traveling companions that we might be headed out to obscurity, or to infinity, or to oblivion, or some obscure place like that down one of those imaginary sagebrush avenues leading to the end of our lives.

“You Americans are all doomsayers, skeptics, and obnoxious pessimists,” Ollendorff denounced and generalized, before loudly belching and simultaneously farting six times. “But a true-blue European aristocrat is more rational, and certainly much more logical about accurate probability, and other exceptional scientific bullshit like that.”

“What do ya’ groom your hair with?” I questioned the Prussian. “I’ll bet ya’ use a *sage*brush because you’re so damned smart. Your goddamned ancestors must’ve been two-tonic knights!”

“Ollendorff ain’t got no damned hair for neither a comb nor a brush to groom with,” the equally baldheaded Ballou cackled while slapping his knees. “And I understand that these friggin’ Prussian dudes are so low-browed that they’ll even comb or brush their bald heads to try and impress us all-too-savvy Americans.”

I thanked the Lord that we were still alive while anxiously riding in that forsaken stagecoach, we being nature’s cold victims freezing our asses’ off in the middle of an unmapped and uncharted desert wonderland (wasteland). I suppose imagining having a sheet of ice shoved-down one’s back could graphically make the reader understand the intense chill that penetrated my fragile heart, my immortal soul, and also, my frozen dick and my frosted buttocks. We yelled for the driver to stop the damned stagecoach so that the passengers could get out, stretch our legs, take pisses in the snow, walk around, and test the ground, and then attempt to build a roaring sagebrush fire to melt any icicles that might have begun forming inside our already-frozen assholes.

“Let’s build a fire!” Ballou authoritatively bellowed. “I gotta’ warm-up my ass and pecker before I can move and climb my genitals back into the damned stagecoach.”

“That’s an exceptionally good idea,” the amiable driver agreed. “I need to thaw-out this nice bottle of frozen blackberry brandy over a roaring campfire.”

“I had no idea I was traveling with a gang of accomplished alcoholics!” the half-drunken Ollendorff bitched while facetiously condemning his alleged immoral traveling associates. “Give me a scenic beer garden in Munich any goddamned time over rank drunks like you three whiskerandos lost out here in an ugly American desert during the fucked-up blizzard of the century.”

“Okay, you three ingrates. Let’s get the fire started,” I constructively suggested. “First we gotta’ assemble some sorta’ dry sagebrush, and stack it into an orderly pile.”

"What are we gonna' do after we gather the sagebrush fragments?" the driver curiously inquired. "How's the pile gonna' ignite? The damned sagebrush is all wet and saturated from the fuckin' snow!"

"Indians used to scrape sticks together to create a spark," I academically stated. "Ollendorff here seems to be an authority on working his stick."

"We'll rub our dicks together, and the friction might generate a lucky spark to ignite a fire!" Ballou inspirationally replied and laughed. "If that esoteric strategy doesn't work, we'll then try and piss fire out of our shriveled-up fadorkinbenders!"

"You're full of shit!" Ollendorff criticized Ballou.

"We'd all have to have hard-ons, and with this freezing frigid temperature," Ballou laughed and coughed, "that phenomenon would be virtually impossible. Not even the fuckin' Abdominal Snowman could get and maintain a regular erection in frigid weather like this freakin' blizzard!"

"For your information," the very disciplined Prussian clarified, "it's the *Abominable Snowman* and not the Abdominal Snowman. And besides Mr. Ballou, I'll just shoot my pistol into the sagebrush and lots of sparks will be created, and then a magnificent flame will automatically result," Ollendorff nonchalantly volunteered. "There is indeed a rational solution to our dilemma, you know!"

"Have ya' ever done such a thing and started a fire that way?" I reasonably asked the know-it-all European visitor. "Ya' seem like a damned tenderfoot to me that's shot his damned ankle at least several times by accident."

"No; but once I read in a book about it being done," the serious-faced, intoxicated Prussian confidently answered. "In fact, I read about it several times in a couple of different books."

"What was the name of the first damned book?" Ballou nastily queried. "Was it *Shooting Off My Mouth?*"

"I believe the book's title was *Flames in Paradise*," Ollendorff grimly replied. "And the setting was on a beautiful, picturesque, tropical Pacific Island."

So, then we all crouched-down and huddled together on our knees in the two-foot-deep-snow, while swirling snowflakes eddied and spiraled all around our heads in an oddball atmosphere that seemed to transcend all of our previous boring and dull experiences on planet Earth. I perceptively scanned my immediate surroundings, and observed that Ballou, Ollendorff and the bewildered stagecoach driver all looked like paralyzed, white, stooping statues, taking royal shits out in the middle of an unknown, hostile, barren, frigid frontier.

After five minutes of assiduously arranging the assorted sagebrush twigs into a handsome heap, we all retreated fifteen paces as the genius Ollendorff applied his pistol to the mound, pulled the trigger, and next an array of sparks flew all over the damned place, except inside the friggin' sagebrush twig pile. The crazy Prussian (in maniacal frustration) then emptied the remaining five bullets into the center of the mound, blowing the entire pile clear out of the Nevada Territory as if he had been using extremely potent dynamite sticks.

The four of us heard a wild neighing, and then quickly realized that the gunfire had frightened the resting team of horses. The alarmed animals panicked and took-off, leaving the driverless unhitched stagecoach behind them, and also abandoning the four of us humans to our miserable, pitiful, lonesome fate; all lost in the biggest blizzard of that entire cold and frigid winter.

"Got any other clever brainstorms?" Ballou defiantly asked General Ollendorff. "How many malignant tumors did ya' say ya' got inside your fucked-up, infected brain?"

The beleaguered Prussian attempted to transfer blame for the failed incident to the now dumbfounded and innocent stagecoach driver. "Why the hell did *you* dismount the stagecoach before I fired the gunshots into the sagebrush mound?" Ollendorff boisterously yelled at the accused defendant.

"That was not half as stupid as *you* blastin' the shit out of the mound and destroyin' what was supposed to make the goddamned fire!" I countered in defense of the poor, persecuted stage driver. "When brains were distributed by the Almighty, ya' must've stupidly gotten in the asshole line *a second* time!"

"Those cocksuckin' unhitched horses are off to the races, and we'll probably never see those frightened bastards again," Ballou lamented and noted. "We gotta' be at least two hundred miles from the nearest populated whorehouse!"

"Those lying library books," Ollendorff disgustedly complained. "They all stated that horses always remain close to their masters for companionship and for support during times of crisis," the Prussian regretted and commented. "I apologize to you, Mr. Driver, for lambasting your character about not staying up there perched in the stagecoach's driver's seat."

The four stranded travelers, with our faces turning purple from the frigid cold, were now transformed into four marooned nomads. We endeavored building a second fire, and after a mound of sagebrush had finally been gleaned and gathered into a classic heap, Ollendorff again obliterated the semi-wood pile by depositing six errant bullets into its center. "Let's try rubbing some sturdy sticks together," the shit-for-brains Prussian recommended. "I gotta' feeling that the widely acclaimed pistol method I had read about in library books is ineffective in subzero weather at precisely midnight in the midst of a terrible desert snowstorm."

"No fuckin' shit!" Ballou nastily replied to the loony, drunken European dude. "You're about as useful as a dried-out turd on a paper plate that's baking in an oven! What pecker-headed library did ya' go to over in Munich, *The Duncecap Academy's!"*

Mr. Ballou methodically dug deep into his pants and produced four healthy matches from a fifth pocket, which the retard never knew he had. In the meantime, the other three of us reviled all native American Indians; frontier hunters; *pioneers;* cake-in-ears; island cannibal; uncivilized savages; friendly barbarians; happy Eskimos; books, and anyone or anything else that inanely maintained that fire could be made by systematically rubbing sticks together.

"Four matches are better than four bars of gold bullion at this particular place and time," I stated to break the stone-cold silence that prevailed at that very moment. "Any kind of money right now is useless, with us being stranded here outside of civilization!"

"That's right," the stage-less stagecoach driver concurred. "Money, silver, platinum, and gold are completely useless right about now. Survival is the only damned thing that really matters."

"If we ever survive this cursed ordeal," Ballou promised with his hand over his heart, "I'll buy everyone a big steak dinner, a horny prostitute, and a bottle of your favorite whiskey when we finally return to civilization."

Mr. Ballou lit the first match, but it burned-out in ten short seconds. The second match was extinguished by a sudden gust of howling wind that sent a series of chills up and down my vulnerable spine and shrunken pecker. The third match was on the imminent brink of being a wonderful success, when suddenly, it too faded and then eventually expired.

The group all huddled closer together, hoping that we could block the effect of the overwhelming wind for the fourth and final match. Mr. Ballou scratched the igniter tip on his rough, jagged, belt, and the baby flame burning blue and true, and then astoundingly, flared into a robust little inferno. Gentle tongues of fire formed on the edge of the sagebrush mound, and the four of us were all instantly optimistic that our improvised campfire would wondrously ignite-up into a nice glowing blaze.

Ballou was so absorbed in watching the sagebrush that the absurd dingleberry had forgotten that the match was still burning in his right hand's fingers. "Ouch!" the senile cretin loudly shouted as his curled fingers and knuckles became scorched. The excessive breath from the old blacksmith's exclamation traveled out of his mouth and onto the sagebrush, causing the tiny fire to immediately lose its original robust vitality.

"Nice goin', you totally incompetent fuck-head!" the normally dispassionate Ollendorff uncharacteristically cursed at Mr. Ballou. "Who's good at diggin' graves without a goddamned shovel! And I don't mean any goddamned snow shovel either!"

Then, no one else dared to say a word for a full five minutes as the strong northern wind howled, and the chaotic snowflakes swirled around our heads, and slammed into our exposed faces. We all peered into each other's saddened eyes, and as midnight encroached under an ominous full moon, all of us realized that the horribly unbearable darkest hour might be our last one staying alive upon the apathetic Earth. In my heart, I knew that each of us shared the same fearful conviction, and that our ultimate demise was probably inevitable, if not imminent.

Ollendorff began all of the stupid solemn bullshit that followed, by him sanctimoniously stating like a bizarre, fucked-up church minister: "Brethren; let us perish together in this frozen wasteland, and let our hearts discard any animosity or discord, so that we may forgive all of those that have sinned against us," the Prussian fool began an unwelcome dissertation.

"Shut the fuck up!" Ballou yelled at the inebriated Prussian.

"I fully realize that some of my charming companions might still hold a grudge against me for bragging about the truth; for me being more academically gifted; and for me exploring the circumference of circles with a mile-long-diameter here in the brutal desert blizzard," the delusional Prussian preached. "But as you all are aware, I meant well and never intended to bring harm or insult to any of you. I confess that I did have some hard feelings toward Mr. Ballou for calling me 'a carnival stooge', which, of course, has no significant worthwhile meaning on the entire European continent," Ollendorff pontificated and elaborated. "Let it be known right here and now that I forgive our simpleton companion, the illustrious Mr. Ballou, with all of my heart, and with all of my soul."

"I said shut the fuck up!" Ballou reiterated as the infuriated blacksmith clenched his fists. "If I only had my anvil available to tie around and hang from your big fat neck!"

Ollendorff then became emotionally disheveled, broke-down, and began sobbing like a weak wimp: Prussian, American or otherwise. Ballou's eyes were creating crocodile tears, too; and then the weeping, muscular blacksmith apologetically told Ollendorff, "I forgive you, too; even though you were, are, and always will be, a fucked-up asshole!"

The pathetic Prussian then ceremonially removed a full pint of powerful whiskey from his interior coat pocket, and instead of twisting-off the cap and quickly swallowing-down a major chug, the haughty fool pledged, "I'll never again take another gulp of this poison if my life is super-mundanely spared from this impending calamity. I shall be totally reformed, and shall dedicate all of my energies to assisting the poor; to nursing the infirmed, and to lecturing various civic service clubs about the need to practice temperance," Ollendorff wholeheartedly promised in a weird type of perverted prayer. "I will first and foremost be an exemplary fine example for today's misguided youth; for them to model their easily tempted lives after."

Then, the penitent Prussian threw-away the bottle of sinful liquor, which Ballou, the driver, and I desperately needed to drink in order to stay alive. Next, it was Mr. Ballou's turn to describe his vices and to forgive all his myriad enemies of their particular trespasses, transgressions, offenses, crimes, and excessive sins, along with innumerable violations against him.

Ballou reached inside his external coat and removed a new deck of playing cards. "I never made a habit of gamblin'," the old bald-headed blacksmith began his repentance. "But I admit I've played a game or two of poker with righteous bankers, preachers and undertakers from time to time. No man is without sin or vice, and I am consistent with that particular axiom of life. Therefore," Ballou proceeded, "I pledge and vow to discard these virtue-less gamblin' cards, and hereby abandon all immorality for the remainder of my tenure on this sometimes cruel and unusual planet. I am *obsoletely* (absolutely) certain that the Almighty's benevolent mercy will fairly and impartially judge my soul on the scales of truth and wisdom."

The blacksmith's sorrowful nomenclature affected him as if the ideas he had presented had actually been very intelligible and erudite remarks. Ballou openly cried, shook like a Quaker, and then quivered as if possessed by a plethora of diabolical, evil demons; and then the distressed gambling fanatic strenuously hurled his new deck of cards out into the desert wilderness, in the same direction that Ollendorff had thrown his full pint of whiskey.

The aggrieved stagecoach driver then professed to sacrifice his future existence (should he successfully live through our present hardship) by giving-up sex with men, with children, with space aliens, and with horny women, and then having some kind of perverted sex operation performed, and finally entering a secluded convent as a novitiate hermit nun, or some highly peculiar religious function like that.

My own remarks were laden with remorse for practicing a thoroughly unfilled and unrewarding life. "I, like you three honest gentlemen, am also in the presence of death," I prefaced. "And with all honorable and sincere motivations, I hereby proclaim to separate myself from my former dependence on tobacco." I then threw-away my corncob pipe in the same direction as Ollendorff had tossed his whiskey bottle, and that Ballou had heaved his new deck of poker playing cards. "If only I could be spared a few additional years on this majestic Earth," I pleaded; "then the new reformed me could engage in charitable and civic service enterprises of all kinds." Next, without any indication of faltering, my fake fortitude suddenly collapsed, and I lost my sense of manliness, crying like a hysterical widow at her damned bankrupt husband's funeral.

The four of us put our weary arms together in a tight circle as if we were faggots or lesbians, or bona-fide fucked-up people like that; and then each of us bade the other a final farewell. "Take us dear Death!" I implored to the distant and merciless heavens. "Let us struggle and suffer no more!"

I shuddered, and was aware of other certain, non-spectacular neurological sensations, and then a queer numbness spread inside all of my appendages, including my shriveled-up, limp penis. A gentle anguish gathered-in and dominated my spirit, and my intense shivering quickly ascended into violent trembling. 'This is the envelopment of my soul, ready to be transported into the afterworld,' I sadly surmised. 'It's the macabre encroachment of Death! We'll all soon be tasty meals for starving coyotes!'

Soon, my hallucination was brought back to reality by an emphatic statement from Mr. Ballou's lips. "Will one of you fine gentlemen have the decency to kick me really hard in my stupid ass?" the aged blacksmith astonishingly uttered like a fallen, disgraced angel.

I rose-up from my position lying on the snow-clad desert ground, and to my right, outlined inside the gray dawn, my eyes perceived a stagecoach station, and inside stood the team of four horses (that had abandoned us) and our weatherworn *Overland Stagecoach.* At first, I doubted my eyes' veracity; thinking that I had been observing a desert-snow mirage, or some sort of tricky optical illusion.

An arched igloo fractured before my amazed eyes, and out of the white shell popped the unmistakable figure of Ollendorff, and to his right hatched the equally white form of the convivial stagecoach handler. The whole situation was so abnormal and so unreal in appearance that the four of us simply stayed there staring at each other with our mouths agape.

"Where the fuck are we?" Ballou shouted.

"This scene has got to be a fantastic supernatural apparition!" Ollendorff shrieked. "It's gotta' be akin to a mass hallucination!"

"We've all been fuckin' fools confessin' our sins and vices to each other like church children, while we were only standin' and shiverin' a mere fifty-feet away from the next stage station!" the thoroughly embarrassed novice stagecoach driver uttered.

"We really *were* goin' around in monotonous circles after all," I concluded and indicated. "We should've known the horses knew where they were goin' all the damned time, and we shoulda' trusted *their* natural instincts."

I have hardly exaggerated in this descriptive narrative any pertinent details of the three travelers' most absurd stagecoach misadventure. It all occurred in precisely the exact chronological order as I have personally recalled, and have professionally authored. We had actually held a midnight holy prayer vigil in the snow-covered desert, and nearly had died twenty paces away from a warm stage depot with lots of wood and matches (inside the building) situated near a hot, black, potbelly stove.

The four new arrivals entered the fairly warm stage station, sat apart in four creaky wooden chairs, and contemplated the entire fiasco in disgust, soon silently experiencing two full hours of suffering personal humiliation. Then, Ballou had the courage to finally initiate a conversation.

"Well men," the elderly anvil-slammer said before clearing his abominable throat. "It's now evident why our horses deserted us. The animals were seeking shelter from the fierce snowstorm, and galloped under that shed outside in fifteen-seconds-flat," the blacksmith lectured. "Those horses must've been neighing their asses' off anticipatin' us grown men makin' silly public confessions like we had become reformed alcoholics at a woman's temperance meeting!"

Ballou discovered some coffee and eggs inside a cupboard, and the new arrivals shared a rather delicious breakfast that ordinarily would be quite a utilitarian-type morning meal. Zest again saturated our spirits, and we all discussed how we had been complete, contrite assholes, just several hours before.

As Ballou rather adroitly and expertly persisted in busting Ollendorff's balls, I ruminated about how I had been enamored with the sensation of again smoking my corncob pipe, and how I had missed the attendant pleasure more than I had craved delicious lobster-tail, or having non-stop-sex with the best piece of ass in the universe. 'The spirit is as weak as the flesh!' I thought. 'I want to smoke my corncob pipe right now. I need the vice of tobacco at this moment more than I need to listen to either Ollendorff or Ballou's illogical bullshit. And that ain't no goddamned *pipe*dream, either!'

I sneaked out of the rickety old stage depot and wandered around the building's barn pretending to be inspecting the condition of the four horses should one of my colleagues happen to accidentally discover my wayward solitude. Satisfied that no one had espied my escape from the insular stage station, thirty minutes later, I embarked on an important mission to locate the singular corncob pipe to which I had become addicted.

I shortly found my legs honoring my compulsion to meander about the nearby snow-laden sagebrush growths in a noble attempt to zero-in on my wonderful missing corncob pipe, already filled with tobacco. I amazingly fell upon my objective and avariciously repossessed it, first caressing the common item, and then stashing it securely inside my tan cowhide overcoat. 'Why are all of these footprints around the exact area where I've found my pipe?' I wondered. 'There must be phantom ghosts haunting around these parts besides phantom stagecoaches and phantom horses!'

I guiltily hid behind the dilapidated red barn that housed the fatigued horses and the weatherworn stagecoach for a while, fearing that I might be spotted by my ruthless companions, who would then proceed to tease and verbally crucify me to no end because I had been caught red-handed abandoning my promise never to smoke again, a mere three hours or so after I had made it. 'Oh, what the hell?' I conjectured. 'Who gives a flyin' shit if Ballou, Ollendorff or the driver catches me in the damned act of smoking!'

I frantically lit the pipe (with some matches I had taken from the depot), and felt the resplendent joy of pure evil surging throughout my entire being. 'Selfishness is a virtue,' I imagined as I diligently puffed-away. 'There's definitely more pleasure in sin than there is in abstinence!' I rationalized. All that artificial, pious justification because I was ashamed of being trapped inside my own self-centered, pitiful, subordinated ego. I dreaded the notion of Ballou or Ollendorff peering-out the stage station's side window and seeing me violating my heavenly pledge, so I advanced to the edge of the old red barn and turned the corner. Straight ahead I detected old Ollendorff turning the opposite corner simultaneously, and I was immediately cognizant that we had coincidentally caught each other's furtive acts.

Between our positions was naughty Mr. Ballou sitting in deep concentration on the snow-covered ground, playing what he considered an exciting game of solitaire. 'I reckon the old gent's simply enjoying the fine sensation of just feeling those very special poker cards in his hands!' I instinctively imagined.

I glanced over at Ollendorff. He stared me straight in the pupils and then winked. The militant Prussian was first to articulate rhetoric.

"I'm not goin' to tell anybody about this un-fortuitous encounter, and about all of that reform bullshit we had initiated; and about being a good model of behavior for the upcoming generation to imitate," the traveling European baron dishonestly stated.

"And I know *you* enjoy your whiskey as much as Ballou down there likes his cards, and just as much as I savor my indispensable corncob pipe," I all-too-honestly returned.

"We're all fucked-up in our own separate ways," Ballou injected as the brawny, retired blacksmith temporarily escaped his stupor while still gazing at the cards in front of him, that remarkably and ironically represented both chance and uncertainty. "My lips are sealed except for imbibing sassparilla (sarsaparilla), eating the finest pussy, and swallowing-down the best of foods that this goddamned planet has to offer," the elderly blacksmith solemnly promised.

“Punch, Brothers, Punch”

No sir; I’m not exaggerating one iota when I’m now reporting that my formerly invincible brain had been hijacked; that my cerebral functions had been temporarily held hostage, and that my immortal soul had been sabotaged just by reading a stupid-ass, extraneous jingle-rhyme a dozen consecutive times in the morning newspaper. Those poetic, catchy, fucked-up words took advantage of my mental vulnerability, and waltzed through my brain for an entire week every time I ate breakfast, lunch, and dinner; or every time I took a stroll or began writing a story, or even took a perfunctory short piss or a long healthy shit.

To be sure, I was a defenseless prisoner of rhyme without reason, and was relentlessly tortured by this diabolical, freaky singsong meter and verse. Now, I guarantee you that the whole childish business will at first appear fuckin’ innocuous, and will seem absolutely trifling to *your* mature sensibilities, too. I caution you to have your guard up before you continue reading this authentic recounting of an amazingly true and bona fide episode of emotional anguish. Please beware: Here’s the fucked-up language that I had incidentally read in that morning newspaper edition.

Conductor, when you receive a fare,
Punch in the presence of the passenjare!
A blue trip slip, for an eight-cent fare,
A buff trip slip, for a six-cent fare,
A pink trip slip, for a three-cent fare,
Punch in the presence of the passenjare!

Chorus
Punch brothers! Punch with care!
Punch in the presence of the passenjare!

Sitting calmly at my breakfast table (where I always break my overnight fast), I couldn’t clearly recollect whether or not I had eaten anything, although there were plenty of random crumbs on my ceramic plate, and upon the tablecloth, and also scattered all over my lap napkin. I had been assiduously outlining and organizing the chapters to a newly-contrived, thrilling novel just the night before the distressing incident had occurred, so I rose from my kitchen chair and then casually rambled over to the den to continue my arduous, brain-drain literary work.

After I lifted my pen to gently apply to my writing paper, all I could get the goddamned authorial utensil to jot-down were the dumb-fuck silly-ass words, “Punch brothers, punch’ with care! Punch in the presence of the passenjare!”

My vulnerable mind grappled with *that* catchy verse bullshit for a full hour, but my basic mental resistance was totally useless. My captivated brain could not refrain from refraining, “A blue trip slip, for an eight-cent fare; a buff trip slip, for a six-cent fare; a pink trip slip, for a three-cent fare; punch in the presence of the passenjare!” My disoriented mind could not achieve any peace or respite from that barbaric and inhospitable rhyming word invasion.

Well, my day’s responsibilities and plans were positively ruined, and I could see the futility of any combative effort on my part quite lucidly. I voluntarily surrendered to my ‘word poem enemy, and after sauntering downtown, I soon realized that my feet and my strolling pace were keeping cadence and measure to *that* same asinine, relentless jingle. When I couldn’t tolerate that bothersome and irksome bullshit any longer, I altered the rapidity of my steps, but my ascending anxiety was to no avail. Those annoying beat rhymes easily accommodated themselves to my new stride, and the vexing verses harassed both my left and my right foot, as I staggered along the pavement, looking like a drunken mendicant.

Exhausted from my hour-long ordeal, I trekked home, and mentally and emotionally suffered all afternoon; and next, even cried right through dinner, and was even passively farting in the bathtub to the jingle’s accursed rhyming scheme. In bed, I rolled and tossed all night long. So, I arose at midnight, picked-up a non-fiction book to read, but astonishingly, there was nothing visible upon the pages except the confounded bullshit words, “Punch brothers; punch with care; punch in the presence of the passenjare!”

And when the rising sun finally appeared in the east, I got-out of bed; remembered to dress and put my shoes on; ventured downtown, and everyone I encountered marveled at my reiteration of the stupid fucked-up hypnotic phraseology, “Punch brothers; punch with care; punch in the presence of the passenjare!” The total strangers that I confronted, besieged and bombarded, were even more upset and pissed-off about that moronic verbal shit than I was!

Two days later, on Saturday morning, I exited my bed to honor a scheduled appointment I had made the week before. After brutally scarring-up my face while shaving, I dressed, and as a mobile tottering wreck, met my valued friend right on time in front of the local pharmacy. My walking associate happened to be the dignified and esteemed Reverend Mr. Biggins, whom I had agreed to accompany on a ten-mile-long walking excursion to the Talcott Tower over in Simsbury, Connecticut.

After we initiated our physically demanding ramble, the honorable Reverend Mr. Biggins kept talking, talking, and talking, as was his predictable wont. But I stated and heard nothing, since my mind was definitely preoccupied in its fascination with the fucked-up repetitious trolley car rhyme. At the end of the first mile, the garrulous minister commented, "Mark; I know you're a devout atheist and an occasional agnostic, but I've never seen you looking so haggard and so fatigued, not to mention you being profoundly absent-minded. I encourage you, Mark. Please say something salient to break the monotony of my mediocre monologue!"

Drearily and without any evident enthusiasm, I unabashedly muttered, "Punch brothers; punch with care; punch in the presence of the passenjare!"

The Reverend Mr. Biggins stared at me blankly through his thick bifocals, looking both pretty damned perplexed and amused, simultaneously. "I can't comprehend your entire drift, Mark. There doesn't seem to be any particular relevance or significance to your strange utterances. Certainly, it wasn't anything melancholy you had mentioned, and yet, perhaps it was your dull droning intonation that had negatively affected my auditory perception. Truthfully Twain," my heaven-bound friend indicated, "I've never heard anything so alluring, yet so pathetic. What is...."

But my ears were deaf to the Reverend's most perceptive statements. My weak and wimpy mind was already being held hostage with, 'A blue trip slip, for an eight-cent fare; a buff trip slip, for a six-cent fare; a pink trip slip, for a three-cent fare; punch in the presence of the passenjare!'

Now, I don't recall what had transpired immediately thereafter during the remainder of the lengthy ten-mile hike, but then the exasperated Reverend Mr. Biggins placed his right hand upon my left shoulder and shouted into my ear, "Wake up Mark! Don't daydream all day long! Here me now, my apostate companion. We've finally arrived at the splendid Talcott Tower, man! I've talked myself deaf, dumb, and blind the last several hours. And I never received any legitimate response from your lips except some nonsensical gibberish that you kept repeating, over and over again," Reverend Biggins remarked and reminded me. "Just look at this majestic landscape and admire the full panorama! Just reflect for a moment and feast your eyes upon the magnificent foliage, and gaze-upon the fabulous shrub arrangements! You've traveled all over Europe, and I challenge you, Mark, to compare what you're witnessing now to what you had seen in Venice and Rome! Come now, my dear Mr. Twain. Give me your honest evaluation of your sensational surroundings! What specific parallels and particular opinions do you have?"

I sighed wearily and then reluctantly and lethargically declared, "A blue trip slip, for an eight-cent fare; a buff trip slip, for a six-cent fare; a pink trip slip, for a three-cent fare; punch in the presence of the passenjare!"

Well now, Reverend Mr. Biggins, who never deliberately cursed a word of profanity in his life, just stood there biting his tongue. His face expressed a very concerned and gravely alarmed configuration. Then, the very distinguished man of the cloth commented, "Mark; there is something remotely appealing about your ongoing declaration that I cannot fully understand. Those are the identical words you've been reiterating this entire, laborious amble over here to Simsbury. There doesn't seem to be any special substance to them; it's all rhyme without any pertinent reason, so to speak! Yes, it's all basic form without content or substance; that's exactly what you're communicating! Those nebulous-sounding words of yours nearly break my heart. How do they go? Punch in the, sorry Mark, but I just can't accurately remember."

I gathered my sanity and slowly articulated the simple lines six consecutive times with perfect enunciation. The astute Reverend's face lit-up and beamed as if it was an illuminated electric sign. "Why Mark, that's an exceptionally captivating and intriguing jingle you've just related! It's almost musical; not exactly Mozart or Brahms, mind you, but almost classical musical! Its unique pattern has a certain magical flow to it! I've nearly memorized all of the words myself. Say them just one more time, just for the sake of redundancy, so that I'll be able to fully master the entire sequence."

Well, I accommodated the inquisitive Reverend with those fucked-up, melodic words, and then the victim attempted to say them all by himself, but made one minor mistake in his delivery, which I immediately and expertly corrected. The second time, the esteemed minister got them all perfect in the proper order, and at that rapturous moment, a great burden seemed to tumble right-off my formerly oppressed shoulders. The torturing jingle had miraculously escaped my conscious and subconscious minds, as if I had been a lustful vampire supplying a new red-blooded candidate with my dreaded, uncouth, red-cell-sucking deportment. Suddenly, a graceful sense of tranquility descended upon and enveloped me, simultaneous with the transference of the rhyming malady from me to the readily-available and victimized Reverend Mr. Biggins.

I was so lighthearted, and I sang some popular song lyrics on the entire ten-mile-long trek home. Then, my emancipated tongue proudly rediscovered the art of speech again, and my formerly pent-up thoughts were finally liberated into viable oral sentences. Those joyous, buoyant words gushed-out gregariously, until my mental fountain was dry and empty. I shook the Reverend Mr. Biggins's right hand at our parting and politely related, "Haven't we had a royal jolly time? But Minister. You haven't said a palpable word ever since we stepped away from the Talcott Tower grounds! Say something lively to break your boredom."

The Reverend slowly turned towards me like an automaton with a lackluster pallid face, and then drew a very deep breath into his flaccid lungs. And without exhibiting either apparent animation or alert consciousness, the church official uttered, "Punch brothers, punch with care; punch in the presence of the passenjare!"

A disconcerting pang of rare sympathy shot through my being as I assessed, 'Poor fellow! He's got the dreaded symptoms of that same contagious mental disease right now! I hope he fuckin' remembers where the hell he lives, before the reverend's picked-up on the street for vagrancy; white collar or no white collar; Minister Biggins should immediately and violently rip the damned collar off during a hectic moment of frantic madness!'

* * * * * * * * * * * * *

I didn't see Reverend Mr. Biggins for an entire week, but then on a Tuesday evening, the pious, self-righteous, sanctimonious, usually confident individual staggered into my presence and met me at my residence for an unscheduled social visit. The about-to-be-appointed bishop looked pretty damned haggard, pale, and basically, an exhausted wreck. The holier-than-thou fellow opened his bloodshot eyes enough for me to observe that the perplexed son-of-a-bitch appeared to have a double case of pinkeye.

"Ah, Mark. It was a terrible ruinous investment I had made in memorizing those horrendous and devastating rhymes you had maliciously taught me," my disgusted friend prefaced. "They've haunted my psyche like a perpetual nightmare both day and night;

horrible hour after horrible hour, right up to this present rendezvous. In fact, I'm inconsolable about experiencing the whole ordeal."

"Well now, Reverend. Why don't you gather your wits, and then tell me what happened after our pleasant journey to and from the Talcott Tower," I suggested. "Things are never as bad as they often seem at first evaluation!"

"That's what the hell you think!" the soon-to-be-ordained bishop unexpectedly cursed. "Last Saturday evening, I had received an urgent telegraph message, and had to hop aboard the evening train to Boston as a result of the emergency. An old friend of mine had died, and his family had requested that I preside over the funeral, and give an extemporaneous account of my former close companion's marvelous contributions to his family and to American society."

"So, what's so extraordinary about that?" I diplomatically asked, before casually popping a chocolate candy into my mouth. "Your actions were quite humanitarian and altruistic. Essentially, you were acting in compliance to your religious job description."

"Well Mark; I took my damned seat in the first Pullman car, and began organizing the precise text for the sermon," continued Reverend Biggins, who to my knowledge, never before had ever uttered a syllable of either obscenity or vulgarity. "But unfortunately, I never got beyond framing the first paragraph, for then the car wheels rubbing against the goddamned rails began their characteristic and very distracting clack-clack-clack; clack-clack-clack; clickety-clack; clickety-clack, background noise," Reverend Biggins sadly expressed. "Right away, those odious rhymes you had conveyed to me came into my mind's play, and the bullshit things dominated my brain as the train wheels and tracks provided my ears with ample musical accompaniment."

"Sounds like a pretty familiar story to me," I assessed and stated, as I perfunctorily reached for a second sweet chocolate. "Nothing too serious, I believe, that could warp your logical thinking," I added, adroitly-but-suavely busting my holy guest's sensitive testicles. "It was just an inconsequential annoyance, that's all."

"That's what the fuck you think, Mark!" Reverend Mr. Biggins screamed-back into my face, with his bloodshot eyeballs nearly popping out of their sockets. "After an hour of deep contemplation, and progressively nodding my head to the inane train track rhythm, I was more fagged-out than a goddamned gay fag after twelve-hours of continuous immoral and illicit homosexual, sodomizing sex. My noggin felt like a freakin' overflowing crapola, and I truly felt like a goddamned fucked-up shit-head," my religious guest insisted. "My colossal headache was splitting my skull apart, as I restively sat there in total anguish like a mother-fuckin' zombie. I stretched my naked ass out in my upper berth, but all my rapidly-disintegrating, degenerate brain could contemplate were those corny infectious fucked-up rhymes you had evilly mentioned to me last week."

"And exactly what were those rhymes?" I further baited the Reverend Mr. Biggins, deftly feigning innocent ignorance. "I can't recall all of them."

"Well shit, Mark," my incensed, usually pious friend loudly bellowed. "It occurred to me that I had a one-track mind, just like the fuckin' train did! 'Clack-clack-clack; a blue trip slip; clack-clack-clack, for an eight-cent fare; clack-clack-clack; a buff trip slip; clack-clack-clack; for a six-cent fare, and the abominable and atrocious agony continued; and so on, and so on, and so on. 'Punch in the presence of the passenjare'!"

"Could ya' nod-off and catch forty winks, I mean, while you were simultaneously nodding your head to the rhythmic beat?" I politely asked, as I cruelly winked at my visitor and directly-but-courteously mocked his pathetic plight.

"Sleep! Did you have the audacity to fuckin' say 'sleep'!" my saintly and usually extremely devout friend vociferated. "I was a total lunatic when the locomotive finally pulled into the goddamned Boston station. The next morning at the funeral, I did the best I could with my prepared oration, but every bitchin' sentence I uttered was tangled, laced, and woven with 'Punch, brothers, punch with care; punch in the presence of the passenjare!' And Mark; my totally fucked-up delivery, which is normally quite eloquent as you well-know, well; my entire pronunciation dropped into and matched the undulating rhythm of those cock-sucking rhymes you had shared with me. And my tired eyes actually caught the dumb-fuck assholes in attendance, sitting there in the church pews, and mechanically nodding their heads to my fucked-up elocution."

"Sounds like some heavy, unprecedented, super-religious bullshit to me," I amiably replied, before pouring myself a cup of hot coffee. "It's a good thing you weren't addressing your congregation here in Springfield, or else your name might've been swiftly removed for consideration for your upcoming hierarchal promotion."

"Well Mark; much to my utter astonishment, the entire audience, the stone-faced undertaker, and the grim-puss hearse driver included, were bobbing their dumb-fuck heads up and down; all in unison in response to my entirely fucked-up speech," Reverend Mr. Biggins woefully added. "After I finished uttering my ludicrous and embarrassing spiel, I had a wicked panic attack, and anxiously rushed into the anteroom in a state of absolute frenzy. A well-intentioned, aged, old maid approached me as I was breathing heavily into a white-cloth-church-moneybag. The elderly maudlin bitch, who incidentally was also from Springfield, quite ruefully whimpered, "Oh, oh. I'm so sorrowed that my friend Barnaby has passed-on. I regret that I didn't have the opportunity to see him before he died of malaria and small pox. His sudden departure is oh so tragic!"

"You loved him then back in Springfield, even when he wasn't a streetcar passenger being savagely punched," I strangely answered. "I mean Madam, you had known the deceased well-before old Barnaby was a streetcar passenger having his ticket punched."

"Loved him? Loved who?" the confused elderly, retired, incontinent whore asked during a moment of pure short and long-term memory loss. "Who the hell are you talking about?"

"Why poor deceased Barnaby Hampton, of course!" I exclaimed before again raising the empty white-cloth-moneybag up to my mouth for some additional, improvised self-therapy.

"Oh him; yes, him, Barnaby Hampton," the hoary, mentally-deranged bitch replied. "Certainly; I had loved Barnaby; God rest his gentle soul. The man did have a rather big dick! I hope that when St. Peter meets and greets him at the Pearly Gates, the main guard doesn't ask Barnaby for his entrance ticket, so that St. Peter can punch it in the presence of the eternal passenjare!" Reverend Mr. Biggins testily communicated to me exactly what the elderly, retired, hoary bitch-whore had mentioned to him in the church's anteroom.

"Did the old, retired, bitch-whore ask you if you had been present when Barnaby got pissed-off with the world, and voluntarily gave-up his ghost?" I facetiously asked my religious visitor.

"Yes, and I explicitly explained to her that she ought to find the nearest bag to breathe into before she fuckin' died from a lack of oxygen in the anteroom," Reverend Mr. Biggins explained. "I told the nosy bitch-whore, whose overall inquisitiveness was mercilessly annoying the hell out of me: 'Barnaby's last dramatic words to me were, 'Punch, brother, punch with care; punch in the presence of the goddamned passenjare'!"

"And what the hell did the hoary, retired, bitch-whore say in response to your most intelligent declaration?" I curiously inquired.

"She said," the Reverend Mr. Biggins whispered and then coughed. "She fuckin' said, 'A blue trip slip, for an eight-cent fare; a buff trip slip, for a six-cent fare; a pink trip slip, for a three-cent fare;

punch in the presence of the passenjare!' That's exactly what the fuck the old retired dry-cunt bitch replied."

I desired to get Reverend Mr. Biggins to step outside as soon as possible, because my disturbed and fazed friend looked as if his frazzled brain needed an immediate enema, or else his head would probably explode right-off his neck, and swiftly propel into the upper atmosphere. In the flickering hall gaslight, the Reverend's hopeless, bloodshot eyes met mine for a pregnant moment, and then the essence of his shallow thoughts were verbally revealed and essentially conveyed.

"Mark; you've been rather reticent and laconic during my whole gut-wrenching revelation to you," Reverend Biggins angrily objected. "You offer me no solace or solution to my aggravating melody-malady. It's just as fuckin' well, I suppose. You couldn't help me in a million years, after spending ten millenniums being a dedicated student in a goddamned psychiatry university!"

"Well Reverend; your ugly tongue isn't doomed to wag that pathetic jingle for all eternity," I optimistically consoled. "I do have in my possession an adequate remedy for your gross condition, if you have the patience and the wherewithal to listen to my special cure. It's really not too-damned-complicated after all; that is, once you exhibit some self-discipline and get the full hang of it!"

"I'll do anything short of divorce from my wife, or castration of my genitals, or decapitation by guillotine to resolve this fucked-up jingle crisis of mine!" Reverend Biggins sincerely exclaimed. "Cure me, Mark, and I'll make you a goddamned revered saint once I become bishop!"

"Well, you don't have to go that far," I maintained with a degree of humility. "Just put me in charge of your Sunday collection baskets, that's all I ask."

I then disclosed to the next ordained Connecticut Bishop how to rid himself of his debilitating-but-dispensable mental illness. The next week, I arranged with a college professor acquaintance of mine for the afflicted Minister to give a vital seminar at the nearby university. Reverend Mr. Biggins, whom I had the distinct pleasure of introducing to the impressionable assemblage of college juniors seated in the huge lecture hall, wonderfully performed his oral routine rather terrifically.

The man-of-the-cloth had inadvertently discharged the burden of his persecuting rhymes into the ears of the euphoric and receptive students, and naturally, the imbeciles gladly accepted the profundity of his inspirational rhetoric, and soon acquired mastery of the mantra-like poetic verses. The annoying and irritating rhyming street trolley pestilence had been expertly transferred to several hundred ecstatic young asshole college recipients, and Reverend Mr. Biggins was once again a sane American citizen ready to advance in his chosen profession to much bigger and better things.

“The Jumping Frog”

When Samuel Langhorne Clemens (a.k.a. Mark Twain) was a barefoot lad growing-up in Hannibal, Missouri, the boy worked as a typesetter for his older brother Orion’s newspaper, the *Journal.* Later, the master storyteller ventured-out onto the muddy *Mississippi River* and learned the challenging trade of riverboat pilot under the expert tutelage of Horace Bixby.

Then, the tragedy of the *American Civil War* broke-out, so the mighty *Mississippi* was closed-down to commercial navigation in 1861. Out of his piloting job, Mark Twain packed his bags and headed west, seeking a new career as possibly a gold prospector, or an aspiring newspaper journalist. In May of 1864, Twain left the Nevada Territory and journeyed to San Francisco, where the industrious journalist penned his first (and most famous) classic tall tale, “The Celebrated Jumping Frog of Calaveras County”. The innovative, satirical work appeared in the New York *Saturday Press* on November 18, 1865, and the cynical humorist Mark Twain became an overnight sensation. Herein, lies a vain retelling of the literary giant’s inimitable landmark story.

A stranger rode his horse into Angel’s Camp, an old dilapidated mining village situated in Calaveras County, California. The visitor was seeking information about a friend of a friend of his, and the former Angel’s resident was reputed to be one Leonidas W. Smiley.

The traveler tied-up his horse at a hitching post and entered the nearly deserted Angel’s Saloon, where the visitor came across an old geezer sleeping and snoring in a rickety, antique, wooden chair that looked as if it indeed had rickets. Upon waking up, the fat, elderly bald-headed, gentleman introduced himself to the itinerant eastern guest as the Honorable Simon Wheeler.

“Where can I find Leonidas W. Smiley?” the visitor to the camp inquired. “He was a boyhood friend of a close friend of mine, and supposedly, later became a devout minister of the Gospel; and that’s the Gospel truth, and not random bullshit. Last reports indicate that this Smiley character was prospectin’ for gold right here in Angel’s Camp, Calaveras County.”

“Well, howdy there, stranger,” old garrulous Simon Wheeler casually greeted his unexpected visitor. “We don’t get too many easterners visitin’ us out here in fool’s gold country. That gold rush everyone’s in heat about is nothin’ but a big bust. Yessiree stranger; that’s exactly what the hell it is. A big bust!” Simon Wheeler emphasized as his dilated pupils turned to a wall calendar and intensely scrutinized a big-breasted nude woman massaging her impressive, huge tits, featuring big brown succulent nipples.

"Well, Sir, what about Leonidas W. Smiley?" the eastern dude with a distinctive New England accent asked Mr. Wheeler. "That is to say, the Reverend Leonidas W. Smiley."

"You must mean old Jim Smiley!" the bald-headed, slightly addled old codger exclaimed. "I've known cucumbers and eggplants that are smarter than him. Well anyway, Stranger," Simon Wheeler disclosed. "Jim Smiley's the only Smiley I've ever had the pleasure of knowing here in Angel's Mining Camp, so just sit back and relax while I tell ya' all I can think of about that stupid asshole."

The friendly stranger pulled-up a chair and sat-down between a cracker-barrel and a hot potbelly stove, politely listening to the exaggerated tale manufactured and presented by the pot-bellied old whiskerando, Simon Wheeler. The old feller' leaned forward in his creaky chair, corralling and blockading the visiting dude in one trapped corner of the cobweb-infested saloon.

Old Wheeler never smiled or frowned, nor did his voice vacillate or waver one iota. The camp orator began his contrived narrative without any noticeable enthusiasm or animation, as if his utterances were of some worldwide significance or academic profundity. The stranger dared not interrupt the loquacious speaker by stating any declarative or interrogative sentence, preferring to absorb the total impact of the preposterous story that *he* suspected was being facetiously fabricated and related.

"Reverend Leonidas W., well now, yes; Reverend Leonidas. Well Sir," Simon Wheeler began with a forced smile, "in the winter of '49, or maybe in the spring of '50, I ain't no goddamn historian ya' know; so, I don't recollect the time and date exactly. But I remember the giant mother-humpin' water flume that existed back then wasn't finished being built yet, when Smiley took his first half-hour piss in Angel's Swamp, and nearly killed all of the brave pike and the shiners swimmin' around in there. Smiley was the most curious jerk-off ya' ever wanted to see or meet, but above everything else, the asshole loved to bet and gamble on anything and everything."

"Bet and gamble?" the visitor challenged. "But I had deliberately said that Reverend Leonidas W. Smiley was a minister of the…"

"That's right, Stranger," Simon Wheeler asserted and stubbornly maintained. "This pud-puller Smiley was only happy when he was gamblin', playin' poker, or rollin' the friggin' dice. But the young bastard was lucky, uncommonly lucky," the old storyteller continued.

"And that freakin' ball-buster would bet on anything from whose wife had the biggest knockers, to whose dick was the longest, either when soft or hard. Smiley would take any side he pleased, and when he wasn't bettin', he was always scratchin' his pimply ass or rubbin' his hairy balls; whichever happened to be closest to his overanxious right hand."

"Sir, in all due respect," the all-too-polite visitor earnestly insisted, "your description doesn't seem to match the Reverend Leonidas W. Smiley I was asked to...."

"Never mind that nonsensical, stupid bullshit!" Simon Wheeler exclaimed as if the chatty storyteller was a renegade mental patient exclusively hanging out at Angel's Saloon. "Now if there was a horse race, the lucky shit would either be flush, or be a big fuckin' loser at the end. Smiley even bet on which mare would have the most colts or fillies, claiming to be a sort of a *stud'* meister himself. But let me tell ya' Stranger," the old, whiskered fellow indiscreetly added, "I ain't never seen him stickin' his tiny dick inside of the old gray mare that ain't what the hell she used to be; now that she's authentically dead. And if there was a ..."

"Now just wait a minute," the sophisticated eastern Yankee visitor passing through Angel's Camp objected. "I come from a genteel Atlantic Coast town where all the folks are mannerly and docile, and I'm not used to hearing this sort of slang language being..."

"That's fuckin' perfectly all right!" reasserted old Wheeler as the accomplished speaker shoved his astonished guest back into *his* squeaky wooden chair. "Now, as I was stipulatin', this shit-head Smiley would bet on dog fights, catfights, chicken fights, female mud wrestlin', and on jerkin-off and female masturbation contests to see who would come to an orgasm first, or who would pop the biggest load the farthest. That son-of-a-bitch was the luckiest son-of-a-bitch I've ever..."

"I think I've heard enough!" the appalled visitor decided, and as the insulted guest attempted to rise and to vacate the premises, old Simon Wheeler roughly pushed him back into *his* chair to continue his remarkable dissertation.

"Now Sonny," the bawdy, risque narrator proceeded, "once there were two birds sittin' their asses on a fence, and instead of bettin' which one would fly away first, old Smiley bets the mayor which bird would take the first crap. Then, this fella' Jim again bets the mayor which bird would shit the most turds in the first half-hour. And once a straddle-bug was skitterin' all over the shit-eatin' wood-planked floor, right here in this armpit saloon, and old Smiley bet the visitin' governor of Vermont where the bug would eventually skitter to. Well," Wheeler elaborated. "The bug skittered its way right up the governor's wife's stockings, and tickled her crotch and aroused clit really good, until the cultured bitch wiggled and wriggled her fat fanny all over this here crowded saloon lookin' like a drunken hooker. The damned governor laughed so fuckin' hard that he gladly paid old Smiley the fifty dollars *he* had bet just to..."

"Now Sir, I believe I've heard enough of this barroom vulgar conversation coming from your filthy mouth," the embarrassed stranger balked. "So, if you don't mind, I'll be on my..."

Old Simon Wheeler forcefully knocked the red-faced guest back into *his* rickety chair, that actually looked like it had a worse case of rickets than the storyteller's flimsy rickety chair had. "Now Sir, like I was pertinently sayin', this bitchin' bastard guy named Jim Smiley would bet on anything. Once he bet Parson Walker when the preacher's wife took sick that she would die of malaria, and when she did pass away, the grievin' Parson had to pay Smiley a hundred dollars, and Smiley insisted that the bet be mentioned in the woman's obituary in the local *Gazette.* Smiley was a lot smarter than your average everyday ass-wiper, that's for damned sure. And also, when he..."

"Please Sir," the new arrival angrily-and-bitterly protested. "I have an important appointment in San Francisco and I must be on my..."

"Never mind about trivialities!" Simon Wheeler yelled in a very contrary tone as the saloon proprietor manhandled the thin, weak dignified visitor back into *his* creaky, rickety chair. "Ya' ain't leavin' until I get to finish the whole damned friggin' story. Now, this here Smiley had a mare he called the fifteen-minute nag, that reminded Smiley of *his* dead wife that he had shot in the head six times with a revolver because the nasty bitch always *nagged* the hell out of him. Anyways," Wheeler editorialized, "this female horse always would lose the goddamn race because she was pregnant and had distemper and asthma, and everything' else; so, Smiley had it all figured-out. The genius at betting used to give the old gray mare that wasn't what she used to be a hundred-yard head start, and the goddamn bitch would win the race every time by a lousy cunt hair; yes, she would. And the curious folks around these parts..."

"Sir, please excuse me, but I must take my horse to the livery station because he needs a new..."

“Now just a cotton-pickin’ minute,” chastised old Simon Wheeler as the aged control freak twisted the stranger’s arm and thrust him back into *his* unstable wooden chair. “I thought you eastern guys was notorious for courtesy and for manners. You is actin’ mighty uncivil and rude by wantin’ to leave this here cozy room before I’m done with my intriguing tale. Now then,” Wheeler commented and transitioned, “this asshole Smiley has this here bull hound dog pup he owned, and to look at the freak, ya’ wouldn’t want to give two red cents for his leash and collar, let alone for him. But Smiley had the vicious pecker-headed pup trained, ya’ understand. As soon as money was placed down on the table in the form of a bet,” the long-winded speaker elucidated, “the mutt’s under-jaw, nose, and impressive dick all stuck-out straight ahead, and then the energized canine was a totally different *animule* altogether.”

“What did Smiley call this weird-looking dog?” the stranger asked, exhibiting s degree of mild curiosity.

“I’m getting to that important detail,” Wheeler mildly scolded. “Smiley named em’ Andrew Jackson as a joke, because *he* knew his dog would do something *unpresidented (unprecedented).* When Andrew Jackson would get into a mean dogfight that was bet on, the old rascal would win every time by latchin’ on with his choppers to the other dog’s hind legs, and then bullyraggin’ the other mongrel all over the damned place, until the other dog was whimpered into fuckin’ submission,” Simon Wheeler explained. “Andrew Jackson really knew how to kick ass really swell, and if his sharp teeth missed the other dog’s hind legs, then the mutt would viciously bite the other cur’s dick off, and swallow the tasty morsel just like it was a little hot dog wiener.”

“Did Andrew Jackson ever lose a dogfight?” the stranger wanted to know. “I hope that this is the end of the Leonidas W. Smiley story!”

“Now I was getting to that prominent detail when *you* so rudely interrupted me,” old Simon Wheeler reprimanded. “One day, Andrew Jackson got shucked-out bad, because the shaggy mutt the critter had to fight was as ferocious as a grisly grizzly bear. And besides that rather fairly-pertinent fact, the new dog everyone was bettin’ on against Smiley had no friggin’ hind legs; and when old Andrew Jackson went to bite the bitchin’ freak, he didn’t know what the fuck to do!” Simon Wheeler described in detail. “So, the other damned dog took the initiative, and bit and beat the shit out of old Andrew, and then bit *his* tender loins off and chewed them up good. Then, Smiley’s dog just curled-up and died, and it always makes me feel remorse for old Andrew Jackson; yes, it does, the way it all ended for him and the way his fightin' career was radically terminated."

"Well, then," the totally dismayed stranger interrupted. "Did Smiley change his evil gambling ways after what had happened to his precious dog, Andrew Jackson?"

"No indeed!" Simon Wheeler testified. "Smiley became even more intent on bettin' and riskin' the damned odds. This here Smiley had rat terriers, and chicken cocks, and tomcats, and all them kinds of dip-shit varmints, and the addicted gambler would throw all of the nasty cantankerous *animules* into this here cock fightin' pit, which was really like a fuckin' *animule* sports' arena. The seven or eight species would have a big brawl," the storyteller expounded, "and everyone would put their dollars-down and bet which one would be the last creature standin'. That's how fucked-up Smiley was, and how fucked-up he had made everyone else stayin' here at Angel's Camp, preposterously prospectin' for fools' gold."

"Look Mr. Wheeler, I appreciate your fine hospitality," the uneasy visitor mentioned and exaggerated, "but I think I've heard enough equivocation about your Jim Smiley when I really need some tangible biographical data on the Reverend Leonidas W. Smiley."

When the visitor attempted to rise and escape *his* captivity inside Angel's Saloon, Simon Wheeler kicked the newcomer in the testicles, and then punched the stranger in the gut, knocking the air out of *his* lungs. Then, the eastern traveler had to sit there in excruciating pain and listen to the remainder of corpulent, bald-headed Simon Wheeler's stellar description of Jim Smiley's immoral and illicit betting exploits in Angel's Camp.

"Well Stranger," the old talkative fellow proceeded. "This here Smiley catched a frog down at the swamp one day, which was easy to do, because the swamp was swamped with frogs. The obsessed gambler then took the creature home and teached him how to jump great distances, even though it wasn't fuckin' leap year anywhere in Calaveras County. Old Smiley educated that frog in all the basics of jumpin', settin-up a pole, and next increasin' the pole's height each time. That fantastic frog even whirled in the air like a dizzy doughnut, doing somersaults and tumble-saults, and table salts, and the like, and the critter always came-down flat-footed like a smilin' Cheshire cat that intentionally falls outa' a tree."

Although the exasperated stranger was still in agony from the flurry of blows that had been administered to his solar plexus, which the decent gentleman had received from the incomparable Simon

Wheeler, *he* still had the wherewithal to ask a rather relevant question. "Did Smiley's frog have a name?"

"I was just getting to that pertinent point, so don't fuckin' *jump* to conclusions!" the senile storyteller bristled and acknowledged. "Old Smiley would train this friggin' frog by makin' the thing leap-up and catch flies the master would dangle above the jumpin' poles. The two practiced the art and the science of jumpin' every single mornin', noon, and night until the fuckin' frog was the most skillful *hopper* in the whole damned area, even though he didn't look anything like a goddamned toilet!" Wheeler amusingly ascertained.

"But did the frog have a damned fuckin' name?" the frustrated fit-to-be-tied visitor, also a dedicated minister of the Gospel cursed.

"Well, Sir; I saw Smiley place old Daniel Webster down on the planked floor of this here dusty saloon: incidentally, Daniel Webster was the fuckin' flyin' frog's name, and then Smiley would yell out, 'Flies, Daniel, flies!' Well Sir," Simon Wheeler euphorically pointed out, "there weren't any damned flies around anymore to reward the damned hungry frog, but old Daniel Webster would jump-up a storm anyway, and break all existin' records, and win lots of cash for everyone interested in bettin' on *his* phenomenal leapin' ability!"

"Look Shit-head!" the virtuous, self-righteous minister turned ordinary person in and around Angel's Camp yelled. "How did the son-of-a-bitchin', mother-fuckin, cunt lappin' frog ever lose a turd-eatin'-bet for Smiley?"

"Well, Stranger; now you're finally talkin' my language!" Simon Wheeler answered and commended without even using a single curse word. "Ya' never did see a frog so modest, so humble, so gifted, and so straightforward as this fucked-up Daniel Webster was. Yes siree; when it came-down to fair and square jumpin' on a dead level plane," Wheeler boasted, "Daniel could cover more ground in one leap and hurtle over any obstacle better than any other non-royalty frog of his mediocre breed. Smiley would ante-up two twenty-dollar bills, and everyone else in attendance would cough-up and bet the incredible sum of forty dollars against Daniel, just to attempt bankrupting Smiley, so that *he* would quit gamblin' and bustin' everyone's friggin' stones all the goddamn time."

"Well, you crazy old, demented mother-fucker; what the fuck happened next?" the irate and now belligerent traveling minister demanded in a totally out-of-character rant.

"I'm getting to that particular highlight," Simon Wheeler promised. "But Stranger, ya' gotta' oblige me with some old-fashioned western patience. Old Smiley was monstrous proud of his special frog, and he kept it in a latticed box', I guess more of a cage than a goddamned box. One day, a feller,' a real wise-ass in the camp came across Jim Smiley carrying his box containin' Daniel. The braggart asked Smiley rather matter-of-factly, 'Say, what the fuck does ya' got in that peculiar box'?"

"Look Mr. Wheeler, I really have to..."

"Just sit-down and fuckin' relax your testicles before ya' make me have conniptions!" Simon Wheeler insisted, as the saloon owner smashed the visiting minister back into *his* rickety wooden chair. "And Smiley answered the feller' sorta' indifferent like, saying, "It might be a parakeet; it might be a mongoose, or it might be a castrated canary, but it's not. It's a goddamn fuckin' ordinary, non-fancy frog sittin' quietly inside this silly box!' And then the camp newcomer looked at the frog careful-like, slowly turning the latticed box all around this way and that, and the jerk-off starkly says to Smiley, 'Say, Buddy; so it is a goddamn fuckin' ordinary, non-fancy frog. What's he good for'?"

"And what the fuck did that stupid asshole Jim Smiley say in response?" the almost-livid visitor to Angel's Camp asked from his imprisonment in the rickety wooden chair.

"Oh well," Wheeler genially replied. "Smiley says rather easy and carefree. "He's good for one thing, I should ascertain; and that is he can out-jump any other goddamned frog in Calaveras County'."

"This story is absolute bullshit!" the visitor-minister vociferously objected. "I'm getting' the hell outa' here right now!"

Old Simon Wheeler administered a frenetic flurry of expert karate and judo' chops to the parson's neck, diaphragm, groin, penis, and ass, and soon the stranger was once again seated, slouched-down in his all-too-familiar squeaky, creaky, rickety, wooden chair.

"Now then," the tale's principal narrator proceeded speaking to his now unconscious audience of one, "the rookie passin' through Angel's Camp peered-inside the latticed box and cleverly says to Smiley, 'I don't see any points about your asshole frog that's any better than any other asshole frog I've ever seen'!"

"Maybe ya' do, and maybe ya' don't know didley-squat about frogs and am-fib-ians," Smiley said to the limp and listless injured stranger. "Maybe ya' don't understand the science of frogs, or maybe you're still a rank amateur just like most local assholes are. I'll risk ya' forty dollars sayin' that old Daniel Webster here can out-jump any other frog in Calaveras County. Well Stranger, the new fellow studied the latticed cage and its sole occupant for a full minute, and then aptly answered Smiley, 'Sir, I'm only a dumb greenhorn here in Angel's Camp, but if I had a healthy frog, I would surely bet ya'!"

After a brief pause, old Simon Wheeler continued his expository narrative. "Then Jim Smiley felt compelled to favorably respond to the suave man's blatant challenge. 'That's okay, that's all right!' the native resident said. 'If you'll hold this lattice box for a minute, I'll hustle-down to the swamp and catch ya' a comparable frog that will jump against old Daniel'!"

The listless stranger that had been brutally assaulted, mugged and molested by Simon Wheeler was now regaining full semi-consciousness. The parson shook his head and reacquired some semblance of sensibility. "What the fuck happened?" the groggy minister asked in reference to *his* recently administered pain and suffering, and not requesting more details about Simon Wheeler's hyperbole involving Jim Smiley and Daniel Webster.

"Well Sir," Wheeler characteristically blustered, "the feller' put-up his forty dollars next to Smiley's bet, and then he sat-down to wait for Jim to return from the pond with a capable specimen to jump against Daniel Webster. Then the wily jerk-off got a most brilliant idea," Simon Wheeler indicated with great admiration. "He took a teaspoon out of his coat pocket, filled it up with quail shot, and meticulously poured the special ingredient down Daniel's throat. The guileful asshole repeated this deceitful act with the spoon at least twenty shit-eatin' times, until Daniel finally weighed at least five more pounds than usual!"

"Look Asshole!" the stranger-minister defiantly blurted-out. "I don't give a shit about Jim Smiley or his mother-fuckin' frog. I only came here to fuckin' find-out some information about the Reverend Leonidas W. Smiley."

"I'm getting' to that essential idea, so just mind your p's and q's, and I'll tell ya'. My God, Mr.! I ain't never met somebody as rambunctious and as spoiled rotten as you are, and with such a goddamned short attention span! Anyway," Wheeler snorted after spitting a large green lunger into a floor spittoon. "Smiley stepped out to the swamp and slopped-around in the mud like a happy pig in shit. Jim catched a nice-lookin' frog, and brought it back to this here saloon where the thrillin' jumpin' contest was goin' to be held."

"If you don't tell me about Leonidas W. Smiley soon," the perturbed Reverend threatened, "I'm gonna' tear this fuckin' saloon apart and crush your goddamn balls into mince-meat!"

"I'm tellin' ya' about Leonidas in a minute, so stop threatenin' my ass," Simon Wheeler pledged and demanded. "Smiley hands the new frog to the stranger and commands, 'Now when you're ready, set your critter alongside Daniel, and I'll give the startin' numbers.' Well, the greenhorn did exactly as Jim had dictated, and then Smiley yelled out 'One, two, three-jump!' The new frog from the pond hopped off lively-like, but old Daniel had indigestion and couldn't budge an inch; just like he was anchored into the floor planks. Smiley was surprised and disgusted, but Jim didn't have no clue as to what the fuck was wrong with old Daniel!"

"I wanta' know what the fuck ever happened to that evasive bastard Reverend Leonidas W. Smiley!" the visitor-Preacher screamed like an incensed maniac.

"Just hold your damned horses, and I'll tell ya'!" wildly exclaimed Simon Wheeler. "The scamming feller' took Smiley's forty-dollars and paced to the swingin' doors over yonder, and turned and bellowed, 'I don't see any points about your asshole frog that's any different or better than any other asshole frog I've ever seen before'!"

"Damn it! What about fuckin' Leonidas W. Smiley, or I'll rip your balls right out of your scrotum and then fanatically choke you to death with my bare hands!" the normally passive Minister deliriously boomed at Wheeler.

"Now then," the master storyteller calmly proceeded, "Smiley just stood there scratchin' the damned dandruff out of his scalp; lookin' at Daniel Webster for the longest time and sayin' over and over again, 'What the hell's wrong with this fuckin' frog!' at least five hundred times. Jim catched and lifted the fat frog by the neck and saw that the critter weighed at minimum five pounds, and understood that Daniel couldn't leap worth a damn if *his* hopping-mad life depended on it. And then," Simon Wheeler paused as the old codger inhaled a large quantity of air. "Jim Smiley turns the frog upside-down, and the *animule* belched-out two handfuls of heavy quail shot. And then Jim became madder than all hell that's being full of aggravated hornets. Smiley threw the frog onto the planked floor, and sprinted-out through the swingin' doors, runnin' hard after the abominable, clever feller' that sneakily tricked him; but Smiley never catched-up with him and…"

"But what about that stupid jerk-off asshole, fuckin' Reverend Leonidas W. Smiley?" the traveling Preacher insisted.

"Well, Stranger," Wheeler tersely added. "The greenhorn with the victorious frog happened to be your Reverend Leonidas W. Smiley. He's the one that broke Jim Smiley's balls but good with the quail shot trick, and also in the process, broke Smiley of his terrible gamblin' habit, too!"

Just then, wrinkled-face Simon Wheeler heard a saloon patron calling his inglorious name from the other end of the bar. “Just stay where ya’ are, Stranger. I’ll only be gone for a second once I serve that drunken lush a double-shot bourbon. I just gotta’ tell ya’ about this here mother-jumpin’, one-eyed, quill-less porcupine that didn’t have no tail or testicles, but only a short, stumpy projection, and a nose that was a weird cross between a very green banana and a very ripe watermelon.”

At that junction, the traveling-Minister became so fed-up with, and so pissed-off at old Simon Wheeler that the itinerant Preacher reached his right hand down to the old timer’s huge testicles, and squeezed with all his might. The man effectively and literally crushed the storyteller’s balls, as those nuggets had never been crushed before. “There Fuck-head!” the traveling Parson triumphantly hollered. “Just like Jim Smiley had been cured of gamblin’, I hope that you’re balls bein’ busted will ultimately cure you of your idiotic exaggerated storytellin’, you obnoxious, arrogant, egotistical asshole!”

And with those magnificent words, the self-satisfied Preacher limped-out of the almost-empty western saloon, unhitched his black stallion, and climbed atop *his* faithful horse, leaving old Simon Wheeler bent over in sheer agony inside Angel’s Saloon.

The recipient of the minister’s vengeful wrath was wishing that he had the balls to tell the old drunk seated at the bar the fascinating story about the quill-less porcupine without a tail and having a nose that was a weird cross between a green banana and a ripe watermelon. Fortunately, discretion prevailed, and old, agonizing Simon Wheeler remained perfectly silent as the bullshitting Western bard poured the old drunk a delicious double bourbon.

About the Author

Jay Dubya is author' John Wiessner's pen name. John is a retired New Jersey public school English teacher, having diligently taught the subject for thirty-four years. John lives in Hammonton, New Jersey with wife Joanne and the couple has three grown sons.

Counting *Twain: Tattered, Trounced, Tortured and Traumatized* along with its companion books *Poe: Pelted, Pounded, Pummeled and Pulverized* and *O. Henry: Obscenely and Outrageously Obliterated*, John has written and published sixty-two total books. *Pieces of Eight, Pieces of Eight, Part II, Pieces of Eight, Part III* and *Pieces of Eight, Part IV* all contain short stories and novellas that feature science fiction and paranormal plots and themes. *Nine New Novellas, Nine New Novellas, Part II, Nine New Novellas, Part III, Nine New Novellas, Part IV, One Baker's Dozen, Two Baker's Dozen, Snake Eyes and Boxcars and Snake Eyes and Boxcars, Part II* are short story collections all written in the spirit of the *Pieces of Eight* series.

Other Jay Dubya adult-oriented fiction are the works *Black Leather and Blue Denim, A '50s Novel*, and its exciting sequel, *The Great Teen Fruit War, A 1960' Novel. Frat Brats, A '60s Novel* completes the action/adventure trilogy. Jay Dubya also has produced two irreverent Biblical satires, *The Wholly Book of Genesis* and *The Wholly Book of Exodus.* A third satire *Ron Coyote, Man of La Mangia* is a parody on Miguel Cervantes' classic novel, *Don Quixote* published in 1605. *Thirteen Sick Tasteless Classics, TSTC, Part II, TSTC, Part III* and *TSTC, Part IV* are satirical works that each corrupt thirteen classic stories from American and British literature and from Greek mythology. *Fractured Frazzled Folk Fables and Fairy Farces* and *FFFF & FF, Part II* satirize and corrupt famous children's literature stories. *Mauled Maimed Mangled Mutilated Mythology* is another popular adult-oriented satirical/parody work that pokes fun at twenty-one famous classical myths. Finally, *Shakespeare: Slammed, Smeared, Savaged and Slaughtered* and *Shakespeare: S, S, S and S. Part II* lampoon the famous works of the great playwright.

The author has also penned a young adult fantasy trilogy: *Pot of Gold, Enchanta* and *Space Bugs, Earth Invasion. The Eighteen Story Gingerbread House* is a collection of eighteen new children's stories. And last but not least, two Jay Dubya non-fiction works are *So Ya' Wanna' Be A Teacher* and *Random Articles and Manuscripts*.

Author Biography

Born in Hammonton, NJ in 1942, John Wiessner had attended St. Joseph School up to and including Grade 5. After his family moved from Hammonton to Levittown, Pa in 1954, John attended St. Mark School in Bristol, Pa. for Grade 6, St. Michael the Archangel School in Levittown for Grades 7 and 8 and then Immaculate Conception School, Levittown, Pa. for Grade 9. Bishop Egan High School, Levittown Pa was John's educational base for Grades 10 and 11, and later in 1960, the aspiring author graduated from Edgewood Regional High, Tansboro, NJ. John then next attended Glassboro State College, where he was an announcer for the school's baseball games and also read the nightly news and sports over WGLS, GSC's radio station.

John Wiessner had been primarily an English teacher in the Hammonton Public School System for 34 years, specializing in the instruction of middle school language arts. Mr. Wiessner was quite active in the Hammonton Education Association, serving in the capacities of Vice-President, building representative and finally, teachers' head negotiator for 7 years. During his lengthy teaching career, John had been nominated into "Who's Who Among American Teachers" three times. He also was quite active giving professional workshops at schools around South Jersey on the subjects of creative writing and the use of movie videos to motivate students to organize their classroom theme compositions.

John Wiessner was very active in community service, being a past President of the Hammonton Lions Club, where he also functioned for many years as the club's Tail-Twister, Vice-President and Liontamer. John had been named Hammonton Lion of the Year in 1979 and in 2009 received the prestigious Melvin Jones Fellow Award, the highest honor a Lion can receive.

John also was a successful businessman, starting with being a Philadelphia Bulletin newspaper delivery boy for two years in the late 1950s in Levittown, Pennsylvania. After his family moved back to New Jersey in 1959, John worked at his grandparents and his parents' farm markets, Square Deal Farm (now Ron's Gardens in Hammonton) and Pete's Farm Market in Elm, respectively. He later managed his wife's parents' farm market, White Horse Farms in Elm for three summers.

Also, in a business capacity, for 16 summers starting in 1967 John Wiessner had co-owned Dealers Choice Amusement Arcade on the

Ocean City, Maryland boardwalk and also co-owned the New Horizon Tee-Shirt Store for eight summers (1973-'81) on the Rehoboth Beach, Delaware boardwalk. In addition, “Jay Dubya” was a co-owner of Wheel and Deal Amusement Arcade, Missouri Avenue and Boardwalk, Atlantic City. And then, for 18 summers beginning in 1986, John had been the Field Manager in charge of farm crew-leaders for Atlantic Blueberry Company (the world's largest cultivated blueberry farm), both the Weymouth and Mays Landing, New Jersey Divisions.

After retiring from teaching in 1999, writing under the pen name Jay Dubya (his initials), John Wiessner became the author of 62 books in the genre Action/Adventure Novels, Sci-Fi/Paranormal Story Collections, Adult Satire, Young Adult Fantasy Novels and Non-Fiction Books. His books exist in hardcover, in paperback and in popular Kindle and Nook e-book formats.

In January of 2022, John Wiessner (Jay Dubya) was nominated into Marquis Who’s Who in America, and in April of that same year, was one of nine distinguished Who’s Who in America members honored with Lifetime Achievement Awards, all nine sharing an article of recognition appearing in the Wall Street Journal.

Google: Jay Dubya books.

www.ingramcontent.com/pod-product-compliance
Lightning Source LLC
Chambersburg PA
CBHW070504120726
47910CB00003B/1113

* 9 7 8 1 5 8 9 0 9 6 8 7 5 *